FOREVER HOPE

FOREVER HOPE

HALF MOON BAY BOOK 4

ERIN BROCKUS

Green Sage Press

Copyright © 2022 Erin Brockus

This is a work of fiction. Names, characters, businesses, places, events, locales, and incidents are either the products of the author's imagination or used in a fictitious manner. Any resemblance to actual persons, living or dead, or actual events is purely coincidental.

All rights reserved. No part of this book may be reproduced or used in any manner without the prior written permission of the copyright owner, except for the use of brief quotations in a book review.

Cover design by GetCovers

Edited by Misha Carlstedt

Ebook ISBN: 978-1-957003-04-7

Paperback ISBN: 978-1-957003-06-1

Hardcover ISBN: 978-1-957003-07-8

CHAPTER 1

July...

HOPE COLLINS WENT from asleep to awake in an instant. Its weight was the first thing she noticed. The *difference*—yesterday morning compared to today. It wasn't a heavy thing, but its import was tremendous. She opened her eyes as a smile slid across her face. On the other side of the bedroom was a wall of floor-to-ceiling windows, and streaming light caught her eye. The white sand beach and ocean of the western shore of St. Croix were brightly lit by the morning sunshine.

What time is it? She glanced at the clock, which informed her it was after 7 a.m. Her smile became a smug grin.

Guess we did have a pretty late night. Well, Alex will be long gone by now.

Finally, she couldn't deprive herself any longer. Hope raised her left hand and the grin turned into slack-jawed wonder as she gazed upon her engagement ring. After returning home the previous night, she had inspected it closely. The showstopper was a large princess-cut diamond, surrounded by a square of smaller, similar-cut diamonds. A white-gold band held the ring firmly to her finger. Even in the soft morning light, the diamonds glimmered. It was perfect.

But today was a workday for Hope, just as it was for Alex Monroe, the dive-operations manager and head dive guide of Half Moon Bay Resort. And as of last night, also her fiancé.

Her breath caught at the thought.

My fiancé. We're getting married! *I'm getting married!*

But workdays generally meant Alex rising before the sun. *Well, I have a few minutes before I need to get up. I'll just snuggle up with his pillow.* Turning on her side, Hope yelped as she came face-to-face with a pair of crystal blue eyes and an enormous grin.

"Like it, huh?"

The hand in question was now pressed against her bare chest as she tried to quell her racing heart. "You scared me to death!" Then her smile reappeared. "I didn't think you'd still be here."

"I thought it might be worth hanging around to see what you'd do when you woke up. Definitely worth it, even if you do sleep until noon." Alex faced her, raised up on one elbow with his head resting in his hand. Morning stubble lined his chin and his short, sandy hair was sticking up like someone had run her hands through it. Repeatedly.

She smacked his chest. "Give me a break. It's barely seven." She kissed him, morning breath be damned. "And I don't like it—I love it. Mr. Monroe, you really knocked it out of the park with that proposal."

"Meh. It was all right, I guess." His grin got bigger.

Last night he'd taken her on a night dive to Salt River Bay, on the north shore of the island, and proposed to her underwater amidst an extraordinary display of bioluminescence. The water around them had been an explosion of illumination, provided by countless numbers of light-emitting sea creatures. Hope still couldn't believe it had really happened.

She brushed a finger over the ring. "I'm amazed at how well it fits."

"A woman who worked at the jewelry store was my hand model. She was about the same size as you."

Hope shook her head as amazed laughter burst through. She'd had no idea his proposal was coming. Her experiences with men had kept her from dreaming too big, but Alex had proven time and again he was worth dreaming for. He rolled onto his back, and she settled on his chest. "I can't believe how lucky I am."

Alex's chest shook as he laughed, exuberant and long. "Ok, let's get this straight. I'm marrying a woman who owns her own oceanfront resort and has made it a resounding success. She just happened to find a cave which contained a treasure worth who-knows-how-much. Not to mention she's brilliant and drop-dead gorgeous. I'm just a dive guide."

"Oh, God. Not this again." Hope counted on her fingers. "Dive guide, rescuer of multiple persons—myself included, defender of justice against employee thugs, expert diver capable of finding hidden treasure, and sexier than hell. Am I forgetting something?" She slapped her forehead. "Oh yeah! Former Navy SEAL and war hero. Alex, shut up."

"Yes, ma'am." He turned, pressing the length of his body against hers.

"Uh-huh. And there's the real reason you stayed in bed so long." She pressed back, stretching like a cat.

He ran a finger down her arm. "I've told you before. I've got no self-control around you."

"Then I guess it's a good thing I don't either. Let's start this day in style."

∼

An hour later, Hope breezed into the lobby office where general manager Patti Thomas was at work. She sat at her own desk and woke her computer. "How's it going?"

"Fine," Patti replied, frowning at her screen as she drummed her ebony fingers on the desk.

"Any more problems with Princess Tinkerbell?"

Patti laughed, a deep, rich sound, before she continued in her lilting accent, "No, nothin' since the Cockroach Crisis yesterday."

They had a very high-maintenance guest named Annabelle Smythe. Her boyfriend escaped on the daily dive trip every morning, leaving her free to terrorize the staff. The previous day, an errant beetle had dared to race across her front porch, and she stormed into the office, demanding Patti fumigate the bungalow immediately. Fortunately, Patti convinced her bugs were occasional visitors, and nothing could be done about them.

Patti typed some more, then groaned, clutching a hand to her salt-and-pepper halo of hair. "Annabelle sent us that detailed itinerary of her activities, and I've been tryin' to keep ahead of any problems that might crop up. But now I *cannot* find it."

Hope brought up the email. "Really? It's still in my inbox."

Patti pointed to her terminal. "Take a look. Nothin'. She probably found a way to retract it, so she could complain some more."

Hope rose and leaned over Patti's computer, verifying there was no email before looking closer. "Oh, look." She pointed at the screen. "You're in the deleted folder, Patti."

Patti inhaled sharply as she grabbed Hope's left hand, pulling it close to her face. Her eyes grew steadily bigger as they met Hope's.

"Oh. Alex and I have some news." Hope grinned just as the power went out, plunging them into dim twilight. Both women glanced at the television on the wall, which normally showed landscape photos of St. Croix but was now black.

"Wonder how long it will last this time?" Hope said as she marched toward the front desk. Several areas of the resort were linked to backup generators, which became active immediately upon the occasional loss of power. The front-desk computer was one. Martine, their front-desk agent, sat on a stool behind the counter, her very pregnant abdomen pressing against the counter in front of her.

"Is your computer still up, Martine?"

She nodded, pulling her black braids into a ponytail, already preparing for the heat. Hope gave her a thumbs-up and continued, heading out of the lobby to the restaurant just behind. As she walked through the swinging doors into the kitchen, the lights cast a brilliance over the clean room. Sous chef Pauline was cutting up a pineapple.

"Looks like all's well here?"

"Just fine," Pauline said, her black hair pulled back into a tight bun. Gerold Harrigan, their executive chef, had hired her several months previously. She was a local from Christiansted who was grateful to learn under the tutelage of such a talented chef. "The fridges and freezers are workin' just fine."

"Ok, sounds good."

Hope headed back to the office. As soon as she opened the lobby door, a raised voice radiated out. A tall young woman wearing a white terrycloth resort bathrobe stood in the middle of the lobby, both hands propped on her hips. The left side of her long blonde hair was perfectly flat-ironed and glossy, but the right side was a dull, frizzy mess that stuck out everywhere.

Hope bit down hard on the inside of her cheek to keep from laughing.

"How can the power just go out? I need it back on now! Greg and I have a photo shoot this afternoon. I can't go looking like this, now can I?" She glared at Patti, who stared back with her usual even, calm expression.

Hope took a deep breath and approached. It was her turn. "I'm so sorry, Annabelle. We live on a small island in the middle of the ocean, so power outages happen from time to time."

Annabelle turned her blazing eyes to Hope. "Why wasn't I informed of this ahead of time? I never would have come to this third-world hellhole if I'd known that!"

"Well, many of our guests think it's part of the charm of discovering a new place. But don't worry, we'll make sure you look perfect for your photo shoot. We have several outlets that are powered off the backup generators, just in case. When is your session?" A quick glance at the clock informed Hope it was 11 a.m.

"It's at three o'clock. Greg is on the dive boat now. And that damn dive guide better not keep him out late again. Yesterday they took forever because of some stupid rare fish or something."

"Yes, a pod of pilot whales is a pretty rare sight," Hope said. "Greg was very excited when I saw him."

Annabelle rolled her eyes. "I don't understand the appeal at all."

Of course you don't. Your hair would get wet.

Patti broke in. "If the power's still out after lunch, bring your hair supplies and find us. We'll make sure you look incredible for your photos, ok?"

"Well, I'd better, or there will be hell to pay." With that, Annabelle huffed, spun around, and marched out of the lobby.

"Is it too early to drink yet?" Hope asked.

"I may join you." Patti turned to her. "Is everythin' ok elsewhere?"

Hope nodded. "I didn't go down to the pier to see if the air compressor is still powered. I don't have a clue how the thing works. Alex can look at it later."

At Alex's name, Patti grabbed Hope's left hand. "We got interrupted by the power failure! You two are engaged?"

A smile threatened to crack Hope's face as she nodded. Patti wrapped an arm around her shoulders as she steered them back to the office, beckoning Martine to join them. "Come on then, child. We need to hear all about this."

CHAPTER 2

Just before noon, Hope strolled down the wooden pier, smiling at a family playing in the ocean. The power outage wasn't causing them any problems. Halfway down, she passed through a tunnel created by the compressor and gear-storage room on her left, and the dive shop and scuba classroom on her right. The resort spa formed the ceiling, spanning both rooms overhead. Unlocking the door on her left, Hope poked her head in and glared at the large behemoth of an air compressor before shutting it again. "Nope. Not messing with that thing. Alex can handle it."

After reemerging into the sunlight, she turned and continued past the dive shop to stand at the base of the stairs leading up to the spa.

Selena, their massage therapist, was at work on the covered outdoor deck at the top of the stairs. Her light-blue staff shirt was vivid against her dark skin, and her black hair was slicked back into a tight bun. Her family had lived on St. Croix for generations, and she had just graduated from a local college. She returned Hope's thumbs-up, affirming everything was fine, so Hope returned to the dive shop, unlocking the door and propping it open.

Stifling heat and the scent of neoprene hit her immediately, and the usually brightly lit room was dim. After verifying the computer was operational, she moved past a wall of fins, masks, and snorkels to open a window for some breeze. Several circular clothing racks were scattered over the floor. Rash guards, T-shirts, and sweatshirts hung from each, and a display of wetsuits adorned one wall.

Hope continued through an open doorway into the scuba classroom. She opened its window, passing by three tables and stopping at a whiteboard to admire Alex's intricate drawing of a Leatherback turtle. A clutch of baby turtles had hatched on their beach a few weeks prior, and he'd given a lecture about them before allowing the guests to watch the hatching under his strict supervision.

Hope's attention was diverted by the many books lined up in the corner bookcase where Alex kept an astonishing reference library. She'd left an item off her list that morning—he was also a marine biologist.

As she returned to the dive shop, voices could be heard, and she moved to the doorway. The boat was back, and a large group of divers walked up the pier and back toward the resort.

She hurried to inform them of the power outage. "Hopefully it will be back on soon, but your bungalows might be pretty hot. Open the windows and the cross breeze will help a lot. The restaurant is fully powered, so lunch will be served as usual. And most importantly, the beer is still cold!"

Hope smiled at the resulting cheers before pulling Greg aside as the others moved on. He'd paled during her explanation, finally closing his eyes as he swallowed.

"Annabelle told me you have a photo shoot this afternoon," Hope said. "We'll make sure she has access to some working power outlets so she can prepare."

Greg's eyes flew open. "I'm sure she's beside herself. She can come on a little strong sometimes."

No! Really?

"She just has high standards," he continued. "Thanks for helping her out."

"Of course. That's what I'm here for. Why don't you two have lunch, then—" Hope was interrupted by the sound of the air-conditioning units on top of the building whirring to life, and a relieved smile rose on her face. "The power's back on! Enjoy your photo shoot. Looks like a beautiful day for it."

Greg relaxed his shoulders and hurried off to placate his princess.

After a deep sigh, Hope walked toward the end of the pier, where *Surface Interval* was tied up. It was a hive of activity as Alex, divemaster Robert Davis, and boat captain Tommy Williams unloaded the boat. Their laughter rang halfway down the pier, returning the smile to her face—the three were a close-knit group. Alex stood at the open section near the stern and saw her, softening his eyes in a look that made her heart soar.

Tommy saw his face, then turned as Hope climbed aboard. He scowled and shook his head. "I shoulda known. He only gets that stupid look when you're around." Tommy was a St. Croix native, a large man with even larger personality and heart. "And what did he eat for breakfast this mornin'? He's been bouncin' off the walls and grinnin' like an idiot all day."

Robert, another local, tossed a pile of wetsuits onto the dock, then ran a hand over his shaved head. "Yeah, he didn't even get mad when one of the divers didn't secure his tank and it fell off the bench."

Hope slid up to Alex as he put an arm around her. "Are you keeping secrets from these fine gentlemen?" she asked.

"I didn't say anything. I thought we'd tell them together."

Tommy and Robert both straightened at that. Hope held up

her left hand and waggled her fingers. "Alex and I are getting married."

Tommy crushed her in a hug as Robert shook hands with Alex, then they switched. She let Alex tell the story this time.

"Nicely done, man," Robert said. "Salt River Bay, good time of year for it."

She and Alex exchanged a quick kiss. "It was *very* nicely done," Hope said. "But today hasn't been as great. I've told you guys before—you have all the fun. We've been dealing with a power outage all morning. It came on just after you got back."

"Is the air compressor working?" Alex asked, his smile falling.

"I have no idea. That monstrosity is solidly in your domain, not mine."

"I better go check it out. Can you guys finish up here?"

After their answering nods, Hope and Alex made their way back to the compressor room. They donned protective ear cans before Alex pressed the green button on the large machine, relaxing as it roared to life. Standing four feet tall and ten feet long, the compressor filled ten whips with compressed air, topping up scuba tanks as they sat in a water bath against the nearby wall. After verifying everything was working properly, Alex turned it back off and they removed the ear protection.

"I've always wanted to ask, why do you put the tanks in water to fill them?"

"It helps keep them cool," Alex said. "This room turns into a sauna. Even in water, the sides of the tanks get very warm to the touch. They're kind of like you that way." He pulled her close and kissed her, opening his mouth to slide his tongue over hers.

Finally, she pulled away with a soft moan. "Hmmm, are my tonsils still there?"

"Present and accounted for, ma'am."

Hope laughed, swatting him on the ass. "Come on. Let's get some lunch before we interview that kid for the dive-shop job."

As Hope and Alex left the restaurant after eating, Annabelle and Greg were heading into the lobby. She wore a flowing yellow dress, and her hair was a perfect, glossy mane that swept after her every move. Greg swept after her too.

Hope breathed a long sigh . "I am so glad they're leaving tomorrow."

Alex followed her gaze as they climbed onto the pier. "He seems ok. Pretty decent diver."

Hope rolled her eyes. "We've already been over this. You have the fun job, remember? You can't imagine what Patti and I have been through with her. Patti more than me."

"I don't envy you. Though if you're so eager to do my job, I'll give you a call the next time the boat sinks and I have to keep a group together for four hours in the open ocean." Alex was grinning now, his arm draped over her shoulders.

"Really? You're still playing that card?"

"Still getting mileage out of it, baby."

He ushered her into the dive shop. Robert and Tommy had left, and Hope closed her eyes as the blast of delicious air conditioning hit her. They continued into the classroom, arranging the chairs. Hope checked her watch. "Ok, Zach should be here any moment. What do you know about him?"

"He's a high school senior, born here, and related to Tommy. He says Zach's a good kid."

"As long as he doesn't have a criminal record."

"Definitely not. I think we've proven not everyone is as trustworthy as Clark."

After a minor scrape with the law, Clark had proven himself a talented bartender and was preparing for the annual St. Croix mixology contest the following month. The previous year, he came in second, and he was determined to win it this time. The bartender had proved far greater success than their other rehabilitation attempt, which had resulted in Alex being shot in the shoulder while defending Hope.

"Even if we get someone to help in the afternoons, that still leaves us with no one to work in the morning while we're on the dive," Alex said. "We're getting too busy to close up when we're gone."

Hope cocked her head. "I've opened up the shop a few times when people needed something. Why don't I start filling in for a few hours every morning? Patti can certainly handle office duties without me. And I can work from home in the afternoons while I'm baking the guest snacks." She had recently rediscovered her love for baking and been able to take some of the workload off Gerold and Pauline.

"You sure?"

"Yes. You're right—we should have the dive shop open all the time."

The door opened, and a young lad with mahogany skin entered. He was maybe five feet, five inches tall, and Hope doubted he weighed a hundred and thirty pounds. His close-cropped black hair was neat, and he had a delicate, earnest face.

Can he even lift a scuba tank?

They exchanged introductions and sat in the classroom. Zach took a seat behind the middle table. He placed a manila file folder on the surface and clasped his hands over it. Hope sat in front of him as Alex took his usual position, sitting on the front table with his legs on the seat of a chair.

"We're looking for someone to work a few hours in the afternoon, four or five days a week," Alex said, all business. "You'd be splitting your time between the dive shop and filling tanks—also loading and unloading the boat if there's an afternoon dive trip. That sound like something you'd be interested in?"

Zach smiled, his face shining as he watched Alex. "I'd love to. I could work here after school. I'm real dependable."

"That's what Tommy told us."

"Uncle Tommy told me all about the boat sinking and being rescued."

Alex smiled slightly. "Well, I don't think you'll need to worry about anything that dramatic."

"Zach," Hope said. "This is going to be a pretty physical position. Scuba tanks weigh a lot, and you might have to carry them to the end of the pier. Are you ok with that?"

Am I going to end up with a huge L&I claim if I hire you?

Zach laughed. It was infectious and made Hope smile. "I know I don't look like much, but I'm stronger than you'd think. I can do it no problem. I've been around the water all my life. I'd love to do this!"

"You have any interest in learning to dive?" Alex asked.

"Oh yeah! I'll do whatever you need if you can teach me to dive. I can paint, and I've even got restaurant experience if you need it. I know you used to be a Navy SEAL, and I'd love to learn divin' from you." Zach was nodding so hard Hope was afraid he'd break his neck. She was finding it harder to stay serious, but Alex had his game face on.

"Well, that doesn't make any difference regarding how I teach, but if you do a good job, I'll put you through the open water class." Alex glanced at Hope, and she gave him a small nod, trying to put as much enthusiasm into her eyes as possible. He held her gaze for a long moment, his face impassive before turning back to Zach. "Ok, we'll give you a shot."

"Thank you! You'll be happy you did. I promise."

The manila file folder contained his completed job application, and Hope promised to process it immediately. "We'll run a background check, then be in touch within a week to nail down a start date."

As Zach left, Hope wasn't sure his feet were even touching the ground.

Alex sighed, staring at the door. "I hope I don't regret this. A stiff breeze could blow that kid over."

She laughed. "Let's give him a chance. I love his attitude. And he'll do anything to stay on your good side. You've got a new fan."

"At least he's pleasant."

"Hey, I didn't even know my scuba class was being taught by a former SEAL. He's already got an advantage over me."

A gleam entered Alex's eyes as she shifted his attention to her. "You were on a need-to-know basis back then. I would've had to charge you double to divulge that. You couldn't have afforded me."

She stood and slid close to him. "Is that right? Well, I can afford you now."

Alex stopped any further conversation with a kiss. Hope made an appreciative rumble in her chest and said, "I'm calling it a day. You coming with me?"

"In a bit. I need to make sure everything's ready for tomorrow."

She strolled down the beach, past the four southern bungalows, and studied their house in the distance. It was several hundred yards away from the last bungalow for plenty of privacy. Painted white with green trim, the main feature of the cottage-style house was the full-length covered porch, which provided a glorious ocean view.

Hope caught movement on the beach and grinned as a medium-sized yellow dog with floppy ears bounded toward her. "Well, hi there, Cruz!" She stopped to scratch his short coat. "You're coming farther down the beach all the time."

Shortly after her arrival, a very skittish Cruz had appeared out of the jungle next to her house. Over several months, she'd convinced him to trust her, and now he was tightly bonded to her and Alex. After her recent emergency surgery, he had overcome some of his aversion, stepping up his guarding duty while she was recuperating. But he was still wary of other humans. The dog was a mystery. Being housebroken, he couldn't be feral. Most likely, someone had dumped him on the side of the nearby highway.

Now he climbed the stairs to the porch with her, stopping as she unlocked the sliding glass door. "Not sure we'll ever know your full story, sweetie."

Cruz replied with a thumping tail against the wooden planks, but kept his mystery to himself.

CHAPTER 3

The sky was ominous, with low-hanging, dark clouds. Hope took a deep breath, shaking out her hands. Small birds flapped through her stomach. "I'm not sure why I feel nervous." To distract herself, she frowned at the old car's interior. "With the auction proceeds, maybe you can buy a car that was actually built during the last half century. I'm surprised this thing still runs."

Alex shut off the ignition of his blue Land Cruiser, and his face tightened, a gasp escaping. "What? This is a classic! It runs like a charm."

She shot him a dubious glance. "If you say so."

"I bought this right after I got assigned to SEAL Team Four. No way am I parting with it."

She couldn't resist a small smile. She'd known the car was tied to his SEAL days, but not the specifics. "If you're happy, I'm happy."

"I'm more than happy. And I'm not getting a new car."

Hope finally laughed. "Sorry I brought it up. Let's get back to business." Her stomach promptly flopped. "And now the nerves are back."

They turned their attention to the building before them. It was a plantation-style detached office painted a soft green with cream trim. Several steps led up to a covered landing and a door made of local hardwood. A shingle outside prominently displayed the building's main occupant: Alistair X. Montgomery, Esquire.

Alex turned back to her. "Well, our last interaction with lawyers wasn't much fun. Hopefully, this will be less dramatic."

"Definitely. No more trials, please."

Montgomery had represented former resort owner Steve Jackson, who had left the attorney's contact information behind for Hope, so he was a natural choice. Steve's surprise visit the previous month had come before she and Alex realized they needed legal services, so Montgomery was unknown to them.

Hope exited the car, smoothing her tailored skirt. Alex placed his hand on the small of her back as they climbed the stairs. He was dressed formally today in khaki pants and a dark-blue button-down shirt she'd picked out. Alex was hopeless where fashion was concerned.

They entered a homey lobby where a middle-aged receptionist sat behind a large wooden desk. After checking in, they walked across a squeaky wooden floor to sit on rattan couches. The receptionist's phone buzzed and after speaking for a moment, she rose, smiling brightly at them. Her white teeth were dazzling against her dark face. "Alistair is ready now. Please follow me."

The squeaky floor continued as they traveled down a white-painted corridor. Black-and-white photos of St. Croix adorned the walls. The receptionist stopped before the last door and ushered Hope and Alex in as she shut it behind them.

The homey, small-town décor ended at the office door. The large room beyond was paneled in a rich wood, and bookcases packed with legal tomes filled an entire wall. Directly in front of them was an enormous mahogany desk with two opulent wing-back chairs arranged in front.

And gliding from behind the desk and making his way toward

them was Alistair X. Montgomery, Esquire. He was a tall, thin man, dressed in a canary-yellow, perfectly tailored suit complemented by a gray and white polka-dot tie. Hope liked him already. He was completely at ease in attire that would look ridiculous on anyone else.

Montgomery, who was middle-aged with short, tightly curled hair and dark skin, shook hands with Hope. "It is a pleasure to meet you, Ms. Collins."

"You as well, Mr. Montgomery."

He held both hands up. "Please, call me Alistair. Or Al, if you prefer." He spoke with a very faint Caribbean accent, nearly unnoticeable. Hope couldn't imagine calling this refined, elegant man Al.

He turned his attention to Alex, who held out his hand and introduced himself.

"Yes, I know who you are, Mr. Monroe. I keep abreast of all local law proceedings. Your composure under cross-examination was admirable. Mr. Camarino has been known to unsettle many witnesses." He moved his eyes to Hope. "And you too, of course, Ms. Collins."

"Thank you. But if we're going to call you Alistair, then I insist you use our first names as well."

"As you wish." Alistair indicated the two wingback chairs as he made his way back around the mammoth desk. He regarded Alex. "Your particular skills have come in handy since you moved to our island. Even at the trial of the man who attacked you."

Alex sat still, his face neutral. "Unfortunately, yes. Though the last thing I expected was Charles going after the bailiff's gun."

"You and everyone else. I'm afraid the bailiff was encouraged to find a new line of work. A particularly thorough tongue-lashing from Judge Cosgrove convinced him." Alistair shook himself. "Enough of that. How may I help you?"

"We're here about an asset-protection matter," Hope said,

sinking into the luxurious black leather. "I understand that is one of your specialties?"

"Yes. Living on an island with a rich history like St. Croix presents opportunities regarding valuable items. From time to time, people request advice about them."

Hope and Alex shared a quick glance. "Well, that's what brings us here. Alex and I would like to consult you about a highly confidential matter."

Alistair inclined his head.

"He and I have made a rather astonishing find, deep in a cave on the resort property."

Alex leaned forward, clasping his hands between his knees. "Hope discovered the cave. Much of it is flooded, and I dove it on the initial exploration, then brought her in. To make a long story short, we found a box of Spanish treasure."

Hope had brought up a video on her phone while Alex spoke. "He wore a camera when we discovered it, and I edited the resulting footage. It would be easier to show you rather than try to explain it. The video is only a couple minutes long."

She handed Alistair her phone, and he watched a time-lapsed video of their journey through two underwater passages. Then the video slowed to real time, emerging into an enormous cavern. Its floor was a river of stone meandering through masses of stalactites.

The attorney widened his eyes steadily, and he nearly dropped the phone at the section showing a disintegrating wooden box, its contents spilling out over the floor. "Good heavens!"

The final clip showed the trove after she and Alex had separated it into gold and silver coins, jewelry, plates, and a stack of solid-gold ingots. Alistair handed the phone back to Hope and sat there, blinking.

"Now you can understand why we'd like some advice about our next steps," she said with a small smile.

"To be sure." Alistair pulled himself together. "This cave is on your property, Hope? Entirely?"

She nodded as Alex spoke. "I wore an advanced diving GPS at one point and mapped the entire route. The whole thing is on her property."

"That settles the issue of ownership. And your find appears to be a treasure of some antiquity and not recent unclaimed property, which simplifies matters." Alistair alternated his gaze between Hope and Alex. "Are you still the sole owner of the property, Hope?"

"Yes," Alex said. "The treasure is one hundred percent hers."

Hope glanced at him, tightening her mouth before turning to Alistair. "Alex and I are engaged. And that treasure would never have been found without his expert diving skills. We're splitting it fifty-fifty."

"Of course it's up to you to divide it however you wish, but I must be clear that under the eyes of the law, it belongs *only* to Hope. At least until you become married." Alistair leaned forward and clasped his hands together on the blotter. "Where exactly is the treasure currently located?"

Hope glanced again at Alex, who sat stiffly with a tight jaw. "Alex carried it out of the cave in a series of technical dives, and it's now divided into two safe-deposit boxes at different banks. And let me assure you, Alistair, I have no doubts whatsoever about Alex's motives. He's the most honorable person I've ever met."

Raising both palms, Alistair flashed a warm smile. "Yes, I am aware of his background. However, it is my duty to inform you both of the legalities of this situation, is it not?"

"Of course," Alex said. "On multiple occasions, I have told Hope I'd be happy to sign any document you might recommend that states her full ownership."

"Well, based on what Hope has already stated, it doesn't appear that will be necessary." Alistair waited for her answering nod. "I presume you're here to find out how to proceed with selling some or all of this?"

"Yes," Hope said. "We'd like to sell a portion of the items. Definitely not all of them. And we'd like to do it anonymously."

"My biggest concern is the safety of the cave," Alex said. "If word gets out that we found treasure in there, it's going to be crawling with people who think they're experts. So I've started investigating contractors to build metal gates over the passages. The primary reason I'd like us to remain anonymous is so we can keep the site unknown."

Alistair arched a brow. "The cave is accessible at the moment?"

"Yes," Alex said. "It's hidden and off the beaten path, but someone could get in there without too much trouble. Securing the site is a priority."

"Excellent. I suggest you proceed with haste. Can you fence in the area?"

"I think so," Alex said. "It's off the highway quite a bit, but we'll try to surround the rock pool."

Alistair nodded as he turned his attention to Hope. "Regarding your comment about anonymity, it makes the issue of provenance more difficult, and may result in lower prices when you do sell or auction the items. Authenticating the pieces should be a simple matter, but buyers expect to know the story behind them. Do you have any idea where the treasure came from?"

Hope smiled, trying to hold in the smugness. "We know exactly where it came from." She removed several typewritten pages from her purse. "Alex and I found a handwritten letter deep inside the cave from the man who was marooned there and placed the treasure. I transcribed it."

She handed Alistair the letter, and he began to read. Hope's eyes drifted to the white wall behind him with several framed diplomas and certificates, including a law degree from Yale University.

"This is really quite remarkable." Alistair rubbed a manicured fingernail back and forth over his brow.

Alex grinned, relaxing back in his chair. "Yeah. Captain Morgan's little brother buried our treasure."

"Is there any possibility the Morgan family could claim ownership of it?" Hope asked.

"No. This letter is dated 1671. I would venture the Morgan family has had ample time to reclaim their lost property if that had been their wish. The statute of limitations has long passed. If the original letter can be authenticated, it should easily prove provenance of the find."

Hope indicated for him to keep the pages.

Alistair's voice poured out like honey. "I have arranged auctions for items of a similar nature, though nothing quite this extensive. I'll make some discreet inquiries about how best to proceed with liquidating a portion of your find. At the moment, my conjecture would be one of the large auction houses in Miami." He paused, straightening his cuffs. "In the meantime, you can investigate securing the site."

Alex nodded. "I'll get it scheduled as soon as possible."

Alistair looked back and forth between them, a smile forming. "Congratulations. This is quite an extraordinary find. Well done."

CHAPTER 4

The sun was nearing the horizon as they drove home, and Hope's stomach growled, prompting her to suggest dinner at a beachside bar and grill north of Frederiksted. Alex tensed at her suggestion, pausing before he agreed. Never a man who enjoyed notoriety, he had gained a measure of fame around the island due to recent events. Alex had made great strides in facing his painful past, and agreeing to something as simple as a romantic dinner demonstrated that.

Breakers was a popular bar and grill, but being locals, they were assured a table even without a reservation. The hostess gave Alex a long look before leading them to a front-row table nestled in the sand. On the glass tabletop, a candle glowed in a red glass jar while waves lapped the shore just twenty feet away.

"You want a bottle of wine tonight?" Hope asked.

"Red sounds great."

She ordered a bottle of Cabernet, and they were quiet as the server poured. Hope raised her glass in a toast. "To a successful meeting with Alistair."

"I didn't know what to think of that guy to start. I've never seen a yellow suit before, but he seemed pretty sharp."

Hope broke out into laughter. "He wasn't what I was expecting either, but I was impressed." She took a drink of wine, savoring the velvety smoothness. "So you're planning on hiring someone to install the gates over the passage and not doing it yourself?"

Alex's brows flew up. "I don't have a clue how to do that." Then he grinned. "If you need the gates blown up, I can manage. But we'll leave construction to an expert."

"Let's try not to blow them up. Perhaps you can obtain the keys."

He watched her over the rim of his glass. "That takes all the fun out of it."

"I'm sure you can find other ways to have fun." She sent him a blistering look that he returned with interest. Then they both broke into smiles. "I still can't believe it!" Hope said. "How are we going to handle all this?"

Alex sobered. "Carefully. And slowly. First, we'll see what Alistair comes up with, then we make a plan."

"A plan, huh? That reminds me, there's another minor matter we haven't had a chance to really discuss yet."

"Oh? What might that be?" His eyes sparkled in the candlelight.

"You know exactly what I'm talking about. What kind of wedding would you like?"

"I'm the groom. I don't get an opinion."

"You're going to make this difficult, aren't you?"

His eyes softened as a tiny smile rose. "I wanted to give you a little time to think about it, and I'm happy with whatever you want. All I care about is that you show up."

She set her glass down, laughing. "I think that last sentence is supposed to be my line."

He took her hand, rubbing his thumb over the ring. "That's a pretty major promise sitting on your finger right now. You don't need to worry about me showing up."

Her heart melted. She was well aware of how he felt about promises. "I know. And I hope you know I feel the same way."

"I do." He pulled his hand away as their entrees came and they settled in to eat. "What's your idea of the perfect wedding?"

"I've never been a traditionalist, and I think we're a little old for a big formal affair anyway," Hope said. "My perfect wedding would be a small, casual ceremony at sunset on the beach of our resort."

An enormous smile spread across his face. "That sounds perfect to me."

"You don't have your heart set on an underwater ceremony?" she teased. "I've heard they're popular with divers."

"No, the underwater proposal was good enough for me." He became serious, sending her a look that went straight to her heart as he tightened his hand around hers. "I can't imagine anything better than marrying you on the beach at sunset."

Alex let go for another drink of wine and broke out laughing again. "Did I ever tell you how I came to certify Tommy?"

"No, you haven't."

He sat back in his chair, his voice becoming animated. "We had two guests who did want an underwater wedding—they'd been here a bunch of times. This was after I'd been at Half Moon Bay a couple years. Since Tommy was a captain, naturally they wanted him to perform the ceremony. I got him certified just so he could perform that wedding."

Hope's smile grew as he told the story.

"And when it came time to actually do it, he was so petrified he made me go down there with him. I kneeled off to the side like an idiot for the whole thing. I have no idea what Tommy thought I'd be able to do, but he insisted on me being there."

"Did he get through it ok?"

"Yeah, he did a great job. Though he said he never wanted to do another one."

"Wait a minute. You're a boat captain too. Why didn't you just do it?"

Alex reared back. "Oh, hell no! It wasn't common knowledge back then that I had my captain's license, and I didn't want anything to do with it. Tommy still gives me crap about that every now and again."

They paused as their plates were cleared away, then Alex met Hope's eyes again, serious now. "There's one other thing I'd like to know about."

"What's that?"

"What do you want me to wear?"

Hope tilted her head, deciding how to answer. "I know you're a pretty casual guy, but I'd dearly love to see you in a tuxedo."

She'd guessed correctly. Alex's mask came over his face immediately, and he was studiously neutral. "If that makes you happy, it's fine by me."

Hope couldn't hold back anymore and laughed. "You should see your face! You're a master at hiding your emotions, Alex, but I know you too well." She squeezed his hand. "I want you to wear whatever you're most comfortable in. Casual is fine—as long as it looks presentable. I firmly draw the line at board shorts."

He grinned, lifting his glass again. "I can work with that. But I'm not exactly a fashionista, you know. I might need a little help."

"It would be my honor."

∽

After dinner, they were driving north on the highway when Alex made an unexpected left turn onto an unmarked dirt road, headed west. He shifted into four-wheel drive as he maneuvered over the rutted, uneven surface. His car might be old, but it was made to handle roads like this.

"What are you doing?"

"I feel like a walk on the beach with my girl. There's a great one ahead that's usually deserted because this road's so awful."

They bounced over a large rut and Hope's seatbelt locked, holding her in place as her teeth clacked together. "If you say so. We do live on a beach, you know."

"I'm in the mood for a little more privacy tonight."

At that, she turned to him. He kept his eyes on the road but wore a small smile.

"That sounds intriguing." An excited shiver ran down her spine.

After a mile that felt like ten, the bumpy track opened onto a flat area of scrubby brush. Alex stopped the car and they got out, walking to a small stretch of white crescent beach a hundred yards long. Hope stopped just above the waterline, admiring the view as the moon threw a pale stripe on the ocean. Alex took her hand and pulled her close. He kissed her hard, plunging his tongue around hers.

She could hardly breathe. "I thought you said you wanted to walk?"

"Changed my mind. We can walk on our own beach. How about a swim?"

"A little late-night skinny dipping?" Hope nipped his bottom lip, sucking it into her mouth before letting go and returning his kiss fully. She peeled off his shirt and ran her hands down the hard muscles of his back, discovering the pistol holstered inside the back of his pants. She wasn't surprised. "I have to admit, I feel better knowing you've got that. Just in case."

He studied her closely. "I told you. I'll never put you at risk again like I did that night in Frederiksted."

"You're not going to wear it in the water, are you?"

He laughed softly as he pulled her shirt off and removed her bra, flicking his thumbs expertly over her breasts. "No, it's attached to my pants."

"Well, you definitely won't be needing those. Wait. What if someone sneaks up and takes it while we're in the water?"

He sighed, staring at her. "Hope, I've looked over the area pretty closely since we got here. We're alone."

"And here I thought you were concentrating on me." She skipped her fingers over the smooth skin of his defined chest.

"I'm good at multitasking." He sobered, cupping her face. "We're safe here. I promise."

"That's all I need to know."

Hope returned her mouth to his, electricity sparking through every cell of her body. She traced her tongue around his and he answered with a groan. Rushing to get his pants open, she took hold of him as he breathed in sharply. They quickly removed the rest of their clothes and pressed their naked bodies together.

He was breathing like a freight train as Hope explored his mouth. She took her time lowering to her knees and enveloped him, using her mouth just how he liked.

"Oh my God, Hope."

His breathing indicated he was getting close, so she pulled away, meeting his eyes with a smile before turning and jumping through the waves. The water was warmer than the air, immersing her in its soft caress. She dove underwater, swimming lazily before rising in waist-deep water to find Alex already in front of her.

Standing tall, she ran both hands through her hair and arched her spine—his eyes were glued to her full breasts. She walked forward and pressed her lips to his wet chest, which was skin hot and slick under her tongue. He moaned, thrusting his hips against her, hot and hard between them.

DRAPING her arms around his neck, she boosted herself up and wrapped her legs around his waist, tilting back and watching him. Admiring his strong, handsome face. His eyes were filled with desire and so much more. "You have no idea how much I love you." She nipped his lower lip.

"Yes, I do," he said, smiling against her mouth.

"Stop arguing."

He moved his mouth back to hers before she could say anything further. Holding her tight against him, he walked back to shore with her legs still wrapped around his waist. They fell to the sand together.

A slight breeze sent tendrils down her back, which caused exquisite shivers. Alex felt her tremor and pulled away, smiling. "Sometimes I can't believe you're real. How did I get so lucky?" He crushed his mouth to hers, kissing her feverishly as he ran his hand up her thigh. Goose bumps rose on her skin and their heavy breath filled the night air.

Alex moved his mouth to her breasts, moving his tongue in rhythmic circles as she ran both hands through his silky hair. Hope looked at the Milky Way above her as his head continued downward, then closed her eyes and arched her back with a cry. He moved in tighter, relentless now, using his fingers and tongue to full advantage.

She was still breathing in decreasing, moaning gasps when he finally climbed back up, kissing his way up her body. He reached her mouth again and then pounded into her, both of them crying out.

Hope was still on fire, sensitive in every nerve.

She opened wider, making him groan even more as their bodies became slick with sweat. Hope rolled them over and sat up with one knee on either side of his hips. He stared at her with half-open eyes, breathing fast and riveted to her. Hope moved slowly, just shifting from side to side.

Alex closed his eyes, pressing his hips against her. "That feels so good. Please don't stop."

She exaggerated the movement, faster and faster, watching him as his climax built. Then she leaned down and kissed him deeply as his breathing became ragged. He broke the kiss and pressed his lips against her ear, clamping his mouth shut as he held her head tightly.

"We're all alone here, love. Make as much noise as you want."

He did.

Hope lay sprawled on top of him, and sand sprinkled to the ground as Alex moved his hand over her hip. "We're both covered in sand now," she murmured languidly.

"Mmmm. Worth it."

She moved off him and raised up on one elbow, running a finger down the center of his chest and tracing its firm contours. She brushed her fingers over his abdomen, smiling.

Alex's blue eyes met hers. "What are you thinking about?"

"What a beautiful man you are. And how much I want to be your wife."

He brushed a lock of hair away from her face. "I can't wait, either."

Then he grinned, wrapping his arm around her neck as a pleased rumble vibrated in his chest. "I am *so* happy I finally got to carry you naked out of the ocean."

"I didn't realize that was on your to-do list."

"Oh yeah, since the beginning. When we were eating lunch on Horseshoe Key, it was all I could think about. Then, when I finally got you where I wanted you, I was too scared my damn hip would collapse again, so I led you out instead."

"Well, I'm happy to fulfill your fantasy." Her smile turned into a full grin. "Mine was on the boat after we dove the Chapel, when I finally got to boss you around for once."

He pulled her back down for another fluttery kiss. "You can boss me around like that anytime you want. Come on, let's get this sand off and head back."

CHAPTER 5

After finishing work the next afternoon, Hope dug her phone out from her back pocket and flopped down on her porch couch. She stared at it as excitement brimmed. She'd been waiting for a quiet moment alone to do this. As she pressed the green circle, a smile nearly cracked her face.

Her sister Sara picked right up. "Just so you know, if I hear any more complaints about how hot the sun is or how you track gorgeous white sand through the house, I'm going to hang up on you."

"Would you feel better if I told you it's a perfect sunny afternoon with a lovely breeze and I'm sitting on my porch, listening to the palm trees rustle?"

"No, that doesn't make me feel better at all. This morning, I cut a lady's hair and gave her exactly what she had asked for. She about ripped my head off, then refused to pay. And it's pouring buckets in Charleston right now. Maybe I'll hang up on you after all."

Hope twirled a lock of hair around her finger. "You don't want to do that. Maybe you need another sisterly visit."

"I'd love to, but I need a couple more months to build my

vacation time back up. My salon sucks—the new owner is horrible. Besides, why do you need me to come down there? Did you kick Alex out for tracking in too much perfect white sand?"

"No, he's even more of a neat freak than I am."

"Not possible."

"Really, he is. You should see the scuba-gear room." She paused, trying to bite back a grin. "Here's the thing. I do need you to come down here, but I'm not sure exactly when yet."

"Oh, I get it. Now that the bungalows are done, you're finally planning the renovations for your house?"

The grin broke through. "Nope. More like planning a wedding."

There was a huge, pregnant pause.

Then, "OH MY GOD!"

Hope winced and held the phone away from her ear as Sara continued to scream. "Seriously? He popped the question?"

"He did!"

"Did he do a decent job of it? Hope, if he let you down with a shitty proposal, he's going to get both barrels from me."

"I have to say, he did all right." She explained the bioluminescent spectacle.

Another pause. "That sounds pretty amazing. Ok, I'm putting the shotgun away. You haven't set a date yet?"

"No, but we're having it on the beach here at the resort. The more I think about it, the more I'd like to completely shut down for a few days and reserve the bungalows just for the wedding party. So that may determine the date. It won't be in the next month or two, that's for sure. I need to check the bookings. We usually slow down a little in the fall, so hopefully I can block out a few days."

"Well, you can count on me for spectacular hair and makeup. You'll look amazing. Alex has no idea how lucky he is."

~

Two weeks later, Hope said goodnight to Patti and left for the day, stopping by the mailbox. Since neither she nor Alex had checked it in several days, it was brimming. A soft package was wedged on top. She tucked the mass under one arm and headed toward the house. After dumping the pile on the kitchen table, she started sorting. At the sound of the slider opening, she looked up. Alex walked in and gave her a kiss hello. He was moving toward the shower when she stopped him. "Wait a second. You've got an envelope from the scuba agency and this package."

Alex brightened when he took the soft plastic parcel from her, holding it up. "You're going to want to see what's in here. I'll be back out in a bit."

A short while later, he returned, freshly showered. He was dressed in cargo shorts and a sage-green button-down shirt, carrying a black shirt in one hand. He set the black one down and held his arms out, turning in a circle. "What do you think of this?"

Hope widened her eyes as she took a slow trip down his body and back up. "I think you look delicious." The shirt was a linen weave with wide, very subtle vertical stripes. Each stripe had a pattern of leaves in it, barely visible. "This is really nice. I like it a lot."

"Good. The black one is the same. Which color do you like better?" He peeled off the green one and pulled the black on over his broad shoulders. It looked spectacular, contrasting his blue eyes and tan skin.

"Honestly, you could wear a garbage bag and you'd look gorgeous. I like them both, though I think we'll avoid black for the wedding. And I'm not going to pick out your exact outfit, you know. I'll give you some selections, but I don't want to know what you'll be wearing."

"Well, don't leave too much of the decision to me, or I might show up in the garbage bag and ugly shorts."

"We've got three months. That's plenty of time."

Hope had wasted no time in checking the resort booking system. She'd been afraid there wouldn't be any open dates left, but she got lucky and found one three-night stretch in mid-October that was completely open. She immediately blocked out the entire resort for all three days. After discussing it, they decided to have the ceremony on the last evening, leaving the prior two for family celebrations and preparations.

With that, October twelfth became their wedding date.

"It's less than three months now, so I want to get moving on the wardrobe," Alex said as he opened a large envelope from the scuba-certifying agency.

"What's that about?"

He sighed. "They're updating the teaching standards. They do that every few years, so they can justify constantly raising the rate on my instructor's license. This goes over the new procedures, and next week there's a meeting in Christiansted I need to go to."

"The teacher gets to go to school, huh? Come on, let's go eat. I ran for twenty minutes on the treadmill during my lunch, so I'm hungry. It was slow, but I'm getting my strength back."

He put down the envelope with a smile. "It makes me very happy to see you healing so well."

"That certainly wasn't how I wanted to have my hysterectomy, but I'm feeling much better now." She tossed Alex a mischievous grin. "And not having a period anymore has other advantages too. Hello, spontaneity."

He took her in his arms and squeezed her tight, not smiling back. "You scared the hell out of me."

"I know—it scared me too. But it's behind us now. And we've got so much to look forward to."

THEY SAT at their usual corner table and ordered. Soon the tall, thin form of Clark was headed toward them with two tall hurricane glasses on his tray. The drink looked like a chocolate milkshake.

"Good evenin', guys. Can I interest you in a cocktail?"

"It looks like you've got one ready for us," Hope said. "Is this your contest entry?"

He set the two glasses in front of them and bowed. "It is. May I present Half Moon Dream? It's based on a mudslide, but I've made some changes."

The drink had a frothy top with a palm tree etched into it, similar to what baristas did with coffee. The frozen blended cocktail was a rich chocolate color and garnished with his trademark—a banana section, its stem split and a cherry wedged between. The arrangement strongly resembled a dolphin holding a ball in its mouth.

Hope lifted the glass with equal parts anticipation and trepidation. Clark had made a wonderful drink last year, but it went through some dreadful phases getting there. She inhaled some courage and took a long sip from the bamboo straw.

The icy flavors separated in her mouth, tickling every taste bud before melding together again, layer upon layer of subtleness. She tasted chocolate, Irish Cream, something citrus, and a layer of something deep and rich underlying it all. Another sip confirmed it—Half Moon Dream was incredible. And completely different from last year's drink.

"Wow," Alex said. "That's great, Clark. I like it even more than Half Moon Hope. I can taste the orange in it, but there's something else there I can't quite figure out."

"I agree. I love it!" Hope said.

Clark gave them a sly look. "You're tastin' my secret ingredient. It's what makes the difference." Then he grinned, his silver tooth gleaming against his dark skin before he turned back to the bar. "Enjoy now!"

Hope took another long sip, closing her eyes as she drummed

her feet on the tile floor. "This tastes just like a milkshake. I wonder if I can get another one."

"It's not a milkshake! It's probably nothing but alcohol. And I don't want to carry you back, so slow down."

She grinned. "Oh, all right. Did you set up the meeting with the contractor?"

"Yes, it's in a few days. I told them we needed two underwater passages closed off, and wanted to fence off an area reserved for guest use. Which isn't a bad idea—guests would love that rock pool."

As she sipped Clark's magical cocktail, Hope's thoughts meandered from the cave to Alistair. Excitement brimmed, threatening to spill over. *I wonder if he's found anything out.* Selling a Spanish treasure didn't sound like a simple process.

∼

ALEX GAVE a final wave as the truck drove away, *Apex Underwater Construction and Salvage* prominently displayed on the door. He had just spent several hours with one of their project managers, detailing how he wanted the cave site secured. The two men dove the rock pool and large entry cave, then hiked around the area. Alex expected a very expensive bid to come in the mail shortly for a tall perimeter fence and two heavy-duty gates over the underwater passages.

Hope is gonna love this . . . But it was a necessary expense.

He continued down the pier, thoroughly enjoying the tropical afternoon breeze as tanks clanged in the gear room. The compressor roared as he ducked his head in. Zach stood in front of the filling station, wearing ear protection like he was supposed to. Alex had to admit he was working out well. The kid might get knocked over by a falling leaf, but he was a hard worker.

Alex continued into the dive shop. He did *not* miss filling tanks every day. It was a hot, loud, mindless job he was happy to turn over. Even better, Zach seemed to think it was a blast for some reason. Alex grinned as a memory flashed into his mind—when he'd discussed a new employee's duties with Hope.

She had been confused, both hands parked on her hips. "Why not get another divemaster? That would free all morning for you to work in the dive shop and get the tanks filled early."

He reared back, horror-struck. "Leading dives is the fun part of the job! Don't take that away from me."

She laughed. "I wouldn't dream of it. I'm the last person to tell you how to run the dive operation. I don't know the ins and outs of it." She reached up to kiss him. "Just ignore me."

"Oh, I know better than that, Boss Lady."

Now, his smile turned into a low whistle as he looked over the bookings for the next week. "Wow. Good thing we've got a big boat."

Both he and Robert were going to have their maximum group size of eight divers each. And Alex thought eight was too many—he preferred six. They were getting more bookings from locals and tourist divers who stayed in condos or other non-dive accommodations. It was partially because his experience was a known commodity now and people liked the novelty of diving with a former Navy SEAL, but he still never brought his past up.

There had been a steady stream of people coming into the dive shop while Hope was there, and regular phone calls wanting to book morning dive trips. She'd mentioned several people interested in an introductory scuba class, so maybe hiring another divemaster wasn't such a bad idea. They would be qualified to teach intro scuba classes, not to mention lead a third group if necessary.

The dive-shop door opened, and Zach's face lit up as he walked in. "Hey, Alex. You're still workin'?"

"Heading out now. I just stopped in to check the census for tomorrow. Everything going ok? Any questions for me?"

"No, I'm learnin' the ropes pretty well, I think. Robert is

wrappin' up, and I'm finishin' up the tanks. I wish I could be here in the mornin', so I could see it when it's busy. Maybe I could work extra on a weekend morning? You don't have to pay me. I'll do it for free."

Alex couldn't help but smile. "I'm sure we can work something out, but you'll be paid for every minute you work here. It's illegal otherwise."

And Hope would have my head on a platter.

He turned his gaze back to the dive schedule. "Robert's leading an afternoon dive tomorrow. You can ride along on the boat if you want."

He managed to keep a straight face as Zach's eyes got huge. "Really? That would be awesome! Thanks. Too bad you're not leadin' it. I want to see you at work."

"It's the same as Robert." Alex was uncomfortably aware the kid had a case of hero worship going on, but he didn't know how to stop it without crushing him.

"No way. Plus, I looked at the website and your bio doesn't even mention you were a SEAL."

Alex leveled a stare at him, and Zach's smile fell. "That's because I don't like to talk about it, Zach. And some guest divers might find it intimidating that their guide was a SEAL, so we keep it under wraps, ok?"

"Oh, I never thought about that. Right on—you can count on me."

"Thanks. I need to get back to the house, so I'll leave everything in your capable hands. You're doing a great job, Zach. Keep it up."

Zach's smile was back as Alex walked out of the shop, and he joined Robert, who was leaving for the day.

"Hope you don't mind," Robert said. "I got a last-minute photo shoot, so I called April to fill in for me tomorrow."

"Don't mind at all. I'll tell her Zach might tag along on the afternoon dive, so he gets some experience. Your photography business is really taking off."

Robert grinned at him. "It is. If I keep gettin' gigs like this, you're goin' to have to hire another divemaster."

They parted ways on the beach and Alex rubbed the back of his neck as he walked home, deep in thought about his expanding dive business.

CHAPTER 6

Hope relaxed in her chair, enjoying the simple routine of lunch with a friend. She sat on the outdoor brick patio of the Red Fort Grill, one of her favorite lunch spots. The bustling restaurant sat alongside the promenade in downtown Frederiksted and overlooked the long wooden pier, a main feature of the town. A giant cruise ship was pulling away, and as the horde of tourists departed, the town had the feel of a collective breath being let out.

Cindy Pearce's long black braids were piled into a loose bun on top of her head and her brown eyes were full of warmth. "Well, you're lookin' great. You feelin' ok?"

"Yes, I'm pretty much recovered now. I just picked up two photos from Vera's shop and was able to carry them the short distance to the car. I'm doing some short treadmill runs and plan on starting the group runs soon." Hope sighed, darting a glance at Cindy. "Just between you and me, that whole experience was really scary. I try not to think about what might have happened if I'd started bleeding an hour later, after Alex had left."

Cindy squeezed her hand. "But that didn't happen, so just put it out of your mind. No use worryin' about something that never was."

Hope laughed as warmth crept up her neck. "Thanks. I said similar words to Alex not too long ago. Guess I should listen to my own advice."

"So, how are the weddin' plans comin' along?"

"Good! We've got our date set and I blocked out the resort, so it will only be us there. Of course you're invited, but it's going to be a very small wedding. My sister and Alex's sister will be the only family. My mom's been gone for a while now and Alex's parents were killed in a car accident more than ten years ago."

"That's too bad. I'm sorry."

"Thanks. At this point, it's water under the bridge for both of us."

"Are you gonna do the big formal dress?"

"No. Nothing fancy. I'm thirty-seven—the long train isn't right for me. I'll find something simple and classic. I guess it's time to start looking."

Cindy leaned forward and crossed her arms on the table. "Let me know if you want some company."

"Thanks! I'd love your support. I've never been much of a clothes shopper. I just need to keep Alex in line. If you need a new wetsuit, he can go on for hours about fifteen different models, but he's hopeless at dressing himself." She shook her head with a fond smile. "He's actually been very sweet, asking my opinion about everything. He's agonizing over pants versus shorts now. I really don't care either way. I just want everything to be fun and low stress."

"No Bridezilla, huh?"

"Not if I can help it."

∽

When Hope got home, she was sweltering in her long-sleeved shirt. It had been cool that morning when she'd left for Frederiksted, but now she couldn't wait to change into a blue floral-patterned sundress.

Alex's garment bag in the corner of the closet enticed her. She unzipped it and pulled aside the suit jacket Alex had reluctantly worn to Charles's trial. Behind it hung his old white and blue dress uniforms and a daily uniform shirt she would dearly love to wear. She ran a hand over the long-sleeved desert camo shirt, which was adorned with his last name on a patch on the right breast. He didn't mind her wearing his sweatshirts, but this was a very personal item, so she was reluctant to bring it up. She regretfully closed the garment bag. "We've got the rest of our lives. I'm sure I'll get to wear it eventually." He'd caught her peeking twice since the trial, and though he hadn't been bothered by her snooping, she had felt guilty and brushed it off.

Alex was teaching an open water referral course that afternoon, so he wasn't available to help with her next errand. She dialed Robert. "I've got the two pictures in the back of my Jeep, but I probably shouldn't carry them all the way down to the dive shop. Can you meet me by my garage and help me out?"

"Absolutely. On my way."

A few minutes later, Robert joined her in the garage at the back of her Jeep. "Here they are. I'm so excited to hang them!"

Robert carried the two unwieldy cardboard boxes while she picked up a much smaller one. They walked into the dive shop as Zach was selling a dive-themed resort T-shirt to a woman who left as they entered. The shirts had been hot sellers, and after working in the dive shop, Hope had ordered additional styles. Patting the glass counter in front of Zach, Hope turned to Robert. "Ok, lay them here and let's take a look."

She used a box knife to carefully cut the tape on the thin cardboard boxes, revealing two modern glass-printed photos, each twenty-four by thirty-six inches. One was a photo of a bright-pink leaf scorpionfish, photographed with the dark ocean behind it, making the colors even more vivid as it clung to a crimson piece of coral.

The other photo was a stunning reef landscape with multicolored corals and schools of blue, yellow, and orange fish. It was shot from below with the sun shining beams of light over the reef.

"Oh, Robert, they're spectacular. They're going to look great in here."

Zach gave a long whistle. "Yeah. These are somethin' else."

Hope inspected the large expanse of white wall next to the door where they would hang. "Tommy is fixing a sticky door in one of the bungalows, but I'll get him to hang these tomorrow."

Robert turned to her, rubbing a hand back and forth over his shaved head. "You sure you want to do this? Seems like you're the one who's spendin' all the money here. I just collect if they sell."

"Of course I'm sure. I've got cards we can place next to each picture listing the price. If a guest wants to buy one, I'll take it back to the shop and Vera can mail it to their home—at their expense, of course. We just need to decide on a price. I was thinking $500 each."

Robert's jaw dropped. "I was thinking more like twenty-five dollars! Nobody would pay that much. And you want to split it in half with me?"

"Yes! Don't underestimate yourself, Robert. These are amazing. I'm sure we're going to sell them. In fact, I plan on raising the price on the next bunch. And these glass prints cost a lot more than twenty-five dollars, you know. Trust me—this is going to be a huge success. I've got four more in the works now, landscapes of St. Croix and beaches that will hang in the restaurant. They'll be for sale too."

Hope unwrapped the small cardboard box she'd carried down. She tried to keep her grin to a minimum as she held up a smaller glass photo. "I had this specially made. It's your bio. I took it straight off your website. We'll hang it here next to the photos, so the guests know how amazing it is they get to buy one of your works."

Robert dropped his gaze to the floor, clearly touched. "Thank you. This means a lot to me. I've always loved takin' photos. It's kind of amazin' people want to buy them. Since you hung the first ones in the guest bungalows, I've sold a bunch of digital files off my website."

"Good. That's the idea." She'd been thinking for a while about selling Robert's pictures so they both benefited, and was pleased with her solution.

The door opened, and she turned as Alex walked in. He was shirtless and shaking out his staff shirt as he prepared to put it on, but then he stopped, widening his eyes at the small crowd. Hope inhaled sharply as she took in his tan shoulders and chest.

"What's going on in here?" He smiled and held her eyes—her thoughts must have been showing on her face.

"Come look! Hope's goin' to hang some of Robert's pictures to sell to guests." Zach beckoned him over.

To Hope's disappointment, Alex put his shirt on, but made up for it by pressing his body against the back of hers as he leaned over her shoulder to look at the photos. She fought to keep a neutral expression.

"Wow." His breath was hot on her neck. "This is a beautiful sight."

"Uh-huh," Robert said. "Get a room, you two."

Hope couldn't help smiling at Zach's confused expression.

Alex straightened. "Zach, I left the gear from the class at the beach end of the pier. You feel like putting it away?"

"Oh yeah. On it."

He trotted out of the dive shop as Alex turned to Robert. "I'm sure these will sell. They're both incredible."

"We'll see. Your fiancée wants a fortune for them."

"Don't argue with Boss Lady. She knows what she's about."

After Robert left, Hope waited for Alex to finish up. As they headed up the pier, she nearly stumbled at the sight before her. Cruz walked at Zach's side as the boy pushed a cart of scuba equipment toward them.

"How about that! He likes you," she said, stopping.

"He's come down here a couple of times when I've been workin'. He moves away if I try to pet him, though."

"Believe me, that's a miracle," Alex said. "It was a month before he stopped barking at me. He hated me from day one." Cruz came over and sat on Alex's feet, looking up at him adoringly.

"Yeah, I can see he doesn't like you at all." Zach laughed and moved on to rinse out the gear.

"This morning I dropped off the signed proposal at Apex Construction," Hope said, Cruz joining her side as they continued. "They can start on the fence next week. We definitely need to sell some of that treasure now. Seventy thousand dollars for a chain-link fence seems ridiculous."

Alex grinned. "Hey, you're the one who wanted to put it in the middle of the jungle and keep it hidden. That costs some serious bucks."

"In related news, Alistair's office called. He has an update for us, so I made an appointment for tomorrow afternoon."

"I finished the checkout today, so that works for me."

Hope took his hand and they walked down the beach. A steady breeze rustled through the palm trees as her mind ran over scenarios of what Alistair might have found out.

∼

THE WOODEN FLOOR was still squeaky under Hope's feet as Alistair's receptionist greeted them. Hope was delighted to learn her name was Clara and she was his wife. "We've been in this buildin' for almost twenty years now," Clara said, smiling over her shoulder as she ushered her and Alex into Alistair's office.

Once again, he met them at the door to shake hands before leading them to the wingback chairs in front of his desk. Dressed in a robin's-egg blue suit and orange tie, he unbuttoned his jacket before sitting behind the opulent desk. The jacket draped around him like an anchorman delivering the evening news.

"Please accept my sincere apologies for the delay in progress. I had hoped my requests would bear more fruit."

"That's quite all right," Hope said. "We've had plenty to keep us busy."

Alex leaned back in his chair, crossing one ankle over his knee. "The construction company starts next week, so we should have the pool contained soon."

"Excellent. I contacted several auction houses in Miami, but because my lines of inquiry were rather vague, some of their responses were rather tepid. Due to the need for secrecy, I was . . . reluctant to divulge the exact nature of your find. But, of the three establishments I contacted, one was very promising." Alistair frowned at his crooked blotter. The frown disappeared once he straightened it.

"This company is the most respected name in the business of auctioning antiquities. I explained you would prefer to remain anonymous, but provenance of the find could be readily obtained. The man I spoke to, a Mr. McCandless, assured me that should present no hindrance, and we discussed the next steps."

"Well, this sounds encouraging," Hope said.

"Quite. My recommendation is for you to determine a representative sample of the items you wish to sell, and we will arrange for Mr. McCandless to fly here to inspect them in my office. If he agrees to host an auction for you, his expenses will be included in the general commission Prodigy Auction House will charge, which is twenty percent."

Alistair raised a manicured finger. "Now, I should point out that if he decides not to proceed, he will present you with an itemized bill of his expenses to be paid upon receipt. However, I think that is highly unlikely once he sees your discoveries."

Hope looked at Alex, who nodded. "That sounds fine to us. Let's go ahead."

"As you wish. I will contact him immediately and let you know as soon as he has an opening to meet with us."

CHAPTER 7

Alex parked and turned the ignition off. A week had passed since the meeting with Alistair, and construction was underway at the rock pool, freeing him to prepare for this task. The scuba-instructor meeting was at the local community center in Christiansted, a squat dark-brown building which could have been a prison in a past life. The last of these meetings had been three years ago, and Alex had enjoyed it. He'd talked with several other instructors, and they'd gone out for a beer afterwards, bitching about all the problems they had to deal with. Back then, he was just one of the guys.

He had a feeling it was going to be different this time.

Alex grabbed the thick, legal-sized envelope and a pen, then made his way inside the building, wincing at the moldy smell assaulting his nose. He found the room and checked his watch. He was a few minutes early, but there was no point in standing in the hall like a kid on the first day of school. The hum of voices could be heard from outside the door. Dive professionals were generally a friendly, talkative bunch.

Alex opened the door and stepped into a bright room with a dozen people sitting behind individual desks. A man about forty years old with short dark-brown hair and a trimmed beard stood behind a table at the front of the room, writing on a yellow legal pad. The natural buzz of conversation halted as Alex entered, and he stiffened as people stopped to look at him. He tried to ignore the hairs rising on his neck as he made his way toward the back of the room, acutely aware of the eyes on his back.

He passed Mark Lowry, one of the guys he'd shared a beer with last time, and sat at the desk behind him. *I feel like the new kid in junior high.* Mark ducked his head and didn't even meet his eyes. But at least conversation started back up again as a young man came in and took a seat near the front of the room.

The bearded man looked at the wall clock. "Ok, folks, let's get going. I'm Cody Davis, and I'm your regional representative. I live on St. Croix, so I'm familiar with most of the dive ops on the island. You guys should be proud of yourselves. We've had very few complaints or infractions. I'm here to talk about some changes we're making to the open water certification standards, but before we begin, let's go around the room and introduce ourselves."

Alex closed his eyes. *That's all I need.*

Fortunately, no one seemed to want to talk about themselves overmuch, except the guy who came in at the last minute, who informed them he was highly qualified because he completed his instructor course in Michigan and was experienced in cold water. He looked all of twenty-five years old. Alex tuned out his bluster and tried not to think about what he'd been doing at that kid's age.

Then Mark, with his brown hair peeking from under his baseball cap, introduced himself from the seat in front of Alex. "Mark Lowry from Ocean Surf Resort. I've been there for seven years and an instructor for ten."

Finally, it was Alex's turn and once again, people turned in their chairs, an expectant air hanging in the room. Alex was stiff as a board as he took a deep breath. "I'm Alex Monroe. I'm an instructor and guide at Half Moon Bay Resort."

The few heads that hadn't turned around did so now.

Oh, this is just great.

At the front of the room, Cody snapped his head up and brightened. "Nice to finally meet you! For anyone who doesn't know, this is the guy you want around if your boat sinks. Alex is our own resident Navy SEAL."

"Not anymore. Just an instructor like everyone else here."

"Oh, come on! I bet you've got some great dive stories."

"Nothing I can talk about." Most people got the hint with that.

Cody grinned. "I'm not asking about classified missions. What was your favorite part of being a SEAL?"

"Nobody cares." Alex crossed his arms and put some steel into his stare, willing his heart to slow.

"Ok, ok! We'll move on. But you and I need to talk—you could be great for the agency here. I've got all kinds of ideas."

"I don't think so." Alex kept his tone even.

The Michigan super-diver narrowed his eyes at him. "You were really a SEAL?"

Alex was on the verge of walking out when Mark slammed his hand on the desk. "Come on, people! He clearly doesn't want to talk about it, and that's not why we're here, anyway. Let's move on, ok?"

Quickly, the woman next to Alex introduced herself.

Alex leaned forward. "Thanks."

Mark whispered back, "That agency guy is a real asshole. I can't wait to hear about the changes."

But Mark's outburst broke the logjam, and the meeting went on. Like most bureaucratic changes, some made sense and others were completely ridiculous. There was spirited discussion about several issues, such as the order in which students should be taught skills.

Alex didn't take part, instead sitting at his junior high desk, taking deep breaths as he fought against the rising memories of other planning sessions.

This is why I spent eighteen years fighting? Why I almost died? So people could argue whether mask clearing should come before neutral buoyancy skills?

He sat back and closed his eyes.

Of course not. The reason why is sitting at home right now.

Alex might not have known Hope then, but he was protecting her just the same. He dropped his shoulders as a sense of calm washed over him.

Finally, Cody finished, and everyone began gathering up their things. Mark turned around. "You want to have a beer like we did last time?"

Alex hesitated before remembering Mark had been the one to stand up for him. "Sure, let's go."

They walked down the street to an outdoor bar with an industrial theme, full of wrought iron and hard chairs. Their server brought over two Leatherbacks and Alex took a long pull.

Mark looked him in the eye. "Sorry I kind of ignored you at first, but I didn't know what to say. I've been following your story. You've been in the paper quite a bit."

Alex snorted. "Not by choice."

"No, I wouldn't think so. Still, it sounds like your resort's doing well. We've gotten guests who wanted to stay at Half Moon Bay, but you were totally booked."

"That's Hope's doing."

"Hope?"

Alex took another drink and smiled. "The resort owner. Also, my fiancée."

"Congrats."

Alex nodded as he panned his eyes around the busy bar. "It's not just the bungalows, either. The dive op is going gangbusters. I need another divemaster, and it isn't easy to find a decent one."

Mark sat back and watched Alex steadily. "I might be able to help you out there. I've got a new guy and he's impressed me. He just moved to the island, and I don't have enough work for him. I'm sure he'd be happy to pick up some hours. His name is Jack Powell—you want his number?"

"Sure." Alex pulled out his phone and entered the info into his contacts. "I'll have him tag along on one of my dives and give him a trial if he's interested. I can definitely give him some work."

The two men toasted a productive afternoon, Alex finally feeling like it had been worth coming.

∼

On the drive home, Alex pulled off the highway, stopping at a sand pullout overlooking the turquoise ocean. He smiled at a sea turtle bobbing at the surface near shore, then took out his phone and dialed. His sister, Katie Fletcher, answered after one ring. "How's Baltimore life?"

"Busy as usual. Dave's out of town at a conference, Jason's got soccer, and Monica's in dance lessons and has a recital this week. And guess who's in charge of getting everyone to their respective places on time and fed? Oh, and I've got a big prospective client I'm pitching to in a couple days too."

Alex laughed. "Sounds like you've got your hands full."

"We should have moved in with you guys and stayed there."

"You'd waste away in the slow lane."

"Doesn't sound like it's so slow to me. You guys have been through a lot in the last couple years."

"It's kept me on my toes."

"Uh-huh. Typical answer from you, vague and self-deprecating. What about now? Anything exciting going on?"

Alex twitched the corner of his mouth. *Was that an innocent question, or is she fishing?* "Maybe. Not sure I want to tell you after that last comment."

"You really are an asshole, you know. Did a new regulator model come out that's got you all atwitter?"

Alex sighed into the phone, glad she couldn't see his smile. "Katie, if you're just going to insult me, I'll hang up now."

"Ok, fine. I'll ask nicely. How are things in tropical paradise?"

"Much better. I'm getting married, Halfpint."

There was a moment of shocked silence, then Katie started laughing. "I knew it! Hot damn—Dave owes me a steak dinner!"

Alex snapped his open mouth shut. "What are you talking about?"

"Dave and I made a bet on the plane ride home after we visited you. He didn't think you'd propose for at least a year. My money was on the next three months. The time in between was a kind of demilitarized zone. The Alex-Hope DMZ."

Katie's laughter had subsided to a few occasional snorts. "How about that? Big brother's getting married. When we visited, it was hard to miss the way you two looked at each other. And I've *never* seen you look at a woman like that, Alex. Certainly not when you were fresh out of high school."

"That was a stupid mistake. Taught me a lesson about looking before I leap, though. I took a pretty thorough look this time, and I've never been surer about anything."

"That was about the only stupid, impulsive thing you've ever done in your life. But watching you around Hope those few days was like seeing a brother I never knew."

"Jeez, Katie. Was I that obvious?"

She had to stop for another laughing fit as Alex scowled at the ocean. The sea turtle dived to eat some grass in the shallows. "Alex, when you were a SEAL, you used to practically trip over yourself in a rush to tell me any woman in your life was 'just a girlfriend, nothing serious.' Pretty sure those were your exact words.

"But every time I tried to prod you about Hope, you clammed up, which told me loud and clear she was very different." Katie gave another teasing laugh. "And when you kept looking at her with those ridiculous lovesick eyes of yours, it didn't help keep the secret either."

Alex let a smile slip out as a flush crept up his face. "You're kind of pissing me off here. I'm thinking about hanging up again."

"Oh, come on! We're finally having normal conversations again. Don't dish it out if you can't take it."

"Uh-huh. Well, I guess I deserve a little teasing after what I put you through."

"Congratulations. I mean it—you two are great together. And it's about time you allowed yourself a little happiness again. When's the party?"

"October twelfth. We're really hoping you guys can come down here. We're having it on the beach at the resort."

"Count us in. Nothing could keep me away, Alex."

~

IT WAS NEARLY six when he got home, and Hope wasn't in the house. Alex frowned when she wasn't on the porch either, then he saw her standing at the waterline with the waves tumbling over her feet. The sun was heading toward the horizon, bathing the sky in splashes of orange and pink as she stood in a light-green dress, radiant, as the breeze blew her hair back. He didn't know whether to kiss her hello or throw her over his shoulder and head for the bedroom. But his common sense asserted itself. He had a tendency to startle her, so he stopped several feet away. "Do you have any idea how beautiful you are right now?"

She turned toward him with a smile and his heart swelled at the sight of her eyes, filled with golden light.

"I was just thinking about you, and now here you are."

He began walking without thought, and she was in his arms before he knew it. He swiped his lips over hers with a whisper-soft touch before settling in for a longer kiss.

They held each other, watching the sunset for several minutes before she said, "How was your meeting?"

"Fine. The usual crap they think they have to change. Oh, I had a beer with another instructor afterwards. He gave me contact info for a possible new divemaster. I'd really like to have someone else to draw on when we need it."

"Sounds good to me." She pulled back to look him in the eye. "The meeting went ok for you?"

"Yes. They got into my past for a little bit, but it blew over, and everything was fine. I need to learn to get used to people talking about it."

She watched him carefully.

"Really," he said. "I'm fine, not to mention starving. Let's go eat dinner."

She inclined her head. "There's the Alex I know and love. Come on, maybe I can talk Clark into making me one of his secret contest drinks."

CHAPTER 8

Hope spent the following morning working in the lobby office and trying not to clock-watch. As she left at midday, she passed the front desk and said goodbye to Corrine, the new front-desk clerk. She was a waif of a woman in her early twenties, with platinum-blonde hair and skin so pale Hope couldn't figure out how she survived in the tropical sun. Martine had delivered a healthy boy the previous week and Corrine was doing a great job filling in. Patti had hired her during Hope's recovery.

Hope picked up lunch for two from the restaurant and deposited it in their refrigerator since Alex wasn't home yet. She cleaned the kitchen, trying to fill the time but so eager for this afternoon's meeting she couldn't hold still. Unable to resist any longer, she headed toward her home office. On one wall hung a watercolor painting of four resort bungalows. She swung the painting open to reveal a wall safe. After opening it using the combination lock, Hope shook her head, awe prickling through her at its contents.

She and Alex had visited one of their safe-deposit boxes and removed an assortment of items to bring to this afternoon's meeting with Alistair and Mr. McCandless. They were taking a gold ingot, an assortment of gold and silver coins, a solid-gold necklace with a large pendant, and one gemstone—a large, faceted emerald. The two golden chalices studded with emeralds and diamonds sat in the back of the safe. Hope had no intention of parting with either.

Despite the wonders inside the safe, Hope's eye was drawn to a small, crushed-velvet box sitting front and center. She picked it up and opened it, entranced.

"Hey, you're not supposed to inspect that before the wedding, you know."

She nearly leaped through the ceiling at Alex's usual silent approach. He stood across the room in the doorway. "There are no prohibitions against seeing the ring," she said. "Plus, it's just sitting here in front. How could I not?"

Like the engagement ring, her wedding band was made of white gold. It featured a row of six diamonds side by side. Alex had designed the custom-made set using a diamond he found in the cave. The jeweler had cut the enormous stone to a smaller size for the solitaire, but there was still enough material left over to make the six smaller stones. An included appraisal revealed the solitaire was nearly two carats and of incredible quality.

Alex stood relaxed and self-assured, his face lit from within. She couldn't resist a big smile. "You make me very happy, you know that? Even without amazing diamond rings."

"I aim to please."

She held up the box. "How did you know what I would like? This is exactly what I would have picked."

"I'm relieved to hear that because it was a guess. Well, an educated guess." He leaned against the doorframe with a grin. "For the past few months, I've been stealing glances on the dive boat at every woman's hand, getting an idea of what you might like and what seemed popular. And I admit, the jeweler helped too."

"I hope none of those women saw you checking for wedding rings. That might send the wrong message, you know."

Alex's smile grew. "Oh, I can be subtle when I need to. Stealth used to be a specialty of mine, remember?"

"It still is. You could get a second job as a creeper." She arched a brow. "Speaking of rings, there's one rather important wedding item we haven't discussed yet."

"What might that be?"

"Yours. You are planning on wearing one, aren't you?"

He became serious. "Absolutely."

"Well, what do you like? Have you thought about it?"

"Oh, yes. Titanium. It reminds me of our relationship. It's light and yet so strong it's unbreakable. And it never loses its luster."

As usual, his response made her heart melt into a puddle as their gazes held for a long moment. "Do you have one picked out?"

He shifted position against the doorframe. "I've got a few different ones I like. We'll head to the jewelry store sometime and make the final pick together."

"That sounds perfect."

Alex laughed and shook his head. "I still can't believe it. You really had no idea I was ready to propose?"

Hope's smile dropped off her face as her gaze fell to the floor. Alex crossed to her, cradling her face in his hands. "Hey, what's wrong?"

"Nothing. It couldn't be righter. It's still hard for me to believe sometimes—that this is real. That it's happening to *me*."

His eyes softened as he stroked her cheeks with his thumbs. "You've been treated so badly by men. I intend to spend the rest of my life making up for that."

Hope slid her arms around him and rested her head against his chest. "You don't have to do that. I know how you feel. I'm sorry—these bouts of self-doubt still creep up once in a while. Your job isn't to prove you love me. I already know that."

"Hey, don't tell me my job." She could hear the smile in his voice.

"I'm your boss. I can and I will."

"Is that right?" He blew in her ear, sending a jolt through her. "Are you about to start bossing me around?"

Hope stepped back and firmly smacked his chest. "We don't have time for that. Come on. I've brought lunch. Let's eat before we head out."

∽

McCandless wasn't what Hope had been expecting. She thought he'd be an older, wire-rimmed-glasses-wearing academic in a tweed coat with elbow patches. Instead, he was about her age with tousled dark-blond hair and warm brown eyes and dressed in a crisp dark-gray suit.

They met in Alastair's conference room, seated at a round teak table with six chairs. To Hope's disappointment, Alistair was dressed sedately in a royal-blue suit, but at least he sported a lavender and pink striped tie. He introduced McCandless, who stood and shook hands warmly. Alex carried their selected pieces in a non-descript gym bag and placed it between his feet.

McCandless sat across from Hope and settled in. "I'm excited to see the items you've turned up. Alistair wouldn't say much. Let me give you my bona fides. I have a PhD in European History with a focus on the Spanish Conquest. I'm also a certified antiquities expert and appraiser, and I've worked for Prodigy for over ten years."

He paused to alternate his gaze between Hope and Alex. "Alistair tells me you found some items you might be interested in auctioning. Now, I should warn you people often find what they think is a priceless treasure, but it just turns out to be a bunch of highly circulated Buffalo nickels—worth nothing. Why don't you show me your treasures and I'll let you know if this is worth pursuing? Or if I'm just going to send you a very expensive bill for my expenses." He softened the last sentence with a smile, handing them each his business card.

Alex nodded and unzipped the bag. "What do you think of this?"

He placed a gold ingot in front of Bryce, who stilled, his smile fading as he darted his eyes all over it. The gold bar was six inches in length, oval shaped, and had several markings with an engraved stamp on one end. Bryce picked it up, turning it over in his hands. Alex dug back into the bag and placed the coins, the necklace with the gold pendant, and the large-cut emerald in front of him.

"Any Buffalo nickels there?" Hope asked.

"Ok, you have my full attention." Bryce blinked several times before smiling at them. "This looks very promising."

He reached down and then placed a black leather bag on the table. Opening it, he took out a jeweler's loupe and placed it in his eye, then held the ingot up for closer inspection. He pointed to the engraved stamp. "This is the Lima Treasurer's stamp, marking this as an official gold bar of the Spanish empire—from Peru. I'd have to check my sources to determine a more precise date, but off the top of my head, I'd say it's mid-seventeenth century."

Bryce dove back into his bag, removing a small black scale topped with a circular plate, and placed the gold ingot on it. "Just over five ounces. The Peru mines produced incredibly pure gold. Last month we auctioned off a similar bar for over sixty thousand dollars."

Hope took a deep breath and tried to keep a neutral face.

Bryce traded the ingot for the emerald and examined it under his loupe, his mouth opening and closing. "Wow. This is Columbian. The color's extraordinary . . . emerald cut, really well done. Whoever made this was an artist." Bryce set the stone on the scale and tapped on a calculator. "Six point five carats." He looked up, his eyes wide. "I don't know what this would sell for, but I'd set the minimum at seventy thousand." He set it down and touched two coins. "You have more items like this?"

"Some," Alex said, his face expressionless. "How do you handle security?"

Bryce relaxed. "Oh, during a live auction we have a heavy guard presence, and all items are kept in a secure vault prior to that. You don't have to worry about security."

Hope snorted and covered it with a cough. *You don't know Alex.*

"How would the items get to your auction house?" Alex asked.

Bryce sat back in his chair and shrugged. "However you want. We take responsibility for the lot of items once it reaches our premises, but we're not involved in transport."

"Mr. McCandless, we will discuss transport amongst ourselves and come to an arrangement." Alistair's voice poured out like maple syrup.

Bryce picked up the golden necklace. "Where did all this come from? Can you prove provenance?"

Hope explained how they found the trove, though not its exact magnitude, then described Barnaby's letter.

"Henry Morgan's little brother? Seriously? Ok, the values I quoted were too low." Bryce was on fire with excitement as he began packing his things back into the black bag. "When you've settled on the items you want to include in your auction, give me a call and we'll get the ball rolling. Prodigy takes a twenty percent commission of total gross proceeds." He settled his gaze on the items lined up on the table. "But if you have more items of this quality, I think you could be looking at clearing six figures."

Hope let out a shaky sigh, her heart trying to explode, but Alex was still straight faced.

"We'll decide which items are worth auctioning and give you a call," he said.

After McCandless left, Hope turned to Alistair. "How do you suggest we get this to Miami?"

A small smile crossed his face. "In prior auctions I've assisted, they simply carried the items on board a regularly scheduled flight to Miami."

Alex was already shaking his head as Alistair held up a hand. "Yes, I realize your items have a much larger monetary value, making alternative arrangements a necessity."

"Well, we can't just send them via overnight mail, and it's a little far to swim," Hope said.

"A boat is also out," Alex added. "The trip would take too long."

"You might want to look into chartering a private aircraft. The cost would be substantial, but it has several advantages."

"I think Alistair's right." Alex looked at Hope. "From a security standpoint, if we fly private, we can avoid the commercial terminal all together, and I'm sure I could get permission from the charter company to carry onboard."

"Carry what?" Alistair asked.

"I think Alex just volunteered for security detail," Hope said.

"I wouldn't even *think* about transporting this without an armed escort," Alex said.

"Yes, I agree," Alistair said. "I was going to suggest hiring one or two persons to accompany you, but you would most likely be sufficient, Mr. Monroe."

"More than sufficient," Hope added with a smile.

"I'll call the airport and ask about chartering a plane," Alex said, then they gathered up their things and left the conference room. Hope's head spun with possibilities as they climbed into Alex's car.

Driving out of Christiansted, they passed a billboard for a Jump Up, to be held in a few days. "What's that about?" Hope asked.

"It's a nighttime street festival held in Christiansted several times a year. I've never been to one, but it sounds like a lot of fun. It's popular with locals and tourists alike. You want to go?"

Hope sat up so fast her seatbelt locked. "Yes! After what I've been through the last few months, a fun night out is just what I need. I can't wait."

CHAPTER 9

Hospital Street in Christiansted was transformed into a pedestrian-only riot of sound, color, and local flavor. Hope couldn't stop smiling. Even though it was fully dark, streetlights lit up the area like it was noon. Strings of party lights zigzagged over the street from lamppost to lamppost.

Hope craned her head up, laughing at a mocko jumbie, who wore a green plaid suit as he danced down the street. Stilts vaulted the figure to eight feet in height, and several others paraded up and down the promenade. A different steel drum band played on each block, their mellow, lyrical sound filling the night.

Alex squeezed her hand. "Don't look so sad. I'm sure the party will pick up soon."

"I love this! We should use it in our advertising more."

"Do you ever stop thinking about business?"

Hope let her eyes smolder. "Why, yes I do, from time to time."

"Uh-huh. What sounds good for dinner?"

Food trucks were scattered over several blocks, giving the revelers a wide variety of choices. Hope had already seen tacos,

Indian curries, Thai, and jerk chicken. "It all does. I don't know how to choose."

"How about that one? It's close." Alex pointed to the Thai truck across from them, and ten minutes later they stood at an elevated table sharing pad Thai and green curry. Two Singha beers washed down the spicy food. A street performer dressed as a pirate and breathing fire at periodic intervals passed in front of them, fortunately not too close.

"Has the guy from the charter-flight company called you back yet?" Hope asked. They stood away from the music so were able to speak quietly.

"Yeah, this afternoon. I told him we had something expensive and private to transport and assured him it was legal. After explaining my background, he said carrying onboard shouldn't be a problem. He recommended a small jet." Alex leaned closer, winking at her. "Maybe we can join the mile-high club."

"Of course that would be your primary objective. You're also taking great care to avoid the question I most want answered." She arched a brow at him.

"Yeah, it's pretty expensive. We only need a one-way flight—we can fly commercial on the way back. But we're still looking at twenty grand."

Hope winced, setting her fork in the empty container. "I guess we'll add another item to the auction."

"I know it's a lot. But it's the safest option." Alex reached for her hand. "Come on, I want some ice cream."

They strolled to another truck painted with a snowman sporting dreadlocks, then stood in front of a steel drum band to enjoy their dessert. Hope people-watched for a while, approving of the solid mix of tourists and locals.

They resumed ambling down the street, their arms wrapped around each other. She continued people-watching, trying to decide if a nearby man was a sitcom star. Out of the corner of her eye, she noted a couple passing by before turning her attention back to the potential star. He had similarly groomed hair and capped teeth, but he wasn't the celebrity.

A male voice called out behind them. "Monroe? *Alex?*"

The astonishment came through loud and clear in the man's voice, and Alex went rigid under her arm. In slow motion, he turned around and Hope did likewise, their arms falling to their sides.

It was the couple who had just passed by. Shorter than Alex, the man was around their age and fit, with brown hair and bright-green eyes. The blood drained from his face as he gaped at Alex. The woman was about Hope's height and very chic-looking, with highlights streaking her long blonde hair. She glanced back and forth between Alex and the man beside her, her eyes growing wider and wider.

Hope turned her gaze to Alex as the most extraordinary succession of emotions crossed his face. Shock, grief, desperation, yearning, and finally . . . the hint of a smile. Hope was uncomfortably aware she was the only member of this little quartet who didn't understand what was happening.

"Baker," Alex said in a tight, even voice, his pulse throbbing in his neck.

"Oh my God! It *is* you. I can't believe this!" Baker's eyes were still bulging, and he heaved the words out. Rushing forward, he crushed Alex into a hug, laughing now. At first Alex just stood there, then he slowly raised his arms to return the embrace. Soon they were thumping each other's backs. Hope and the woman exchanged awkward smiles.

Baker stepped back and held Alex by his upper arms, looking him up and down. "You look great! Healthy, man."

"I am. How you doing, Mike?"

Mike just shook his head and laughed again, finally saying, "We all need to go have a beer. Right now."

Then he noticed Hope, and that jolted Alex into action. As he turned to her, wonder slackened Alex's face. The shock was still there too. "This is Mike Baker. We were on the same SEAL Team."

The air rushed out of Hope and her knees weakened, understanding now what she'd just witnessed.

Alex put an arm around her and drew her close. "This is Hope, my fiancée."

Mike had been smiling, but when Alex said "fiancée," he started laughing again before finally getting it back together to shake her hand. "Pleased to meet you, Hope. This is my wife, Emma."

Now it was Alex's turn to laugh, and soon both men were slapping each other's backs again while Hope and Emma frowned at each other, wondering what the joke was.

Alex broke away and held his hand out to Emma. "Sorry, Emma. It's really good to meet you."

"Same here, Alex. Mike's told me a lot about you."

Mike glanced around the street as another mocko jumbie danced by. "There's got to be a bar around here somewhere."

"Yeah, I know one. Follow us." Alex took Hope's hand and gripped it tightly as he walked quickly up a side street. Energy came off him in waves, and she had a hard time keeping up.

Fortunately, their destination was only a block off the main street, an outdoor bar with lit tiki torches scattered around the square tables. A short wooden fence enclosed the area. They found a table for four and sat, ordering drinks.

"What are you doing here?" Alex asked Mike.

"We're on vacation and thought we'd come check this out tonight. You guys visiting too?"

Alex laughed, brushing his shoulder against Hope. "No, we live here."

"You're kidding!" Mike frowned. "Wait, you did tell me you were moving to some Caribbean island right before you dropped off the face of the earth. What do you do here?"

"I'm a dive guide."

At that, Mike belly laughed, clutching his stomach until Emma elbowed him. People were starting to stare. "God, that just figures. A dive guide."

Alex smiled, relaxing as he took a drink. "What about you?"

"I'm still in the DC area. I work for a defense contractor in Alexandria."

Hope was beginning to feel like a fifth wheel. "What about you, Emma? What do you do?"

"I'm a lobbyist for an environmental company. I work at the Capitol. How about you?"

"I own the resort where Alex works." Hope shot him an acerbic glance, feeling a bit left out, and he just grinned at her. She couldn't help smiling back. There was no mistaking his happiness about this reunion.

"How much longer are you down here?" Alex asked.

"A few more days," Mike said.

"You should come over tomorrow. We could go diving after I'm done with the afternoon trip." Alex turned to Emma. "Do you dive?"

"No way. That is *not* for me. I'm more of a sit by the pool and drink margaritas kind of girl, though I like the water. Besides, I have an afternoon booked at the spa. But feel free to take Mike off my hands."

Mike smiled at her, and Hope could see the genuine affection between them. Not to mention one of those marital looks where couples pass information without speaking.

"I know!" Alex opened his eyes wide, leaning forward. "We can dive Washing Machine! I never get a chance to do that—it scares most people." He turned to Hope. "Oh. I'm sorry, baby. I'm not sure you'd enjoy this dive."

Hope's eyebrows rose toward the sky. "I'll sit this one out. Diving a site called Washing Machine with two Navy SEALs is *not* my idea of a good time."

. . .

As Alex drove them home, he was still thrumming, shifting in his seat as he swapped hands on the steering wheel. Hope stared at his animated face—this reunion might have gone very differently even one year ago. "So, what was all that laughing about when you introduced me?"

Alex rubbed his neck and grinned sheepishly. "Well, I might have told him about a hundred times I'd never get married again."

"Oh? You've never struck me as a *girl in every port* kind of sailor."

"No! It wasn't that. More that I didn't want any distractions. I was pretty focused on the job." He laughed. "Mike, on the other hand, was a bit of a player. I never thought he'd settle down either."

"Uh-huh. So I guess that explains your laughing fit."

Alex shook his head, now down to one hand held casually on the wheel. "I cannot *believe* we ran into them out here."

"You were ok seeing him again?" Hope crossed her fingers that Alex's nightmares wouldn't come back.

"Yeah, after I got over the shock. It was great to see him, and I can't *wait* to dive with him tomorrow."

"You were close, weren't you?"

His eyes took on a faraway look. "Every platoon has one guy. The guy who holds it all together. Who can joke when it's needed, or open up a can of whoop-ass when that's more appropriate. Mike was that guy. He was my best friend."

CHAPTER 10

Alex climbed the stairs to the pier with Mike, who was craning his neck around, trying to see everything.

"Damn! What a beach," Mike said. "Nice place—how many bungalows?"

"Eight. There's plenty of room to grow, but Hope likes the small feel of the resort. Though I wouldn't be surprised if she decides to expand at some point." *Especially after an influx of cash.* They entered the dim tunnel. "Come on. I'll get you some gear."

They entered the room, and Mike made a beeline for the compressor. "Sweet. Looks like it can do the job. No membrane system?"

"No, we only dive with air. I'm thinking about getting one, though. Our dive op has really picked up and guests are asking for Nitrox. I'd rather use it too." Within minutes, they were back on the pier, Mike's arms filled with a wetsuit, mask, and fins.

"You dive much?" Alex asked.

Mike shook his head. "Haven't in several years. Last time I dove was in Chesapeake Bay—three-foot visibility and nothing to see but mud."

"Well, I think we can do better than that today."

Mike darted his eyes everywhere as they approached *Surface Interval*. "I was expecting a glorified panga. Sweet boat, man."

"Got lucky." Alex grinned and let the double entendre—and the memory—wash over him. "We needed a new boat and the owner of this one needed to sell, so we got a great deal."

Mike threw the lines, then Alex headed straight west toward open water. The ocean was calm, and the day was sunny, with an occasional cloud racing across the sky. A perfect St. Croix afternoon.

After thirty minutes, Mike threw him a skeptical glance. "Where are we going? Mexico?"

"We're almost there. It's a seamount in the middle of nowhere that does ridiculous things to the currents. That's why it's called Washing Machine—the fish love it. In addition to strong lateral currents, you can get some pretty good up and down drafts. I've dived it several times with my friend Robert, but not in years. It's a rush." He turned to Mike. "You're not scared, are you? We can go snorkeling if you'd prefer."

"Oh, kiss my ass. I can outdive you any day of the week."

Alex laughed and watched his depth finder and GPS unit, slowing the boat. He reached the top of the seamount but had to keep the boat in gear to stay above it. The current was *moving*. "I need to moor the boat, and the ball's submerged. I'm gonna need you to hold her in place while I do it."

"You want me to keep the props running?"

"Yeah, you'll have to—the surface current's running pretty good. Just don't run over me, ok?"

"No promises."

Alex grabbed his mask and fins and proceeded to the bow, picking up the mooring line coiled on the fiberglass deck. Once ready, he saluted Mike and dove in. Alex looked down at the top of the seamount. The force of the current caused the line with its attached mooring ball to hang straight sideways instead of floating vertically.

Free diving toward it, he grinned as the water slammed him to the left, and he angled his body and kicked hard to stay atop the mount. Ten feet down, the current switched, throwing him to the right, and he had to pivot the other direction. Soon he had the boat line secured to the mooring ball, tugging the attachment several times to make sure it was tight.

Satisfied, Alex held onto the rope and studied the area, excitement building. An enormous school of horse-eye jacks floated motionless above the mount—a wall of fish, hundreds strong. The size of dinner plates, small flicks of their tails held their sleek silver bodies stationary in the strong current.

On the other side of the mount, a school of bluefin trevally was harassing a shoal of small silver fish. The silver and blue forms of the trevally darted in and out of the dense ball as they hunted for a meal. Much deeper, a dozen reef sharks circled. Then Alex needed to breathe.

He surfaced, giving Mike the ok to shut the engine off as he drifted to the stern before climbing back aboard. "It looks great down there. Visibility's a good hundred feet and there's lots of fish around. I saw a school of sharks down deep. The current is running one way for the first ten feet, then switches. We'll just see where it takes us, but if we can get deep, maybe the sharks will get curious and come check us out."

As they descended, they were slammed and pulled by the current. It changed directions four times before they reached one hundred feet and levelled off. Alex studied the small, suspended particles always present in ocean water. They were drifting downward, and he added extra air to his BCD as he was in a downdraft. Fortunately, not a strong one—the lateral current was much stronger.

The two men exchanged ok signals and Alex relaxed, for once able to enjoy the dive without having to worry about anyone else. He turned back around and the school of small fish he had noted earlier was *flying* toward him. Within moments he was surrounded by them, silver fish all around as the much larger trevally zipped in and out. He was sure the hunters would collide with him, but they always managed to veer away at the last second.

Smiling, his heart hammered as a loud *whooshing* came from his other side.

Alex spun around and the entire school of tiny fish had reversed direction as one and was speeding by him again. This time they were chased by an eight-foot blue marlin, its swordbill passing within feet of him.

Mike's "*Yeah!*" came through plenty loud, and Alex held up a hand for a high five.

He led them around the seamount and the current picked him up and threw him forward, sling-shotting the men around one side of it. Not wanting to be swept away, Alex finned hard to stay near the side of the reef and soon the moving water slackened. Mike followed just behind.

This was where he'd seen the sharks. Now in calmer water, they moved away from the seamount and were rewarded when the sharks ascended to investigate them. The divers hung motionless in the water as the six-foot silver predators slowly circled, watching them with black, alert eyes. They were curious, but never threatening.

The two men moved up to eighty feet and Alex gestured to Mike, asking how much air he had. Mike flipped him off, and Alex returned the gesture with a grin. Next, Alex smacked his fist into the open palm of his other hand, the signal for current. Mike nodded and Alex turned around, letting the powerful stream carry him around this edge of the seamount. Once again, they were picked up and thrust forward into a raging river in the middle of the ocean. Alex whooped, his eyes wide and his heart surging.

Ahead and to their right was an enormous column of colorful fish milling about off the point of the seamount. At a glance, Alex counted a dozen varieties. From previous dives, he knew another strong current ran in the opposite direction on the other side of the fish column, creating a narrow area of calm water for the fish to relax in. He signaled to Mike, and they turned out of the river and into the still corridor, the fish gently parting around them.

Alex was completely surrounded by fish in all three dimensions.

They tolerated his presence, not wanting to enter the fast-moving water to get away from the divers, and he kept his motions slow and gentle to avoid startling them. A Moorish Idol swam right in front of his mask, its yellow, black, and white stripes vivid in the water as its lengthened dorsal fin trailed behind. The two men hovered, enjoying the serenity of the fish drifting around them. It was like being inside a natural aquarium. But eventually, they'd had enough.

Time for some more excitement.

With his heart pounding again, Alex signaled Mike and they swam back toward the current they'd just left. The seal of his mask began to weaken from the force of the water, so Alex turned and let the water rush him forward once again.

Ahead was an expanse of agitated, frothing ocean. It swirled, bubbled, and churned as the two currents collided, creating a whirlpool eighty feet below the surface.

Alex was thrown into the maelstrom, the water spinning him around and around as it pulled him downward. Mike slammed into him, and both laughed in sheer exhilaration as they were turned and tumbled, bumping into each other again and again.

His computer—and his ears—verified they'd been swept down forty feet, so Alex swam hard to escape, reaching the perimeter of the tornado with Mike just behind. They were spit out and thrown in the opposite direction by the new current. His face hurt from his grin, and once again, he flew by the column of fish. Adjusting his body position, he angled up toward the top of the seamount.

They'd been down for an hour, and this wasn't a dive conducive to good air consumption. Despite his skills and bluster,

Mike hadn't dived in a while and Alex wasn't eager to buddy breathe if he ran out of air. The current swept them over the top of the seamount and the mooring line rushed toward Alex.

Only gonna get one shot at this. Better not miss.

He reached out and grabbed the line, holding tightly as the current whipped him around the rope. Now he faced Mike, who was too far to one side. Alex held out a hand and Mike gripped it at the last second, both of them laughing as Alex pulled him in. Finally, Mike reached for the line himself.

During their safety stop, both men hung in the water like two flags on a flagpole. The school of jacks came over to check them out, effortless in the current as the sunlight glinted off their silver bodies. Hundreds of them milled around the two men.

They climbed the mooring line hand over hand until they surfaced, then let go. Before the dive, Alex had thrown out a trailing line. The current sped them past the boat, and they grabbed the rope, pulling themselves back to the stern and climbing back on board.

"Holy shit—that was awesome! Did you bring two more tanks?" Mike whipped his head around the stern of the boat, a big smile on his face.

"No, I didn't even think about it. Told you it was a rush." Alex stripped off his wetsuit, tossing it on the deck before securing his tank. It was still warm and sunny. Minimal waves slapped against the boat, giving no hint of the raging water below.

"Ok, maybe you're not an idiot for doing this for a living."

Alex laughed. "That is definitely *not* a dive I take guests on. I don't get opportunities like this very often. Thanks, Mike."

Grinning, Mike turned toward him, then saw Alex's left shoulder. He froze, meeting Alex's eyes as his smile disappeared.

The two men stared at each other for a long moment.

"Cut myself shaving," Alex said.

The gunshot wound wasn't as obvious as it had been a few

months ago, but Mike had seen enough of them to know what it was. "Hell of a razor, Monroe."

"I had a little tussle with a guy last year. I ended up with this souvenir and he ended up in prison."

"I guess being a dive guide's a little more exciting than I thought."

"Not by choice." Then Alex shook his head, gazing at the horizon. "No, that's not really true. I barely existed down here until recently. That fight gave me a glimpse of who I used to be. And something woke up in me. Something I didn't know was still there."

Mike looked steadily at him. "It'll always be there, Alex. What happened in the last year to change things?"

Alex twitched a corner of his mouth. "I found Hope. In both senses of the word. Come on, let's head back and we can relax with a beer."

The sun was low on the horizon and warm on his shoulders as Alex headed home, his spirit lightened.

CHAPTER 11

Alex leaned over and took a six-pack out of the fridge, noting Hope had liberally stocked it. It was after 5:30 and he was surprised she wasn't home yet. Returning to the back porch, he set the beer on the table and sat across from Mike. They toasted and took a long drink, both thirsty after the challenging dive. "How long have you been married, anyway?"

"Two years." Mike laughed. "Bet that surprised you, huh?"

"Probably no more than I surprised you."

"After I retired and got a real job, I began to see the advantages of a steady relationship. Then I met Emma and knew she was the one. You and Hope live together?" They opened two more beers.

"Yeah." Now it was Alex's turn to laugh. "You saw the signs for the spa, down on the pier?"

Mike nodded.

"That used to be my apartment. A hurricane damaged it, so I moved up here and Hope *repurposed* it. Sometimes I think she engineered the whole thing just so she could build a spa."

Soft feet climbed the steps behind him.

"I did no such thing. I simply took advantage of an opportunity." Hope leaned down for a kiss. "Looks like you survived the Washing Machine and you both look freshly scrubbed to boot."

"I used your guest bath to get cleaned up," Mike said. "I tried not to make a mess."

"I'm sure you didn't." She turned to Alex. "I have to get changed and then I'm heading to the manager's reception. I might have dinner in the restaurant afterward." She glanced at the nearly empty six-pack. "You boys try not to have too much fun. I expect you to save me a beer when I'm done tonight."

"Yes, ma'am," Alex said with a wink.

After Hope went inside, they cracked open another round. "When are you two getting married?" Mike asked.

"Mid-October. We're having the wedding here at the resort."

"I can see why. Makes it hard to find a honeymoon destination, though, when you live in paradise."

Alex smiled as he swept his gaze over the beach. "We haven't even talked about that. It was hard enough finding time for the ceremony. Maybe someday we'll get away for a bit, but I doubt it will be right after the wedding."

They made small talk, and Mike told him about his job as a consultant specializing in tactical weapons. Alex had the feeling he was tiptoeing around a bit. At 6:30, footsteps came from behind him and he turned, surprised Hope would be back so soon. Instead, head server Charlotte was walking across the porch, carrying a steel bucket and two closed Styrofoam containers.

With a nod, she set the bucket filled with Leatherbacks between them and a container in front of each man. "Hope wanted to make sure you guys had dinner, so enjoy." She smiled and left, heading up the beach.

They each opened their containers to a bacon cheeseburger and a huge order of fries.

"Oh yeah. I see why you're marrying this woman!"

Mike dug in while Alex stared at his meal, ridiculously touched. But he was starving and dove in too.

By the time they had finished and opened the next round, they had an impressive collection of empty bottles and cans on the table. There were still a couple in the bucket, and Alex kept one in reserve for Hope. The next time there were steps behind him, he turned with anticipation and was rewarded when she climbed onto the deck. When Hope had left for the reception, she'd just kissed the top of his head from behind—he hadn't actually seen her.

She was wearing a flowing tank dress in multiple shades of blue that swirled around her like ocean waves as she walked, and she smelled like tropical flowers. The low neckline showed the full swell of her breasts, and she was wearing several gold chains from the cave.

He couldn't take his eyes off her.

Hope sauntered over to the table and rested her hand on his shoulder, raising a brow at the empty beer containers. "You gentlemen have been busy, haven't you?"

Mike smiled at her. "Thanks for the hamburgers. Give my compliments to your chef."

"I'll do that." Hope watched Mike and tilted her head. "Shall I prepare the guest room for you tonight?"

His smile fell as he took in the empties on the table. "Uh, no. I'll be ok to drive."

"Oh, I'm afraid that's not an option."

Mike's face went blank, and a huge grin spread across Alex's. "I don't recommend arguing with her. It doesn't end well."

"I can't allow someone who has drunk—let's see, five beers—to drive home. I'm sure you understand. I can drive you, but our guest bed is quite comfortable, I've been told." She spoke in her usual low, husky voice. Alex crossed an ankle over his knee and relaxed, enjoying the battle of wills and knowing full well who would win.

"I'll just get a cab then."

"Good luck with that. They tend to be rather selective after the sun goes down."

Mike opened and closed his mouth a few times as Hope stared steadily at him. "Well, let me call Emma and make sure she's ok with me staying here."

"Of course. Take your time."

Mike rose, eyeing Hope as if she might be dangerous, and walked down to the beach as he pulled out his phone.

Alex laughed, trying to keep quiet about it.

Hope turned to him, frowning as she parked a hand on her hip. "I hold you responsible. You should know better."

He held up a hand. "Tomorrow's my day off, so I don't have to get up early. Besides, we're sailors. We haven't even gotten started."

"Wrong. You're SEALs. I have higher expectations."

"Believe me, SEALs are even worse."

She harrumphed and he bit down on his lip to keep from laughing any harder as Mike's muted voice came from the beach. Alex had already been thinking of asking Clark to give Mike a ride home after closing the bar, but her solution was better.

Lips pursed tightly, Hope fished out a bottle before sitting in the third chair. Then she turned those amazing eyes to him, so he leaned forward and gave her his biggest, sunniest smile.

"You are truly impossible."

Alex didn't miss her faint smile as she lifted the bottle to her mouth.

Mike made his way back, sitting in his chair with a frown. "Emma told me to stay here. That she'd find a way to live without me for a night. Next, she informed me there was a last-minute cancellation at the spa tonight, so this gave her the opportunity to take it." He glared at Alex. "This is probably going to cost me $500, Monroe!"

"Well, it sounds like you're a man who needs to drown his sorrows. Open him another beer, Alex. You two are officially off the leash now."

Mike took the beer and sat there, blinking at Hope's change in attitude.

Alex stood. "There's another six-pack in the fridge. I'll be right back."

After returning, he kept one for himself and buried the rest in the ice-filled bucket as Hope told Mike the story of winning the resort. She was animated now, talking with her hands and smiling. Alex just leaned back and watched her.

He moved his gaze to her neck and shoulders, her skin tan and healthy again and no longer sickly pale. It would be silky soft and warm under his fingers. He settled on her cleavage. The dress showed plenty and when she leaned forward to articulate a point to Mike, it showed even more. With his shorts getting tighter by the second, Alex imagined running his tongue slowly down that valley. How her skin would taste just the slightest bit salty from her time in the warm air.

"Monroe! Earth to Alex!" He started at Mike's shout and immediately darted his eyes to Hope's. She was looking at him with a smile and a private gleam in her eyes—she knew exactly what he'd been thinking about.

"Sorry. Was thinking about this afternoon's dive. What were you saying, baby?"

"I was asking Mike how long the two of you served together."

"About ten years," Mike said. "When I was assigned to the Team, Alex had just made lieutenant and was bossing everyone around and driving us all up the wall. I took him under my wing to loosen him up a little."

"Huh. That doesn't sound like Alex at all."

Mike laughed and took another swig of beer as Hope

squeezed Alex's knee under the table, saying, "Yes, I've met Commander Monroe a time or two."

"I'm surprised you're still together." Mike grinned, and still looking at Hope, pointed a finger at Alex. "You realize you're marrying a total nerd, right? For God's sake, he got a master's degree because he thought it was *fun*. Hopeless overachiever, sitting over there."

"Yes, I've noticed he's rather determined."

"He's probably not the worst dive guide in the world, though."

"Still in his probationary period, I'm afraid. Not sure I can trust him on his own just yet." Alex pressed his bare foot on top of hers. With her free foot, she kicked him in the shin without missing a beat. Then she leaned forward, crossing her arms on the table. "Alex told me his specialties were sniper and diving. What was yours?"

"Demolitions."

"If you need something obliterated, Mike's your man," Alex added.

"I'll have you know, it involves a lot more finesse than most people think." Mike nodded to Hope. "It's not just blowing shit up."

Hope turned back to Alex. "You never told me. What made you want to be a sniper?"

"I didn't. I got volunteered. Our platoon sniper retired, and our CO thought I was the man for the job. What I thought didn't enter into it, though it ended up suiting me, so I guess he was right. It's a very precise, mathematical skill."

"All SEALs can shoot," Mike said softly. "You don't make it if you can't. But SEAL Sniper School is something completely different. One of the hardest classes in the military to pass. You should be really proud of Alex, Hope."

She locked her gaze with Alex's. "Believe me, I am." Hope finished her beer. "But I've had a busy day. I'll get the guest room ready, then I'm turning in." She stood and kissed Alex, brushing her finger down his nose before heading for the door.

A delicious warmth spread throughout him. "Is this where you tell us not to stay up too late?"

Hope turned back, serious. "No. Stay up as long as you need to."

CHAPTER 12

After Hope disappeared inside, Alex turned his attention back to Mike, who was staring right at him.

"I still can't get over running into you," Mike said. "At least you're happier to see me. The last time we met at Walter Reed, you pretty much threw me out of the room."

"Well, don't feel too special. I did that to pretty much everyone." He barked a laugh, but it didn't last. "Seriously, though, I'm sorry. I never thought I'd be anything but a SEAL, and I was pretty messed up. I got my recreational scuba instructor c-card so I'd have something to do while I was on leave. Never thought I'd do it full time."

"Seems like it's worked out well for you."

Alex smiled. "Yeah, it has. I'm happy with my life now. For the first time . . . since."

"Except for gunfights, maybe. How did that happen, anyway?"

Alex explained the altercation with Charles Reed. "The funny thing is—and you're one of the few people who can understand this—being in that fight made me feel alive again. Defending Hope gave me back my purpose." He laughed and shook his head.

"Getting shot was one of the better things that's happened to me in a while."

"All this sun has scrambled your brains. Like I said earlier, hopeless overachiever." Then Mike sobered, leaning forward as he gave Alex a piercing stare. "You know none of us blame you for Syria, right? Please tell me you know that."

Alex closed his eyes, unsure how to respond. But he was very aware the primary emotion surging through him wasn't anger or grief, but relief. "I'm still trying to get a grip on that. There's no getting around I was responsible for it."

"Like hell you were. ISIS was. That was a really high-level target we were going after—you know that. It was worth the risk."

"There are eight men who might not agree with you."

Mike hissed through his teeth. "Bullshit. They knew what they were getting into, same as you and me. And there are a lot of other guys who are damn grateful you were there. Even those civilians owe their lives to you." He crushed his empty beer can and opened a new one, his brows drawn. "That Navy Cross they gave you was total horseshit. If what you did that night didn't deserve the Medal of Honor, I don't know what does."

Alex shifted in his seat. "Doesn't matter. It's not like I'm going to wear it, anyway."

"You don't have to, but you sure deserved it."

"Maybe I'll believe that someday."

Mike shook his head with an exasperated groan, jabbing his index finger at him. "I know you, Alex, and I'm betting you've spent the last six years down here hating yourself. You can't change what happened, but you made a hell of a difference that night. *Let it go*, man."

"I'm trying to." Alex fished out another beer and met Mike's eyes. "Thanks. It helps. . . hearing this from you."

"We have a group text going. All of us who were there in Syria, except for you and Gregson, who also dropped off the face of the earth. Can I loop you in on it?"

Goose bumps rippled down Alex's arms. "No. I'm not ready for that yet. I've only been able to deal with any of this in the last year. If it weren't for Hope, I'd still be unable to face it." He took a deep breath. "But I will be ready. I just need some more time."

"Of course. Can I at least tell them you're doing ok? They'll really want to hear about this. I could text the photos we got today."

"Sure. Tell them I'll be in touch when I'm ready."

Mike settled back in his chair, his face relaxing. "You got it. The pictures that kid took of you and me on the pier are pretty good. What made you hire him, anyway? Can he even reach the top shelf in the dive shop?"

"It was mostly Hope, but Zach's working out well. She's got a soft spot for strays and misfits."

"Well, that's obvious."

Alex threw an empty can at him, but Mike swerved, laughing. "You're not going to ghost me, are you?"

"Not much point in that. You know where I live now. You'd just come down here and bust my balls."

"Damn right I would."

"You're too late, anyway. Someone's already got that job."

∽

THE NEXT MORNING, Alex woke with a mouth that tasted like he'd eaten a dead rodent. After crawling through the Sahara for a week. Then the pounding headache announced itself. The final indignity appeared when he opened his eyes to broad daylight. It was nearly 8 a.m. Unsurprisingly, Hope was already up. He shuffled to the bathroom and drank a large glass of water, took some ibuprofen, and changed into a T-shirt and shorts.

He trudged into the kitchen, where Mike and Hope sat at the

table. A fresh cup of coffee was brewing for him, and he crossed to it. *I love you, Hope.*

"Good afternoon, princess," Mike said. "Did you get your beauty sleep?"

"Shut up, Baker." Alex took a big drink of coffee, then kissed Hope. "Morning, baby." He shot Mike a dirty look, then sat down while Mike grinned at him.

"Been a while since you've had a late drinking night?"

"Yes. It has."

"Well, I hope you don't feel it's something you need to make a habit of," Hope said.

He rubbed his temples. "Definitely not. Besides, it was your idea."

"It was not. I merely left you two to your own devices. How much you drank was purely your own decision."

"You plied us with liquor," Alex said. "You can't blame us for what happened."

She shot him an arch look. "When did you finally stumble into bed, anyway?"

"Not sure."

"It was about two," Mike added.

Hope finished her coffee and stood. "Unlike you two, I don't have the luxury of just sitting around all day, wallowing in my misery. Some of us have to work, you know." She walked toward the bedroom, trailing a hand over Alex's shoulder to let him know she wasn't really mad.

"I should probably get going too. Emma might actually want me to come back at some point."

The coffee was working. His headache was much better. "It was great seeing you again, Baker. I'm glad you came over."

"Me too. I had a great time diving."

"Thought I was gonna have to rescue you a couple of times, but you pulled through."

"Yeah, bite me."

They both started laughing at the same time, then were on their feet, giving each other a back-slapping hug.

"I'm not going to let you push me away this time," Mike said.

"You won't need to. I'm on a new path now."

"Alex, if you ever need anything, call me. Day or night. I don't care."

"I know. Thanks. But you'll probably just use it as an excuse to get a tropical vacation."

"You might get sick of me. Next time Emma and I will stay here. I'd like to stay in one of those bungalows."

"There's always room for you. You can stay with us if the resort's booked." They walked to the front door. "Let me get Hope. She'll want to say goodbye."

She was pulling on a staff shirt and quickly followed Alex to the front door. She wrapped Mike in a big hug. "I'm so glad I got to meet you. Next time you'll have to stay here, so I can get to know Emma better."

"Only if you can peel her out of your spa."

"Thank you, Mike." A long look passed between them, and Mike nodded, confirming something Alex had been wondering about.

After another quick hug from Alex, Mike was on his way. With a deep breath, Alex turned to Hope, enfolding her in his arms. He kissed her, a soft, tender press of lips. When she started to pull away, he deepened it, letting the feel and taste of her course through him.

She drifted back with a smile. "What was that for?"

Alex brushed a finger down her cheek. "My way of saying thank you. You just confirmed you orchestrated his staying here. We had a great night."

"I wouldn't go that far. I put some extra six-packs in the fridge while you were diving. Thought you guys might be thirsty after."

"We were. And we talked about all sorts of stuff last night.

Rehashed a lot of old times. And we even talked about Syria some."

"A good talk?"

A faint smile crossed his face. "Yeah, it was. He gave me a lot to think about." Alex kissed the top of Hope's head and went to shower off his hangover.

CHAPTER 13

Warm waves splashed over Hope's feet as she walked home along the beach, carrying her sandals in one hand. It was late afternoon, and the resort was quiet as guests recovered from the day's activities and prepared for the night's. Hope's day had passed uneventfully, but she was glad Alex wasn't working. That morning, the line between his brows had been deeper, and she doubted it was from the hangover. His visit with Mike might have been cathartic, but he had a lot to digest.

Hope and Mike had talked for a while before Alex awoke. "I'm so glad you two got to spend some time alone," she said. "I'm sure it meant a lot to him. He told me you were his best friend."

Mike smiled. "It meant a lot to me too. I've missed him. Watching that guy in the water is something else."

"Oh? I thought maybe that was a SEAL thing."

"No, that's an Alex thing. After Syria, we all went through a rough time . . . but not like Alex. I let him push me away." He met Hope's eyes. "That's not going to happen again."

"I think he's finally realized how many people care about him. Thank you for staying last night. I think spending time with you was the best possible medicine."

"I talked to Emma a lot about Alex. She knew what it meant to see him again. When I called her last night, she practically forced me to stay here. Alex and I had a lot of fun yesterday, almost like old times." He glanced down for a moment, then twitched a corner of his mouth as he turned his attention back to Hope. "I owe that guy a lot. He's kind of an ass, but he gets under your skin."

"He definitely does." They'd both had a laugh, and then Alex could be heard moving in the bedroom and Hope got up to make his coffee.

Now, she opened the slider and walked into their house. Alex sat at the kitchen table with his Navy box open before him.

He looked at her with a smile. "Welcome home. How was your day?"

She was very relieved he was smiling as he looked through his medals. "A good day. No emergencies to deal with, which is always a good thing. Reminiscing?"

"Yeah. Thought I'd look through this some more."

Three photos sat in a stack off to one side, and the box containing his SEAL insignia was open on the table, along with several other medals she hadn't seen before. "What are those?"

"Active campaign medals." He pointed to each one. "Afghanistan, Iraq, and Syria. I've been to Syria more than once." The light glinted over another large pin resting in his other hand.

"What are you holding?"

"Parachutist pin. I was kind of a middle-of-the-road paratrooper."

"Uh-huh, sure." She turned her attention from the pin to his eyes. "You doing ok?"

He set the small box down and leaned back in his chair, pausing. "I think I am. I went for a two-hour swim this afternoon—that helped clear my head. It was great spending time with Mike again. It brought up some memories but sorted other things too. My head's kind of a whirlwind right now." He placed everything back in the box and stood. "Let's head to dinner. It's probably a good idea to call it an early night."

∼

ALEX FELL into a deep sleep immediately, his breathing slow and regular. Hope read for a while, but she was lulled by his comforting breaths and turned off the lamp, falling peacefully asleep. That lasted until 2 a.m., when the quiet night was split wide open by a soul-gutting shriek from Alex.

He vaulted upright in bed, screaming "No!" over and over as he pressed the heels of his hands against his eyes. Sweat poured off him, and his hair was plastered to his head. The shouting soon stopped. Worse was the agonized keening sound Alex produced with each gasping exhalation. He'd had a terrible nightmare several months ago, but this was much worse.

Hope sat up and placed her hands on his shoulders as he heaved with every breath, and his torment quieted a bit at her touch. Lying down, she pulled him with her to cradle his head on her breast. Last time, this had quieted him, and they'd ended up making love.

Tonight was different.

Once he was wrapped in her arms, instead of calming, Alex's breathing escalated. The keening began again. Hope gripped him tighter as his deep breaths became gasping spasms, convulsing through his body. Each jerky inhale was followed by a long, lamenting exhale.

Until finally, seven years after the ambush in Syria, Alex broke down into enormous, wracking sobs, crying out his grief and anguish against Hope's breast.

His whole body shuddered with the force of it. Hope's own tears coursed down to mingle with his on her chest and she clutched Alex tighter, sharing his grief. He wrapped his arms around her, holding tightly as he poured out his agony. Muscles all over his body clenched as he wailed against her, releasing the misery and self-loathing he'd carried for so long.

Eventually, the painful cries became softer sobs, and he shifted position, clinging even more tightly to Hope as he took deep, hitching breaths. He was wrapped around her, both arms pulling her tight as his legs entwined with hers. Finally, he depleted himself and quieted at last.

Hope pressed a long kiss to his forehead as she wiped her face with one hand. She quickly returned it to his back, needing to touch him. His sweat had dried, and her hands moved smoothly over his upper back.

Alex lay heavy against her, drained and not moving for several minutes before taking a deep breath. "The dream is always the same. Just sometimes it's more . . . intense." He spoke in a flat, exhausted voice. "I hear the explosion and run out of the APC. When I start toward the lead Humvee, it gets hit with a mortar and explodes in front of me. I don't know if it's an actual memory or just my brain trying to put the pieces together."

"I don't suppose it matters. It's real enough." She kissed his forehead again. "You'll get through this, love. I'm here for you."

"Tonight, the dream was a little different. The guys in the Humvee were screaming at me to get them out."

Hope closed her eyes, trying to remain calm. "I'm so sorry."

He snuggled closer and buried his face further against her neck. "I'm pretty sure that part didn't actually happen. That was just my mind conjuring up something special tonight. The psychiatrist at Walter Reed said I could take it as a good sign if the nightmares got worse, because it meant I was working through it. I hadn't had any in a couple years until they started again last year."

"You are working through it."

He kissed her skin, still wet from his tears. "Thank you for helping me through this."

"I told you before—you're not alone anymore. Never again."

His jaw cracked with an enormous yawn.

"Sleep, my love. I've got you now."

His body relaxed as he drifted off, head against her breast.

She was awake much longer.

THE NEXT MORNING, Hope awoke just after 5:30, but Alex's side of the bed was already empty. She padded to the kitchen and discovered her mug on the counter, but he was nowhere to be found. After brewing her cup, she made her way to the porch. Alex stood on the sandy beach, dressed in shorts and a sweatshirt with the hood pulled up as he faced the ocean. He held a steaming mug of coffee in one hand.

He smiled at her approach and pulled her to his chest with one arm, kissing the top of her head.

"How are you feeling this morning?" she asked, watching him closely.

His face smoothed, a slight smile rising. "That's why I'm standing out here. I'm trying to figure out how I feel—the ocean always helps me with that. I'm worn out, for sure. But there's something else. I feel . . . a little lighter, I'd say."

He took a drink, gathering his thoughts. "I was looking at that Navy Cross yesterday. That medal has always represented my worst failure. I still couldn't look at it for long. But that dream last night . . . I've never had a nightmare that bad. It was like my mind was throwing the worst it could at me." He glanced behind them to the east. "And yet the sun's still about to rise over those mountains. And I'm still here. More importantly, you're still here."

"And I'll always be here. Remember? We're a team. And you're a man who knows a lot about Teams."

"Yes, I do. Especially when I'm part of a great one."

CHAPTER 14

August...

HOPE AND ALEX walked along the resort access road toward the highway. Construction had recently finished at the rock pool, and Hope couldn't wait to see it. Cruz danced in circles around her, excited about their adventure. She frowned at him. "Don't get too wound up. We're going to try a leash today, so stay close."

"I admit I'm curious," Alex said. "He didn't seem to mind the collar much, so maybe he's leash trained, too."

"Time to find out."

They were nearing the highway. Hope bent down and clipped the leash to the dog's collar before she began walking again. Cruz followed at her side for a bit, then took off toward the side and felt the pull of the leash. He sat and whined.

"It's ok. I just want you to wear it when we cross the highway, ok?" He tilted his head at her. "I'll take that as a yes. Let's go."

She marched on, catching a glimpse of Alex's smile. "Careful, or I might put a leash on you next."

His smile got bigger.

Alex hadn't suffered any further nightmares in the weeks since, and she studied him now. She was still trying to put her finger on it, but maybe Alex's explanation was the best. He was lighter since that night. Finally releasing all that guilt and pent-up grief had eased him tremendously.

After a few pulls on the leash, Cruz trotted at Hope's side and soon they were stopped at the highway, waiting for a break in the traffic.

"Ok, this looks good," Alex said, and they rushed forward. After another tug, Cruz ran happily enough, staying at Hope's side. She unleashed him as soon as they entered the cool jungle on the other side and he bounded away, rejoining them periodically as they progressed.

The tree canopy swayed in the breeze above them as they made their way along the faint trail. After nearly half a mile, they came across the eight-foot chain-link fence that crossed the track. Cruz was busy sniffing along the length of it.

A padlocked gate was directly in front of them, flanked on both sides by *No Trespassing* signs. Alex produced the key and ushered them through.

"That gate looks secure enough," Hope said.

Alex nodded. "It is, and we have the only keys."

THEY FOLLOWED the dim track for another quarter mile before approaching a clearing. A sandy beach led into the clear rock pool. As Hope looked at it, a small smile rose on her face. "The last time I was here, I was still a free woman."

"Ouch. You sure know how to make a guy feel good."

Her smile turned sultry as she sidled up to him, pressing her body against his. "Well, I'd like to think I know how to make one guy feel good."

"Ms. Collins, I think you're trying to distract me."

She cocked her head. "You're not going to be able to call me that much longer. You'll have to start calling me Mrs. Monroe."

Alex crushed her to him, squeezing her so tightly she could hardly breathe.

"Alex," she squeaked. "I can't breathe."

He loosened his hold, smiling at her as he cupped her face. "I wasn't sure you wanted to take my name. Being a businesswoman, I thought you might prefer to keep your own."

"No. I can't wait to be Mrs. Hope Monroe. Maybe I'm more traditional than I thought."

He pulled her to his chest. "You just made me very happy. I wouldn't mind if you kept your maiden name, but I love the idea of you taking mine."

"I want to make you happy. You have no idea how much."

"I am. And I'll do my best to keep your misery to a minimum."

Hope laughed as she looked into his eyes. "Well, there's a declaration of love."

His eyes softened as he smoothed her hair. "You know how I feel. And I'm trying to remember you're a butterfly who needs to rise."

"I can't do that without you."

Hope climbed onto a nearby boulder, shading her eyes with her hand as she stared into the jungle. "This is perfect. I can't see the fence at all. It goes all the way around to the hillside?"

Alex nodded. "They did a good job. On both sides of the hill, the fence abuts a steep section, so there's no way to get around it. The only way in is through the gate where we entered." He removed his backpack, pulling out a pair of swim fins as well as a mask and weight belt. Next, he pulled out a mask, snorkel, and fins for Hope. They stripped to their swimsuits and eased into the pool.

"You haven't been in here since they installed the gates?" Hope asked.

"No, I thought we'd check them out together."

Hope put on her snorkeling equipment, and they swam to the nearby gate. It was submerged ten feet, covering a wide opening that led off the rock pool to parts unknown. Alex took a deep breath and sank, free diving to the gate and inspecting it closely. Hope followed, peering into the mysterious passage beyond, but didn't stay long. All she could see was dark rock that faded to blackness.

Alex made sure the hinges and padlock were secured before surfacing next to her. "Seems good to me."

"Are you planning on exploring that passage?" Hope asked.

"Maybe someday, but I'm in no hurry. Let's head to the cave."

They swam to the enormous cavern, free diving to the tunnel opening fifteen feet below the surface. This depth was more of a challenge for Hope. She needed to clear her ears several times and had to grip the cool bars of the gate to stay submerged. It was also nearly dark here. The passage was located along the back wall of the cavern, and both she and Alex wore headlamps to provide some light.

Hope stared into the black tunnel, now blocked by the large metal gate. Memories of both the good and bad times that had occurred deep within rolled through her mind. The bad time had involved a terrifying lapse of concentration, which led to her silting up a small room. A potentially fatal outcome, but a cool head and exhaustive training from Alex had allowed Hope to find her way to safety.

Just as importantly, Hope's cave incident had forced Alex to face his fear of losing her as he had his eight comrades in Syria. He had finally understood he couldn't protect her from all harm. Moreover, that she didn't want him to.

Happier memories were the good times, which had led to their two treasure-filled safe-deposit boxes. Then Hope's musings were interrupted by her lungs, which insisted this was an excellent time to breathe. She headed toward the surface.

Alex stayed down considerably longer, inspecting the gate carefully before rejoining her at the surface. "Looks solid. Nobody's getting through either of those without the key. You want to head back?"

Hope nodded—she was nearly shivering. Without a wetsuit, the cool water temperature was very noticeable, and the dim confines of the cave made it seem even colder. They headed toward shore where Cruz stood wagging his tail in abandon. Then he leaped into the pool with a splash and swam toward them.

"Look at you!" Hope grinned as he paddled a circle around her and all three made for shore.

As soon as they were back on land, Alex enfolded her, rubbing the goose bumps on her arms. She exhaled a happy sigh and melted into his warmth. "You always know what I need."

"Well, I try. It's kind of my main job, you know. Dive guide's taken a back seat since I met you."

Soon they had redressed and were heading back down the animal track. "How are things coming for Clark's contest?" Alex asked.

"Good! I upped our game this year. I bought a better-quality banner and display for Clark's table. Everything's all set for next week."

"He has a great drink. He should do well."

Thoughts of the resort caused Hope's mind to return to her email inbox. "I got an interesting email yesterday. A man asked if he could rent space to tie his sailboat to our pier for a few days. He lives on it and travels around the Caribbean, but has to conduct business on land now and again. Can you think of any reason that might be a problem?"

In front of her, Alex shrugged as he scanned back and forth. "No, as long as he doesn't impinge on *Surface Interval's* space. It's a pretty common practice down here."

"I'll email him back and tell him to let me know when he's

coming. Sounds like easy money to me. Speaking of money, have you contacted the private-jet company?"

Alex pushed a vine out of his way, holding it back for her before continuing in front. "Yes. I went down in person and showed my credentials, and they're ok with me carrying on board." He snorted. "For once, my so-called notoriety came in handy. They knew who I was. We didn't set a specific date. I plan to give them short notice, though I didn't tell them that. I don't want anyone knowing about this in advance—it's the highest-risk part of the whole operation. The less people involved, the better."

He spun around, walking backwards as he stared pointedly at her, then turned and led on.

Hope was free to grin since he couldn't see it. Alex had just sent her a message, but was smart enough not to say it out loud. "Pout all you want. I'm coming with you and that's final."

"Like I said when Mike was here, I know better than to argue with you."

"It sounds like we're ready to go ahead with this. Just so I don't feel left out, I'll take care of booking our return flight back to St. Croix."

Alex nodded. "I'll call Bryce in Miami and see when he's available. And I don't need to tell you—we need to be on high alert on this trip. I'm treating this as a mission, ok?"

"I wouldn't expect anything less."

She smiled fondly at his back. *We're flying to Miami on a private jet. Relax, Alex! Compared to what we've already faced, this will be easy.*

CHAPTER 15

Alex stood in the dive shop, watching the computer screen as he moved a flexible wand around the inside of a scuba tank. There was a lighted camera on the end, and its image was displayed on the terminal. Zach finished building the display for the new fins Alex had ordered and came over.

"What are you doin'?" Zach asked.

"Visual inspection. Scuba tanks need to be inspected visually every year to make sure they aren't deteriorating inside. I set aside a few each month, so we don't end up having to do a bunch at once."

Zach's voice dripped with eagerness. "Can you show me?"

"Maybe eventually. But this is more intricate than filling tanks. So far only Robert or I do it."

"Did you learn to dive in the Navy? Or were you already certified?"

Alex answered without looking away from his inspection. "I grew up in the Florida Panhandle, on the gulf. I got certified as soon as I could, when I was fifteen, and became an instructor in the Red Sea while I was in the Navy."

"You've been all over the place, haven't you?"

"It was part of my job description for a long time."

This tank was good. Alex withdrew the camera and pressed a plastic sticker on the tank, which indicated the month it would expire next year.

"I could see myself makin' a career out of divin'," Zach said, watching closely.

Alex turned to him with a smile. "Yeah? You live in the right place, that's for sure. It's been good for me."

Zach glanced at Alex from under his brows. "It's hard for me to believe you used to be a SEAL. You seem so normal."

"I am normal!" Alex grinned. "My SEAL days are in the past now. I've learned to relax a little more." His smile faded as he regarded Zach. "It's a pretty long road to becoming a scuba instructor, but you can work your way up through divemaster without leaving the island. I can teach you that far, and it would get your foot in the door. Who knows? Maybe you'll end up leading dives here at Half Moon Bay someday."

Alex handed him the finished tank and Zach carried it out to start the afternoon's air fills. He rose and exited the shop, walking to the side of the pier. His gaze was drawn up the stairs to the spa, and visions crashed down on him. Of all the miserable times he'd spent in that apartment, closed off and too afraid of losing anyone else to let people near him.

Shouting erupted from the shallows, and Alex snapped his head over. But it was just a couple of guests playing in the ocean and he relaxed again. After the conversation with Zach, he was in an introspective mood. Alex was forty-one, but at Zach's age, he could never had imagined the turns his life would take.

I'd never go so far as saying the bad times have been worth it, but I'm finally believing good times can follow bad ones. And that maybe Syria doesn't mean a life sentence after all.

The catharsis resulting from his soul-rending nightmare had provided a new peace and perspective for him. He still had no intention of speaking freely about his SEAL days, but now it was similar to his active-duty time. The reluctance to speak about it was more of personal preference and the unwritten code of a very small cadre of men, instead of a traumatic response to avoid facing his guilt and pain.

Turning up the pier, his footsteps thumped on the wooden boards as he turned his mind back to the conversation with Mike. When he had explained the fight with Charles woke something up in him, Mike assured him it had never left. Alex was finally able to see that for himself.

Maybe it's time to join that group text. I'll have to call Mike about it soon.

As he walked up the pier, his trigger finger itched. Alex headed into the house to change. He hadn't been to the gun range in a while.

~

WHEN HE ARRIVED at the long-range target area, Alex sighed. A small crowd of men stood clustered around one guy lying prone, giving him advice. *Maybe I should have called ahead.* There was a fitful breeze, and the sun blazed overhead. Targets were placed in a grassy field, with scattered flame trees providing color to the scene.

The shooter pulled the trigger, then swore, and the crowd around him piped up with all kinds of contradictory advice. From where he stood, Alex recognized several problems with the shooter, but wasn't about to rag on the poor guy. The crowd quieted and the man fired again. And missed again. He was aiming for the thousand-yard target—that might have been a bit ambitious. He was closing one eye and not compensating enough for the wind.

"Aw hell, Bill," the man said. "You put in a longer target than this one? Nobody's gonna hit that damn thing. I can't even hit a thousand yards. You really think anyone can hit two thousand?"

Alex whipped his head around and narrowed his eyes, looking down the field. He could barely see a new target laid out. It was *very* long range. That got his attention. Still, he didn't feel like waiting around for the local contingent to finish and was contemplating the two-hundred-yard lane when the range boss, Bill, saw him.

"Alex! Come show this joker how it's done. We installed something just for you."

"I don't want to break up your party."

Bill took in the metal box Alex carried and his smile widened. "I think the party's just getting started." He turned to the prone shooter. "Brian, put your rifle away. It's almost time for cold range."

Alex kept his face expressionless as Brian tossed him a cocky grin. The man stood and disassembled his weapon. It wasn't the best choice for a long-distance shot anyway—a rifle civilians loved, but Special Forces operatives wouldn't touch with a ten-foot pole.

As Bill went down the aisle and called cold range, allowing shooters to enter the range safely, Alex nodded to a couple of other guys. They were also vets and he'd had a beer with them a time or two. They and Bill knew he'd been a SEAL. He didn't know Brian, who had now flipped his camo baseball hat to the usual position of brim in front.

He leveled a steady gaze at Alex, evaluating him. "You think you can hit that long target?"

"Won't know until I try."

Bill hollered hot range and Alex opened Betsy's case, quickly assembling the sniper rifle then moving to the firing line.

"What kind of rifle is that?" Brian asked from behind him.

"A lot different from yours, Brian," one of the others replied, a smirk in his voice.

"MK13," Alex said, and could tell from Brian's blank expression it meant nothing to him. *Fine by me.*

Alex lay prone on the ground, resting the rifle in its rest and dialed in the scope on the thousand-yard target. After months of regular shooting, he was fully confident again. He pulled the trigger five times in quick succession, chambering and shooting all five rounds. All hit center target.

With a satisfied smile, Alex moved the rifle, looking through the scope for the next mark. "No fifteen-hundred-yard target?"

"Nope, didn't see the point." Bill had come back to watch.

"Easy for you to say," Alex said. "You're not the one shooting."

He sighted the two-thousand-yard target. The distance was over a mile and one hell of a challenge. Bill had built up a large dirt berm behind the target to catch any stray rounds.

An anticipatory tingle ran through Alex's body as he sighted down the scope and dialed in the target. He let his sight broaden, taking in the environment around the target—the direction the leaves and grass were blowing, a small rise midway between himself and the target, and many other things he wasn't even conscious of anymore. They were part of a routine built of long experience.

He narrowed his focus again to the target, not changing his breathing at all. Keeping both eyes open, he waited until he exhaled and pulled the trigger, hitting the target in the second band. Murmurs of appreciation sounded behind him and Alex imagined the sets of binoculars pressed to eyes.

But he had better shots in him.

He repeated the procedure, shooting three times in rapid succession and hitting the inner band with all three.

"Holy shit!" Brian exclaimed behind him, but Alex didn't relish having an audience.

He shot three more magazines, the wind blowing several rounds off the target. But he was pleased overall. Bill warned him hot range was nearly over, so he returned to the table and disassembled Betsy.

Bill came over again after calling cold range. "A few of us are having a beer at Charlie's. You want to join us?"

Alex hesitated before saying, "Sure. A beer sounds good."

If he wanted to be treated like one of the guys, he needed to act like one instead of the Lone Ranger. He could practically hear Hope saying the words inside his head.

On the way to the parking lot, Brian told a dirty joke and everyone laughed. Alex's smile lingered, realizing how good it felt to be part of a group again. Just a bunch of guys getting together for a beer.

CHAPTER 16

Trying to act nonchalant, Hope worked to quash a smug smile as she examined the booth next to theirs. The hand-painted banner and sad display were no match for the new Half Moon Bay Resort setup. She turned back and frowned. "No, up more. Keep going." Taking a step back, she evaluated the straightness of the banner Alex was hanging. It was crooked, even after his adjustment. "It *still* needs to move up more."

This time, he clearly lowered it two inches.

"Alex! That's the wrong direction. Dammit, you're doing that on purpose."

He turned around and grinned. "About time you noticed. I was starting to wonder if I was going to be up here all night." He lifted to his toes and affixed the banner perfectly as she scowled at his back, determined not to smile. A snicker came from next to her, and she whirled to glare at Clark. He promptly got busy unpacking the blender.

Clark's table was covered with a navy-blue cloth, and Hope had created a pleasing contrast by draping a square of aqua fabric over it. A large photo banner of the resort hung from the front of the table and formed the lower section of the booth. Taken from the ocean, it showcased the pier with the beach and bungalows behind. And a little extra advertising wouldn't hurt—it was a beautiful photo. Robert's, of course.

This year, the St. Croix mixology contest was being held in a different ballroom of The Buccaneer Resort, one that was brightly lit and actually had windows overlooking the grassy lawn. Last year, the resort had performed admirably, hosting the event shortly after the hurricane. But a dim, stifling-hot expanse of space was all that had been available.

Alex had been able to stand the claustrophobic room only for a short amount of time at the end of the contest, but this time his posture was relaxed, and he looked very pleased about putting one over on her. It was more than the new room too. He was more at ease and not as troubled by the memories a dark, enclosed space brought back.

She turned a critical eye to her bartender, satisfied once again. "Clark, you're much calmer than last year."

He was very handsome, dressed in black dress slacks paired with his light-blue staff polo shirt. "Well, I'm an experienced veteran now, aren't I? Got the rookie jitters out already."

"Glad to hear it." Hope was skeptical he'd stay calm, but kept her thoughts to herself.

Still on the step stool, Alex tugged on the upper banner, making sure it was secure.

"Hey now, you're gonna rip it," said a voice from behind. "Leave it to a damn dive guide to screw up hangin' the banner."

Alex dismounted. "If you would show up when you're supposed to, I wouldn't have to do the dirty work all the time."

Hope turned around and embraced Tommy, then his wife Priscilla, standing just behind him and wearing a colorful dress. Her black braids hung loose down her back. They hadn't been able to make it last year, but were determined to show their support for Clark now.

"Let me take a look at this and see how bad you messed it up."

Tommy poked and prodded, but couldn't find anything further to complain about. "It'll probably hold long enough for the competition." He pointed at Alex. "Don't go gettin' cocky on me, though."

"Who, me?" Alex and Tommy shook hands.

"I'm sorry we're late," Priscilla said. "Maria was going to a sleepover tonight and was late gettin' ready."

"You're not late," Clark piped in. "As long as you don't miss the competition, nothin' else matters, right?" He was lifting liquor bottles from a box on the floor to his table, lining them up with precision next to the blender. Arm in mid-air, he froze, frowning as he looked several times from the box to the lineup of bottles.

With a gasp, he spun to Hope, the whites of his eyes clearly visible. "I forgot the Irish Crème! I can't make Half Moon Dream without it!"

Hope hurried to double check. Sure enough, no Irish Crème was in sight. "Don't panic, Clark. I'm sure we can get some. You stay here, and I'll head to the bar here at the resort. I'm sure they'll have a bottle I can buy." Tapping her fingers on her crossed arms, she turned to Alex. "Monroe, you're with me. We've got a mission to complete."

Without waiting for Alex's response, Hope turned on her heel, stopping to grasp Tommy's upper arm and whispering to him, "Keep Clark under control, ok?"

"You got it."

Hope marched on, checking her watch, and turned back when Alex lagged. "Get a move on! We have less than an hour until the competition starts."

"Yes, ma'am. And you call *me* bossy."

She grinned as he caught up to her, offering his elbow. They walked inside the main building, which was painted bright pink with white trim. She dragged Alex across the floor of alternating black-and-white tile, finally entering the bar.

The bartender sported an impressive set of dreadlocks tied back with a pink and white ribbon. Hope approached with a smile. "Hi. We're part of the competition tonight, and our bartender forgot the Irish Crème. We're sunk without it. Can I buy a bottle from you?"

The bartender's smile fell as he shook his head. "Sorry, ma'am. I just poured the last of my bottle. All our extras went down to our booth at the competition."

"Is there another bar I can check?"

"No, but there's a liquor store just down the highway to the west. They should have some."

"Ok. We'll give that a try. Thanks."

"Good luck tonight!" he called as they hurried out, trotting across the lawn.

Alex breathed an exasperated sigh. "Jeez, next time, let me do the talking. Rule number one on a mission—don't let the enemy know who you are, for crying out loud! I'm surprised you didn't tell that guy what Clark was making."

"I'm sure he wasn't lying. I didn't see any bottles of Irish Crème behind him."

Alex studied the pink building. "Maybe I can sneak into their storeroom and steal a bottle. You want me to try?"

Hope stopped dead. "Alex. You are *not* stealing a bottle of liquor from one of St. Croix's most famous resorts. We've got plenty of time to go to the store. I left my purse at the booth. Do you have your wallet and keys on you?"

Alex's face fell, but he confirmed they were fully operational for the next phase of their mission. Soon he was driving them to the liquor store. Hope peered at him, still not sure if he'd been joking about trying to steal a bottle. *I'm probably better off not knowing.*

Before long, they were parking in front of a small liquor store. They entered and Hope headed straight for the liqueur section. "Let's see, crème de menthe, orange liqueur, coffee liqueur . . . here we go!" She pointed to the tag for Irish Crème, but there was nothing except wide empty space on the shelf above it. Her stomach dropped to her feet. "They *can't* be out!"

They started digging behind all the other bottles on the shelf, but there was no Irish Crème. Panic sent tendrils throughout her abdomen now. "Ok, we need to think fast here. Follow me, sailor." She beckoned, marching toward the checkout counter.

A middle-aged local man dressed in a green and white tropical shirt stood behind the counter and brightened when Hope approached. Alex stopped just behind.

"Sir, I'm really hoping you can help us." Hope wrung her hands together.

The man lit up at being addressed as *Sir*. "How can I help you tonight, dear?"

Hope leaned both hands on the counter, leaning toward the man. "We're in desperate need of a bottle of Irish Crème. One of our best friends is competing in the bartending contest tonight, and he forgot his bottle. It's nearly a life-or-death situation. His late father's greatest wish was that Clark win this contest."

A cough sounded behind her and she kicked her foot back, making solid contact with Alex's shin. Hope looked at the man's nametag before turning beseeching eyes to him. "There wasn't any left on the shelf. Jasper, is there any chance at all you might have some in your back room? Could you *please* check for us?"

"Oh! You poor things. We've had a real run on that the last few days." He patted Hope's hand. "You two just wait right here and I'll go check."

Jasper whisked through a swinging door behind him as Alex moved next to Hope's side. She wagged her eyebrows at him. He winked back, trying to bite back a grin as a loud "Ah-ha!" emanated from the back room. Loud sounds of scurrying followed, then Jasper burst through the swinging door. With a wide smile, he held up a bottle in victory. "I had one bottle left in my case! One bottle—can you believe it? Let's get you rung up."

"Oh, thank you! You're an absolute lifesaver." Hope's relief poured off her in waves. She wasn't lying, after all. Well, except for the part about Clark's father.

After Hope secured their treasure, they exited, assuring Jasper they'd do their best to ensure Clark won. Hope slid into the passenger seat and sent a smug grin Alex's way. "And that, my dear, is how you do that."

Alex burst into laughter as he started the car. "Ok, I'm impressed, though I'm pretty sure you gave me a bruise on my shin."

"I simply did what I had to. At least my idea didn't involve grand larceny."

He snorted. "If that clerk had been a woman, you never would have gotten that far."

"Then I would have turned the floor over to you, so you could try out your acting skills." Hope couldn't help the laughter that erupted.

Alex checked the time and sobered as he pulled back onto the highway. "We have less than fifteen minutes before the competition starts. Buckle up, master thespian."

CHAPTER 17

They rushed into the ballroom with five minutes to spare.

Patti had arrived and was gripping Clark's upper arms with both hands. He stared at her, near tears, as he opened and closed his mouth repeatedly. When he caught sight of Hope, his stricken expression turned to one of desperate anticipation.

She held up the bottle triumphantly as everyone cheered. "Here you go, Clark. Piece of cake. Told you we'd find another one."

She and Alex were both panting after running from the parking lot. Clark took the bottle and held it like a priceless treasure.

God, don't drop it!

But he didn't, carefully bringing it behind his table. Clark reverently placed it in line with the others, then closed his eyes and swiped a hand over his forehead.

Hope followed him, placing both hands on his shoulders as she turned him to face her. "Clark, you doing ok?"

"I am now. I was getting a little nervous for a while."

Hope glanced at Patti, who was fanning herself with a

brochure, and could just imagine how nervous he had been. She squeezed his shoulders. "Remember, you've done this before, and you make drinks every day. Don't be nervous—you're ready for this. I'm really proud of you, Clark. I don't care if you come in first or last. I think you're the best bartender on the island."

Clark burst forward and wrapped his arms around her. Smiling, Hope looked over his shoulder and locked eyes with Alex.

The look on his face floored her.

Alex was an expert at hiding his emotions, but he wasn't now. He must have heard her little pep talk, because the love and admiration on his face was unmistakable. Tears sprung to her eyes as she gazed back at him. But as the master of ceremonies began introducing the event, Clark pulled back and broke their reverie.

"I'd better join everyone else. You've got this, Clark. Break a leg!"

She walked back to the group of light-blue polo shirts and slipped next to Alex, who pulled her in tightly and kissed her ear, whispering, "You have no idea how incredible you are."

The room applauded as the competition got underway. There were sixteen entries, several more than the previous year. Eight booths were lined up on each side of the ballroom, with the crowd milling around in the middle. After the competition finished, each mixologist would make his or her drink available to the audience members. But with only one bottle of Irish Crème, Clark would be calling it an early night.

People will just have to come to the resort to order it. Hope smiled.

As the previous year's reserve champion, Clark was given a prime position in the center of the line, with last year's winner on the opposite side. The judges were the same three from the last competition, two women and one man. They began at one end and proceeded down the line, not spending much time in conversation. *How do they keep from being hammered by the end?*

Patti, who was Clark's aunt, appeared on Hope's other side.

"Thanks for findin' that Irish Crème. Clark was about to completely lose it."

"It ended up being more of an adventure than we'd planned. There wasn't any here on the resort and we had to drive to a liquor store. I pulled out my high school drama-club skills and procured their last bottle."

"Clark is very lucky you did."

Hope hadn't seen Clark's wife, but wasn't surprised. "Kamila stayed home, huh?"

Patti sighed, nodding. "This pregnancy is much harder on her than the last. She just had an appointment, and the doctor told her to take it easy if she wanted to stay off bed rest. With over four months to go, they decided it was better for her to miss it."

"That's a shame, but definitely the right decision. I feel bad for them—she was visiting family last year. Now she has to miss this year too. But I'm sure it will be worth it in the end."

WHEN THE JUDGES got to Clark's booth, it was a repeat of last year. He was charming and confident, mixing the three drinks with a quick wit. But he didn't get much response from the judges—also similar to last year. As with the other contestants, they gave no indication whether they loved or hated the drink, just wrote their impressions on a scorecard attached to their clipboards. Then they moved to the next booth.

Hope sighed. "Well, now we wait."

Alex squeezed her shoulder. "How about a walk?"

Patti turned sharply, and Hope just smiled at her, mouthing, "He's ok."

Patti relaxed and peered around the ballroom. "I should check in with my relatives."

"That'll take until next week," Alex said, as he steered Hope toward the exit. They held hands as they left the building and ambled down the walkway. "Let's head to the sugar mill," Alex said.

They came upon a grassy expanse with a tall, tapering rock cylinder and climbed the steps to enter, their footsteps echoing inside the structure. "This is one of the oldest mills on the island," Alex said. "This used to be a plantation, and slaves burned the sugar cane here."

"There's a lot of history on this island, and not all of it is positive. There are many of these scattered around." Hope ran a hand over the interior wall, the stone rough and chalky under her hand. When she turned around, Alex stood motionless with his hands in his pockets, just watching her.

"Are you doing ok?" she asked as she slid her arms around his waist.

He nodded. "I was watching you with Clark tonight. You weren't going to let anything stop you from getting that bottle for him. You should have seen his face when you hugged him." He pulled away to tuck a lock of hair behind her ear. "You have no idea the effect you have on people. I just stood there, unable to believe you agreed to marry me."

He cupped her face and kissed her deeply. She tightened her hold on him and their kiss deepened. Alex ran his hands through her hair as he pulled her tighter. Then voices approached and they broke apart with regretful smiles.

"Probably not the best place to get too carried away," Hope said. "Let's keep walking."

They continued along a paved path on the golf course. "You're wrong, you know," Hope said.

"About what?" Alex took her hand again.

"I'm the one who can't believe you want to marry me. Sometimes I have a hard time believing I've brought anything good to you. Since you met me, you've had a boat sink, a tree fall on you, been shot, and almost had me drown—twice."

"Well, when you put it like that, you're right. I'll take my ring back now."

Hope smacked him hard on the shoulder and he staggered back a few steps, laughing. "Ouch!"

"You deserved that. You weren't supposed to agree with me."

He took her hand again as they continued walking. "You didn't even come close to drowning the second time. You were amazing in that cave."

He paused, gazing around the beautifully manicured area. "This is hard to explain. I've tried before but haven't done a very good job. Before you moved here, I just went through the motions of life. I loved the diving, and the responsibility of leading dives made me feel good, but it was easy—I didn't have to get too involved. Then you had your accident, and I realized I still had feelings inside."

They passed a monkeypod tree glowing with small white lights. "When the boat sank, I immediately slipped back into command structure. I *knew* what to do. It made me feel alive again. When we met Charles that night, that got amplified a thousand-fold, because the person I was protecting and fighting for was *you*.

"It all gave me the courage I needed to finally start facing my past and come to terms with Syria. That's going to take more than a year, but I've gotten a long way. I guess that's what this long-winded ramble is about. Since I met you—since I fell in love with you—I feel proud of myself again."

Hope stopped and turned toward him. "You should. I'm glad to hear you finally say that. Maybe now I can stop hammering you over the head with it."

"Probably not. Remember, nothing but cement up there."

"Uh-huh. I love you."

"I love you too."

She raised onto her toes to kiss him. His lips were warm and soft and everything she needed in life. "We better head back."

When they entered the ballroom, the three judges were clustered with the master of ceremonies on the stage, located at one end of the room. The Half Moon Bay crew stood loosely in front of their booth. Gerold was there now too.

At their approach, Patti raised a hand to her breast. "Finally! I was startin' to worry you weren't goin' to make it back in time."

"Seriously?" Alex asked. "I might have spaced out, but do you really think Hope would?"

"No, I guess not."

Hope patted her shoulder. "I'm going to check on Clark."

When she approached, he beamed and gave her a hug. "I'm so glad it's over. I'm sorry I forgot that bottle. How dumb."

"It's fine. Shouldn't be long now. You're not going to faint or anything, are you?"

"Maybe. Not sure." Hope widened her eyes and Clark laughed. "I'm doin' ok."

"Well, if you get dizzy, let me know. I'll have Tommy or Alex catch you. You'd probably just knock me over."

"Dunno. They're pretty far away. I think it's you or nothin'."

The master of ceremonies started tapping on his microphone.

"Oh, look at that!" Hope said. "Saved by the microphone. I'd better leave you to the spotlight now. Good luck!" After a quick embrace, Hope returned to stand between Alex and Gerold.

The MC cleared his throat. He was an older man with gorgeous silver hair, dressed in a red smoking jacket and black pants. "Good evening again, ladies and gentlemen. We've had an excellent turnout, with four more entries than last year. So, in the interest of brevity, I'm only going to announce the top three placings." Hope's nerves ramped up and she leaned into Alex, who wrapped an arm around her shoulders.

"In third place, with Pink Paradise, is Bob Jenkins of our host hotel, The Buccaneer!" The large retinue of pink shirts across the aisle clapped and whistled.

Hope's heart hammered.

"And our reserve champion, with Moonlight Midori, is Angelique Salinas of Paradise Cove Resort!" The whole crowd erupted, and a general buzz spread throughout the room, murmurs rising and falling like a tide. Hope darted a look at Clark. He was doing his best to keep a neutral face.

Either he won or he didn't place. This is killing me!

She exchanged a glance with Alex, who looked expectant but not nervous. *Of course not.*

"And we would like to present our congratulations to this year's grand champion, with Half Moon Dream, Clark Bailey of Half Moon Bay Resort!"

Clark's face went blank with shock, and he slapped both hands to his cheeks in a comical gesture. Hope laughed even as she applauded so hard her hands hurt. All the light-blue shirts rushed to his booth as one, giving Clark their love and support.

Hope stood back and let the others approach.

First there was Clark's aunt Patti, who had always supported him. Then Gerold, who had worked closely with Clark for years and whose culinary talents had planted the seed in him to try his own drink recipes. Next was Tommy, who always put everyone at ease with his good-natured joking. And finally, Alex, who gave him a back-slapping hug. They had always been friendly and traded barbs. Clark still refused to try scuba diving, much to Alex's disappointment.

Then everyone looked at Hope.

"Well, what are you doin' clear over there?" Clark asked. "You're the one who made this possible, you know."

Alex held an arm out to her. "Get over here, Boss Lady."

Hope walked over and joined the embrace of these people who meant so much to her. Who were her family every bit as much as Sara.

CHAPTER 18

Hope adjusted her swim goggles and gazed at the flat turquoise sea in front of her. The sun had just risen over the peaks to the east, throwing a golden shimmer over the surface. "I'm shooting for thirty minutes total, easy pace. Feel free to go on ahead if I'm too slow."

Alex turned to her with a deadpan expression. "I believe we've already had the conversation where I explain I'm not leaving you behind."

Hope couldn't help the smile that came to her face. Or the warm feeling that spread through her chest. "We have. Let's go, then."

Hope dove in and began swimming as half a dozen blue tangs drifted across the white sand twenty feet below. Now mostly recovered from her surgery, she had recently started swimming again and felt the layoff.

After fifteen minutes, they turned around and started back, Alex at her side the entire way. By the time they were back at the pier, Hope was breathing hard, and fatigue coursed through her body. She climbed the ladder and toweled off as Alex took a drink from his water bottle. "Good job. How did that feel?"

Hope returned his high five. "Tiring. I'm wiped out, like when I first started swimming after moving here. Some things are different, though."

She pulled him in for a long kiss.

"Very different. Such as your shopping trip today, for example?"

Hope threw her head back and laughed. "If you had told me after that first swim that a year and a half later I'd be shopping for a wedding dress, I would *never* have believed you."

"Even less that you'd be marrying me?"

Hope's smile fell. "I never thought I'd get married, period. I never believed I could trust a man enough. That it wouldn't all come crashing down on me. Even with you. That's why I never asked about marriage—I was too scared to risk what we have."

Alex took her in his arms. "I promise, whatever comes, I'll always be here for you."

"I know. I promise the same."

"Can I make one request? About your dress?"

"Of course."

"Whatever dress you decide on, make sure it's the one *you* want. But I'd love it if your tattoo showed, at least a little."

Hope's smile returned. "Oh? Are you planning on having carnal thoughts about it during the ceremony?"

Alex remained serious. "No, it's not that. I know what it symbolizes for you, and if ever there were a day you should display it, it's our wedding day. Besides, it's kind of symbolic for me too. My journey hasn't been the same as yours, but it's similar. Your tattoo reminds me of that."

"We're so good for each other. And I'll do my best to find a dress that doesn't cover it." They held each other for a long moment. "This is the first time I've had to make an appointment for shopping. The shop owner is a cousin of Patti's, so that makes me feel better about it. Cindy's meeting me at the shop for moral support. Wish me luck."

"You don't need luck. You'll be beautiful no matter what you wear."

∼

Coral Coast Bridal Shop was located on a narrow pedestrian street of downtown Frederiksted near the waterfront. Painted white with pink trim, wedding bells and cherubs decorated the two windows on either side of the door. Hope took a deep breath to tamp down the flutters and pushed the door open, bells jangling over her head as she entered.

The shop was brightly lit and blindingly white. In front of her, Cindy leaned on the counter as she talked to a very thin middle-aged woman wearing a light-blue dress, her black hair just brushing the shoulders of it.

The older woman greeted Hope with a smile—her teeth were dazzling. "You must be Hope! I'm Coral. Patti's told me so much about you."

Hope shook her hand, smiling at the double meaning of the shop's name. Coral inspected her closely, moving her eyes up and down Hope's body. "I'm sure we can find you the perfect weddin' dress. Today we can get an idea of what you like and if you don't find what you're lookin' for, we can order it in. I've got lots more available than what I can stock, don't you know." Coral tilted her head. "What style of dress interests you? White or ivory? High neck or tank? Can I get you coffee or tea? Cookies? Come on, don't just stand there!"

Hope blinked several times before shooting a pleading look at Cindy, who put her arm around Hope's shoulders and led them over to a small sitting area. She pushed Hope into a white embroidered chair as she sat in a matching one, a box of shortbread cookies on a small table between them. Coral sat in the middle of a couch opposite them.

"I'll pass on the coffee or tea. Thanks." *Caffeine is the last thing I need. I'd probably just spill it all over the front of some horribly expensive dress.*

"What style of dress would you like to look at, dear?" Coral sat with her hands clasped, bobbing her head up and down. She had a rather large nose, reminding Hope of a woodpecker.

She tried to keep a straight face. "I'm not sure exactly. Something simple and classic. And white. I'm thirty-seven years old, so I can't see myself in anything too fancy."

"That's enough to get me goin'. You two just wait right here. I'll be right back." Coral got up and bobbed away, presumably to find a tree to attack.

Hope closed her eyes. "Maybe I should just join Alex with the board shorts and T-shirt."

Cindy laughed. "I'm sure we won't need to resort to drastic measures. You'll do fine. You have to admit, this is pretty excitin'. Let's see what she comes back with."

"Exciting isn't the word. Unreal is more like it." Hope breathed in some courage and looked around some more. To her right were three seven-foot-tall mirrors side by side, the two on the ends slanted to show multiple angles.

Coral returned with an armload of white dresses. She handed Hope one and herded her toward the changing room. Afraid Coral might peck her shoulder, she hurried. Then she was alone in the small room and disrobed. She'd worn a strapless bra today, not sure what style of dress she'd end up with.

The first one was white satin with a high lace neckline. Hope pulled in on, then returned to the three-way mirror as Coral buttoned up the back and Cindy looked on, tapping her finger on her chin in appraisal. The lace was very sheer, and Hope checked out the rear view, verifying her tattoo was visible. It had a fitted waist and draped to her knees, but nothing about the dress really spoke to her.

"It's ok, I guess, but I'd like to keep looking."

"Of course. Here's number two." Coral thrust it into her hands and sent Hope back to the changing room.

This dress was more promising, a classic tank style, very fitted while showing some cleavage, but not too much.

Cindy stood up to get a closer look. "I like that one. It seems like you."

Hope met Coral's eyes in the mirror. "This one makes the short list."

"Agreed. It's beautiful on you. Let's move on! More dresses to see." She clapped her hands and thrust another one in Hope's arms, pushing her back to the changing room.

But dresses three and four were both busts, not her style at all. Number four actually had a train, which Hope had insisted she didn't want. She was tiring, nearly ready to go with dress number two and call it a day. Never a big clothes shopper, this wasn't changing her mind.

Dress five was similar to two—Hope liked it immediately. It was also a fitted tank dress and showed most of her tattoo with the strap bisecting it, but this one went all the way to her feet. "I like this one too. But I don't want to try too many, Coral. It just makes it harder to choose."

Cindy nodded. "Yes. Both of these are nice. Maybe we should stop here."

"Wait! I want you to try one more. It's a different style, but I think it would be great on you. You need a dress that shows more cleavage—show off those assets!" Coral started rifling through the white dresses on a rack in front of her, finally exclaiming "Here we are!" as she pulled a dress off the rack and bobbed back to Hope, pressing it in her arms. "Come on. Off you go!"

With a sigh, Hope went back to the small room yet again, staring at her reflection. "Really? One more?"

The dress she currently wore was really nice—she liked the floor length of it for a wedding, rather than knee length. *Maybe I should just stop here.* Then she thought about returning to the mirror area and having Coral flap her wings and peck at her for not trying on the last gown. She surrendered, unzipping.

Hope stepped into dress number six, able to zip this one up herself. Catching her reflection, her breath caught with a sharp inhale.

This is it!

She knew it immediately. Staring at her reflection, she was hardly able to believe it as her gaze traveled from head to toe. A glance over her shoulder confirmed her tattoo showed too. Inexorably, Hope's gaze was drawn back to the mirror, and tears filled her eyes. Her breath hitched as she studied herself.

"I'm getting married. In this dress. To Alex," she whispered in the tiny room.

Then a smile lit up her face. *He's going to love it!*

Now full of confidence, she opened the door, eager to see it in the big mirrors. Cindy and Coral were chatting and turned as she entered with her arms spread out, twirling around.

Both stood still, mouths agape and eyes wide.

"Wow, Hope. That's it!" Cindy said.

Hope nodded, looking at her reflection. "Oh, yes."

"Oh, my dear." Coral rose to her feet. "You look enchantin'. I don't think we need to look any further."

Coral met Hope's eyes and both broke into wide smiles. She poked and prodded at Hope's sides, then lifted her breasts with fussy expertise. "This will need some alterations. It needs to be taken in at the waist and let out at the bust. You're made for this dress! Let's get you rung up and you can leave it here. I'll alter it myself—don't you worry about a thing."

Hope's head was still spinning as she and Cindy walked to their cars, and not just from the experience. The dress was expensive. But worth it.

And we might have a lot more money soon...

"I wish we could have lunch, but I've got to head to class," Cindy said.

"Next time, then. We should set up a day to go diving. Seems like ages since I've been."

"I've got midterms comin' up. But next month I've got more free time. I'd love to go with you."

Hope got into her Jeep and headed toward the resort, still not believing she was actually planning a wedding. Not to mention arranging to sell an honest-to-god treasure.

∼

AFTER RETURNING TO THE HOUSE, Hope checked her inbox and quickly responded to Sandra, an upcoming guest who had been peppering her with questions about the resort. Fortunately, the woman was friendly and decidedly un-Annabelle like.

The latest email asked about her renovation of the guest bungalows. Hope responded with some before and after photos. She never minded answering guest questions. Managing expectations was an important part of the job, and this woman was enthusiastic. Another email came in, this one from the sailboat owner, requesting their wine list, specifically French wines. That was a question for Gerold, so she forwarded it to him.

After closing her laptop, she headed down to the dive shop, entering the cool, inviting room. Alex spoke intently on the phone while Zach hung T-shirts on a circular rack. She exchanged a quick smile with Alex and approached the boy. "Are those the new T-shirts I ordered?"

"Yeah," Zach said. "I really like them."

They featured a drawing of four resort bungalows, complete with palm trees and their white sand beach. The ocean with a diver and coral reef anchored the bottom of the design, with the new resort logo in the lower right corner.

"Thanks, April," Alex said. "I know it's short notice. Something came up quick and I can't work. It's a good group—you shouldn't have any problems."

Alex hung up and Hope turned to him with brows raised. "April's filling in for you tomorrow?"

He smiled. "Yes. You and I are going on a little surprise road trip. I've already talked to Patti about you needing tomorrow off." They held eye contact and Hope nodded back, understanding. Still flush from her opulent wedding-dress purchase, she couldn't wait.

"Perfect!" Hope said. "A relaxing road trip is just what we need. I can't wait."

A very posh, extravagant road trip on a private jet!

CHAPTER 19

The early morning was clear and fresh, with just a few high clouds forming over the mountains. Hope climbed the stairs and entered the private jet. With a smile, the flight attendant waved them forward. The inside was smaller than she expected, with a cream-colored fuselage and six beige leather seats, one on each side of the aisle. Two pairs of chairs faced each other, with a wooden table between them. A single pair of seats was just behind.

Alex had simply parked his Land Cruiser outside the general aviation section of the St. Croix airport, and they walked right up to the plane. Hope slid into the butter-soft leather seat, smoothing her white blouse and tailored gray skirt. But she'd drawn the line at heels, dressing in sensible flats instead. Alex sat across from her, the rich, wood-grained table between them.

The flight attendant, a very polished blonde woman in a blue uniform, appeared in the aisle next to them. "I'm Ann. I know it's only 7 a.m., but can I get you a glass of champagne before we take off? Or tea or coffee?"

"I'll have some coffee. Thanks," Hope replied. "Cream, no sugar."

"Black coffee, please," Alex added.

An excited thrill rose inside Hope. Champagne would have been a wonderful way to start their luxury adventure, but Alex wasn't in the mood. She was always secure with him around, but she sighed as he settled in, darting his eyes around and scanning their surroundings. *Oh, honey. Relax for once! I doubt we'll run into any terrorists today.* But she knew better than to voice her thoughts out loud. This side was a part of his makeup—he couldn't change it. But it wouldn't distract her from enjoying herself.

Ann was soon back with their coffees, steam rising from the white porcelain mugs. "Our flight to Miami is three hours and fifteen minutes, and I have breakfast to serve you after we've reached cruising altitude." She smiled and disappeared into the cockpit.

Alex adjusted the drab blue messenger bag, keeping it next to his side. The plain fabric gave no hint of what was inside. Dressed in loose khakis and an untucked dark-blue polo shirt, he lifted the cup to his lips. "At least they serve decent coffee for our twenty grand."

As they taxied to the runway, Hope smiled. Memories came to mind of her only other flight with Alex, the turbulent twenty-minute journey to St. Thomas. "This plane is even smaller than the one we took to pick up *Surface Interval*, but I'm much more relaxed this time."

"It's a bit more comfortable."

"We got to skip the security check altogether. No manual pat downs for you. That must have been a disappointment." He gave her a small smile in return, but didn't respond. He wouldn't relax until their treasures were safely delivered to the auction house.

The plane lifted smoothly into the air and headed northeast. An hour into the flight, Ann was back with more coffee. She served them a meal consisting of a breakfast sandwich, fresh fruit, and assorted pastries before retreating.

Not knowing when they'd have a chance to eat again, Hope

ate heartily, though she went light on the coffee. "So, did you reserve a Rolls-Royce to pick us up at the airport?"

"Nope, just the service's base sedan. The less conspicuous, the better."

Hope smiled, tolerant of Alex's tendency to prepare for the worst. Besides, what that messenger bag contained was extremely valuable. He was prepared for anything. Maybe overprepared.

"I've been thinking lately about your story of Tommy doing the underwater wedding," Hope said. "What do you think about asking him to perform our ceremony? At least he'd stay dry."

Alex smiled slightly. "If I asked him, he'd probably refuse and toss me overboard. If you asked him, he'd probably fall all over himself saying yes."

"Oh, sure. Put it all on me."

"Hey, you're the one who can talk folks into anything. I just piss people off."

Hope grinned. "Steve being a case in point?"

"That was mutual, but we parted on civil terms. We've texted a few times since his visit."

The plane bumped through some light turbulence but settled quickly. "Are you going to invite him to the wedding?"

Alex sighed and poured himself more coffee. "Yeah. At least invite him. Then it would be up to him whether to come or not. Tommy forgave him, and I'm a bit more at ease these days. It's the right thing to do."

Hope ran a hand over the rich leather seat. "I agree. And back to Tommy. You don't like the idea of him doing the ceremony?"

"Not at all. I think he'd do a terrific job. I'll muster up the courage to ask him. By the way, are you planning on having a maid of honor?"

"I haven't decided. If I do, it will be Sara, for sure. What about a best man?"

"Well, I'd thought about Tommy, but if he performs the ceremony, he's out."

"Robert?"

Alex met her eyes. "I was thinking about Mike, actually."

Hope straightened, nearly spilling her coffee in the rush to set her mug on the table. "That's a great idea! I love it. You should ask him. I can talk Sara into wearing a fancy dress—she lives for hair and makeup."

~

THEY LANDED at a private executive airport near Miami. As they taxied across the tarmac, a modern glass terminal appeared in the oval windows, a long row of expensive private jets lined up in front. Hope frowned, a little sad the experience was ending.

Alex slid the messenger bag across the table to her. "I'd like you to carry this, so my hands stay free."

An excited shiver rippled through Hope, and she considered a smartass comment about being secret agents. A look at Alex's face changed her mind. He wasn't playing at anything. He had a job to do and had cleared his mind of all distractions. It was what had made him such a good SEAL.

"Our mission has been planned to perfection?"

He twitched a corner of his mouth. "As well as it can be. There's an old military saying that no plan survives first contact with the enemy. I'm sure something won't go as intended."

"I choose to be optimistic—nothing will go wrong. So there."

Alex just gave her a small smile.

Ann breezed down the aisle and opened the rear door, lowering it to the tarmac. They said their goodbyes and Hope and Alex descended the plane.

And with that, their private-jet trip was over.

The air here wasn't as humid as in St. Croix, and the day was sunny and already hot. A hive of busy service workers moved around the plane, refueling, adding more catering, and performing other mysterious tasks. A young white man wearing dirty coveralls and a Buck Aviation baseball hat attached a hose to the jet wing and began fueling it. He nodded to her.

Returning it, Hope swiveled her head around the tarmac, looking for a car that wasn't there.

"This is just great," Alex muttered as he dug his phone out of his pocket and dialed. "Yeah, we're here in Miami. Where is our car?" He listened, stiffening. "We're not waiting on the damn ramp for an hour. Are you kidding? Just cancel it—we'll get a cab." Alex hung up, shaking his head.

Buck Aviation Guy approached them. "I overheard your conversation. My brother's a limo driver and is usually in this area. You want me to call him?"

Ooh! A limo. We can continue in style.

Hope was about to agree when Alex told the man curtly, "No. We'll get a cab." He pressed his hand into the small of her back, ushering her ahead of him as they walked toward the glass terminal.

She clutched the handles of the messenger bag, her heart sinking. "I don't understand." Hope took one last look back. Buck Aviation Guy turned away, talking on his cell phone. "What's wrong with a limo? That would have been perfect."

"And who knows where we might have ended up? No, we'll find the taxi line and pick one."

Hope scowled as Alex opened the terminal door. But she brightened again once she looked around. The cool interior was brightly lit, with shops on either side of a wide central corridor. A quick glance at the stores made her very aware she was at a private-jet airport in Miami. They passed Gucci, Chanel, Coach, Rolex, and Prada, among others. It was fun to pretend she was part of the one percent as a woman passed by in huge sunglasses, wearing a full-length faux mink coat and carrying a Chihuahua.

Alex sighed behind her. "God, these people."

Hope bit her lip to keep from laughing. Not everyone was

high society, though. A man in a gray hooded sweatshirt walked by. *Hey, it's a normal person.*

They passed under a *Ground Transportation* sign that pointed ahead. Hope stole a quick glance at Alex. He constantly moved his eyes around, evaluating everything.

Are you worried about getting brained by a Gucci handbag?

Next up was an ocean-themed art gallery, next to the bathrooms. Hope craned her head around as they passed it, captivated.

"Hold up a second, ok? I need to use the men's room. If you'll wait here, I'll be right back."

As Alex walked away, Hope turned her attention back to the art gallery. It was right next to the bathroom, so she walked to the wide-open entrance. There were several sculptures as well as a number of oil paintings and watercolors on the wall, all featuring scenes or figures of the ocean and its creatures. After assuring the saleswoman she was just browsing, Hope studied the carvings, staying at the entrance so Alex wouldn't have to search for her when he came out.

Her breath caught at a stunning glass figure of a dolphin captured in a vertical jump. It was located front and center at the entrance, five feet in height, including the glass wave pedestal it leaped out of. Soft-gray color faded from its back to its white belly. It looked so smooth, almost soft. *Would it feel warm or cool?* Unable to resist, Hope set the messenger bag down to run her hands over the dolphin's side, a tingle radiating through her fingertips. It was cool, and decadently smooth.

This would be perfect in the lobby—the first thing guests see when they enter!

She couldn't detect any seams between the different colors of glass. The figure was beautiful, though she had a sinking feeling its blue eyes were made of sapphires, making her doubt it was in her price range.

Then again, it might be very soon.

Delight made her breath catch as she stroked a hand over it again. Ready to approach the saleswoman and get her card, Hope bent down to pick up the messenger bag.

It was gone.

CHAPTER 20

*A*lex washed his hands, glowering at his reflection. He wanted to get to the auction house as soon as possible, and at least now he could concentrate on the next leg of the operation. *You know better than to drink coffee for a whole flight.*

He wasn't happy about the car not being there, but was used to adapting on the fly. And changing from a car service to a taxi wasn't any great hardship. He turned and headed out of the restroom.

Just outside, Alex stopped dead. In the middle of the corridor, Hope rushed past, her face a mask of anger. She wasn't running, more like trying to hurry without drawing attention to herself. Both her hands were empty.

Oh, shit.

Stomach plummeting, he followed her furious gaze to an average-looking man in a gray hoodie. He was walking quickly through the terminal, and their blue messenger bag was clutched in his right hand.

Instantly alert, Alex zeroed in on the familiar young man, having marked him earlier as being out of place. The hood draped over his shoulders, and greasy blond hair curled up at his neck.

Alex followed, staying far to one side of Hope, and was impressed she wasn't yelling bloody murder at someone to tackle the guy. The last thing Alex wanted was attention. He was used to stealth.

Gray Hoodie hadn't noticed Hope. He fixed his eyes straight ahead as he tried to look invisible. They came to a T-intersection and the man headed right, Hope in close pursuit. The man craned his head around and Alex turned to look at a tropical-shirt display, watching through peripheral vision as he slowed. Hope didn't though, and Gray Hoodie widened his eyes at her, realizing he'd been spotted.

He shot off to the left and burst through a set of white double doors. Hope ran in hot pursuit. Alex stifled a groan and followed much more quietly through the doors. The trio were inside a long, deserted, white-painted corridor. Gray Hoodie and Hope raced down it, their footfalls echoing off the brown tile floor.

"Hey!" Hope shouted. "That belongs to me. Drop it, asshole!"

At the end of the hallway, the man disappeared through another set of double doors, sunlight streaming beyond. Alex couldn't help the smile that rose as Hope sprinted in her tight gray skirt.

What is she going to do if she catches him?

Then she was out the door too. Alex followed at his slower pace, stopping on a sidewalk just outside. A narrow lane ran next to it, a large truck motoring by. Gray Hoodie ran down the sidewalk with Hope on his heels.

The man swerved into the lane and took off down a wide-open cement area. Hope ran just behind him, her face red as she scowled. Alex could easily outflank the guy and started running to intercept him, fully confident in the situation.

There were gray cement buildings all around, but the area was deserted. The only sound was the occasional rumble of trucks in the lane behind them, and the sound of pounding feet and rapid breaths.

Alex ran much more quietly. *Neither of them has a clue I'm here. I can't believe she's got such stamina after not running much since her surgery—must be the adrenaline.* A smile tried to rise on Alex's face, but he quashed it, concentrating on the pair.

HOPE REACHED for his hood but missed. "Goddammit, stop! Give me that back. It's *mine*, asshole!"

Gray Hoodie hit the brakes, stopping, then whirled around toward Hope. She skidded to a halt and took a big step backwards.

"You want me to stop? You got it!" He was in his mid-twenties, and spoke with a deep Southern accent.

Alex slowed and approached silently, ready to move quickly if necessary. He withdrew his Sig from the holster at his back.

"Why do you want this bag so much, bitch? It's heavy as hell." Gray Hoodie took a step toward Hope with a snarl on his face, but Alex was almost there, approaching on their nine o'clock.

Hope's expression changed from anger to shock as Gray Hoodie produced a four-inch switchblade and flicked it open. But that was nothing compared to the shock on the man's face when Alex appeared at his side, pressing the barrel of his pistol into his left kidney.

Gray Hoodie knew exactly what it was and froze. He darted his eyes to Alex, who leaned close, giving him a lethal glare. "Didn't anyone ever tell you never to bring a knife to a gunfight?"

The guy started panting, sweat dripping down his cheeks. "Look! I just grabbed the bag. I didn't mean anything by it."

"Drop the knife. Now."

Gray Hoodie opened his hand and the knife clattered to the cement. Without moving his eyes, Alex kicked it aside. "Hope, pick up the knife."

She was gasping, and a lock of hair was pressed against her sweaty face. With glazed eyes, she picked up the knife.

Alex stepped closer, between her and Gray Hoodie, and

jabbed the gun in more. "You have something that belongs to us." He spoke in an even voice, dripping with menacing intent. "We want it back. Now. Hand it to the lady."

Gray Hoodie rushed the bag out with one hand and Hope snatched it back. She gripped both handles without flinching at the weight, though her hands shook wildly.

Gray Hoodie hadn't moved his eyes from Alex's, like he was hypnotized.

Alex was several inches taller and stepped closer, being as intimidating as possible. "Now apologize for calling her a bitch. That's not nice."

The guy wrenched his eyes to Hope's and started babbling. "Look, lady. The bag was just sitting on the floor next to you, so I grabbed it."

Alex dug the gun in harder, increasing his glower.

"I'm sorry I called you a bitch! Ok? I'm sorry!"

"How did you know where she was?"

Gray Hoodie ratcheted his head back to Alex. Once more he was mesmerized, like an antelope staring at a lion. His mouth opened and closed, but no words came out.

Alex narrowed his eyes and moved until his face was an inch away, gripping Gray Hoodie's arm with his non-gun hand. "I'm not going to ask again. And I hope you realize I know how to use this gun."

"It was Rocco, ok? My friend Rocco! He's a refueler at the airport. I case the terminal and he alerts me when a potential mark comes in. People who fly on private jets usually have stuff worth stealing. I'm sorry! Don't shoot me, please."

Alex pulled back and let his eyes soften a little. "All right. Was that so hard? And this is your lucky day. We don't have time to get the police involved, so get out of here. Now!"

Alex shoved Gray Hoodie hard and he stumbled away, then started sprinting and was soon out of sight. He re-holstered his weapon as he scanned the area, relieved they were still alone. Alex turned to Hope, who was still breathing hard as she watched him with wide eyes.

"Hand me the knife. I'll take care of it."

Hope stared at her hand, as if surprised there was a switchblade in it. Jerking, she gave it to Alex, her hands trembling wildly.

"What exactly was your plan?" he asked, keeping his voice even. "What were you going to do after he pulled the knife on you?"

Her bottom lip began to quiver. "I didn't think that far ahead. I just took off after him." Her eyes filled with tears, and a terribly guilty expression transformed her face. Alex's irritation evaporated immediately.

"I put the bag down to look at a dolphin sculpture. When I went to pick it up, it was gone. He was carrying it and hurrying away. I'm sorry. I just wanted to get it back."

"Come here." Alex drew her into his arms and was surprised at the smile spreading across his face. Hope never lacked for courage, but her planning could use some work. He should be mad as hell at her, but all he felt was relief and a weird, giddy pride. "We got it back. That's what counts. Come on, let's get out of here and get that taxi."

Alex kept his arm around her as they returned to the terminal, again moving his eyes everywhere. He didn't think Gray Hoodie had any partners, but was on high alert now.

They continued along the sidewalk, passing a lidded garbage can. Alex wiped the knife clean with his shirt before tossing it in. When they reached a corner, the front glass facade of the terminal appeared on their left. A line of taxis sat out front. Alex picked one at random and they entered the back seat. He gave the driver the address for Prodigy Auction House.

As they left the curb, the cabbie played Latin music on the radio, giving them some privacy. Hope clutched the bag tightly under one arm as her other trembling hand plucked at non-existent lint on her skirt. She refused to look at him.

Alex leaned over and kissed her temple. "Stop worrying. Everything's fine."

Finally, Hope turned big, haunted eyes to him. "Because you were there and knew what to do. You were suspicious from the start, weren't you? That's why you didn't want the limo ride."

"I think they use a two-pronged approach. If the mark gets in the limo, that guy robs them. If they go in the terminal, they get Gray Hoodie. I haven't decided if the car service was involved. When we're done today and back at the commercial airport, I'll make an anonymous tip that they need to take a close look at our friend Rocco."

"I thought you were just being overprotective again. I was pretending to be rich and famous, and was mad I didn't get to ride in the limo."

"I am overprotective. But occasionally, I know what I'm doing too."

Her eyes held the glassy look of shock and she'd need some time to process what had happened. "It's just like the cave. I'm sorry for jumping to conclusions and not trusting your judgement." Hope squeezed his hand in a vise grip.

"I'm sorry for occasionally coddling you."

"I'm a complete idiot."

"Hey, that's my line."

She gave him a small smile, finally relaxing her shoulders. "Maybe we deserve each other."

He pressed his leg against hers and returned the smile. "Always?"

"Count on it, sailor."

CHAPTER 21

Hope stared out the window of the cab, acutely conscious of the messenger bag safe at her side. Goose bumps rose as she pictured the man flashing his knife—the realization she was all alone with an armed thief. How incredibly stupid that was. Hope was so shocked at the situation and herself, she hadn't even been able to react. She'd just stood there gaping at the knife.

Then Alex was there, cool and lethal.

She leaned her head against the seat. *Did I chase after him because I knew Alex would find us and be there to save me?* She was highly suspicious the answer was yes, but if the timing of the theft had been a little different, her mistake might have been even more stupid. She might have been stabbed.

Hope looked at the man next to her. Alex stared at his phone, pinching the screen—zooming and widening it. It was a map of the vicinity they were traveling through. He was double-checking the driver's route, making sure he didn't take them off course.

She leaned her head on his shoulder with a thump. "I'm sorry."

He kissed her head, then went back to his map. "Stop apologizing. Everything's fine now. Besides, I have to do something once in a while to make you think I'm worth keeping around." He craned his head at the skyscraper next to them. "We're almost there. Put it out of your mind, baby. It's go time."

She straightened and took a deep breath, making a conscious effort to pull herself together and prepare for their appointment. There was a box of tissues in the seatback pocket, and she used one to wipe her still-sweaty face. Then she ran her hands through her hair, putting it back in order.

The taxi came to a stop in front of a dark-brown granite building with smoked windows. Hope paid the driver, and they pushed through a large revolving doorway into an expansive lobby. Prodigy Auction House was on the twelfth floor, so they proceeded to the elevator. The doors snicked shut and they moved smoothly upward. It even smelled like money.

Alex glanced at his watch. "11:55. Even after all the excitement, we're right on time."

Hope's negative energy finally dissipated as excitement replaced it, and she gripped the messenger bag tightly.

The elevator opened to a small but very opulent lobby. The floor was Calcutta marble, and the walls were a light-gray shade of granite that contrasted the floor beautifully. Across from them sat a receptionist behind a large wooden desk. As they approached, the young woman with her dark-brown hair in a stylish bun quickly dismissed Hope to turn her attention to Alex, lavishing him with a full smile. "How may I help you today?"

Hope stared steadily at her. "We have an appointment with Bryce McCandless. Hope Collins and Alex Monroe." She gave the receptionist her best fake smile. As usual, Alex was completely unaware of his effect on the opposite sex.

"One moment, please. Have a seat and I'll ring Bryce." The receptionist was coolly professional now. Hope and Alex moved to the seating area, sinking into a dark-gray leather couch. Framed photographs of ancient coins, Chinese vases, and gold crosses hung on the walls.

They didn't wait long before Bryce appeared in the lobby, dressed in a navy-blue double-breasted suit and red power tie. His face brightened as he shook their hands. "Welcome to Miami! I trust you had a nice flight?"

"Wonderful," Alex said. "We're eager to get moving on this."

"I'm sure you are. So am I." Bryce flashed another excited smile before leading them through a hallway to a small conference room, which was dominated by a rectangular wooden table that seated eight. A wall of windows overlooked the buildings across the street and a tall stone statue of a humanoid figure hulked in one corner. As Bryce showed them to their seats and sat across the table from them, an older man with well-groomed silver hair entered the room.

Bryce stood again. "I'd like to introduce Henry James, our senior vice president in charge of Latin American auctions. He's going to be an extra set of eyes today." They shook hands all around.

"We'll tag each individual item in your lot. Between Henry and I, we should be able to determine a minimum opening bid for each and give you an itemized list before you leave today. Next, we'll set the date for the auction, which will be both in person and online. We get a lot more response that way. The items will be placed in a locked box and secured inside our vault, which I assure you has bank-level security. Does that sound acceptable?"

"Sounds fine to me," Alex said.

Bryce rubbed his hands together. "Ok, let's see what you've got."

Hope hefted the messenger bag onto the table. Unzipping it, she removed a slightly smaller bag, her arms flexing at the weight. It was made from fabric that couldn't be ripped or cut, and was padlocked shut. She slid the bag to Alex, who produced a key and unzipped it. The sound echoed in the silent room.

One at a time, he removed twelve gold ingots, twenty gold chains including one with a solid-gold pendant four inches long, a plastic zip-closed bag filled with gold coins, another with silver coins, and eight gold and silver dinner plates.

Bryce's eyes bulged.

Alex absently handed Hope another zip-closed bag filled with gemstones as he removed two gold crosses, one twelve inches tall and encrusted with emeralds. The other intricately engraved cross was eight inches tall.

Henry inhaled sharply.

A manila file folder was next, Alex setting it between Hope and himself. Hope opened her zip-closed baggie with a shrug. "This seemed like the best solution at hand." She removed the gemstones it contained, placing them in a neat row. Many large rubies and diamonds, as well as a dozen emeralds, one as large as her palm, glittered in the soft light.

As she finished, Alex withdrew the final item from the fabric bag and held it up. It was a ten-inch-tall gold figurine with a large head and folded arms and legs, engraved with an intricate headdress suggesting feathers. It gleamed in the light, no tarnishing anywhere. Its back was engraved with a robe enhanced with diamonds and emeralds. Even from where Hope sat, the stunning artistry of the figurine was apparent. Alex's arms bulged as he set the idol between the two men.

Bryce and Henry both stared at it in open-mouthed astonishment.

"My God," Henry said. "What is that?"

"I thought you were the expert," Hope said with a raised brow and smug grin.

Bryce reached out and stroked a finger over it, as if afraid it would disappear. "Inca, for sure. Classic period. Probably a temple god. Incredible workmanship." He looked up between Hope and Alex. "Any minimum bid we come up with for this is just a wild-assed guess. It's priceless. You sure you want to part with this?"

"We talked about donating it to a museum," Hope said. "But we got lost trying to decide which one. We've kept some pieces for . . . sentimental value. We're ok parting with this one."

Henry snorted. "Plenty of museums have similar pieces—well, kind of like this. You can get a *lot* of money for it. I'd set the minimum bid for this at one million dollars."

The air rushed out of Hope's lungs as her heart pounded. "What? That much?"

Bryce was nodding. "We had a piece last year, not even this nice, that sold for 1.5 million dollars."

He rose and moved to the end of the table, picking up two laptops and a cloth bag before placing one laptop in front of Henry and opening the other himself. From the bag, Bryce took out a scale, a number of white plastic identification stickers, and several sizes of clear plastic bags. He placed the idol in one and attached a sticker to it, noting the item number and opening bid on his computer.

While he did that, Henry picked up the larger cross, turning it over in his hands, his eyes wide. "This is Peruvian, and just *covered* in emeralds and diamonds." He produced a jeweler's loupe from a pocket and inspected it more closely. "So intricate. Late 1500s. Minimum bid, $500,000."

Hope sat back in her chair, stunned. She exchanged glances with Alex, who was expressionless except for the wink he shot her way. Her smile rose in return as their legs pressed together under the table.

Next, Bryce picked up the enormous emerald. "This isn't the same one you showed me in Alistair's office."

Hope pointed toward the table. "No, that's this little one here."

Bryce laughed, placing the huge emerald on his scale before inspecting it through his loupe. He was quiet for several moments, then handed it to Henry. "Look at the color of this thing. And it's over twenty carats. Amazing."

Henry whistled as he looked through his loupe. "Minimum bid, $750,000."

IT TOOK NEARLY two hours for Bryce and Henry to catalog all the items and enter them into the computer. Finally, they finished their tally and Henry printed the total, handing copies to Hope and Alex.

The minimum bids for all their items came to nearly $2.8 million.

And I almost lost it all.

Because she got complacent. And dismissive. Thinking she knew more about what was happening than Alex did. And she'd been dead wrong.

Bryce opened a closet door and removed a large lock box. "We'll place all the items into this box, in your full view, and lock it up. Then we'll place an identification sticker on it, giving an identical one to you. After that, it will be stored in our vault until the auction."

"I don't suppose I can accompany you to the vault?" Alex asked.

"I'm afraid not," Henry said. "It would defeat our security measures if we let people see them."

Alex nodded in acknowledgment.

"However, we do have armed security on the premises. Would you like them to accompany Bryce and myself to the vault?"

"I would definitely like that."

Bryce had been typing feverishly on his laptop. "I'm finding a date for the auction. We don't want to set it too soon, so we can do some advertising and get a good buildup. We've got an opening in early October. I think that would be perfect. Does that sound ok to you two?"

Hope and Alex exchanged shrugs. "It's fine with us. Whatever you think would work best," Hope said as she picked up the manila file folder that sat between her and Alex. "We gave you a copy of the letter already. This is the original. Do you need to do anything special to authenticate it?"

Henry took the letter from her, handling the fragile vellum with great care as he set it between himself and Bryce. Both put in jeweler's loupes and turned on small flashlights, inspecting the document carefully.

"Based on my initial observations, I'd say it's authentic," Henry said. "But can we keep this? We need to run some tests on it to document the actual age. This proves provenance of your find, so fully authenticating it is very important. Only Bryce or I will conduct the tests, and we'll have a guard present at all times. Would that be acceptable?"

Alex tightened his jaw. "Can you run the tests while we wait? We weren't planning on coming back here to pick anything up, and I'd prefer not to . . . just mail it."

Henry and Bryce looked at each other, and Bryce shrugged. "Yeah, we can do that. It should only take an hour or so. We'll escort the box to the vault with guards, then proceed to test the letter. Do you guys want to go grab lunch for an hour or two?"

Hope tensed. "I think I'd rather wait."

"We're ok just staying in this conference room," Alex said.

Henry smiled. "That's perfectly fine—make yourselves comfortable. I'll have someone deliver you some lunch. It probably won't be too fancy, but it'll be edible. We'll be back as soon as we're done."

Bryce placed the items inside the box as Henry called for two security guards. Hope met Alex's gaze, completely stunned. But as he gave her a slow smile, excitement kindled in her gut.

CHAPTER 22

*L*unch was a sandwich and salad with bottled water to wash it down. Hope ate eagerly, a glance at the clock confirming why she was so hungry. It was nearly 3 p.m. Relief and a dizzy happiness washed over her, knowing their treasures were now safely locked in a vault.

$2.8 million! How is that even possible?

Hope looked at Alex. That was how it was possible. The altercation with Gray Hoodie intruded into her thoughts and Hope pushed it away, determined not to let it ruin her hard-won good mood. After all, she'd found the cave in the first place, with Cruz's help. The entire adventure had been a team effort.

Alex returned her look and her smile. "What are you thinking about?"

"How incredible this is. How it took both of us to get here." She leaned forward and brushed her lips over his, and an electric tingle ran through her.

"You sure that's all you're thinking about?"

"Wouldn't you like to know."

"Yes, very much."

"Maybe later. I thought you were concentrating on the mission here, Mr. Monroe."

"The security detail is over. This is the mop-up. I can relax a little now."

Hope leaned back in her chair again. "What are we going to do with all this money?"

"We don't have it yet. Let's just take this one step at a time."

"Eminently sensible advice."

"Told you, I've got to find some reason for you to keep me around." Alex had that gleam in his eye that never failed to get a response from her.

"I don't think you need to worry about that."

Their gazes held for a long moment, then Hope broke the contact by digging her phone out of her purse, moving on with the final phase of their mission. She opened her airline app. "There's a flight to St. Croix that leaves from Miami International at 6 p.m. How does that sound?"

"Good. We need to get back tonight. I only made arrangements to cover today."

"Ok, I'll buy it now." She booked their flight, a faint smile coming to her face. *How about a little surprise for Alex? He's earned it.* She'd just finished when the door opened and Bryce and Henry returned, sliding the folder back to Hope.

"We tore a very small corner off. You can hardly tell," Bryce said. "But we conclusively dated it to between 1650 and 1675, which matches the date on the letter. You guys don't want to auction this?"

"No," Hope said, sliding the folder back into the fabric envelope. "This has sentimental value." It also might come in handy in the future if they sold more items. What they'd brought today was only a portion of the total.

Bryce smiled. "Of course. We took some photographs so we can show it at the auction." He looked between Hope and Alex.

"Do you have any photos or video of where you found the treasure? You said it was in a cave, right?"

Alex nodded. "A wet cave. We dove it through a series of passages and found the treasure in a large cavern. I wore a video camera when we found it."

"You dove it? As in scuba diving?" Henry asked.

"Yes," Hope said. "Alex is an expert diver, and I tagged along after his initial explorations."

Bryce's eyes got bigger at Alex's explanation of his adventures in the cave. "This is great! Collectors want the story behind their items. They don't buy a gold doubloon because of its monetary value, but because the coin has a story they identify with. Can you send me some stills and a video clip?"

Alex looked at her with a grin. "That sounds like a job for Hope."

"I can do that. I already edited down the footage to a couple minutes. I'll double check to make sure Alex and I aren't identifiable, and I should be able to pull some stills out pretty easily."

"We need a name for the lot," Bryce said.

Hope thought of the letter. "How about the Barnaby Morgan Treasure?"

"Sounds perfect to me," Alex said with a smile.

"You want to keep your names out of this, right?" Bryce asked.

Hope and Alex both nodded.

"That shouldn't be a problem." Henry leaned forward, looking at them both seriously. "We have plenty of experience with anonymous clients—it's not unusual. At this point, we just need bank account information to deposit the final payment and for you to sign the contract. Then we're done."

By 4 p.m., their signatures had been collected and they were finished. Sitting back in her chair, Hope breathed a relieved sigh. Then a shiver of awed disbelief ran down her spine at what they had just accomplished.

"Are you staying in Miami overnight?" Bryce asked.

"No," Hope replied. "We're flying back tonight. We both have to work tomorrow."

"We keep a fleet of vehicles for transporting clients," Henry said. "Since you're officially clients now, we insist on providing transportation to Miami airport for you."

Fifteen minutes later, Hope and Alex left the parking garage in the back of a black stretch limousine.

"You got your limo ride after all," Alex said, with a twinkle in his eye.

"This one feels a little safer too."

The trip to Miami International Airport proceeded uneventfully. They made a short stop at a sporting-goods emporium so Alex could purchase a small, lockable gun case to house his pistol during the flight. He also bought a small, hard-sided suitcase to place the gun case in.

After an easy check-in and pass through security, they were soon clinking champagne glasses together as they settled into their wide leather seats. "First class. You are definitely spoiling me this trip, Boss Lady."

"I thought I'd splurge tonight since we are celebrating, after all. And you deserve a little pampering after this morning."

Alex laughed. "This beats the hell out of a C-17, that's for sure." He leaned over and gave her a quick kiss, and her body jolted as his tongue brushed hers. "You can spoil me all you want."

Hope tried to redirect her thoughts. "It surprised me the check-in agent didn't bat an eye when you checked your firearm."

"I'm sure they're used to it, and I showed him my Navy ID. But I'd be surprised if TSA doesn't look in the suitcase to make sure it's secure."

"And in a few hours, we'll be home. It's out of our hands now. You have a full boat tomorrow?"

"I think so. Both Robert and I are working. Par for the course these days. And the new guy is getting his tryout soon. If he works out, that will be a big help."

After dinner, Alex settled in to watch a movie, but Hope didn't see anything that interested her. The flight attendant came through and refilled their red wineglasses as Alex absently reached over and grasped her left hand in his right. She smiled when he rubbed his thumb over her ring. It had already become an automatic habit.

She studied his hand, considering it. The hand he used to softly stroke hers was the same one that had held a gun against a man just hours ago. Where other men might have yelled in rage at the thief, Alex had exuded an ice-cold, deadly professionalism that was even more intimidating. When the threat was over, he'd simply switched off that persona and gone back to being his usual sweet but protective self.

Hope closed her eyes and leaned against the headrest, considering the stupid mistakes she'd made that day. She should have waited for Alex. He'd had no trouble tracking her and the thief, and certainly hadn't needed her help to get the bag back. Guilt roiled her gut once more. *Why do I do stupid things like that?*

Alex's movie finished, and he returned his earbuds to his pocket. Hope leaned her head against his shoulder. "Why do you put up with me?"

He laughed quietly and kissed the top of her head. "You sure are stealing my lines lately."

"I was just asking myself why I do such stupid things. Why I get mad at you, even though I know you're right?" She shook her head.

"That's what makes you who you are." A smile cracked Alex's face as he gripped her hand tighter. "A lot of marriages break up because the two people try to change each other. We don't do that. I'm always going to be stubborn and protective. You're always going to be impulsive and overconfident." He shrugged. "I'll put up with your faults if you put up with mine."

"At least life isn't boring, huh?" Laughing, she gave him a quick kiss as both leaned back in their seats. She wasn't Predictable Hope anymore. A small smile crept across her face as she relaxed. Alex was correct. Every now and again, he knew what he was doing.

She returned her gaze to his fingers, softly caressing hers, and she focused on how strong, yet gentle, they were. That brought thoughts of what else those hands were capable of, and she shifted position in her seat, heat spreading throughout her. It was a mystery how Alex could arouse her without even trying. But this was one she was happy to leave unsolved.

∽

THE DAYS after their Miami trip were busy. Hope had the manager's reception, which was more interactive than usual, keeping her there late. Alex led several night dives, and both ended their days collapsing into bed. He had just returned and was reading in bed. In the bathroom, Hope, dressed in a silky nightgown, brushed her teeth and smiled at her reflection. *He won't be sleepy when he sees me in this.*

Shutting off the light, she padded to the bed. Alex was already asleep, lying on his back with one arm thrown over his head. With a deep sigh, Hope pulled off the nightgown so it wouldn't get tangled up as she slept. *Not much point in wearing it, anyway.* Cracking a big yawn, she climbed into bed, trying to be quiet. She fell asleep immediately.

HE CAME to her in the dead of night.

Hope awoke on her side as Alex fitted himself behind her. The moon cast slatted shadows through the open blinds, its soft light illuminating the bedroom. His hot rigidness pressed against her as he kissed her tattoo. He traced his mouth slowly up the side of her neck to her ear, and she tilted her head, smiling at the similarity to their first kiss on his deck at sunset.

He flicked his tongue in her ear, whispering, "I can't get enough of you."

"Then you know how I feel." Hope reached back and stroked his hip, tracing the ridges of scar tissue.

Alex rumbled in his chest, circling his tongue in her ear and sending lightning through her. She was already aroused and began to turn around when Alex tensed, preventing her from moving. "No, stay still. This is for you."

Hope relaxed as he moved his lips back to her neck, using one hand to lift her hair as his tongue streaked across the back of her neck, sending a jolt of lightning straight down her spine. He stroked her breast with a light, gentle touch that only inflamed her more. Then he brushed down her stomach, spreading his fingers wide as his legs pushed hers farther in front of her.

"You have no idea what you do to me—how much I want you." He pulled his legs away as he glided his hand slowly over her hip, then down her thigh. With the same slow, soft rhythm, he stroked up and down her thigh. Her skin tingled in its wake, and she breathed deeply now. Finally, he stroked her from behind.

Gasping, she arched her back against him.

He moved his mouth back to her ear. "Oh, yes. You're ready, aren't you?"

"Very."

He whispered in her ear, "I just want to please you." He shifted position, tracing his hand back up her arm and bringing his legs up behind hers again.

With one powerful movement, he was inside her.

She held her lower lip between her teeth, arching again as she felt his motion deep inside, waves beginning to course through her.

His breath was heavy in her ear. "Like that, do you?"

"Oh my God, yes."

Alex moved in a slow, even rhythm, and she was already on fire from head to toe. He moved his hand back to her breast, stroking again, and she moaned. His soft laughter filled the room. "Oh, yes, moans are most definitely encouraged."

Then his mouth was at her ear again. "You turn me on so much. Can you feel it?" He pushed harder, and her breathing became faster, electricity arcing up and down her body.

"Move onto your stomach, baby." She rolled over and he went with her, never dislodging himself, and began moving within her again, rumbling a deep, throaty moan. Mmmm, you feel totally different from here."

He should have been heavy, but he wasn't. He traced his right hand all along her body, moving from her shoulder down her side and hip, before brushing it up to stroke the side of her breast. He breathed heavily in her ear, making her wild. "Please. Open wider. I need to be deeper."

She did and gripped the pillow with her left hand. The pleasure knifed through her, and her breath matched his rhythm.

Alex made a steady rumbling deep in his chest, only stopping when he inhaled. "Lift your hip a bit."

Hope moved her right knee up, creating space beneath her. He immediately moved his hand in, his first strokes making her cry out.

"Oh, my. You *are* enjoying this, aren't you?"

He smiled against her ear and stroked his fingers to match his movement inside her. Now both her fists were bunched on her pillow. He was panting in her ear, and she was escalating quickly, getting louder. Even her toenails were on fire now, sensations rippling through her body.

Then he stopped completely and whisked his hand up to her abdomen. "I know those sounds. Greedy little thing, aren't you?"

She groaned in frustration as he laughed, so softly, speaking again in his throaty whisper. "I love you. I want to show you how much."

"Alex . . . I need . . . I don't even know what."

"That's ok. I do."

He began moving again. Hope was no longer solid. She had melted into the sheets. The pillow grew taut beneath her head as she gripped tighter with both hands.

"You're so soft, so warm." Alex knew exactly how much was too much, never pushing her to where she wanted to be with each growing, desperate second.

Slow, then faster, then slow again.

He kissed from her ear down to her shoulder, his tongue leaving a wet streak behind. "Oh my God, this tattoo. You are the sexiest thing I've ever laid eyes on."

Hope was moaning again. "You feel so good. I can feel you deep inside me."

His hand was still on her stomach, spread across it. He moved it back between her legs, and her body jerked as she cried out. Her peak was building, and she was panting hard.

Alex laughed softly before whispering, "I think you're ready now."

He pounded into her hard, moving his hand in rhythm.

What had been building exploded, rolling in waves up and down. It progressed from her center up to her head before rolling its way back down, all the way to her feet, only to renew itself. Her climax continued as inexorably as the movement of the ocean, never ending. Very dimly, she was aware that Alex had stiffened also, crying out in unison with her. But her response was all-encompassing, nothing she'd ever experienced before, wave upon wave, time and again.

Eventually, the crashing breakers subsided, and she calmed, shuddering.

Her heaving gasps turned to deep, renewing breaths, eventually diminishing to occasional volcanic, whole-body twitches. Alex had collapsed behind her, resting on one arm, his other beneath her, his face cradled next to hers.

She regained the ability to speak. "Oh God. Alex, where did that come from?"

He turned his head and kissed her ear, whispering, "From my soul. It belongs to you now."

CHAPTER 23

September...

ALEX WALKED into the dive shop, glancing around the bright, neatly organized space. Zach was due soon, so he didn't worry about filling tanks. He slid behind the counter and brought up the dive schedule. A group of six who wanted an afternoon dive every day started tomorrow, which was becoming more common.

Best of all, the schedule allowed them to take *Surface Interval* out for a full-day trip, with Gerold preparing packed lunches for everyone. Alex had wanted to start these ever since buying the boat. It was large enough to make a long day comfortable, and the longer trip allowed them to dive sites normally too far away.

He moved his gaze to the wall, where a spreadsheet hung on a clipboard. Zach had made a detailed inventory report so they could track and order items more closely. And the dive shop was spotless. Alex had always kept things clean, but he was pleased at the boy's attention to detail. The physical aspects of the job hadn't caused any difficulties, and he had become a great employee.

Zach walked in the door and set his backpack behind the counter. "Hey, Alex. You want me to start filling tanks?"

"In a minute. You're doing a great job, Zach. I know school just started up again, so if you need to cut back your hours, let me know, ok?"

"I think it'll be fine. I only work for a few hours in the afternoon. Besides, it's fun." Zach's face lit up, his gleaming teeth on full display.

Alex was still mystified at how filling tanks could be considered fun, but he wasn't about to look a gift horse in the mouth. "You still interested in learning to dive?"

"Yes! When can we start?"

"Hold on there!" Alex laughed. "I'll take you through the open water diver class, but we're going to have to sit down and figure out a schedule. We've got some busy weeks coming up, and there's the minor matter of my wedding. But after that, we should be able to start."

Zach's face fell at having to wait, but he was a good kid. "That works for me."

"I don't want to teach you with big time gaps between classes. There's a lot to learn. Because of your school and work schedule, we might have to get creative with the sessions, but we'll get it done, I promise."

～

AFTER GETTING HOME, Alex flopped down on the couch in the air-conditioned great room, absorbing the cool air. He flipped his phone over in his hands, procrastinating. "It's the right thing to do and you know it. Dial."

He pressed the green button and Steve Jackson answered. They circled around each other for a few minutes, discussing pleasantries. Finally, Alex took the plunge. "You got any big plans in mid-October?"

"Not that I know of."

"We set the date for our wedding, and I was wondering if you'd like to come. We'd like to have you there. Both of us."

There was a long pause, then Steve cleared his throat thickly. "I'd love to. Just let me know the date and I'll be there."

Alex gave him the specifics and Steve hinted he'd most likely stay in Christiansted like he did on his previous visit. After hanging up, Alex opened a beer and leaned against the counter. He was lighter now as he gazed at the ocean, sparkling in the late-afternoon sun, and a smile rose to his face.

How about that? The crusty old guy was touched. I'm glad I made the call.

He opened the slider and settled on the front porch with Cruz at his feet. He took a long drink of beer and pulled out his phone once more. *One more to go . . .* He put his feet on the coffee table as a flutter rippled through his stomach. He breathed out the nerves and dialed.

"Monroe," Mike said. "Wow. You know how to text *and* call? I had no idea you were so smart."

"It's a recent development. I'm a late bloomer. You blow up your cushy corner office yet?"

"I can't discuss things like that with civilians."

"You are a civilian," Alex said.

"Yeah, but I've got a security clearance. All you've got is a c-card."

"I'm sitting on my porch with a beer, looking at a white sand beach and listening to the waves wash on the shore. Beat that."

"You're a real bastard, Monroe."

"Yeah, I get that a lot."

Mike paused for a moment. "So, have your ears been burning lately?"

"Uh-oh. Do I want to know what this is about?"

"Actually, yes. I texted that photo of you and me on the pier to the group. I added, 'Look what I found under a rock in St. Croix' and sat back to see what would happen."

Alex's nerves amplified a thousand-fold and now had nothing to do with his purpose for the call. He was afraid to ask, but desperately yearned for the answer. "What happened?"

"My phone *blew up*. I don't mean those annoying texts you glance at before putting your phone back down. I mean, it didn't stop. All night. Emma made me go to the other room."

Alex's heart pounded. He'd spent the past six years convincing himself his Team blamed him and wanted nothing to do with him.

Now was the moment of truth.

He made his shoulders relax, fighting to keep his voice even. "What was the mood?"

"Oh, for God's sake, you have to ask? We've all spent the last six years wondering what happened to you—if you were still alive, even. Alex, they were *thrilled*. I told you that night, none of us blame you. I stayed up until 3 a.m., sending every pic I took of you and talking about our visit."

Tears welled in Alex's eyes, and he let them roll down. Seven years of self-hatred began to dissipate. "Thanks, Mike. I really needed to hear that."

Mike sighed. "Alex, let *them* tell you that."

"Yeah, that's one of the reasons I'm calling you. Can you loop me in? I'm ready now."

"As soon as we get off the phone. Consider it done. Just get ready to have some sore thumbs." Mike laughed. "You said that was one of the things you called about. What else?"

Alex took a deep breath. "This one's pretty personal. I'm in need of a best man and wondered if you wanted the job."

Mike's breath deepened over the phone. "I'd be honored, Alex."

"Thank you, Mike. For everything."

"You're welcome. But it's nothing compared to what I need to thank you for."

Alex swiped a hand over his face, wiping away the tears. "Oh, stop it. Let's not get sappy here. Don't thank me too much. I'll cover your tropical beachfront accommodations, but you're paying your own airfare, pal."

"You always were a cheap son of a bitch."

"Yeah, well, some things never change."

"I'm still trying to figure out how you convinced Hope to marry you."

"That makes two of us, Mike."

∽

AFTER ENDING THE CALL, Alex retrieved another beer before returning to the porch. He was a massive confusion of emotions. Instead of trying to sort them out, he just closed his eyes and listened to the waves wash against the shore. It calmed him.

Then relief flooded through him as he understood at last—maybe he'd been punishing himself unnecessarily.

He opened his eyes, and Cruz was looking at him with his head cocked. The dog shuffled forward, resting his muzzle on Alex's knee with a whine. Smiling, Alex scratched behind his ears. "You're a good boy, aren't you? I'm doing ok, better than I have in a really long time."

Cruz thumped his tail on the floorboards.

Then Alex's text tone went off. Again. And again. Warmth spread through his chest as he picked up the phone. Everyone introduced themselves so Alex could match the man with the phone number. Next, they sent selfies, and they didn't look so different. The group pressured him into taking one, so he sat on the porch rail with the ocean at his back and smiled at his phone. He promptly took a truckload of shit over his sun-bleached hair and was concerned he might have earned the moniker *Surfer Boy*.

It went on for over an hour, and Alex's head was spinning, so he texted he needed to go. But he promised he'd keep in touch.

And Alex believed strongly in promises.

He leaned his head back against the wall, a big smile on his face as he just soaked it in. Eventually, he watched the sun approach the horizon as he absently stroked Cruz's head. The dog perked up, looking toward the beach, and Alex turned as Hope climbed the stairs onto the porch, hanging her head.

Cruz abandoned him to greet her.

Alex patted the cushion next to him. "Sit down, baby. Rough day?"

"A bit of a crisis, but we handled it." She looked at him, guilt lowering her brows. "I'm afraid I volunteered you for a job tomorrow afternoon. The shower faucet in the Jasmine bungalow is acting up again. We can't seem to figure it out and it sprayed all over the place. I'm comping the guests their dinner tonight. But I need Tommy to replace it tomorrow afternoon. Can you drive the boat on the afternoon dive trip? Please?"

"Of course. I enjoy it, and the guests get a kick out of seeing me drive. Speaking of afternoon dive trips, we're getting them more and more," Alex said.

"I've noticed. Word's getting out we've got the best dive staff on the island."

Alex snorted at that. "I've been thinking about the next step for the dive operation. I want to look into getting a membrane system."

"Membrane system? Are you planning on growing pod people?"

"No!" He laughed. "I'm talking about Nitrox. I think we should offer a package to divers that has both a morning and afternoon trip. We'd get a lot of takers. But we need to offer Nitrox if we're going to do that, especially for your dive guides, Boss Lady. When you're diving that much, enriched air makes a big difference—it's much safer."

"Can you give me a quick primer on Nitrox? The kindergarten version, Mr. Monroe."

"Sure. As you dive, nitrogen builds up in your blood, right? Too much causes decompression sickness—the bends. So, if the air you're breathing contains more oxygen than normal air, you accumulate less nitrogen. That's Nitrox, air that's been enriched via the membrane system to a higher percentage of oxygen. Much safer."

"Admirable, concise explanation. And it sounds like a good idea."

He nodded. "I'll start looking into membrane systems after the wedding."

"Seems like the resort gets busier every day. We have very happy divers here, thanks to you." Hope settled closer to him. "The wedding's getting ever closer."

Alex gave a happy sigh as he wrapped her in his arms. The sun had dipped below the horizon, and a velvety purple sky rose before them. "I also completed one other major task today."

"Oh?"

"Mike agreed to be my best man."

She pinned him with those golden eyes. "I cannot tell you how happy I am to hear that."

"There's more. When Mike was here, he told me he had a group text going with the Team—everyone who's left. He wanted me to join in. I told him I wasn't ready for that." He looked down, then met her eyes again. "But now I am. He added me to the group text, and I spent the last hour catching up."

She leaned forward to look at him closely. "And how did it go?"

He pulled her back to his shoulder, kissing the top of her head. "It went great. Really great."

CHAPTER 24

Several days later, Hope was working the front desk when two women about her age walked through the lobby door. They chattered happily as they dragged their suitcases behind them. The brunette made a beeline for one of Robert's large St. Croix landscapes hanging prominently on one wall. She inspected it closely, breathing "Beautiful," before moving on to the next.

The other woman, with short red hair and freckles, approached Hope. "We'd like to check in. The reservation's in my name, Sandra Hoskins."

Hope brightened. "Oh! Glad to meet you, Sandra. I'm Hope Collins."

They shook hands. "I wasn't too much of a pest with all my emails, was I?"

"Not at all," Hope answered. "I'm all for it. We pride ourselves on being a quiet, tranquil resort, but not everyone wants that. If you'd been looking for wild nightlife, you'd hate it here." She finished checking them in. "You're in the Frangipani bungalow. If you head out of the lobby and turn left at the ocean, it'll be the last bungalow."

The brunette tore herself away from Robert's pictures and came over. "Hi, I'm Amy Richards. That bungalow has two beds, right? We're not that kind of couple."

Hope laughed. "Yes. We welcome all guests here, but don't worry, it has two queen beds. And you're both planning on diving tomorrow morning?"

"Yes," Sandra said. "We got certified just for this trip, so we're really looking forward to it."

"I'll see you there. I'm diving with a friend of mine. Maybe the four of us can buddy up?"

"Perfect," Sandra said. "We need all the support we can get!"

Hope handed them their keys. "Just relax today. And don't forget to check out our spa. We've got massages and body treatments. I'm installing a hair and mani-pedi station, but that's not finished yet."

"Trust me," Amy said. "For the next few days, hair is the last thing we're worrying about. See you later."

Shortly after, Corrine returned from an appointment, and Hope made her way to the dive shop, where Tommy was hanging two new glass photos on the wall. One was of the dive site Chapel, showing the inside of a large dome, its many holes in the ceiling admitting sunbeams which burst throughout the cavern. The other was a bright-purple sea fan with two yellow and white butterfly fish highlighted against it.

Tommy smiled at her. "You're gonna need to give me a raise if I have to keep hangin' new pictures all the time."

"Robert refused to believe these would sell like hotcakes. I think he's finally convinced now."

Even after raising the price to $750, the photos had sold well. Hope went behind the counter and pulled out two photo cards and wrote the new price of $1000 on them, attaching them next to the newly displayed photos.

Just then, Robert walked in.

"Here they are," Hope said, pointing to the wall. She had picked this pair. "What do you think?"

Robert laughed, raising both hands. "I'm certainly not goin' to argue with you."

"I just checked in a guest who was studying your photos in the lobby very carefully. She's going to be on the boat tomorrow. Maybe you'll have another sale."

"They seem to be sellin' just fine as it is. I still can't believe it."

Hope bounced up and down. "I'm going to dive with you tomorrow! I haven't been diving for too long and Cindy finally finished her tests. Since Alex is trying out our new prospective divemaster, I get to dive with you."

Robert winced. "Yeah, I know."

"Hey! I'm a good diver."

"It's not you I'm worried about."

"Robert! Cindy is good too. We won't cause you any problems, I promise."

He propped a hand on his hip, frowning at her. "Hope, you couldn't cause me a problem if you tried. Your fiancé, on the other hand..."

"Oh, I get it. Alex needed some prodding to come around to the idea, I agree. But I assured him I'm perfectly capable of diving with someone other than him."

"Not sure you totally convinced him."

Hope laughed as she gathered up the cardboard boxes. "Oh dear. Was it bad?"

He shrugged, smiling again. "I'm still alive. So far."

Robert glanced at the photo and back to Hope. "I've been thinking about a weddin' present for you two."

She rounded on him. "Robert—no! We don't want anything."

"It's not so much somethin' I want to buy you as somethin' I'd like to do for you." He met her gaze. "You have a photographer yet?"

Hope couldn't help the smile that alighted across her face. "No, we don't."

"Just so happens I'm free that evenin'. Someone cancelled all the divin'."

"You really want to?"

"I'm better with landscapes and sea life, but I've shot several weddings."

She embraced him. *How did I get so lucky?* "Oh, thank you! I can't tell you what it means to me."

"I'm happy to do it."

"Where's Alex, anyway?"

"I think he went up to your house. He mentioned filling out paperwork for the new guy."

As she walked into the house, Alex was seated at the table with his laptop and a pile of paperwork in front of him. A pen was tucked over one ear.

"Now you look like me working."

He sat up, pinching the bridge of his nose. "Not my favorite part of the job, I admit. Jack checks out. He passed the background and his divemaster certification is current. We'll see how he does tomorrow."

"Do you have a good group?"

He smiled at her. "It's a good one for testing someone out. A few divers are experts and two more are total newbies. It can be a challenge to lead a mixed group like that." He started gathering up his papers. "I'm done for the day."

She opened two beers, handing Alex one. "I found us a wedding photographer."

He snapped his head up. "Really? That never even crossed my mind. Good thing you're in charge."

"I'd thought about it, but nothing specific. This afternoon, the best possible solution fell into my lap. Robert."

"Robert's going to be our photographer? That's great!"

"He said it was his wedding present to us."

"He's a good guy. He might even be able to make me look halfway decent. I'm off for a shower." Alex headed toward their bathroom as Hope leaned against the counter, her head filled with all the moving parts that were now coming together for their wedding.

∽

IT WAS A PERFECT CARIBBEAN MORNING. The sun was gentle as soft, fluffy clouds bounced across the sky. A light breeze blew against Hope's face as she opened the dive-shop door for Cindy, then followed. Robert stood behind the counter as Sandra and Amy filled out dive waivers.

"Mornin', you two," he said with a smile. Cindy and Robert knew each other from her previous dive trips. He turned to Hope. "Does Cindy need to sign a waiver?"

"No, Alex still has one on file. She just needs equipment."

"Well, let's head over and I can get all three of you set up. Hope, your stuff's already on the boat. And the other couple cancelled this mornin', so it'll just be the five of us."

Hope made introductions among the three women as they headed toward the gear room, pleased they had a small group of four. She spied Alex's tall form already on the boat, talking with a thirtysomething man with tan skin and brown hair who had to be Jack.

Soon they were aboard, and Tommy pulled Sandra and Amy aside to give the boat-safety briefing. Hope eagerly approached Alex for an introduction.

Alex smiled and turned to the man. "This is Hope, the owner of the resort. Stay on her good side or you'll never hear the end of it."

He was good looking, with short, dark-brown hair and enormous liquid brown eyes. "Jack Powell. Pleased to meet you."

"Don't listen to Alex. He's full of lies about me." After shaking hands, she returned to her trio of fellow divers, making sure everyone was set up.

Alex walked forward and rummaged in a cabinet in the bow before returning to Jack. Sandra's eyes followed Alex the whole way. "Too bad we're not diving with him. Hope, you've *got* to introduce me. Yum."

Hope smiled sweetly. "I'd be happy to. He's my fiancé."

"Oh, shit! I'm sorry." Sandra laughed. "This is rather embarrassing."

"Don't worry about it." She couldn't help but warm to Sandra, who had a likable, self-deprecating personality.

Alex raised his voice. "Everyone all set? We're leaving the dock in a sec."

He beckoned to Robert, and the two bent their heads in conversation. Alex smiled widely, but there was something slightly predatory, maybe even *sharky*, in it. Robert took a step back before shifting from foot to foot. Alex quickly glanced at Hope before making his way to the stern and tugging on his wetsuit.

What was that about?

Robert took a deep breath and put on a sunny face, approaching his group. "We only have ten divers on the boat today, so we should have a nice trip. Don't be afraid to spread out. There's plenty of room."

Alex and Jack's group was first to jump into the water, and a small pang tugged at Hope as she watched Alex verify ok signals from his group and slip beneath the waves. She'd never been diving without him.

Hope shook it off and geared up. She and Cindy were fully qualified to dive without any professional present. Robert was a bonus, plus he knew where the animals liked to hide out.

Their first dive was fun and relaxing. Sandra and Amy definitely had some new-diver jitters to work out, but Robert was patient and supportive of them and their posture was more relaxed by the end of the dive. He was an excellent divemaster, finding several well-camouflaged flounders hiding in the sand, though he was more of a mother hen than Hope would have preferred, checking her air several times.

As they slowly motored toward their second site, Robert passed a container of Hope's cookies around and sat with the women as they all drank water or soft drinks from the cooler. Alex and Jack were deep in discussion on the bridge.

"This is an awfully big boat for such small groups," Sandra said.

"Well, we got lucky today," Robert said. "It's usually busier. And we've got room to add a third group too."

"We try not to run a cattle-boat operation here," Hope said.

"I was admiring the two pictures in the dive shop," Amy said, turning to her. "You're smart to have them for sale."

"They are gorgeous, aren't they?" Hope grinned. "And every single one was taken by Robert."

"Really? You've got a lot of talent," Amy said to him with a smile.

"Thanks. It's always been a hobby of mine. Hope's helped me turn it into more of a business." He inspected the landmarks on shore as Tommy throttled down. "We're close to the second site. We'll be first this time, and I need to moor the boat."

Robert pulled his wetsuit up as he shouted to Tommy, "We about there?"

Tommy called down from the wheelhouse, "Yeah. It's just ahead."

"Why are the moorin' balls under the water, anyway?" Cindy asked.

"It's safer that way—they don't get run over by boats," Robert said. "And it looks better too."

"Alex and Robert were instrumental in gettin' them started on the island," Tommy said.

"It was Alex's idea. I just helped with the grunt work," Robert explained.

"That seems pretty smart," Sandra said.

"Occasionally, Alex does somethin' that's not totally stupid," Tommy called with a grin. "It's pretty rare, though."

"Hey!" Hope said. "He's your boss—show some respect."

"He's not my boss. You are! Captain outranks dive guides, you know."

Hope thought about pointing out Alex was much more than that, but Tommy knew it as well as she did. Instead, she leaned back and enjoyed the banter.

"I heard that! I'm not deaf, you know." Alex shot Tommy a dirty look as he and Jack returned to the main deck, and Tommy's grin widened.

"If you two are done," Robert said, "let me go over the dive briefin'."

Soon they were descending through the water. The sun was high overhead, and the reef below sparkled with color. Hope loved the sea fans. The variety was incredible—around her were red, purple, yellow, and brown ones. Some were full and lacy, and others had upright fingers gently waving in the surge.

Several groupers swam with them. They were a large species of fish that appeared in a variety of colors. Around them she spied black, brown, and a bright tan, some with intricate patterns on their sides and others with tiger stripes.

Robert stayed close to the group, particularly to Hope, and checked their air supplies at regular intervals. She was pleased he was so attentive to the new divers, but he should be giving her a little more credit for being experienced.

He glanced toward the sand to their right and stilled, concentrating. Hope followed his gaze to an area of disturbed sand billowing in a cloud. Excited, Robert beckoned them to follow and swam out to the disturbance. As she neared, the frothy sand thinned enough to make out a triangular shape with a long tail behind. It was a large stingray, rooting through the sand for its lunch. It slowly moved forward, its flat head bobbing up and down as its mouth sifted through the sand, searching for creatures to eat.

Hope and Cindy exchanged wide-eyed ok signals, neither having been this close to one before. The ray was unconcerned, ignoring the divers as it continued its hunt. The group watched for several minutes before Robert led them back to the coral reef.

Hope spotted the other group. She stared for a moment, trying to figure out what was wrong, then it came to her. Alex trailed behind, while Jack swam at the front of the group. He must be doing well if Alex was letting him lead.

As if he sensed her, Alex turned his head and they exchanged waves. Calmness washed over her upon seeing him again. Hope turned and could barely see the bubbles of her group in the hazy distance. She hurried to catch up to Cindy and pointed out a cute blue boxfish with yellow spots clumsily waddling through the water. Hope exhaled a happy stream of bubbles, enjoying being completely weightless and able to move in three dimensions.

She hadn't realized how much she'd missed it.

CHAPTER 25

As she left the boat with the other three women, Hope cast a backwards glance at Alex. He was busy talking to Jack, so she continued. Amy turned around, walking backwards up the pier. "You two want to join us for lunch in half an hour? That'll give us a chance to shower and change."

"I'd love to," Hope said.

"So would I, but I have to work this afternoon," Cindy said.

"Oh, that's too bad," Amy replied with a frown. "Great morning, though. It was fun diving with you."

Cindy said her goodbyes and thirty minutes later, Hope walked into the restaurant, dressed in a sundress with her hair twisted in a clip. Sandra and Amy were already at a table, and she joined them, beckoning Charlotte over. "You guys want a beer?"

"Oh, for sure," Sandra said. "We are *thirsty*!"

Clark brought three Leatherbacks, and Amy smiled at him. "Maybe after this round we'll order some Half Moon Dreams. That's a great drink!"

"Clark just won an island-wide competition with that drink, you know," Hope said. "He's the best bartender on St. Croix."

"Ah, it was nothin'." Clark tried to downplay their exclamations and retreated to the bar.

The three women toasted a successful morning of diving. "So, what did you think of your first real dives?" Hope asked.

"Loved it," Amy said. Her curly brown hair hung loose to her shoulders. "The water was so warm and clear. Pretty much the opposite of the quarry where we got certified. And Robert was really great at leading the dives. Very attentive."

"Yes, he certainly was." Hope still thought he went overboard, but Sandra and Amy were happy and that was what counted.

Charlotte brought their entrees and the conversation paused while they ate.

"This resort has a really serene vibe," Amy said. "You've done a great job with it."

"Thank you," Hope said. "I've worked hard, and I've got a great team around me. They deserve most of the credit."

Sandra and Amy exchanged a long look as something passed between them. Sandra leaned forward. "Ok, we have a confession to make. We *are* two friends down here on vacation, but it's a working vacation. Amy's a photographer and I'm a writer for *Entrepreneur Today* magazine. We're doing a special issue on successful businesswomen. When I was doing research for my piece, I came across a press release about a woman winning a resort in a raffle. You, of course."

Hope smiled politely.

"This was a few months ago, but I couldn't get it out of my mind. I stalked the Half Moon Bay website and showed Amy. That's what inspired us to get certified to dive. We've been talking about taking a vacation for ages and thought this would be perfect. And here we are!"

"And you're enjoying yourselves so far?"

"God, yes!" Sandra laughed and rubbed her freckled nose. "Well, except the part where I wanted to hit on your fiancé. Sorry about that."

Laughter rang around the table. Hope always wanted to see happy guests, but she remained perplexed. *Where is Sandra going with this?*

"You were great at answering all my emails, so we wanted to get to know you a little and see what the resort was like," Sandra continued. "We're both really impressed. We'd like to do a feature article about you. I'll do an interview and write the story, and Amy will shoot some pictures of you and the resort. What do you think?"

Hope sat up, her head spinning. "Wait. You want to interview *me?*"

Sandra laughed. "It's a great story. And just looking around this place, it's obvious you're doing a great job. We've talked to a few of the staff, and they love you. That was clear on the dive boat this morning, not even counting your fiancé."

"We wanted to make sure you weren't a dragon queen before we let the cat out of the bag," Amy added.

"So, what do you say?" Sandra asked.

"Sure, I guess." Hope said. "Never thought anyone would want to write an article about me. When were you thinking?"

"How about tomorrow afternoon? After lunch. That will give Amy some time to scout the sites where she wants to photograph you."

Amy was nearly dancing in her seat. "I already know one shot I want to get. Can you wear a business suit tomorrow?"

"Of course," Hope said.

"I want to get a picture of you standing on the pier with the ocean behind you. It'll make a great photo."

Hope could have been watching a tennis match as she bounced her eyes between the two women. "Just tell me where you want me."

"The other articles are already completed," Sandra said. "The whole issue will feature women entrepreneurs and businesswomen. I'm planning to write my article immediately and submit it to my editor. The feature issue is slated to come out next month, so I'm trying to make the deadline. My editor was pretty enthusiastic when I pitched her about you, so I think we've got a good shot at making the issue."

∼

Hope was still dazed when she stepped into the lobby office after lunch. She explained the interview to Patti.

"That doesn't surprise me at all, child. You deserve it."

"It probably won't make the cut, anyway. But if it did, that could get us a lot of business. I'd be a fool to say no."

Hope opened her inbox to another email from Wayne, the mysterious sailboat owner. Last week, he had contacted her again with more details about tying up to the pier for a couple of nights. He lived on his thirty-foot sailboat and traveled around the Caribbean, periodically coming to shore to *walk on dry land,* as he put it.

Gerold must have satisfied his curiosity regarding the wine and menu, because he was willing to eat at the restaurant and pay a docking fee for his boat. It sounded like a win-win to her. His current email said he expected to be there within two weeks. She asked him to let her know when he had the exact date and they'd be ready.

Hope sat back with a smile. There were additional streams of income now. Tourists staying at local condominiums or renting houses were diving here and eating in the restaurant more. Alex was adding Jack to the rotation and thinking about adding a third group to the boat in the morning and another trip in the afternoon.

Now boat owners were looking for short-term docking.

And I'm being interviewed for a national magazine. Oh, and there's an auction coming soon. Don't forget that!

∼

THE WOODEN BOARDS were warm and smooth under Alex's bare feet as he carried an armload of wetsuits toward the dive shop, pleased yet slightly saddened Hope had enjoyed her dives without him.

He dumped the wetsuits into a metal trough filled with water and disinfectant solution, letting them sit for a while. Robert stood over a similar trough next to him, dunking BCDs before hanging them on a rolling rack to dry.

Jack emerged from the gear room and Alex approached. "Good job today. You handled the group well and the divers had a good time."

"Thanks. You have a really nice setup here."

Alex laughed. "Yeah, we've had some major upgrades recently. I'll look over the schedule and give you some dates when I need help."

Jack nodded and waved goodbye. Satisfaction rolled through Alex—hopefully he'd found someone. Jack had been excellent, making sure the new divers were well looked after while acknowledging the experienced divers didn't need coddling. April wasn't filling in as much, so another divemaster would really help.

Tommy was hosing off the boat deck, reminding Alex of his other task. The boat captain saw him coming and turned off the hose as Alex boarded. Now that the time was here, he shifted from foot to foot, unsure how to start.

"What's up, man? You got ants in your pants or somethin'?" Tommy smirked as he dropped the hose.

"You could say that. I need to ask you something."

"Ok. Ask."

Alex opened his mouth and then closed it again, looking at the deck, and Tommy laughed. "I gotta say, I'm enjoyin' this. You're pretty good at puttin' people on the spot, you know. It's kind of nice to see you squirm for once. Maybe you need a light rewired in your house?" Tommy's grin got bigger.

"No." Alex tried to stare him down, then started laughing himself. "God, I feel like a teenager asking my girl's father if I can date her. Ok, I'm just going to come straight out and ask. Will you perform our wedding ceremony?"

Tommy's smile fell and he just stared at Alex. "You realize there's some serious irony in that question, don't you?"

"Yeah, I know you're still sore about the underwater wedding. That was like five years ago, man. And we're having the ceremony here on the beach—no scuba required, I promise."

"That damn ceremony about scared me to death, you know."

"Come on, Tommy. If you refuse, I'm going to have no choice but to bring out the heavy artillery. Hope. You know you can't say no to her. You can save us both the embarrassment."

Tommy continued staring at him.

"It would mean a lot to us . . . to me."

No change. He stood still as a statue.

"Please?"

Finally, a slow smile crept across Tommy's face. "You suffered enough yet?"

Alex raked a hand over his head. "Hell yes."

"All right then. I accept." He drew Alex into a hug even as he started laughing. "That was fun!"

"No, it wasn't, you asshole."

"You guys aren't goin' to do some weird new-age ceremony, are you?"

"Strictly conventional." *I've got no idea what kind of ceremony Hope wants, but I'm not about to say that after what I just went through.* He met Tommy's eyes. "Thanks. It means a lot to have you do this. I never expected to get married."

"I'm really happy for you, and I'd be honored to marry you two. I mean that."

~

Hope took a deep breath of the wonderful scent filling the kitchen and placed the last containers of zucchini bread in the freezer. The slider opened and Alex entered, the sun setting behind him. She quickly moved to give him a proper welcome, which he returned with enthusiasm.

"Well, hello to you too," he said with a sexy smile. "I can't tell you how wonderful it is to come home to you."

She grinned. "You only say that when I've been baking."

He peered around her, searching the countertop.

"Don't worry, I saved a few slices for you."

He lit up before kissing the tip of her nose. "Even without the treats, you're the best part of my day." He picked up a slice and ate it in three bites. "Oh, man. That hits the spot, especially after the conversation I just had."

Hope spun around to face him. "What happened?"

Alex closed one eye, wincing. "I talked to Tommy about the ceremony. After a *very* uncomfortable conversation, he agreed."

Hope grinned. "Made it difficult for you, did he?"

"Yes. Very."

"Well, you're a man willing to do what it takes to complete his mission. I'm proud of you." She leaned in for a long kiss, lingering over the taste of her zucchini bread in his mouth.

Alex rumbled deep in his chest. "Too bad all my missions didn't end like this."

Hope laughed, trailing a finger over his jawline before taking her own slice of bread.

"I could tell you had a good time this morning," Alex said. He picked up a slice and ate it in three bites.

"Yes! It was wonderful to be in the water again. And you'll be happy to know Robert was an excellent guide and very concerned about my welfare. Maybe too concerned. He kind of hovered over me the whole morning." She raised a brow. "Why do I think you had something to do with that? I saw that rather frightening grin you gave him before the first dive."

Alex's face broke into a smug smile. "Well, I might have told him if anything happened to you, I'd serve him his balls for lunch."

"You didn't! Oh, why am I even asking you that? Of course you did. Alex, what am I going to do with you?"

"Love me? You can't help yourself."

"Unfortunately, you're right about that. Poor Robert. If he changes his mind, you're in charge of finding a new photographer."

CHAPTER 26

The next morning dawned in soft-pink splashes, the ocean shimmering like liquid metal as Hope and Alex drank coffee on their porch. She wore one of his sweatshirts and sat with her knees drawn up underneath it to make herself a cozy ball.

"You've got a big day ahead of you," Alex said, as he absently stroked her hair.

Hope curled closer as he drew her in with his arm. "I do."

"I'm incredibly proud of you. I can't wait to see the article."

"There's no guarantee it will get picked for the issue, so it may all be for nothing. At least I'm not being blindsided by the worst experience of my life."

"There's nothing I can do about that. I've accepted it."

Hope had wanted to ask him about something for a while, but had been hesitant to bring it up. "You just said you're proud of me for being interviewed. I feel the same way about your article, you know. I want to shout about it from the rooftops."

"No one cares about something that happened years ago."

"I think you're very wrong about that. You said it yourself. Being a SEAL was important—your article showcases that vividly." She took a breath and plunged in. "I saved a copy of the paper. I would love to frame your article and hang it in the lobby on the wall of staff photos. You should be proud of what you did, Alex."

He hesitated, taking a sip of coffee. "I wouldn't go that far, but I'm not wallowing in self-blame and grief anymore. I'll think about it, ok? Maybe we can frame both articles."

"Thank you."

AFTER A LONG SWIM, Hope headed into Frederiksted for her first stop of the day. Frederiksted Floral Shop was in a strip mall just north of its namesake town. Hope walked in, inhaling the wonderful fragrance as she approached the counter.

A matronly local woman was cutting stems off bird-of-paradise flowers and gave Hope a sunny smile. "What can I do for you?"

"I need to place an order for my wedding. It's going to be a small celebration, so I won't need much. I really just need some arrangements for the aisle, a few centerpieces, and the bouquets for my maid of honor and myself."

"I can do that! Do you want to look through some photo books for inspiration?"

Hope smiled, tapping her hands on the counter. "No, I know exactly what I want."

The woman collected a pen and pad of paper. "How excitin'! Let's get started."

WHEN HOPE ARRIVED at the Red Fort Grill, Cindy was already seated and had managed to secure a table with a full ocean view.

"Are you settling back into your routine?" Hope asked.

"Yes." Cindy rested her chin in her palm. "Only one more semester and I'll be done!"

"You picked a good field. People never run out of sore spots that need to be worked on. You should be able to find work easily."

Cindy's face lit up. "I've got news about that! I just got a job in a local physical therapy clinic. I'll start as an aide, and after I get my certification, they'll promote me to PT assistant."

"That's great! That should make the rest of your classes easier too."

"That's the idea. The runnin' store was gettin' pretty routine. Best of all, the job is Monday through Friday, so I can still lead the group runs on Saturdays."

"I'm really happy for you, Cin. You deserve this—you've worked hard for it."

Cindy took a drink of her soda. "Thanks. Now if I could just get my love life back on track. There are no good men left on this island. I think you got the last one."

Hope laughed. "Don't despair. There are still good ones out there, I promise. Just be patient. Sometimes you find the right guy when you're not even looking for him." Hope's smile faded as she met Cindy's gaze. "I've had some pretty bad experiences with men. I'd given up when Alex came into my life."

"You've hinted at that before. I know it can be hard to talk about."

"Yes, but I've mostly worked through it now, with Alex's help. He'll never understand what a difference he made. My first experience with men was when my father walked out on us when I was twelve. My mom fell apart and I had to grow up fast, working babysitting jobs and delivering newspapers until I was old enough for a real job. That didn't start me off on the right foot."

"No, I'm sure it didn't. How terrible for you."

Hope barked out a humorless laugh. "I'm not done yet. When I went off to college, I got my first real boyfriend. Serious boyfriend. He almost destroyed me, physically and mentally. I ended up in the hospital and pressed charges against him. He ended up in prison."

Cindy stilled, staring at her wide-eyed.

Hope held up a hand. "I'm not telling you this to get sympathy. You're a really good friend and I want you to know. And to give you some hope. I spent years refusing to get close to a man because I'd convinced myself they couldn't be trusted. That they'd either run out or hurt me. Then I found Alex."

Hope shook her head, a small smile on her face. "What I'm trying to say is this. If I can find the love of my life, as screwed up as I was, you definitely shouldn't give up. You're a terrific woman, Cindy, and you don't need a man to tell you that. You'll find your guy when the time is right."

∼

Hope walked up the beach, experiencing the relief that came from sharing something profound with a good friend. Her flip-flops flicked up the sand, and she gave a small laugh, picturing what she must look like as she trudged along in her gray power suit while wearing flip-flops. The three-inch black pumps she carried in one hand weren't great for walking on the sand.

When she entered the restaurant, Sandra and Amy were seated at a secluded table. Amy looked up as Hope sat. "I'll leave you two alone. I'm going to take some shots of the resort. I was waiting for afternoon light, and it looks good out there now. When you two are done, I'll take pictures of you in various places. Ok, Hope?"

"Sounds good." She breathed out the butterflies as she turned to Sandra, who started a voice recorder and had a pad and pen in front of her. "I'm a little nervous."

Sandra looked up with a smile. Her short red hair was still damp from her shower. "Don't be. I'm not here to do some hatchet job on you. I really admire what you've done. Why don't we start at the beginning? How did you enter the lottery?"

Once she got started, Hope's story came easily. She laughed as she explained about Sara entering her in the contest, then moving here only to discover Steve had left the previous night. She moved on to the boat sinking and scramble to find a replacement, then the hurricane, and finally Charles and the trial. She left out the cave exploration, but detailed all the improvements and changes she'd made to the resort and emphasized their new environmental focus, including the nesting turtles and coral-restoration project.

By the end, Sandra gaped at her. "Good God. I can't believe you've been through all that in less than two years!"

Hope smiled. She hadn't mentioned any details of Alex's past other than saying that they had met and fallen in love. That was his story to tell, not hers.

"What would you say is the biggest lesson you've learned from this experience?"

Hope thought for a moment. "That you can't go through life afraid to trust or depend on others. This resort is a special place, and it's because of the people. Yes, it's beautiful and tranquil, but that's because of the hard work by everyone who loves it and each other."

Amy returned, a camera with a long lens hanging from one shoulder. "You guys about done?"

Sandra nodded. "I've got all I need. You ready for your close-up, Hope?"

Amy took Hope to several spots in the resort, photographing her in various poses. They finished on the pier, with the ocean behind Hope. The door to the dive shop opened and Alex stood there with a smile, the pride obvious on his face.

After taking her last picture, Amy saw him. "There you are! I want some of the two of you."

"Hang on a minute," Hope said. "I've got a matching staff shirt in the dive shop. That will look better."

The photographer took several photos of the pair, then finally announced she was done. "Thanks. I'm sure I've got some great shots here."

Hope and Alex walked hand in hand back to their house. "How about that," Alex said. "I might get to be in a famous magazine and known worldwide as Mr. Hope Collins."

Hope laughed and squeezed his hand. "Not for much longer. You'll be Mr. Hope Monroe before you know it."

CHAPTER 27

A few days later, Hope started her day baking shortbread cookies at home. They were her own design, based on a family recipe Patti had given her. Late in the morning, she received a text from Patti that Wayne, the sailboat owner, was tying up his boat at the pier. Hope had just pulled the last cookies from the oven, so she cleaned up and headed up the beach, carrying a tray for the lobby.

Patti was on the pier, directing a very large sailboat alongside it and well away from the end where *Surface Interval* would tie up later. She had the situation well in hand, so Hope continued to the lobby. *I'll introduce myself to Wayne after he has a chance to settle in.* She set her tray of cookies next to the infused water, then waved to Corrine on her way to the office. A half hour later, Patti joined her.

"Everything ok with Wayne and his huge boat?"

Patti wiped her forehead. "Yes, he's all set and goin' to lunch. He was a bit condescendin' if you ask me."

"Maybe he was just tired from being at sea for so long."

Patti made a skeptical noise in her throat before turning to her, a smile bursting through. "In happier news, I talked to the florist, and everythin' is on schedule."

"Thanks for your help. I feel better knowing you're in charge."

Patti's smile widened, and she slapped the desktop. "Oh, I'm havin' the time of my life! When my daughter got married, it was just a family celebration in our backyard."

"So five hundred people were there?"

They both laughed, and the warm sound of two people who loved each other filled the small room.

AFTER A QUICK LUNCH with Gerold and Pauline, Hope pushed through the swinging double doors from the kitchen into the restaurant. She scanned the open-air dining room. A thirty-something white man with slicked-back brown hair and a deep tan sat alone at a table fronting the beach. He wore khaki shorts and a white Ralph Lauren linen shirt, with aviator sunglasses hinged over his breast pocket. Hope made her way to the table.

"Are you Wayne Timmons, by any chance?" she asked with a smile.

He gave her an appraising glance, from her eyes down her staff polo shirt and black capris, then up to her face again. "I am. You have me at a disadvantage—a situation I'd love to rectify. Whom do I have the pleasure of addressing?"

Hope held her hand out, ignoring the emphasis he put on the word pleasure. "I'm Hope Collins. Welcome to Half Moon Bay."

"Thank you. You have a lovely resort." He stood and shook her hand, holding it a beat too long.

"I won't bother you. I just wanted to stop and introduce myself. We're hosting a manager's reception tonight at six, here on the patio. I hope you'll join us."

"If you'll be there, count on it." He sent her a suggestive smile, and Hope countered with a professional one before turning away. She resisted the urge to wipe her hand on her pants.

Great. All I need is this guy hitting on me.

THE TROPICAL EVENING was warm and lush, and the bulbs strung overhead bathed the patio in a pleasing glow. Hope nodded as Clark refilled her wineglass. "How's your wife feeling?"

"Better now," Clark said. "She's still off work until the baby's born, but at least she can move around more."

"That's good to hear. Let me know if you need any time off."

"Hopefully not for a few more months." Clark moved on to the next guest.

Wayne approached from the beach and made a beeline straight for her. She darted her eyes around the patio, but there was no sign of Alex. He hadn't made an appearance at a reception in a long time, so she'd asked him to join her.

She hadn't told him it had anything to do with Wayne, and she still tried to convince herself of that. Fending off advances from solo male guests wasn't unusual, and not something she needed Alex's help with. She wasn't afraid of Wayne, but he exuded the aura of a man used to getting what he wanted and might not be as easily dissuaded as most. She'd be more at ease with a little backup.

"Good evening, Hope." Wayne shook her hand and ran his thumb over the back of it. "Pleasure to see you again."

She pulled her hand back but remained pleasant. "Likewise. Did you enjoy your afternoon?"

"It was mostly business. After lunch, I hired a cab to drive me around Christiansted. I live on my sailboat but stop in the Virgin Islands every few months to keep up with business. I'm a real estate developer, and one of my projects just finished construction on the island. I'm here to check on it." He paused for a sip of white wine, taking in the strands of Edison bulbs overhead before returning his gaze to hers. "It's been about a year and a half since I was last on St. Croix, and never at this resort. Last time I stayed just north of Frederiksted. This might become my new favorite place."

An arm slid around her waist as Alex said, "Sorry I'm late. I had a few things to wrap up at the last minute." His hair was still damp, and he was dressed in black cargo shorts and a yellow button-down shirt.

She wrapped her arm around Alex's waist. "This is Wayne Timmons, the sailboat owner. Alex is my fiancé and runs the dive operation here."

Alex glanced at her before shaking Wayne's hand. They didn't make a display of their relationship, so she didn't normally introduce him as her fiancé. But he picked up right away that she wanted Wayne to know.

The developer brightened as he shook hands with Alex. "Just the man I wanted to talk to! Could you add me to your dive trip tomorrow morning?"

"I'm sure we can fit one more in my group," Alex said. "Do you have your certification card with you?"

"No, I'm afraid not."

"Most of the records have been computerized now. I'll look up your file online."

"I've never taken a formal scuba course," Wayne said, his manner cooling. "But I've been diving for years. It's usually not a problem."

"If it were just you and me, it wouldn't be. But I can't take uncertified divers on our commercial trips. If you'd like, I could dive the house reef with you tomorrow afternoon."

"No, I don't think so," Wayne gazed around, losing interest. "I'll look elsewhere. I'm going to get more wine." He flagged down Clark at the edge of the patio, got a brimming refill, and headed back to his boat.

"I really like that guy," Alex said. "Maybe he'll stay a month."

Hope laughed. "Something tells me Wayne isn't used to hearing *no* very often."

Alex turned to her sharply. "Is that why you wanted me here tonight?"

"Oh, nothing that dramatic. He's a bit of an ass, but doesn't seem dangerous. Though I don't mind him knowing exactly who I'm involved with."

"That makes two of us." He regarded her closely. "If you want me to have a friendly chat with him, let me know."

"I'm sure he's harmless."

※

AFTER THE RECEPTION, Alex headed straight home while Hope stopped by their mailbox, noting a soft package for him. She squeezed it as she walked home. *Shorts or shirt?* The yellow shirt he had worn was one of many that had made the short list for the wedding, which got longer by the day. This parcel must contain his latest contender.

When she entered the house, he was on the couch leafing through a scuba magazine. She walked up and held out the package, squishing it between her hands. "Your latest attempt at haute couture?"

He rose and snatched it out of her hands. "Yes, but you don't get to see this one. I'm keeping it a secret. It's a shirt, but that's all I'm saying. I had to order something new since Mike's going to need one too."

Hope absently thumbed through the mail. "As long as they're different colors."

Alex stopped moving and stared at her, his face totally blank.

"You two can't match. Your pants or shorts can be the same color, but people need to be able to tell who the groom is, you know."

"I wasn't planning on inviting a bunch of strangers. I think they'll know."

"Different colors, Alex."

He frowned at the package.

"It comes in more than one color, doesn't it?"

"Yes. I just don't know which to pick." Alex squeezed the parcel and sighed. "I'll look for another color then."

Hope patted his shoulder as she passed him, heading to the bedroom to change. "I'm sure you'll figure it out. Look on the bright side. You're set for dressy tropical attire for the rest of your life."

CHAPTER 28

Hope threw a tennis ball through an opening in the porch window and Cruz raced down the steps. He hit the ground running, tearing down the beach to retrieve it. She tried not to notice Wayne's boat at the pier, instead focusing on it being her day off.

She had been trading emails with Bryce all morning. The auction was approaching, and he was lining up the details. After obtaining their permission, Prodigy had photographed the items and sent a sneak peek to their elite-level clients. They also performed additional appraisals on some of the more high-dollar items. This included confirmation the idol was indeed solid gold. The auction was on automatic pilot now, needing no further input from her or Alex. They didn't have to be involved at all, only needing to check their bank account when it was over.

They still hadn't told anyone about the rock pool or cave. Eventually, she would like to open the pool and entry cave as an attraction for guests, but that could wait.

She threw the ball again as Sara's ringtone went off. Hope answered with a smile. "It's only one o'clock. Don't you work?"

"I didn't have any afternoon clients today. Besides, look who's talking. All you do is swing in a hammock all day drinking mai tais."

"I'll have you know I'm hard at work right now playing fetch with my dog."

"Sounds exhausting."

"Actually, I had a pretty good run this morning. It's great to feel healthy again. I've started up my Saturday group runs."

"Good. You gave us quite a scare, you know. I'm very glad you have that behind you. Are you a famous entrepreneur yet?"

Hope laughed. "I haven't heard a word. It seemed like a long shot, anyway. Sandra was rushing to make a deadline, so I'm not holding my breath."

"Well, just pretend you're famous. I'm sure you're hard at work as always."

A giggle escaped. "It's my day off and I'm kind of hiding out in our house. We've got a slightly creepy guest here and I'm avoiding him."

"Well, that's mature. You do realize you have your own bodyguard, right?"

"It's nothing that serious. The guy is leaving tomorrow, so I'm just trying to stay out of the way. I'll be sure to see him off, full of well wishes."

"Speaking of your bodyguard, how are the wedding plans going?"

Hope threw the ball again and Cruz leaped off the porch, clearing the stairs in a single bound as he raced over the sand. "It's coming together. Tommy's doing the ceremony, and Robert's taking photographs. Gerold's in charge of the cake and catering, though I haven't discussed the menu with him yet. Patti's organizing everything and going to run the show. All I need is my maid of honor to show up."

"I bought my dress last weekend, and I just got my plane ticket, so you can officially count me in."

"Well, that's a relief. I was worried you'd find something more interesting to do."

"That's always a risk. I don't like to be too tied down to plans, you know."

"Uh-huh. We're checking off another big item this afternoon. Alex and I are going to pick out his ring. In fact, he should be along soon."

Sara sighed. "This really is a problem for me, you know. With Alex marrying you, what am I going to give him a hard time about?"

"I'm sure you'll find something. Maybe related to being a SEAL?"

"No, I think he's had a rough enough time with that."

"Careful, Sara. If you say that to him, he might think you actually have a heart."

"You're right. I need to be careful here."

Cruz had been sitting in front of her for some time, whining, so Hope tossed his ball again. He ran and picked it up, then took off at top speed toward the resort. Alex was stepping off the pier onto the beach. Cruz careened to a stop in front of him, sand flying, and dropped the ball, wagging his tail frantically. Alex picked it up and launched it, throwing his whole body into the motion. Then he dug his phone out of his pocket, both thumbs flying over it.

Hope wrinkled her brow. "My dog is very fickle. I just got dumped for someone with a better arm."

"Oh? I thought Cruz didn't like anyone else."

"That's improving. He's actually made friends with a high school kid we've got working at the dive shop. But the person I'm referring to now is Alex."

Warmth flowed through her abdomen as she watched him. He wore a big smile that turned into a laugh when he threw the ball again and the dog tore after it. "I gotta go, sis."

"Oh, sure. Cruz isn't the only one who's fickle where Alex is concerned, you know."

"Shut up. I'll talk to you soon. Love you."

Hope descended the stairs to meet Alex, who was once again tapping away on his phone. "You look like a man who wants to go ring shopping."

He laughed as he turned his attention to her. "That is one sentence I never thought would apply to me. It's even more surprising how true it is."

His text tone went off again.

"By the smile you've had all the way up the beach, I'm guessing that's the Team?"

"No. Actually, it's Katie. They bought their plane tickets and will be here two days before the ceremony."

"Is Dave coming?"

His smile got even bigger. "Yes. And the kids too."

"I think we should plan a snorkeling trip. Everyone. Kate and her family, Sara, Mike, and Emma. A big, happy family trip."

"Good thing we've got a bigger boat now." Alex's smile lingered. "Come on. Let's go get me a ring."

∾

AN HOUR LATER, they were walking down a sidewalk in downtown Christiansted. Alex opened the door of a brightly lit jewelry shop and Hope entered, the freezing blast of air-conditioning enveloping her. A small man with wiry brown hair rose from his workbench in the corner and smiled as he held out his hand to Alex.

"Mr. Monroe! So nice to see you again." He looked at Hope with wide-eyed expectation, drumming the tips of his fingers together.

Alex laughed. "Yes, it worked. Max, this is my fiancée, Hope."

The jeweler beamed, then took Hope's hand, patting it. "I'm

very pleased to meet you. This is the best part of being a jeweler. May I see it?" He oohed and aahed over her left hand. Max had a European accent, but Hope couldn't quite place it. Maybe Dutch?

He was adorable.

Hope beamed. "It's a beautiful ring. I love it."

"Well, I had very mixed feelings about making it, I must tell you. I still think it was a crime to cut down that incredible diamond. But Mr. Monroe explained it was an heirloom and he wanted it brought into the modern age." He fussed over her hand, tilting it this way and that. "It did turn out rather well, I must admit." Max smiled, looking back and forth between them. "What can I do for you?"

"We want to see those rings I looked at before. And would you please call me Alex?"

"Of course, of course!" Max led them over to one side of the shop and took out a black velvet display that held two dozen rings. "These are all our men's titanium wedding bands. Is that what you remain interested in?"

"Yes, I still want titanium."

Hope moved closer. "Which ones do you like?"

Alex pulled three out of the display. Two were silver colored and one black. One of the silver rings was unembellished but shimmered softly. The other was thinner. It had a subtle line like a wave running up and down the middle of it. The black one didn't have any patterns but shined with an almost glossy finish. They were all beautiful, but she already had her favorite. "Is there one that you can eliminate?"

Alex inspected the three rings. "Max tells me black titanium is very popular, but it's probably my least favorite—too flashy."

"I agree."

Alex looked at her. "Do you have a favorite between the other two? I like them both."

"They're both really nice, but you're the one who has to wear it. Pick the one you like best."

He nodded and pointed to the ring with the wave. "This one reminds me of the ocean. It's my favorite."

Hope smiled and pressed into his side. "Mine too."

"Ok, Max, it's official. We want this ring."

"Of course, Mr. Monroe! Let's get your finger sized." Alex took a breath, but Hope squeezed his arm to stop him from correcting Max's use of his name. He hadn't used her first name either, and she had a feeling it was formal address or nothing.

Max measured Alex's left ring finger. "I need to make it slightly bigger, shave a little off. It shouldn't be any problem at all. Can you give me a week, or do you need it sooner?"

After assuring Max a week would be fine, they paid and were soon on their way.

On the drive home, their conversation turned to the auction, and Hope explained the latest news. "Bryce said they'll email us a detailed receipt shortly after the auction ends at 5 p.m. Their system updates the items live as they close, and the winner must pay Prodigy within seven days. After that, the final payment will be wired to our account within two business days. We could be millionaires before our wedding day."

Alex laughed and shook his head. "It's pretty incredible to think about."

"I'm going to be a nervous wreck waiting for that auction to end. It's online so we can watch."

"Do you really want to do that? I'm not interested in sitting around a computer screen watching numbers scroll. Even big numbers, but you do you."

"You really don't care much for the money, do you?"

Alex shrugged. "I've had some thoughts about the dive operation. The Nitrox system will cost some money, and I think we could run more dive groups. We could think about snorkel tours and sunset cruises too. Maybe buy a second boat someday."

That brought a smile to Hope's face. "Oh? Going to start leading snorkel trips, are you?"

Hunching his shoulders, Alex tapped his fingers on the wheel. Her grin widened, well aware of his thoughts on this subject.

"Look, I don't play the SEAL card very often, but under no circumstances am I leading guests on snorkeling trips, ok?"

"Mr. Tough Guy Diver. Well, I'm sure we can hire a perfectly qualified guide who would be happy to do it."

"Oh yeah, no problem there. As long as it's not me."

"You didn't seem too put out when you were leading snorkel tours with Sara or Kate's family."

He raised an index finger. "I said guests. Family is totally different. I love showing them the ocean. Though you better believe I'll do my best to extoll the virtues of diving over snorkeling."

"I have no doubt. April said she loves snorkeling *and* diving. Maybe she'd be interested."

Alex shrugged. "It's all hers, though I think she's getting busier with her other divemaster job. She's been busy the last couple of times I've called."

Or does it have something to do with you being engaged and getting married soon? But Hope held her tongue, saying instead, "I saw Jack teaching an intro scuba class in the pool. I'm surprised how many people have come into the dive shop to ask about that. They must see you guys take off in the morning and feel like they're missing out. I didn't realize Jack was an instructor."

"He's not. Divemasters can teach the intro courses and refreshers too. That takes some of the strain off me."

Hope nodded, her mind turning back to the impending sale. "You said you didn't want to watch the auction. Do you have a better idea? Maybe a dive together?"

A ghost of a smile crossed his face. "You read my mind. Let's take the boat out and dive that afternoon. Just you and me. I'll block it out so we don't have an afternoon trip. We haven't dived alone since Salt River Bay."

"Don't worry, I won't expect you to top that dive! The perfect distraction. It's not like watching the auction will change what happens." Hope looked at him with a gleam in her eye. "We could dive Chapel again."

"We could, but I was thinking about something else. You'll just have to wait and see."

Alex's surprises were usually pretty good, and Hope was already looking forward to it. Time appeared to be speeding up. The auction was only a couple weeks away, with their wedding shortly after.

CHAPTER 29

The next afternoon, Hope shrugged into a pair of flip-flops and headed toward the pier for a swim. Cruz trotted at her side. "You going to wait for me again?" He huffed at her, which she took as agreement. Lately, he'd accompanied her on a few afternoon swims and lay in the shade until she was done.

Hope ducked her head into the compressor/gear room. Alex sat at his workbench, a regulator open before him.

"I was going to see if you wanted to join me for a swim, but it looks like you've got quite the project going on there."

"I'll have to pass," he said, pointing to the offending piece of equipment. "This reg was free flowing this morning, so I'm rebuilding it. The diver needs it for tomorrow morning's trip. By the way, when is our good friend Wayne sailing into the wild blue yonder?"

"I think this evening sometime. Why?"

Alex put down his tool and stared at her. "That guy actually tried to intimidate me into letting him on the dive boat this morning. After I told him no at the reception."

"Oh, dear." Hope leaned against the doorframe, laughing. "I wish I could have seen that."

"Don't worry, no blood was spilled. Not sure he's going to return, though. We didn't exactly hit it off." He sharpened his gaze. "Though I think he feels a little differently about you."

"Pretty sure he got the message loud and clear at the reception. See you later."

Cruz followed her down to the palapa, but when she put on her goggles and swim cap, he turned back to the compressor room. The dog circled three times and lay down in the shade, closing his eyes.

Hope dove in on the southern side, and the warm water slid over her body as she cut through the water. Since her surgery, she was stronger than ever. A curious silver fish kept pace with her, darting around while she swam. At the twenty-minute mark, she stopped to tread water and rest. She kept the same moderate pace going back. As she reached the ladder, her escort sped off underneath the pier, reuniting with others of the same variety.

Cruz was waiting for her at the top of the ladder, tail wagging, then lay down under the bench as she dried off. Looking up, Hope suppressed a groan as Wayne exited his sailboat and strolled toward her, wearing a Lacoste button-down shirt and tailored slacks. Designer boat shoes completed his *expensive sailboat owner* outfit.

His gaze lingered on her body, traveling up and down. Hope quickly redressed in her T-shirt and board shorts. "Hello, Wayne. Finishing up your preparations?" *How soon are you leaving?*

"Yes, I'm nearly ready. Before I leave, I'd like to offer you a drink. I have some chilled champagne on my boat. We could toast our new friendship."

Hope tried to keep her jaw from dropping. "I don't think so. I already told you, I'm engaged. In fact, I'm getting married in a few weeks."

He smiled and leveled a gaze at her. "I'm just in time then."

"I'm really not interested. Thank you."

A low thrumming sound had been occurring for some time.

Hope looked down, surprised it was coming from Cruz. The dog had never shown any signs of aggression—only fear—but that wasn't the case now. He stood at her side, facing Wayne with hackles raised and teeth bared. A steady, deep growl emanated from his throat.

Hope patted his head, which he ignored, intent on the developer. "I'm sorry. He's never acted like this."

Wayne didn't react. He was staring transfixed at Cruz. Slowly, he raised a finger and pointed. "That's my dog!"

Hope about fell over. "*What?*"

He nodded emphatically. "Absolutely. He lived with me on my sailboat for two years. Until the last time I was in St. Croix, when we anchored in a bay not far from here. He jumped off the bow and swam to shore. I have no idea why, but I never saw him again. I looked but couldn't find him. What a stroke of luck!"

A smile transformed his face as he patted his thighs. "I finally get my dog back. Come on Chauncey. Come here, boy!"

"You named him Chauncey?"

No wonder he ran away.

Cruz hadn't moved from her side, and his growl increased an octave.

"Yes. I'm so glad to get him back." Wayne cocked his head, as if only now noticing Cruz's reaction to their reunion.

Hope balled up her fists. "Well, you can't have him!"

Wayne turned to her sharply, his smile disappearing.

"Look at him!" Hope snapped. "He doesn't want anything to do with you."

Wayne glared and took a large step toward Hope, now less than a foot away. Cruz increased his growl to a menacing snarl, and he stepped forward, holding his left front paw off the ground.

Hope's heart pounded in her ears as she stepped backwards to put some distance between them, more furious than scared.

"What the hell did you do to my dog, bitch?" Wayne reached out and gripped her upper arm.

As soon as Wayne touched her, Cruz launched himself at the man, landing against his torso. Hope staggered back, entangled with an angry man and an even angrier dog. All three toppled over and fell into the ocean, landing with a resounding splash. Hope surfaced, sputtering and splashing. Wayne was nearby, treading water as he focused behind her. She turned and Cruz had already swum toward the beach, which was probably a good thing.

She wiped her face and shot Wayne a furious glare. "Oh, this is just great! The ladder is right there. Get going."

"Fine. But we're not done yet."

They swam over and Wayne climbed up, making no effort to help Hope as she ascended behind him. Cruz must have made it to shore because his constant barking echoed to them, and it was getting louder.

Hope dripped all over the deck. "Would you just get on your damn boat and leave? Cruz doesn't want to go with you and I'm not giving him up."

"I'm not leaving without my dog, dammit." Wayne took a step toward her. "You can't just steal him. I've had him since he was a puppy."

"Oh, bullshit! I'm not *stealing* him. He's been with me for the last year and a half. You must have treated him like hell! He's scared to death of people. I'm not letting you anywhere near him, you bastard." Hope was trying to decide between kicking him or throwing a punch. Plus, the anger kept her fear at bay, which was forming a tight ball in her stomach. *Am I making another stupid move here?*

Wayne lowered his brows, and steam might have exploded from his ears. He grabbed Hope's arm again, wrenching her toward him as she gave an involuntary yelp. Her stomach lurched and her senses sharpened. The barking was getting louder, and she looked up the pier to gauge how much longer she had until Cruz arrived.

But something much more dangerous was headed their way.

Alex was pounding toward them, both hands clenched into fists. Her fear fled and her gut settled. Then it gave a different lurch at his expression. Normally he ran ice cold when angry—quiet and calculating, keeping his emotions well-hidden. That Alex was nowhere to be seen.

His face was a portrait of red-hot rage, his eyes blazing and focused solely on Wayne.

As he slowed in front of him, Alex wrapped his hand around the man's throat. He marched forward and pushed Wayne backwards. They continued, and Wayne windmilled his arms as he stumbled back. He opened his mouth and widened his eyes at the enraged man in front of him. Finally, Alex slammed him into one of the four support pillars of the palapa, still gripping Wayne's neck.

A cold sweat broke out over Hope's body. "Alex, stay calm." She wrapped both hands around his bicep. The muscle was like steel beneath them as she tried to pull him back. Her mouth was getting drier with every second.

Alex didn't even hear her.

Wayne just stared at Alex with huge, terrified eyes.

"Don't. You. Touch her. Ever." Each phrase was punctuated by Alex slamming Wayne against the wooden support post, his hand still tight on Wayne's throat. Yellow pieces of thatch drifted down around them. The developer was breathing, though, so Alex wasn't choking him.

Though he wasn't exactly listening to her either. "Alex!"

Furious barking announced Cruz's arrival, and he latched onto Wayne's pant leg. Snarling, he whipped his head back and forth, Wayne's leg twitching frantically. Next, the dog moved to his shoelaces, shredding them before ripping into the pant leg again. The situation was spiraling out of control.

Hope lost her temper. "God save me from protective males. Everyone! STOP!" She shouted this last word, fists clenched at her sides, and it finally got through to Alex.

He snapped his fingers open, revealing a red hand-shaped mark on Wayne's throat. Even Cruz let go and returned to Hope's side, resuming his low growl.

Alex moved back a step, chest heaving as he darted his eyes to Hope's upper arm. She looked down, shocked at the red mark on it. She rubbed it absently.

"I . . . I'm sorry," Wayne stammered before swallowing forcibly. "I didn't mean to hurt you."

Alex whipped his head back to him, and he stepped close as Wayne widened his eyes again. "You want to try to intimidate me? Fine—hit me with your best shot. Believe me, I've faced worse. You try to rough up a woman? You can bet your ass you're gonna hear from me about it."

Alex moved even closer, nearly nose to nose. "But you lay a hand on the woman I *love*? Consider yourself lucky you're still alive."

"I'm sorry, ok?" Wayne raised both hands and Cruz's growling increased.

"Are you ok, Hope?" Alex asked without taking his eyes off Wayne.

"Yes." Hope grasped Alex's upper arm again. This time he moved back, and she kept contact with him. "I'm fine. Wayne and I had a disagreement, but it's settled now. Isn't it, Wayne?"

"Yes. Keep him, ok?"

Alex stood still, both hands clenched. He was breathing hard, and his eyes were still on fire. Menace radiated from him.

"You need to get back on your boat right now and leave," Hope said.

Wayne jerked a nod and slithered sideways away from Alex before rushing toward his sailboat. Cruz barked at him, but didn't leave Hope's side.

"Don't come back, Wayne," Hope said.

He made fast work of untying his lines. "Don't worry about that."

Hope kept her hand on Alex's arm and Cruz sat on her feet until Wayne was away from the dock and motoring out of Half Moon Bay. She sat with a heavy thump on the bench.

"What the hell was that about?" Alex turned to her.

"A dog."

Hope took in her sopping-wet clothing, the dripping dog, the furious man in front of her, and the entire ridiculous situation, and started laughing uncontrollably, pleased to be laughing and not crying.. The tension diminished with every second. Alex stared at her, his eyes going from narrow to wide at her reaction. Finally, she got a grip and patted the bench next to her. Alex sat and she explained the whole ordeal.

"So, Cruz knocked all three of us into the water. He swam back to shore and was headed out here for round two when you showed up and almost strangled Wayne."

"All that over a dog?"

She snorted again, but got it under control. "Hence my laughter. I don't think Wayne even cared about him. He just wanted his possession back and couldn't stand that Cruz wanted someone else."

Alex had calmed. He watched her steadily, and the throbbing pulse in his temple was gone.

"Thank you for not killing Wayne. I wasn't sure there for a while."

"Don't worry, I wasn't going to kill him. But I was very close to wailing on him."

Alex took a deep breath and rolled his head around on his neck. "I heard Cruz barking like hell and came out to see what was going on. Wayne was looming over you, then he grabbed your arm and all I saw was red. I knew that guy was an asshole, but I still can't believe he'd actually lay a hand on you."

"I was rather surprised too."

He turned to Hope. "I know you think I'm overprotective

sometimes. But don't ever expect me to just stand by if you're in danger like that."

Hope smiled and slid her arm around his shoulders. "No, it's a nice feeling to know you'll always defend me. If you hadn't been here, I think Cruz would have done a pretty good job too."

Laughter bubbled dangerously close to the surface again. "Would you believe Cruz's original name was *Chauncey?*"

With that, she lost it again, bending over her thighs in hysterics.

When she glanced up, Alex was laughing too.

"Oh my God, if only you could have seen it," Hope said between snorts. "Wayne, terrified and standing there with your hand around his neck while Cruz tried to bite his leg off."

Then they were laughing harder, leaning against each other. Hope looked up and jumped. Zach stood slack-jawed nearby, just staring at them.

"You saw the excitement, huh?" Hope asked and Alex quickly got hold of himself, looking serious again, though his cheek was twitching.

Zach approached them, and Cruz moved over to get his head scratched. "Yeah. I saw Wayne get off his sailboat from the dive shop but didn't come out until I heard Cruz barking."

He turned to Alex, and awe washed over his face. "Man, you were *pissed*."

"Well, the whole situation is over now," Hope said. "Wayne is gone, Alex got some extra exercise today, and Cruz solidified his new home." At his name, Cruz made his way back to Hope.

"I better start filling tanks." Zach threw one last stunned glance at Alex as he walked away.

"I can't tell if this helped or hurt his case of hero worship," Hope said, then absently added, "I wonder if Wayne's going to have a hand-shaped bruise around his neck."

Alex snorted and wrapped an arm around her shoulder. "I

don't really care. As long as you're safe, I wouldn't change anything I did."

Hope inspected the handprint on her upper arm, relieved it was already fading.

Cruz shifted position and placed his muzzle on both their knees, whining. Alex scratched his ears as Cruz thumped his tail on the wooden dock. "Ok, buddy. I think you've got a permanent home for sure now. Any guy who defends Hope is all right in my book."

CHAPTER 30

October...

ALEX WAS CLIMBING down the steps of the pier and heading toward the restaurant when movement distracted him. Cruz dug some distance away, sand flying between his hind legs. Alex grinned, able to see the humor in the situation with Wayne, but his smile faded at the vision of Hope with Wayne gripping her arm. Alex shook out his clenched fist, taking a deep breath.

He was glad Cruz got his happy ending, understanding completely why the dog had escaped from Wayne. St. Croix was a small island, but if the developer ever showed his face again, Alex wasn't going to give him a warm welcome. Fortunately, Hope wasn't displaying any delayed trauma response from the altercation, which helped his temper.

He walked through the restaurant toward the kitchen, nodding at several divers who were attending sous chef Pauline's cooking class, then opened the swinging double doors and entered Gerold's spotless domain. "Tour de France called yet, Gerold?"

"They did, but they told me there's snow in France, so I had to turn them down. I'm not doin' snow, man." Gerold was rubbing spices over several whole chickens.

"I hear you. I hate the stuff."

"What? You grew up in Florida."

"I did. That's why I hate cold weather so much. There's a reason I live on a tropical island, you know." Alex made his way over to a large basket of food sitting on the counter.

"I was in a snowstorm in New York once," Gerold said. "It sucked. Have you even seen snow?"

"A time or two."

"Ah, I think you're just a wimp."

"Hey, you try crawling out of a thirty-eight-degree ocean into below-zero air temperatures and see how much you like it."

"Why the hell would you do that?" Gerold transferred the chickens into roasting pans.

"It wasn't exactly my choice. I just went where they told me." Alex started poking through the basket, determined to keep Hope distracted that afternoon.

Gerold stared at him, but let the comment go and washed his hands instead.

"This looks great," Alex said. "Thanks."

"Try to keep the meats and cheeses cold. They're in a small cooler. I'll get the champagne for you." Gerold placed the bottle in an insulated carrier before opening a cupboard filled with glassware. "You want plastic or crystal champagne flutes?"

"Better make it plastic."

"You're a barbarian, you know that?"

Alex laughed. "It's a *picnic*. And we're traveling by boat. Does that sound like a job for crystal?" He picked up the champagne carrier. "This is a decent bottle of champagne, right?"

"Oh yeah. Hope appreciates the finer things in life. Why she's with you, I have no idea."

"You're lucky I've let you try out your low-class food on me all these years." Alex swung an arm under the handle of the basket and picked it up. "Thanks, Gerold. This is terrific—you really outdid yourself."

"You're welcome. You two have a good time."

The late-afternoon sun bathed Alex's face as he strolled down the pier toward *Surface Interval*. After climbing aboard, he stashed the picnic supplies in a cupboard under the canopy.

He returned to the gear room to make sure he hadn't forgotten anything and stopped to inspect the area next to the compressor. He folded his arms, evaluating it for a membrane system. Alex shook his head as he took in the room. One corner was filled with his supplies for the coral-restoration project, and now he was researching a Nitrox system. "How things change." A smile rose as he headed back toward the boat.

Hope was already on board, dressed in her black string bikini with the fishnet cover-up that barely covered anything. As Alex strolled down the wooden walkway, he rumbled deep in his chest. Her hair was longer—her ponytail had more length than usual, and the black swim top only enhanced her full breasts. It was almost sexier than seeing her naked. He was too far away to see her three small abdominal scars, but they were hardly noticeable, anyway. And beautiful to him. All of her was beautiful.

She's my everything.

Hope turned around as he boarded, and he wrapped her in his arms as he walked her backwards under the canopy, leading with his lips. "Ms. Collins, I'm not sure that's proper dive attire."

"I certainly hope not. I had something else in mind when I picked this out."

"Well, hold that thought." She tasted of mango, and he pushed against her hips, making sure she knew her effect on him.

"Easy. You're the one who said to hold on." Hope pulled away a little and glanced down his body. She bit her lip, then gave up the fight, holding a hand to her mouth as laughter tumbled out. "What are you wearing?"

He looked down with a frown. "A rash guard and board shorts. Why?"

"Alex, your shirt is blue and yellow, and your shorts are green!"

"And this is why I like having a job where I get to wear a wetsuit most of the time." She was still laughing, so he took off his shirt. "Better?"

"Mmmm. Much. Can I trust Mike to make sure you look presentable for our wedding?"

He shrugged, grinning. "Probably not. He's more likely to pick out the top and bottom that clash the most, just so I look like an idiot. Don't worry—Patti will be there. She won't let things get too out of hand."

Alex eased the boat away from the dock. It was a beautiful afternoon. The sun was past its punishing zenith, but there were still hours of daylight left. The water was flat calm as they motored north. Alex sat on the padded bench seat, gathering Hope into the hollow of his shoulder.

"I saw Jack worked a couple days," she said. "Did it go well?"

"Yeah, he's good. I talked to him some about the coral-restoration project and he was really interested in it, especially after I told him I had a degree in marine biology." Alex laughed. "I think the fact I wasn't some hack making things up as I went put him at ease. I might give him some instruction and let him take over some of it. Eventually, anyway."

"Does he know the rest of your background? Military?"

Alex looked at her sharply. "Not unless someone else told him. I have no intention of telling him I was a SEAL. Fight club, remember?"

Hope reached up and cupped his face, and he turned to her with raised brows.

"There's so much you could brag about. People have no idea. Yet that's the last thing you want."

"I didn't do it for a pat on the back, and I loved the challenge."

"Well, if I'm going to be your wife, I reserve the right to be proud of you whenever I feel like it. You really don't get a say in this, Mr. Monroe."

"Is that so?"

"Oh, yes."

"You really have no right to call me bossy."

"You know my answer to that. Don't make me prove it."

He grinned, drilling her with his eyes. "Careful now. I just told you I enjoy a challenge."

"Maybe I'll test your resolve later." She held his gaze for a long moment before peering around. "We've been going over half an hour now. Where are you taking me?"

"Told you. It's a secret. But I will say you've never dived there before."

After another few minutes, they passed a familiar purple house, and Alex changed their heading to northwest. The seas were still very calm. Here in open water, it was usually choppy in the afternoons. A smile rose as he sat with one hand loose on the wheel, the wind blowing on his face and his other arm draped around the woman he loved.

Soon, he spotted the stubby trees of the small landmass ahead. Hope straightened, then stood, her hands resting against the wooden console as Alex's grin widened. She turned back and her smile answered his. "Are we going back to Horseshoe Key?"

"Yes. I've always wanted you to dive it."

"That's right! You did say it was a dive site when we were there. I may have been a bit distracted."

He brushed her warm, soft lips, and was almost disappointed to be diving. "I'll try to distract you some more. Later."

He throttled down and angled toward port. They were headed

to a small horseshoe-shaped islet, the open ends facing them as Alex angled the boat toward the left. The base of the horseshoe was a tiny island with stunted trees and shrubs, which provided shade for a stunning white sand beach.

"There's a mooring ball here, so I'll tether us to it."

Hope kept the boat in neutral until Alex reappeared at the surface. He gave her the ok and the area became nearly silent without the boat engine, except the soft sounds of waves slapping against the hull. Hope tugged on her wetsuit and Alex tried to keep his eyes off her black bikini.

"This is one of my favorite dive sites," he said. "The reef slopes down deep, but we'll level off at sixty feet and head toward the southern point. There's a channel that bisects the reef and dumps onto the outer edge of the horseshoe. Because we're in the open water here, the outside drops deep. Really deep. There's a chance to see pelagics—open water animals like marlin, tuna, dolphins, big schools of rays. I even saw a whale out here one time."

Soon they were descending, and Alex's experienced eye immediately saw how much lusher and more vibrant this reef was than those closer to shore. There was a healthy mix of hard and soft corals, with many varieties of each. It was a living rainbow of colors, and the healthy reef meant more fish.

Schools of sergeant majors flitted about the reef, their black bars shimmering in the sunlight. Clouds of blue tangs swooped and dove over the reef, cleaning it, and groups of lavender tube sponges seemed to glow from within. Hope darted her head around, her eyes wide. She gave him an ok signal with both hands and high-fived him.

They reached sixty feet, and Alex led them into the channel. It was fairly narrow, and they had to swim around multiple protruding sea fans. The walls soared on either side of them, and a school of creole wrasse busily swam above them in a long line of royal blue.

Alex shined his light in some of the wide shelves lining both sides, hunting for creatures. He was rewarded when his light revealed a large nurse shark on the sand under a ledge. Over eight feet long, it was a shy creature trying to sleep. Hope practically vibrated as she smiled at him. She'd seen very few sharks and never one this close. Two more rested under a shelf on the opposite side, and he waited patiently, thoroughly enjoying her excitement.

Next, he spied three turtles sleeping in crevices. Two were hawksbills of normal size, but the third was a monster Leatherback nearly six feet long. Hope exclaimed through her reg, and a wide grin split Alex's face.

The channel emptied into a sheer wall that dropped hundreds of feet, with nothing but clear blue ocean in front of them. Alex waited for Hope to emerge beside him. She clasped his hand and squeezed tight.

They turned together and a squadron of ten eagle rays swam by, the nearest just feet away. The tops of their triangular-shaped bodies were covered in white-patterned spots, and the beautiful creatures were nearly eight feet from wingtip to wingtip. Their bodies tapered to a whip of a tail six feet long, and they swept their wings up and down in effortless grace. They disappeared into the haze and Alex turned to follow the wall toward the point just ahead.

There was no current today, making for an easy, spectacular dive. They hovered at the point for several minutes, watching a large moray eel. Then a green sea turtle swam by, ignoring him while watching Hope closely. She exchanged a smile with him—she'd always had an affinity with turtles. They moved up to forty feet and continued around the point, back toward the boat.

Alex heard them long before they became visible.

At first the sounds were faint, a series of clicks and whistles with squeals mixed in. Wide-eyed, he whipped toward Hope, cupping a hand behind his ear, asking if she heard it. She nodded her head, but her brow was furrowed. She didn't know what they were.

Even better! Hopefully, we'll have some excitement soon. Maybe I can help things...

Alex used his metal pointer to slowly bang his tank a few times, and the sounds became louder. The divers moved out from the wall into the water column as his heart rate increased. He looked up and down, then left and right. The direction of sound was almost impossible to discern underwater, and he didn't want to miss them.

The first one zipped by in front of them, with another just behind. Both were eight-foot-long Atlantic spinner dolphins, and a third swept over their heads. Then they were in the midst of twenty, circling and dancing around them.

A male and female twined around each other in a mating display as they swam by. A baby barely two feet long sped right in front of Alex, squeaking as it went, and he grinned from ear to ear. The water was alive with clicks and squeals.

Dolphins were always great for a show. They were expressive, playful animals that turned a dive into a spectacle. The encounters were often short-lived, as if dolphins thought these bubble-producing creatures weren't worth the time once their initial curiosity was sated.

He and Hope had drifted apart a bit and a large dolphin slowly swam between them, clicking loudly. It was an adult male, nearly nine feet long. It continued around the other side of Alex, dolphin and man watching each other the whole time. Alex hovered motionless, not wanting to chase him away. The dolphin spun in a tight circle and slowly swam up to Alex, evaluating him. It continued by, brushing softly against the man.

Alex was shocked, electrified by the touch.

There was nothing threatening in its gesture, but he'd never had an animal act like this. The dolphin turned and brushed against him again. Alex maintained a strict hands-off policy with any marine creature except in extreme circumstances, but he couldn't shake the feeling that this dolphin wanted to be touched. He hardly dared to breathe as it moved past.

The next time it approached, the large mammal slowed nearly to a stop, brushing against Alex yet again. He reached out his hand, hesitating, then touched his fingertips against the large animal in a feather-light caress. The dolphin's skin felt like warm rubber, smooth and silky. It didn't move away, just turned around and came back for another pass.

This time, he held his hand against the dolphin's side, but firmer and with more confidence as the animal swam slowly by, clicking as it went. The vibrations rippled through Alex's hand and a smile rose to his face.

They continued for several more passes, and Alex was awash in awestruck wonder. Finally, the dolphin stopped directly in front of him, turning its head slightly as it faced Alex. They stared at each other for a long moment. The dolphin's eyes were kind and intelligent.

It moved its head in a single nod, and goose bumps broke out along Alex's body.

Then, with a massive thrust of its tail, the dolphin shot over his right shoulder. All the others in the pod were gone. He could still hear them, but distantly. Alex gazed back to where he'd last seen his dolphin, but the ocean was empty.

The animal was gone, and Alex's heart twisted at the loss. This was followed by a deep, powerful upwelling of emotion, and he blinked rapidly.

He turned to Hope, who hovered vertically in the water with both hands held to her chest, her eyes glittering with tears. She swam over to him and took both his hands in hers, squeezing tightly. Alex was nearly overcome as he gazed at Hope. The meaning of the encounter ricocheted around his head.

Though not the same as his other encounter with a dolphin, this one was every bit as special, perhaps more so. And now Alex stared into the eyes of the biggest difference between that time and now.

Wrenching his gaze away, he checked his computer. They had been down for over an hour, and he signaled to begin their safety stop. With reluctance, he took another 360-degree look, but couldn't even hear the dolphins anymore. It was difficult to swallow the lump in his throat.

The dolphin had been trying to convey something meant for him alone. Also the same as last time.

Trying to rein in his emotions, Alex rose toward the surface.

CHAPTER 31

Alex tried to get a grip on himself as he removed his gear. He was embarrassingly close to tears, which was *not* how he had envisioned beginning the next phase of their afternoon. Though he'd cried in front of Hope before, it had been delayed grief following the terrible nightmares about Syria, not because he'd cavorted with a dolphin.

They shrugged out of their scuba gear and wetsuits. Hope kept giving him sidelong glances. He was stiff and halting—reluctant to meet her gaze and unsure why he was so embarrassed about his reaction. She'd had a similar experience with a turtle after her diving accident and understood better than most what he was feeling.

Hope sighed, and when he turned around, she stood before him. She shook her head, giving him a small smile as she wrapped her arms around his waist. Her warm skin melted into his, and he immediately relaxed.

"You stubborn man. Why are you acting all self-conscious? That was one of the most amazing things I've ever seen. Dolphins love you. Was your other encounter like that?"

"Kind of. The other one was longer, but we never touched.

I've never touched any animal like that." He drew her closer, trying to find the words. "I'm emotional because of how different *I* am. When I saw that first dolphin, I was alone and broken. I was only looking for a reason to keep getting up every morning. And he helped me find that. He reminded me how at peace I felt in the water, and I knew coming to St. Croix was the right decision." He paused, then spoke against her hair. "But today . . . instead of lost and broken, I feel . . . finally whole again. Because of you."

Hope shook her head. "Not just me. Because of *us*."

"Us. I'll always be by your side."

"And I'll be at yours."

Alex kissed the top of her head and held her, stroking his hands over her back. It wasn't long before it entered his mind that their afternoon wasn't over yet, and he still had a lot planned. He let go and moved toward the bow. "I'll unmoor us."

"What, we're leaving?"

He caught a glimpse of her disappointed frown before he turned away and smiled, knowing she couldn't see it. His warm flush helped dispel the residual emotion left from the dolphin encounter. "Not far."

He climbed to the wheelhouse and started the engine as Hope followed, sitting on the bench as he stood at the wheel, slowly motoring toward the white sand beach. He got as close as he dared and dropped anchor in the bare sand.

"Mr. Monroe, what do you have up your sleeve?"

Alex looked at her with his best wide, innocent eyes. "Who, me?"

He shut off the engine and climbed down to the cupboards lining the front of the covered section. Hope was just behind. He bent down and pulled out the basket with one hand and the champagne cooler with the other. "Ta-da!"

Hope's face lit up as she bobbed on the balls of her feet. "You brought a picnic?"

He couldn't resist and kissed her, a lightning bolt racing through him as she pressed her tongue to his. "What better place? And not just any picnic. This was personally prepared by Gerold, and he picked the champagne too." He turned to another cabinet and removed the dry backpack he'd stowed that morning, then loaded the food and supplies into it.

"I'll leave my cover-up behind this time. Something tells me I won't need it."

They swam to shore and walked onto the silky white beach.

"Why don't you pick the spot this time?" he asked.

Hope shaded her eyes with one hand and peered around, finally pointing to a different area near the stubby trees that would still provide some shade.

"Your wish is my command." He gave her the blanket to spread while he unzipped the champagne from its container. "Still nice and cold." He popped the cork and poured into their very appropriate plastic glasses. "What shall we drink to this time?"

"New beginnings is still appropriate, I think," she said as they toasted. They drank, and as their eyes met, both broke into laughter. "This was where we truly became a couple," she said. "Now we're going to be married in less than two weeks. I still can't believe it."

"I'm a whole lot more relaxed this time." Alex's smile faded. "That's one of the reasons I wanted to come back here—to try and make up for some things. There's a lot I'd do differently that day. Starting with telling you about my wound when we were eating. I wanted to, but just couldn't bring myself to do it." He glanced at her from under his brows. "And you were pretty effective at pushing me away, you know. I didn't want to open that can of worms if things didn't go the way I wanted them to."

"I'd do things differently too. I should never have been so stubborn about it. I was so scared. I knew how strong my feelings for you were, and that I'd have to jump into the deep end this time." She turned a smile to him. "I tried to play it cool when we got here, but wearing this bikini was *not* an accident. I was ready and I wanted you very badly."

As Hope began slicing Gerold's homemade bread and the artisan meats and cheeses he'd selected, Alex let his gaze traveled down her body. Hope normally wore sporty swimsuits that covered her well, but this string bikini was *not* of that variety. He met her eyes again, but still had some things to say. "I'm sorry I made things difficult for you. Even now, I'm not sure I could have told you about being a SEAL while we were here. I had a hard enough time telling you about my wound. But I didn't handle it well, and I made a lot of things difficult for you." He sighed. "God, I'm an asshole."

She gave him a fond smile but didn't reply.

Arching a brow, he poked her in the knee. "This is where you're supposed to say, 'You're not an asshole, Alex. You're the love of my life.'"

She couldn't hold back the laughter, but tried to cover it by sipping her champagne, staring at him over the rim. "The two aren't mutually exclusive, you know."

He grinned. "Ok, I guess I earned that."

Hope leaned over and kissed him, pressing her palm to his face. "Don't apologize, love. I don't understand why I waited so long to tell you about Caleb. You certainly deserved to know before I told you. And it wasn't like I didn't know how I felt about you, for God's sake."

She gave Alex a crooked smile. "Confession time. I was in love with you when I had my accident, but I was too petrified to deal with it, even to admit it. But everything became very clear when the boat sank. That was the day I stopped fighting my feelings."

"You were all I could think about on the Coast Guard ship—I knew I loved you. For me, there was no going back after that." He took in the trees and beach around them, the water lapping softly against the shore. "I'm not sure you understand what that afternoon meant to me. To have you accept me so completely, yet not feel sorry for me. I got my courage back that day. It just deepened my feelings even more."

"I know, Alex." Then a mischievous grin spread across her face. "But it took you long enough to finally say it."

"Me? You just told me you loved me even longer. Pot meet kettle, Ms. Collins."

"The girl doesn't say it first!"

"You told me you were a non-traditional sort."

"Not about that. No way. Come on, let's eat."

The crusty bread paired deliciously with the cheeses and meats. Gerold had included an incredible pasta salad and fresh fruit as well.

After eating, they started putting the food back in the dry bag, but there was one last small box at the bottom of the cooler. Withdrawing it, Alex opened the lid to discover a selection of chocolate-covered strawberries. "Oho! We've got dessert."

Alex poured the rest of the champagne, as Hope put the box of strawberries between them. They each reclined on an elbow, facing each other.

"Thank you," she said. "This was an incredible surprise."

"I thought it was fitting to return here."

He removed the strawberry and held it in front of Hope's mouth. She placed her hand over his and drew it into her mouth, then pushed his index finger in, creating suction as she gave him an intense stare.

He inhaled sharply, feeling the effects immediately. Desire rolled through him.

Hope picked another up, still smiling, and held half of it in her mouth as she leaned toward him. He needed no further explanation, biting it in half as their lips met. They finished the berry, then their lips came together again. She tasted delicious as he ran his hand over the soft warm skin of her back, untying her bikini top and pulling it off.

After he picked up another berry, Alex rolled her onto her

back and slowly drew it between her breasts. He fed it to her before leaning down and drawing his tongue over the stripe. She tasted of chocolate, salt, and dreams come true. He continued licking at the chocolate as he slid his hand under her bikini bottoms. She arched her back, moaning now. He moved his mouth to the center of her breast and smiled as her moans got louder.

When he lifted up, Hope pushed him onto his back and pulled off his shorts, along with her bikini bottoms. Alex lay back and closed his eyes as she traveled up his leg, tenderly kissing his scarred hip before drawing him into her mouth. The ocean waves subsided as the waves in his body took over. He threw an arm over his eyes as the sparks rocketed through his body. "Hope, I want you so much."

She withdrew, kissing up his stomach. If anything, his throbbing increased. A gentle breeze blew, cooling the wet skin she left behind, and a delicious shiver knifed through him. Straddling him, she traced up his neck and across his chin. Finally, her warm, wet mouth met his and he slid his tongue in, tasting her.

Which gave him other ideas.

He pressed against her shoulders to move her off, but she pushed back, preventing him. They had a little tug of war, but Hope wouldn't move.

He pulled away, laughing. "You know, I am stronger than you."

"Doesn't matter—I'm far more devious. You can't outmatch me. Surrender."

"Ok, fine." He grabbed a handful of her hair and yanked her head down. Crushing her mouth to his, he was determined to make her pay. She groaned, enjoying herself fully. He smiled, then inhaled sharply as she grasped him and guided him inside her.

He was intensely sensitive, feeling everything as she moved above him and around him. Her strawberry mouth softened, brushing against his lips, then opening with her tongue as he reached his toward her.

Hope placed both hands against his face as her breathing became more ragged, starting to match his now. She broke the kiss, and he opened his eyes. She was inches away, watching him.

She grasped his hands, pulling them above his head as their fingers entwined.

They were both panting now, their hands gripping tightly in a mirror image of the first time they made love, here on this very island. Alex's climax was building, and she shifted slightly, allowing him deeper access. He closed his eyes and buried his face in her shoulder.

Hope was moaning louder now—she was close. He moved powerfully beneath her, the privacy of their islet allowing him to give in completely. Hope clung tightly to his hands, pressing them into the warm, soft sand above his head as they rode the wave together.

Gradually, their breathing returned to normal as she rested above him. He stroked her hair, and she nestled her head against his neck. Running her finger in long strokes down the side of his chest, she pressed a kiss against his skin. "You're wrong, you know."

"About what?"

"That first day when we were on this islet. I know what it meant to you because it was the same for me. That was the day I became free."

CHAPTER 32

Hope sat on the blanket with her arms around her knees as Alex breathed deeply next to her. He had a soldier's knack for falling asleep at will. She glanced to her right, where the sun was just dipping below the horizon. Night fell very quickly in the tropics, but Alex wouldn't have any problems driving back in the dark.

She turned her gaze to him. Lying naked on his back with his hands clasped over his stomach, he breathed deeply but quietly, the lines in his face relaxed in sleep. Dark stubble, with some gray interspersed, was beginning to line his chin.

She dropped her eyes to his chest and shoulders. He always made time for his morning swims and a weight-training program several times a week, and the results of both were apparent in his muscular, lean build. The bullet scar on his shoulder was much less noticeable. She continued downward, unable to imagine a more spectacularly built man.

His breathing changed and she looked up. His blue eyes stared back at her in the dim light. "Were you ogling me while I was defenseless in sleep?"

"I don't think you're ever defenseless."

He laughed, tossing an arm over his eyes. "I am around you, believe me."

A breeze came up, rippling goose bumps down her arms. Now that the sun had set, it was cooling off quickly. "We'd better head back. It's dark now and I'm getting cold."

This time, they put their swimsuits back on. After packing everything in the dry bag, they were soon back on board. Hope toweled off quickly, her teeth chattering. Alex hurried to a storage cupboard and removed two sweatshirts. "Here, put this on. I keep a couple on board to wear after night dives."

She pulled the oversized hoodie over her head and paused mid-motion, just inhaling Alex's scent. She was smiling when her head popped out.

He grazed her lips with his. "What are you smiling about?"

"Nothing in particular—just how happy I am. It was a terrific afternoon."

Alex pressed the button to raise the anchor and they were soon on their way back to the resort.

"You're not going to get lost in the dark, are you?"

He shot her a dirty look. "Not unless they moved the resort while we were gone. You've always indicated I know my way around pretty well when the lights go out."

Hope rolled her eyes, ignoring his grin. It was windy in the elevated wheelhouse, and she pulled the sweatshirt tighter. Alex sat down, pulling her next to him as she settled against his warmth. St. Croix was lovely at night. The looming landmass was barely visible against the starry sky, scattered lights the only hint of occasional houses or resorts.

They were relaxing against each other when Alex sat up, jostling her as he alertly looked at the bow. He removed his arm and stood behind the wheel as a loud exhalation came from their right.

"It's dolphins!" Alex called. "Might be the same pod we saw earlier. Spinner dolphins are great on the surface. Too bad it's dark, but maybe I can do something about that." He beckoned to her as he pushed the throttle to full speed. "Here, you take the wheel and I'll man the spotlight."

Above the wheel, a round spotlight was mounted to the ceiling and he turned it on. As he aimed it at the bow, half a dozen dolphins were illuminated as they leapt in the bow wave. "Yep, they're spinners."

"Why are they called spinner dolphins?"

Alex laughed. "Keep watching."

Dolphins were on both sides of the bow wake, jumping through the frothy water. Another shot vertically out of the water, spun around several times, and dropped back in. On the other side, another jumped even higher, completely exiting the water as it whirled around half a dozen times before submerging again.

Hope laughed, then four appeared at the same time, jumping and spinning. "Why do they spin like that?"

"Spinners are the only dolphins that do. There's no biological reason—they must enjoy it." The dolphins certainly appeared to be having fun.

Another noisy breath sounded, and the glimmer of another dolphin appeared alongside them. Hope bent around Alex. "There's another one to our right."

Alex moved the spotlight to illuminate this one. "I recognize his patterns. That's the one I touched."

The dolphin jumped through the waves, matching the boat's speed. He disappeared, only to shoot ten feet out of the water, spinning half a dozen times before descending. Then he did the same again.

Alex leaned against the console with an enormous smile on his face. Dolphin and man once again watched each other for a long moment as it swam on its side. The intelligent mammal squeaked and clicked before veering to the right toward open ocean, then submerged. The rest of the pod followed and disappeared. Alex shut off the spotlight.

"You need to give that guy a name."

"If I ever see him again, I will." His shy smile was back as he dropped his gaze to the deck.

Something important had happened out here this day.

∼

A CLOUD CROSSED THE MOON, throwing the beach into shadow as they walked home. "Your ploy worked," Hope said. "I haven't thought about the auction all afternoon, but I can't wait to check my email now. Hopefully, we'll have the results."

"I have mixed emotions about selling that idol. It was pretty cool." Alex grinned at her. "Good thing we've got two more, huh?"

Hope matched his smile, excitement fluttering through her.

Cruz waited for them on the porch, wagging his whole rear end as Hope petted his head. "You're probably hungry, aren't you? We already ate. I'll get you some dinner." She fed him before rushing to her laptop, Alex looking over her shoulder.

Her most recent email was from Bryce. The subject line read simply: Auction.

Frowning, she brought up the short email.

THE AUCTION WENT PRETTY WELL. See the attached file for the itemized list of entries sold. The buyers have seven business days to settle their payment, then we transfer the net proceeds to your account. I'll update you at that point. Don't hesitate to contact me if you have any questions or concerns. Best, Bryce.

. . .

"Well, that doesn't sound very enthusiastic," Hope said, her heart sinking. "It almost sounds like a boilerplate reply." With her frown deepening, she glanced at Alex.

He just shrugged. "Only one way to find out."

She clicked on the attachment and was presented with the identical spreadsheet they had been given at Prodigy. It listed each item in the lot and the minimum bid price. Only now, the column marked *Final Bid* in bold type had been completed, and the total was tabulated at the bottom.

Behind her, Alex gasped, and her gaze was drawn inexorably to the bottom right corner of the spreadsheet.

The grand total was $3.73 million.

Hope stared at the number, then her held breath exploded out. "Am I seeing this right?"

Alex pressed his hand on the table, leaning closer. "Yeah, it's right. I can't even comprehend that. What do we do with all of it?"

"Nothing to start with. It can just sit in the bank. We need to think about this long and hard." Hope's thoughts turned to Sara in her small apartment in Charleston, then to Kate and her hectic, overscheduled life. "Though I think we both agree that job one is giving some to our families."

He nodded. "Absolutely."

Slowly, she turned her head and met his gaze. His eyes reflected the sheer wonder that had to be in hers. Then a slow smile rose on his face as her heart surged. Alex ran a finger over her tattoo. "I seem to recall there are two chalices in the safe we've had rather good experiences with. Maybe you could retrieve them for a celebratory drink?"

With elation floating through her, Hope rose. "You're just full of good ideas today, aren't you?"

"You have no idea. Yet."

LATER, Hope lay in bed with her head on Alex's chest, watching a quarter moon through the slats in the windows. Its white stripe shimmered on the ocean. Her thoughts had returned to their Miami trip, and she was pensive now. "I almost lost everything. I only set that bag down for a moment, but that was all it took. If it weren't for you, we wouldn't have that money right now."

"We don't have that money right now. We haven't gotten it yet."

"Hey, I'm trying to make you feel important here." Her toes curled as Alex kissed her forehead.

"You always make me feel important." Then his laughter filled the night air, startling her. "When I was following you and Gray Hoodie, I was so proud of you. And grateful you were cussing at someone else for once. I can't believe how fierce you can be." His smile lingered as he glanced at her. "And I admit I was pretty proud when I swooped in at the end and saved the day."

"Believe me, so was I." She kissed his chest. "You've needed to learn you can't always save me from harm. I've learned I need to trust your instincts more, even when I'm not happy with what they're telling you."

"A lot of it is just being aware of what's going on around you. So many people are oblivious to their surroundings, noses buried in their phones. It's never a bad idea to know what's going on around you." He bit his lip, trying not to laugh. "And I got a little lucky. I just happened to be coming out of the men's room when you went stomping by in your tight little skirt."

"I just felt so bad. I wanted to get the bag back—I thought you'd be so mad at me!"

"I probably would've been if it hadn't been so damn funny. You screaming at him to stop and calling him an asshole." He was laughing so hard now, he could barely talk.

"It's really not funny, you know."

"Meh, it kind of is."

"Alex, he pulled a knife on me. And I was so stupefied I just stood there like an idiot! I could have been stabbed at any second. How could I have been so dumb?"

"Don't be so hard on yourself. You weren't in any real danger. I had my gun out as soon as he pulled the knife."

"But you weren't that close yet."

"I was plenty close to shoot the knife out of his hand. If there hadn't been a clear angle, I would have hit him in the wrist. That would have been a disaster, though. I wanted to avoid shooting if I possibly could. Holding the gun against him was plenty effective."

"I didn't even know you were there." She propped herself up on an elbow. "How good of a shot are you?"

He paused for a moment. "Pretty good, Hope."

She sighed. "It really wasn't very smart on my part."

"Oh, but you do keep life interesting."

CHAPTER 33

"How have you liked being on the boat the past few days?" Alex asked.

"It's been great." Jack ran a hand through his thick brown hair as he looked around the boat. "I like how organized you are. I came from a shop in St. Thomas that was pretty much the opposite. And I've liked everyone I've met here—you guys are a good group."

Alex grabbed an armful of regulators as Jack swung a BCD over each shoulder. They stepped off the boat, heading to the rinse tanks. "Do you have any problems teaching Discover Scuba Diving classes? We're getting more requests for those."

"Fine by me. It all pays the same. And I'd love to learn more about your coral-restoration project."

"Sure, I'd be happy to show it to you sometime. We've got a few more dive trips going out, then we're shutting the resort down for several days. But after that, it really picks up."

"Tommy said something about a wedding."

Alex laughed. "Yeah. Mine."

"Oh? I hope you have better luck than I did."

Alex kept his face neutral, surprised Jack would divulge that. "I couldn't be happier and I'm fairly confident Hope feels the same way."

"Hope? Oh. I didn't realize you two were together."

"We try to be professional." Alex grinned. "Try, I said."

"Congratulations." Jack held his hand out and they shook. "Sorry. I got divorced not too long ago and it's still a sore spot. I'm here for a new start."

"I think you'll find this is a good place for that." The two men exchanged a nod and went back to the gear.

～

AFTER HE HAD FINISHED work and showered, Alex headed straight for the kitchen. When he walked in, Gerold and Hope were huddled over a stainless-steel counter as the chef wrote on a pad of paper.

His eyes became round when he saw Alex. "Quick. Tie him up or something! I can never get you two in here together."

"What are you talking about?" Alex asked. "This is where the food is. I'm never far away."

"We're finalizing the menu for the wedding," Hope said.

Gerold threw him a disgusted look before turning to Hope. "The last time I asked him what he wanted, he replied, 'Food'."

Alex grinned and scooped some Caribbean chicken stew into a bowl. "My order hasn't changed, Gerold." Hope met his eyes and he winked at her.

"Gerold and I have settled on a choice of mahi-mahi or filet mignon for dinner," she said.

"How about the cake?" Gerold asked.

"I *loved* my birthday cake. Can you make one just like that?"

"In my sleep."

She laughed. "Try to stay awake, all right? It doesn't need to be big or fancy. We'll probably have fewer than twenty people here."

"What about wine?"

"A white and a red," Hope said. "Something crisp for the white, a dry Riesling or Chenin Blanc. A Cabernet would work for the red."

"Did you like the champagne you had on your picnic?"

Hope flicked her eyes to Alex's and they shared a private smile. "Of course we did, Gerold. It was Moët & Chandon."

Gerold sent another dirty look Alex's way. "Do you have any idea how far out of your pay grade she is?"

"Of course. I'm not stupid, you know." Alex sat down and started eating.

"It's not *your* intelligence I'm questionin' right now."

Hope grabbed a nearby wooden spatula and hit Gerold over the head with it. "Hey! That's not nice."

Gerold rubbed his head. "Man, you two are made for each other."

Hope narrowed her eyes at Gerold before turning to Alex. "Does that menu sound ok to you?"

"You had me at filet mignon and red wine."

"That's settled then." Hope walked over to plant a kiss on Alex's head. "I need to go back to work. You're going to the range?"

"Yes, right after I eat. Might have a beer afterwards."

After Hope left, Gerold busied himself prepping for the dinner service. "You both have family flying in the next couple days, right?"

"That's the plan. There's a pretty good storm over the southeast US right now that might shake things up a bit. At least the forecast is clear for us." Alex leaned forward on his elbows. "Thanks for all your help with the wedding. It means a lot to both of us."

Gerold gave him a level look. "Whatever you need, consider it done."

Patti pushed through the swinging doors. "You got any salads ready for lunch, Gerold?"

"Yeah, in the fridge. Help yourself."

"Patti!" Alex beamed at her, and she raised a brow skeptically. "Just the woman I wanted to see."

Patti put her salad on the table and sat across from him. "That sounds like trouble."

"Why are you always so suspicious of me?"

"Years of experience."

"I assure you, my intentions are entirely above board this time. Has Hope said anything to you about our wedding night?"

"No! Of course not!" Patti's eyes blazed as Gerold doubled over in silent laughter behind her.

"I didn't mean it like that! Jeez, Patti. Did she say anything about *where* we were spending our wedding night?"

Patti's eyes were still narrowed, but most of the heat had left them. "No, she hasn't said anythin' to me. I just figured you two would go back to your house."

"I'd like our wedding night to be somewhere else. I was thinking one of the bungalows. Away from everyone else."

"The further away from people tryin' to sleep, the better," Gerold added.

Patti gave him a long look, and Gerold busied himself cutting a cucumber. She turned back to Alex. "The north-side bungalows will all be empty, so that shouldn't be a problem. Why are you askin' me?"

Alex squeezed her hand. "I was wondering if you'd be willing to decorate it. You know a lot more about that than I do, and I want to make it really special for her."

Patti stared at him with an open mouth, then snapped it shut, eyes glittering. "I'll make it wonderful. Don't you worry." She stood to embrace him, and Alex rose quickly, hugging her ample form as she sniffled against him. "Oh, these allergies! So bad this time of year." She grabbed a nearby tissue and dabbed her eyes as

Alex tried to keep a straight face. Gerold grinned as he moved on to a bell pepper.

"Thanks, Patti. This really means a lot."

"You've been alone far too long, dear man. It's about time you settled down."

"What can I say? I'm particular. It took me a long time to find the perfect woman."

∼

THE NEXT MORNING, Hope sat in the lobby office and hit *send* on her response to the latest guest review. Her feet drummed on the floor—she loved positive reviews.

Next to her, Patti laughed. "From the smile on your face, it must have been another good one?"

Hope did her best to look demure, not smug. "They particularly mentioned how wonderful the staff was, especially Clark."

Patti nodded and thumbed through the mail. "Here, these are for you." She handed Hope a letter and a large padded envelope.

She opened the letter, a small smile rising at the bill from Alistair's office. This was an invoice she was happy to pay. His services weren't inexpensive, but she and Alex had gotten their money's worth. If she ever needed legal help in the future, she knew where to turn.

Next, Hope turned to the large envelope. "Probably another furniture catalog. Everyone wants to sell us something, even after the renovations." Hope ripped the tab and gasped as she tilted out the contents. The envelope fell to the floor as she gripped the magazine in both hands, the glossy pages trembling.

It was the latest issue of *Entrepreneur Today*, and she was staring at herself.

Patti noticed her expression. "What is it?"

"Come here."

Patti stood behind her and froze. "Oh, Hope. I can't believe it!" She clasped both hands over her mouth and laughed.

Underneath the broad magazine title, Hope stared straight at the camera. The photo was taken on the pier, and the sun was low enough to give the scene a golden hue. She stood in her gray business power suit with buttoned jacket and fitted skirt, wearing three-inch black pumps. Standing straight legged with arms crossed and facing the camera with a serious, yet confident expression, Hope could have ruled the world.

"Open it up!" Patti said, poking her in the shoulder. "Come on!"

On the first page of the article, a handwritten message was scrawled on a sticky note.

Hope—here it is, hot off the press. I wanted to get it to you right away. We're shipping another fifty copies by ground. It was great meeting you. Enjoy the article! Sandra

The piece was very complimentary, detailing everything they had talked about during the interview. It ended with the resort's success and that Hope was due to marry the dive manager shortly. Amy's photos were interspersed throughout. The final picture was of her and Alex standing together in their matching staff polos and smiling at the camera. Her left hand rested against his chest, her engagement ring sparkling.

"Oh my. You two are the most gorgeous couple." Patti lifted an arm over Hope's shoulders. "What an accomplishment! Lead article in a major magazine. Let me frame it and hang it on the wall in the lobby."

Hope snapped her head up. "No, Patti. I don't want to brag about this."

"It wouldn't be braggin'. Look at it as free publicity for the resort. You said that yourself, you know."

"The article, not some picture of me on the wall." Hope was uncomfortably aware of how Alex must have felt when she'd discussed hanging his article.

"Come on, just think about it."

"After the wedding, ok?"

"All right. Let's get you married first." Patti gave her a warm embrace before moving back to her desk. Hope stroked a finger down the magazine cover, convincing herself it was real.

CHAPTER 34

*E*arly-afternoon sunshine streamed through Hope's home office windows. She was trying to concentrate on financial reports, but kept getting distracted by what was in the closet. Tearing her gaze away from the closed door, she forced herself to focus. She was evaluating the new spa. The services were being very well received by guests and the facility was making a small profit. In addition to massage therapist Selena, Hope was thinking about hiring a body treatment and facial specialist. The hair station was finished, but she hadn't hired a stylist yet. Though from the comment cards, female guests wouldn't mind ending their spa session with a fancy new 'do.

"I'll deal with that after the wedding." Cruz lifted his head but laid it back down when she didn't have anything further to say.

Before she knew it, Hope was staring at the closet door once again. With a gleeful smile, she pushed back and padded over. She held her breath as she opened the door, even though she knew what was inside. A white plastic garment bag, with Coral Coast Bridal Shop printed in bright-pink loopy script, hung front and center on the rod. Coral's bells and cherubs adorned it.

Hope unzipped the bag to reveal her wedding dress, her

fingers trembling. The fabric was cool and smooth under her hand as she slowly drew it down the bodice.

The ceremony was only a few days away, and Sara and Kate's family were due to arrive the following day, on the ninth. Mike and Emma were coming the morning of the eleventh, after an unexpected work conflict delayed them. Steve was staying at the same resort in Christiansted he'd used on his previous trip, and she was happy he was coming.

Hope re-zipped the bag and turned her eye to the white shoebox on the floor. It contained a pair of pretty white flats with a rosette on the toe of each. Though Hope hadn't decided yet if she should just go barefoot, it was best to be prepared either way.

~

Late the next morning, Hope sat cross-legged on the porch couch with her laptop balanced on her knees. She was flipping between screens of current bookings and a spreadsheet she'd made to keep track of the next few days. She glanced at the deserted pier. Alex and Jack were both working that day.

A group of six divers were their final guests and leaving the following afternoon. The other divers that morning were two couples staying in a nearby condo and diving again tomorrow with Alex. She wished Jack were taking the group, but Alex wanted to work. But after that, they were closed until after the wedding.

Hope checked the St. Croix weather forecast yet again and wanted to applaud when it still showed nothing but perfect tropical weather. The news had briefly mentioned a storm in Florida, but that was far enough away not to affect them.

Best of all, Sara was due to arrive late that afternoon. Typical of her, she hadn't provided her flight number to track, promising to text it while on her layover. A distant drone of the dive boat approaching the pier distracted Hope.

Sara's ringtone sounded, and Hope picked up with a grin. "Are your ears burning? I was just thinking about you. I bet you're sitting in an airport bar somewhere."

"As a matter of fact, I am. Do you want the good news first or the bad news?"

"Sara, I do *not* need to hear the words *bad news* three days before my wedding."

"Good news it is. I made it to Miami! Yay me."

A lead weight plummeted into Hope's midsection. "Miami? Isn't there a big storm in Florida?"

"And that brings me to the bad news." Sara took an enormous breath and rushed through the words. "We were the last flight to land before they shut down the airport—no flights are coming in or out until tomorrow—don't freak out!"

Hope bolted upright, perching on the edge of the couch. "Oh no! I've been concentrating so much on the weather here that I never thought about how that storm might affect travel for you guys. Have you got another flight?"

"Yes. Relax, Hope. Everything's fine. I'm on a flight that leaves tomorrow morning and they're hopeful the airport will reopen by then."

"*Hopeful?*"

"Yes, isn't that nice of them? They're really being very helpful."

Hope rolled her eyes, her heart trying to burst out of her chest. "Doesn't anything ever faze you?"

"What would be the point of that? Besides, I'll still be getting there two days early. Plenty of time!"

"Sara, you're my maid of honor, and you're doing my hair and makeup. Goddammit, I haven't had a haircut in three months because I wanted you to do it!"

"I'll be there. Have a drink and dig your toes in the sand or something."

"Oh, stop trying to cheer me up. Do you at least have a hotel room for tonight?"

"I'll probably just crash here in the airport after I hang out in the bar for a while."

Hope rubbed her forehead. "Oh no, you won't. I'm not going to have you arriving here all strung out and exhausted. The last thing I need is you and Alex at each other's throats. There's a hotel in the airport there. I'll make a reservation and email it to you as soon as we get off the phone. I mean it, Sara. Get a good night's sleep."

"Fine. Has anyone ever told you you're bossy?"

"Yes. I need to make this reservation right away. Before the hotel books up. Keep me updated, ok?"

Within minutes, Hope had a room booked and charged to her credit card. She sent the confirmation to Sara, then scrolled through her emails. Unlike her sister, Kate had sent a copy of her family's flight itinerary to both Hope and Alex. Her stomach plunged further. They were also connecting through Miami. She drew her gaze back to the dive boat and the distant figures of Alex and Jack walking up the dock together.

"It's time for reinforcements. Come on, Cruz."

The dog's nails clicked on the wooden planks as he walked next to her down the pier. Since chasing off Wayne, Cruz had claimed the pier as his own little kingdom. Fortunately, he was a benevolent ruler and let Zach pet him freely now, though he still shied away from the guests.

Some distance away, Alex and Jack faced each other. Alex was discussing marine life at the dive site they had visited, giving Jack tips on what to point out to his groups. She stopped in front of him. "We've got a problem. Both Sara and Kate are connecting through Miami and the storm has shut down the airport. I just heard from Sara, and she's booked on another flight tomorrow morning, assuming the airport reopens. But I don't have Kate's phone number to get in touch, and I'm sure they're stuck too. We need to know what's going on with them. Come on—let's hurry."

Alex raised his sunglasses on his head and placed both hands on Hope's shoulders. "Deep breaths, Boss Lady. Calm down."

She glared at him. "Hasn't anyone told you the *last* thing you should say to an upset woman is *calm down?*"

Alex grinned. "Would you rather I screamed and jumped into the ocean? We've got three days. It'll be fine."

"I'll just finish unloading the boat," Jack said, ducking his head as he turned away.

"Hold on a second, Jack." Hope smiled at him, making a determined effort to relax. "Is there any way you could take the dive group tomorrow? I could really use Alex."

"Sure, be happy to," Jack said as Alex straightened.

"Stand down, Alex," she said. "I'm pulling rank on you."

"Yes, ma'am." A lazy smile spread across his face. "I'd hate to see you get even more flustered."

"Now can I go unload the boat?"

"Of course," Hope said after shooting Alex an appraising look. "Thanks for all your help, Jack. I promise things aren't always this hectic around here."

"No problem. I can handle this kind of hectic. Hope everyone gets here ok." Jack tossed her an easy smile and made his way back to *Surface Interval*.

She shifted her attention back to Alex. "I don't think you're appreciating the seriousness of this."

He drew her into his arms, and Hope melted against him. "I understand just fine, baby. I also understand the only two people absolutely necessary for this are standing here right now."

As usual, he talked her out of her funk. "I think you could make the argument that Tommy's pretty necessary too. I intend to make an honest man of you, Mr. Monroe."

Alex steered her up the pier, taking her hand. "Honest? Ouch."

She smiled, tightening her grip. "It was a turn of phrase. Maybe you prefer the one about the cow and the milk?"

"Definitely not." He paused. "It was never my intention to just set up house, you know. I've known for a while now I'd ask you to marry me. But I'm sorry I wasn't more open about it. I never meant to cause doubts for you."

She shook her head. "I was so afraid this was all going to fall apart. When I saw those words on your dive slate, I couldn't believe it. That it was happening to *me*."

"Well, please don't ask me to repeat it—I don't plan on proposing ever again. Once was enough."

Hope stopped. "What do you mean? You've been *married*."

He shrugged with a slight smile. "I told you, my first marriage was very spur of the moment, not to mention ill-advised. We just talked about it and decided to do it. You're the only woman I've ever asked to marry me."

"Oh." She didn't know why that made her so happy, but it did. "You might be glad to know you're the only man who's ever proposed to me. And that I said yes to."

A gleam formed in his eye. "I wasn't sure for a while. The *saying yes* part."

"You're not going to let that go, are you?"

He took her in his arms and warmth flooded through her body as his lips brushed hers. "I don't plan on letting any part of this go." As he deepened the kiss, Cruz dropped a stick on his feet. Alex looked down as he wagged his tail and hopped his front feet up and down. "Really? Your timing is lousy, dog."

"Come on, we've got other things to concentrate on, anyway."

"I'll call Katie as soon as we get in the house." He threw the stick into the shallows, and Cruz chased after it, happy to cool off.

"Are you ever going to call her Kate, like she wants?"

"Hell, no." Alex grinned. "It irritates her way too much when I call her Katie. That's priceless."

Hope opened two beers and set one in front of Alex as he talked to Kate. "I'm glad you guys at least made it to Miami. Do you have a rescheduled flight yet?" He darted his eyes to Hope before returning them to the kitchen island. "That's good. We'll just keep an eye on things. Oh. Hope wants me to make sure you have a hotel there in Miami." He paused, listening. "Ok, good. Sounds like you guys are set. Keep us updated, ok?" He hung up.

"How bad is it?"

Alex spoke with exaggerated calmness. "Could be worse, for sure. Tomorrow's flight was full. They're confirmed on a flight to St. Croix on the eleventh."

"That's the day before the ceremony!"

"Yes, and it's plenty of time. Mike and Emma are coming that day too. And we're not getting married until sunset, anyway. They could all come in on the twelfth and still make it on time."

"Don't even say that." Hope took a big drink of beer as Alex texted. "Getting an update on Mike?"

"Yes." Alex cupped her face. "It's going to be fine. You'll see."

"I know. I never thought I'd be a nervous bride." Hope heaved a big sigh, shaking out her hands. "Time to pull it together. There's nothing more we can do, anyway."

"That's my girl." His text tone sounded. "They're connecting through Charlotte, and the weather looks fine. They'll also be here on the eleventh in the early afternoon. They're renting a car, so they'll just drive themselves here."

"Well, at least that's one group we don't have to worry about." Hope cracked a playful grin. "So, have you finally decided on what you're wearing?"

"Not completely. Mike and I have discussed it and we'll make the final decision after he gets here." Alex laughed. "Probably an hour before the ceremony." He lifted a brow. "I'm more curious what you'll be wearing."

"A dress. That's all you need to know."

CHAPTER 35

By noon the next day, Hope was regretting her decision to invite family and not just marry Alex alone on the beach. Her morning had started with a text from Sara saying Miami airport was open again and her flight was scheduled to take off at 9:00 a.m. She texted a half hour later—the flight was now delayed until 11:00. Further texts informed Hope of each successive delay. The newest departure time was now 1:20 p.m.

Guess I can't get mad at her for not updating me.

The worst part was the certainty that Hope was far more stressed about the situation than Sara. At this moment, she was probably sitting in a bar having several conversations at once with fellow stranded travelers.

Alex had contacted Steve, but the inclement weather hadn't affected his plans. He was due to arrive the morning before the ceremony and was staying in Christiansted. Hope was pleased he was attending, but recognized it might be awkward for him. *What more proof could he need that Half Moon Bay Resort has moved on without him?*

Alex had managed to talk her into letting him work after all, complaining there wasn't anything for him to do. And Hope couldn't argue the logic, especially since his idea was to drive so he could give Tommy an extra day off to prepare for the ceremony. But Hope wasn't fooled for a minute. He just wanted to be out on the water.

As she made her way to the lobby, the resort was silent. The final group of guests had just departed and now the three southernmost bungalows were being prepared for Sara, Kate's family, and Mike and Emma. Cruz darted ahead, chasing a hermit crab who disappeared into the sand. The dog frantically dug after it but came up empty and huffing. Hope kept walking and he bounded to her side again. They skirted the infinity pool, and Cruz cautiously lapped from the waterfall edge. After a quick trip to the kitchen, he was waiting for her outside and Hope smiled, applauding his courage. He kept his nose to the ground, snuffling at all the delicious scents. "See what you've been missing? You probably could have gotten all kinds of treats if you'd ventured down here before now."

Hope crossed the empty lobby as Cruz hesitated at the threshold. But soon his feet clicked on the tile floor as he trotted after her. Martine was coming back part time in a couple weeks, and Hope was keeping Corrine on full-time so they could expand the front-desk hours into the evening. Patti sat behind her desk and Hope was taking a breath to speak when her text tone pinged.

Sara: I'm on the plane! We're taking off in fifteen minutes!
Hope: Great! I'll be there to pick you up.

"I hope that was good news?" Patti asked.

"Yes! At long last, Sara's on her way." Hope leaned against the doorway. "I just spoke with Gerold, and he has everything needed for the dinner and cake. So everything's humming on that end. Can I help you with anything?"

"All's in order here. The flowers will be ready the mornin' of the twelfth. Same with the chairs and decorations for the ceremony." She pointed to Hope. "You just stop worryin'. Patti's takin' care of all of it. I'm also preparin' one of the northern bungalows for your weddin' night."

Hope laughed, running a hand through her hair. "I've been so consumed by the ceremony and dinner afterwards, I hadn't even thought about that. Thanks, Patti."

"Of course." Patti checked her watch. "I need to run. I'm off for the next two days, but I'll be back with the flowers on the twelfth. Don't hesitate to call if you need anythin'." She nodded at Cruz as she passed through the doorway, and he responded with a happy wag.

～

The sun was angling toward the western horizon when Hope drove her Jeep to the airport. Alex sat in the passenger seat, and thoughts of the auction had preoccupied her all afternoon. "Should we mention the treasure and auction to our families when they're here?"

Alex sighed. "With everything going on, I haven't really thought about it. I'm just glad the money got deposited into our account like it was supposed to. Besides, we don't know what *we* want to do with it yet."

"I know. It's a pretty major subject. Let's just table it for now. I want the focus to be on our wedding. The rest will make a pretty terrific surprise for them later."

Inside the terminal, Hope craned her head, trying to see through the crowd of people exiting the arrivals area. She turned to Alex. "Can you see her? You're taller."

"No one's running and screaming to get away, so she must still be on the plane." He answered Hope's glare with a grin.

"She's going to be your sister-in-law, whether you like it or not. Might as well get used to being nice to her."

"You might give her the same advice. I've always been nice to her."

"You used to hunt terrorists for a living. And you're scared of my little sister?'

"She's much more frightening. There—I see her."

Hope grabbed his arm to steady herself and stood on her tiptoes, then spied her sister walking toward them. Bouncing up and down, Hope gripped Alex's arm tighter. Sara wore a blue tie-dyed dress that swept nearly to the ground, swishing around her as she walked. Her long brown hair was beautifully curled, and her lush figure filled out the dress perfectly. A garment bag was draped over one arm. Seeing Hope, she brightened, and the two sisters ran toward each other. They hugged as Hope tried to avoid Sara's gigantic hoop earrings. "You finally made it! Welcome back."

"Only a day late, and my sister set me up in style. Hello there." Sara embraced Alex.

"Good to see you again," Alex said.

Sara stepped back, frowning as she held his arms in both hands. "I don't remember you being this tall. Have you grown in the past year?"

"Grown, yes. Gotten taller, no."

"Well, I suppose you come in handy whenever Hope needs something on the top shelf."

Alex swooped to Hope. "Ha! Did you hear that? She just admitted I'm useful."

"Don't let it go to your head," Sara said. "I'm just jet-lagged. I'll snap out of it soon."

"Do you have checked luggage?" Hope asked.

"God, I hope so. We'll see if it shows up with the delayed flight. I brought my whole kit with me. Only the best for my sister on her wedding day." She took Hope's arm and began walking toward the baggage claim, absently handing Alex her garment bag. "Come on. You can carry my bags."

Hope cast Alex a big smile as he glared at her, then dutifully followed the two sisters to the baggage carousel. Fingers crossed, Hope breathed a sigh of relief when Sara's suitcase and hair/makeup case both appeared. Sara carried the kit herself and Alex took her suitcase.

He held the passenger door open for Sara, but she refused, getting in the back seat. "Oh, no. I'm not falling for that. You'd be kicking my seat the whole way and I just had several hours of that. We'll all be much more comfortable this way. However, I appreciate the gallant gesture."

Alex inclined his head, then got in front and soon they were headed back to the resort.

Hope had let her hair air dry, and it fell past her shoulders as Sara ran a hand through it. "You really do need a cut, but I can work with this. The sun's given it beautiful highlights. It's pretty dry, though. Do you even use that conditioner I sent you?"

"Sometimes," Hope lied. "I have a resort to run, you know."

Sara turned her practiced eye to Alex. "Your hair looks ok."

"Just got it cut a couple days ago. I was afraid if I let you do it, I'd end up with a shaved head."

Hope pulled off the side of the sand road between the resort and their house and pointed to the wooden structure behind a screen of vegetation. "You have your own private bungalow this time."

"Thank goodness. The last thing I need is the two of you keeping me awake all night."

Hope unlocked the door to the Ixora bungalow and ushered her sister through first. Sara took a few steps before stopping in the middle of the room. She swept her gaze around the white-painted walls. Robert's photographs hung on three of them.

"Wow. This is incredible, Hope. You can keep your guest room—I'll stay here from now on."

Alex laid the garment bag on the bed and set the suitcase on the wooden floor, then returned to stand behind Hope, sliding his arms around her waist and pulling her back against him. "Hope did all the designs herself, then terrorized the construction crew until everything was perfect."

"You always have had good taste, Hope." Sara looked at them with a small smile. "And, as much as it pains me to say this, you two are pretty adorable together. So, what's the plan, Hope? I don't even need to ask if you have one. I'm expecting multiple spreadsheets."

"Today is just relaxing. Tomorrow, Alex's sister and her family come in, as well as his friend Mike and his wife. I thought you could cut my hair tomorrow morning. Then we can all do something in the afternoon. You want to go snorkeling?"

"As long as Alex doesn't throw an octopus at me."

"No promises." Alex grinned at her and squeezed Hope's shoulders. "Afternoon should work. The condo divers begged for one last trip so Jack and Tommy are taking them out again tomorrow morning, but the boat will be free in the afternoon."

"That works." Hope leaned her head against Alex's chest as she glanced at Sara. "I'll spend tomorrow night with you here."

"What?" Alex pulled his arms away and stepped aside so he could look at her.

"We're not spending the night before the wedding together, Alex."

He started laughing. "Um, did you suddenly develop amnesia or something? We've been living together for over a year now."

"Doesn't matter. After dinner tomorrow night, you won't see me again until the ceremony."

Hope couldn't hide a smile as he stood there with one hand parked on his hip, his brows drawn. Then he dropped his shoulders. "What if I miss you?"

"That's the idea." Their gazes held and they moved toward each other like magnets. A tingle spread through Hope's body as they brushed lips.

"Ok! Enough of that. Where's Clark?" Sara breezed past them and headed for the bar.

CHAPTER 36

Alex cut through the water like a blade. Hope had decided on a treadmill run this morning, so he was on his own for a swim. He increased his arm turnover, a slight smile rising as the sand slipped by faster beneath him. Swimming was an important aspect of maintaining his injured hip, and fortunately, it had always been one of his favorite activities. *How many times have I swum this exact route? While just existing in limbo?*

Not anymore.

Alex turned and headed back to the pier, keeping his eyes open but not wearing goggles. He enjoyed the slight stinging of the saltwater in his open eyes. He moved faster until he reached top speed, churning the water around him into a froth and loving every moment.

While toweling off on the dock, he glanced up the pier. Sara was headed toward him, a cup of coffee in one hand.

"Sleep well?" Alex asked.

"Like a rock. It was mostly relief, knowing I made it in plenty of time."

"Hope would have moved heaven and earth to make sure you got here."

Sara sat next to him on the wooden bench. "So would've I. It wasn't a coincidence I was on the first flight out of Miami." She shaded her forehead with her hand, gazing at the placid ocean to the north. "Your apartment roof is out there somewhere?"

He raised his arm. "Right about where I'm pointing. Now it's got a new life as a coral nursery."

"Hope told me. That sounds interesting. Maybe you can show me a video sometime."

"Or maybe you can learn to dive and see it firsthand."

She slid her gaze to his. "Take it easy, there. Just because you won over one Collins sister doesn't mean we'll both become fish people."

They both smiled, and Sara's attention drifted toward the house, visible in the distance. "I'm a pretty free spirit, and don't really care much about getting married. But Hope has always wanted the happily-ever-after. She just wouldn't ever let herself fall hard enough for it to happen. I'm glad it finally did."

"She's everything to me, you know."

"I do. When I came down here to visit, she was in full denial about you. She looked at you like you were on the dinner menu." Sara snorted. "And you were pretty obvious about it too. But she was so scared of being hurt again. I was really happy when she told me you two finally got together."

"We both had our reasons for keeping apart."

Sara nodded. "I knew this was different when Hope told you about Caleb. It scared me too, because if you hurt her, I think it would destroy her."

She paused, staring at the morning's golden shimmer on the ocean. "I'm sorry for what you went through as a SEAL, but I think Hope's the one to help you. She knows a lot about facing things you'd rather bury, especially since she met you. But mostly, I know you're the right one for her because she finally took that leap of faith—for you." She gave him a crooked smile. "I guess what I'm trying to say is, I'm glad you're going to be my brother-in-law."

Alex was floored. He'd never had a serious conversation with Sara before. "Thanks. It means a lot to hear you say that. Hope brought me back from the brink. I'm not sure she'll ever understand what she means to me."

"I think she does." Sara stood. "I'd better get back to my bungalow. Judging from Hope's hair yesterday, I'll need to bring out my heavy artillery, so I better start preparing. See you later."

She'd started to turn away when Alex called to her, "Thanks, Sara."

She smiled over her shoulder. "Don't let it go to your head. I'll still keep you on your toes, don't worry."

∽

JUST AFTER NOON, Alex showed Mike and Emma to their bungalow. "You're stuck between Katie's family and Hope's sister, but the bungalows are spaced pretty far apart. I don't think you'll hear any noise." Emma was walking around the bungalow, running a finger over the furniture and rubbing her fingers. Alex doubted she'd find any dust.

Mike scowled at her. "Would you relax? The place looks pretty nice to me."

"Very nice," Emma said, then turned to Alex. "I'm looking forward to spending some time with you and Hope. Last visit, I wanted to make sure you and Mike had a chance to reconnect. He's told me a lot about you."

"Uh-oh," Alex said with a grin. "That doesn't sound good."

"Don't worry," Mike said. "I lied. I said you were a solid, upstanding guy. So, did Kate finally make it here?"

"Yeah. She and her family got delayed several times, but arrived a short time ago. They're at the pool now. Let's go." They walked up the beach, the gentle breeze stirring the row of palm trees around them.

"Where's Hope?" Emma asked.

"Getting her hair cut."

Jason and Monica laughed as they played in the water, and it brought a smile to Alex's face. After the delays, his nephew and niece couldn't wait to get to the pool. Both had snorkels and masks and were diving for objects with their father, Dave. Katie sat on the edge, dangling her legs in the water.

"Look who the cat dragged in," Alex said by way of introduction.

Katie's face exploded into a smile, and she vaulted to her feet. "Mike! How are you?" They embraced as Alex stood back, warmth spreading through him at this little reunion.

"Been a few years, huh?" Mike said. "You look good. So does the family."

"Thanks. Never a dull moment, that's for sure."

Mike peeled off his shirt and jumped in, Katie following. Alex walked over to grab towels from the rack, and Emma followed him. "Thanks for inviting us," she said. "You can't imagine what it meant to Mike when you asked him to be your best man."

"When Hope and I talked about it, Mike was the only guy I wanted."

"I didn't know Mike . . . before. When he was a SEAL. We've only known each other a few years. But he's always talked like you were his long-lost brother."

"We are brothers. Closer, maybe. At least I hope we will be again."

A distant motor indicated the dive boat was coming back. He grabbed several towels and set them on a lounger near the swimmers. "I'm heading down to the pier. The morning trip's coming back."

"Hold up," Mike said. "I'll come with you."

"Me too!" Jason said. "I want to see the boat again."

Soon, the entire contingent was walking down the pier. Alex nodded as the divers passed them. "You guys have a good morning?"

"Great dives," a man answered. "We're already planning our return trip. We're going to try to get in here next time."

They continued to *Surface Interval*. Tommy and Jack couldn't be thrilled about a crowd milling around while they tried to unload the boat, but these weren't normal circumstances.

Tommy shook Katie's hand. "Nice to see you again. Good flight?"

"No," she said with a laugh. "We got delayed two days. But we're here now—that's what counts."

Alex pulled Tommy aside. "You need anything? For the ceremony?"

"No, don't think so. Hope gave me some suggestions for remarks and a copy of your vows. I think I'm ready."

He clapped Tommy's shoulder. "Thanks, man."

Alex was continuing to the stern when he stopped short. Hope and Sara were descending the stairs from the spa, headed toward the boat. Hope wore a light floral sundress, and he had no idea what Sara had done to her hair, but it flowed to her shoulders in a thick, glossy mane. His breath caught just looking at her—she was stunning. Hope stepped aboard, all smiles as she hugged and greeted everyone. Poor Jack had to dodge everyone as he unloaded BCDs.

Alex moved behind Hope, whispering in her ear. "You look amazing. Did you have fun?"

"Oh, yes. And Sara even gave me a French manicure."

Alex frowned. "That definitely sounds like something I should be giving you."

Hope waved her fingers in his face, showing off the white tips. "Sorry to disappoint you. See for yourself."

He inspected her fingernails, unimpressed, before breaking into a smile. "My idea's much better."

"Good thing we have a wedding night coming up then."

"Comin' through, comin' through," Tommy called as he came between them, carrying a BCD on each shoulder, with Jack right behind.

"Let's move onto the dock and give these guys some room to work," Alex said, and Jack gave him a grateful nod.

After stepping off, Alex pulled Mike and Emma aside as Hope introduced Sara to Katie's family. "Hope and I are thinking about all of us going snorkeling this afternoon. You guys interested?" They were, and the three of them were discussing the particulars as Jack lifted a five-gallon water bucket used for rinsing cameras, raising it onto one shoulder.

He stepped off the boat and tripped.

Time slowed, and Jack appeared to move in slow motion as the entire five gallons of water splashed on top of Sara, drenching her from head to foot.

All conversation ceased.

Alex's first impulse was to laugh, but his protective instincts took over and he was in motion before even knowing it. He grabbed Jack's arm and wrenched him back several steps. "Jack! What the hell?"

Sara sputtered as she dripped on the deck, eyes aflame at their new divemaster.

Jack was mortified—his face was completely slack, and his big eyes were even larger. "I'm so sorry, miss! I tripped. Are you all right?"

Alex took another look at Sara standing like a drowned rat, and laughter lurked ever closer to the surface. He glanced at Hope, who fortunately was completely dry. She was biting the inside of her cheek. Her eyes met his and that was all it took.

Both of them started laughing.

Sara shot a dirty look at Hope, then Alex. Finally, she glowered at Jack before assuming a regal, chin-up expression. "I'm fine. Just getting an early start on the snorkeling."

She turned and flipped her long, sopping brown hair over her shoulder, hitting Jack in the face with it as she strolled off, head held high.

"I'd better go smooth things over," Hope said, scurrying after Sara.

Jack picked up the empty bucket and hurried up the pier, his eyes glued to the decking. Alex followed at a more sedate pace. When he reached the dive shop, Jack was dunking BCDs and his face was crimson.

"I'm really sorry about that. She's family of yours?"

"About to be. She's Hope's sister." He grinned. "Her *very close* sister."

Jack paused, groaning. "Am I about to get fired?"

Alex leaned against the wall of the building and tried not to laugh. "Actually, you just did me a huge favor. Now I look great by comparison. It's probably a good thing you're off for a couple days. With any luck, Hurricane Sara might blow out of town before you come back to work."

∽

A CONTENTED HUM of conversation filled a private section of the restaurant, and Hope gazed around. She and Clark had moved additional pots of the red and yellow bougainvillea into the room, giving it extra color, and soft candles glowed on the table. She snuck a sideways glance at Sara, but her sister—and her hair—had fully recovered from their dunking. The entire wedding party was present and full of happy memories after their snorkeling adventure earlier that afternoon.

Mike and Emma had boarded the boat a few minutes late, and Alex wasted no time letting Mike know about it. Standing on the elevated bridge, Alex put an arm around twelve-year-old Jason's shoulders. "Jason's my first mate today and is going to throw the lines."

"Hey!" Mike said. "I thought I was your first mate."

Alex glared at him over his sunglasses. "You were late. You've been demoted."

"Tough crowd."

With a grin, Jason threw the lines onto the boat and climbed back up the ladder as Alex eased the boat away. He let the boy throw the throttle forward and the boat surged ahead.

Sara sat next to Kate, and Hope joined them. Kate turned to Hope. "Are you nervous about tomorrow?"

"Not yet. I'm sure the nerves will crop up eventually."

"I was a wreck before my wedding. We had three hundred people there. Your idea is much better."

"Was Alex there?"

"Oh, yes." Kate threw a fond smirk up at the wheelhouse. "Throwing that terrifying smile at Dave every chance he could."

"I've seen that smile a time or two. It is rather frightening."

"God help any man who threatens you."

A little late for that . . . What Hope called Alex's sharky smile was nowhere to be seen when Wayne had threatened her. That smile was reserved for when Alex *didn't* perceive a serious threat.

Soon they pulled into a broad, shallow bay, and the coral reef rippled through the clear water. "Hope," Alex called. "Can you come up here and take over the boat while I moor us?"

"Monroe, you're a real jerk, you know that?" Mike glared, both hands on his hips.

He and Jason descended the ladder as he glanced at Mike. "You are well aware of my feelings about being late. You're just lucky I've mellowed over the years. C'mon, Jason. You can throw me the mooring line."

Alex had taken the group to a secluded section of reef that was protected and perfect for the kids. Hope had given Jason and

Monica inexpensive underwater cameras and they pestered Alex the whole time to identify every fish they saw.

It had been a perfect afternoon.

Now, Hope winked at Alex as they paused for a drink. She couldn't help thinking that by this time tomorrow, the same group of people would once again be gathered for dinner.

But her life would be very different.

CHAPTER 37

*H*ope awoke, instantly aware something was different. The mystery was solved when she opened her eyes to the open room of a guest bungalow instead of her bedroom. Her next thought followed immediately.

This is my wedding day.

Dressed in one of Alex's T-shirts and sleep shorts, she got up and wrapped herself in a terrycloth resort robe. Smiling at the fluffy indulgence, she started a cup of coffee as the bungalow phone's orange message light blinked in the dim room. Hope picked up the receiver and pressed the lighted button.

"Good mornin', you two!" Patti's voice said. "On your porch you'll find a breakfast basket. When you're finished, just put it back out front. Press zero, and someone will come pick it up. And Sara, you keep Hope inside. We don't want the bride and groom seein' each other before this evenin', now do we? Don't worry, I've given Mike and Emma the same advice, since Alex is gettin' ready with them."

Hope laughed softly as she hung up.

"Please tell me that wasn't your betrothed on the phone, whispering sweet nothings. I might have to throw up." Sara yawned and threw a leg outside the covers.

"No. It was Patti telling us there's breakfast on the porch."

"Oh. That's much better."

Sara put on her own robe and made herself coffee while Hope opened the front door. She retrieved a picnic basket and metal ice bucket containing a bottle of champagne and a carafe of orange juice. Hope brought them inside to the coffee table, opening the basket to reveal two crystal champagne flutes. Pastries, a plastic-wrapped bowl of fresh fruit, yogurt, and granola were also carefully nestled inside.

"Oh, mimosas!" Sara popped the cork, sending a rueful glance Hope's way. "I know you hate champagne corks." She mixed the mimosas and handed Hope one. "To happy endings, big sister."

Tears flooded Hope's eyes as she took a sip. "This is really happening, isn't it? I'm really getting married tonight?"

"You are absolutely getting married tonight. If Alex runs, I'll personally hunt him down and drag him back by his balls. Though if I have to do that, he might not be of much use on your wedding night."

Hope laughed and wrapped her arm around Sara's shoulders. "If there's one thing I'm confident of, it's that Alex won't run."

"I think he's a good match for you."

"He's the perfect match for me. That's what's so amazing about it. With my history, I need a man I know will keep me safe. And more than anything, I need to know he would never hurt me. And I've found all of that."

She gave a bark of incredulous laughter. "In a man who can be deadly when the situation calls for it. I've seen that with my own eyes. Yet I feel completely safe with him. You wouldn't believe how I've laid into him at times, and he's gotten pissed at me too. But he'd never cross the line and I *know* that."

"As long as he makes you happy, I'm happy. But make no mistake, if he ever screws up, he's going to answer to me."

Hope gave her a smile. "He knows. There isn't much that scares Alex. But you should be proud. You're one of the few things on that list, sis."

"Glad to know I'm not losing my touch." She held up her mimosa in a toast. "Is Cruz taken care of tonight?"

"Yes. He likes to sleep in a bed on the corner of the porch, and Patti will feed him this afternoon before the ceremony."

"You know his full story now. And you were right about Creepy Guy."

Hope shook her head. "That's a good name for him. I totally understand why Cruz ran away. I never want to see the asshole again, either. He's into real estate, though, and has property on the island, so I wouldn't be surprised if we come across him sooner or later. But I'm not letting Cruz anywhere near him."

"Cruz is someone else who found his home here."

"You're right, he is. Half Moon Bay is a great place for a new start."

~

ANOTHER MAGIC BASKET appeared on the porch at lunchtime, this time accompanied by soft drinks and bottled water. Sara laughed. "Apparently they don't want the sisters showing up at the wedding hammered."

"Wouldn't look too good to have the bride lurching drunkenly down the aisle."

Sara got busy unpacking the basket. "Ok. We have a very important topic to discuss."

"I don't know how to tell you this, but I'm not a virgin."

Sara rolled her eyes. "I'm talking about your hair. Do you want it up or down?"

Hope crossed the room to stand in front of the full-length mirror that had mysteriously appeared in Sara's bungalow. Hope wasn't sure where it had come from, but her money was on Patti.

Alex hadn't made any requests about her hair, just her tattoo, so this was her decision. "Up. If nothing else, that will be cooler."

"My sister, the incurable romantic. Lets her decision on *wedding-day hair* be determined by air temperature. Lucky for you, updos are my specialty. Even if you'd said you wanted it down, I wouldn't have listened."

"Of course you wouldn't. What did you think of my new hair station in the spa?"

"Very professional. Two thumbs-up, for sure." Sara sighed. "Since the new owner took over, the salon where I work has become a disaster. My clients are starting to desert me."

Hope tried to sound casual. "You know, I happen to have an opening for a stylist."

"Oh, no you don't. This island isn't big enough for me. Besides, you can't have enough work here for a full-time stylist."

You might not need to work full time for much longer . . . "With your skills, word would get around in no time. You'd have to turn people away."

"Well, I'm honored you have such faith in me."

They settled on a couch and ate their lunch of cold chicken and Caribbean potato salad. Gerold's touch was apparent throughout the meal.

Finally, Sara clapped her hands. "Let's get this show on the road. You can have first shower."

Hope wiped the foggy mirror, revealing herself. She was dressed in sheer white lace panties and matching strapless bra. There was no need for the pushup variety. For a very brief time, she had entertained the idea of garters and white stockings, but the thought of that in the tropical heat had changed her mind in a hurry.

She rewrapped herself in the robe and exited the bathroom. "Ok, boss. What's next?"

"I'll blow-dry your hair, then shower myself. I don't want your hair to air dry and do something ridiculous. We don't have time for that." She pointed to the makeshift salon she had created out of the bungalow desk. "Sit down, missy. Let's get to work."

∼

SEVERAL HOURS LATER, Hope and Sara stood side by side in front of the full-length mirror. Sara was dressed in a pale-blue floor-length strapless gown. It was elegant and understated, wrapping around her ample curves, the perfect maid of honor dress. Her hair was up and styled with artfully placed ringlets. Hope had been amazed, watching Sara arrange her own hair in the mirror. She truly was an artist.

The only monkey wrench in the proceedings had come just as Sara was finishing her hair. The power failed. With her own hair already arranged, Hope had quickly opened the windows. "Usually they don't last too long, but you never know."

Sara stared at the curling iron in her hand. "Good thing it didn't happen an hour ago. I don't need power for makeup. But what if it stays off all night?"

"The kitchen runs on backup generators, so dinner will be fine, and we can light candles for the table. Alex and I don't need light for what comes later." She and Sara exchanged grins. "It kind of adds to the adventure. As long as we don't start sweating like pigs, anyway. But the worst of the heat is over. I think we'll be fine."

NOW, the power was still out. But with the windows open, the bungalow temperature had remained comfortable. Hope met Sara's eyes in the mirror. "The Collins sisters look pretty good, don't we?"

Sara stood slack-jawed, staring at her sister in the mirror. "Oh,

Hope. You look incredible. Alex is going to fall over in the sand when he sees you."

Hope turned her attention to her own reflection. Her hair was up in a similar fashion to her sister's, though more ornate. Sara had accented her sun-kissed highlights beautifully by adding scattered tiny pearls throughout Hope's hair. They matched perfectly with her dress.

Hope slowly drew her gaze downward.

Her wedding dress was white silk, with a tightly fitted strapless bodice that showed ample cleavage, but not too much. The torso clung tightly before falling in a loose drape from her hips to her feet, flowing as she walked.

Its crowning glory was the swirling pattern of embroidered pearls. They were sewn from underneath her breasts to where the silk flared over her hips. Several lines oscillated around the torso of the dress, and the pearl embellishment was subtly reminiscent of ocean waves.

Hope had loved it from first sight.

The dress was the essence of classic beauty, simple and yet completely timeless. She turned slightly in front of the mirror. The turquoise and yellow colors of her tattoo, a chrysalis becoming a butterfly, were on full display. The gown fit her like a glove. Coral had known her business when she altered it.

Hope exhaled an awed sigh. "Wow."

"That, dear sister, is an understatement," Sara breathed. Then she shook her head, snapping herself out of it. "What is Alex wearing, anyway?"

Hope laughed, lifting her hand to her mouth. "I have no idea. I helped him with a selection of shirts, and last I heard, he had decided on dressy shorts. He has built up a huge collection of shirts to pick from."

"Well, he'll look pretty stupid if he shows up in a staff shirt and board shorts."

"I informed him board shorts were off the table."

"That's a relief."

A glance at the clock informed Hope they were less than thirty minutes away, and butterflies had begun to flit around her stomach.

"Are your shoes in that box?" Sara asked, pointing to the floor.

"Yes. I bought a pair of flats. I didn't want to wobble through the sand in heels, but I'm leaning towards going barefoot. Alex is going to tower above me no matter what, so I might as well be comfortable."

"If you're going barefoot, so am I."

"Deal."

Sara grasped Hope's face, tilting it back and forth.

"What?"

"Just making sure you don't need a touch-up. It looks fine."

Hope returned to the mirror, confirming Sara had done a wonderful job. Hope had told her she wanted to look beautiful, not made-up, and her sister had delivered, deftly applying subtle tones to her eyes and cheeks. A soft, pinkish-red color graced her lips—smear proof, of course.

Hope opened the small refrigerator to check on the bouquets, their fragrant scent wafting into the room. They were similar but Hope's was much larger, a burst of stargazer lilies and white roses with baby's breath interspersed between. She relaxed after verifying they were still fresh and shut the door, conserving the coolant.

Then the air-conditioning unit whirred to life as the ceiling fan and lights came back on. Sara grabbed Hope by the shoulders and steered her to the unit near the corner. "Here. Stand in front of this and stay cool until it's time. I don't want my makeup running all over your face."

"Technically, it's my makeup now."

"Don't argue with me."

They swayed before the cool draft, and before they knew it,

there was a knock at the door. Hope and Sara exchanged a wide-eyed look, and Sara rushed to the door.

Patti entered and smiled at Sara. "You look beautiful, dear. It's time. You'll go first, then I'll come back for Hope. Where is she?"

"Right here, Patti," Hope said from the corner.

She turned, inhaling deeply as her gaze traveled from Hope's head to her feet, then up again. Her eyes brimmed with tears as she held both hands out to Hope, and they squeezed tightly. Patti closed her eyes briefly, tightening her jaw as she fought back emotion. "Oh, child. What a vision you are. Just perfect."

Hope swallowed the lump in her throat.

Patti reached up and stroked Hope's cheek before turning and draping her arm around Sara. "Let's get goin', shall we?" Just before she shut the door, Patti threw back over her shoulder, "I'll be right back for you, child."

CHAPTER 38

Hope gave Patti a final embrace, then her wedding coordinator hurried ahead to take her own seat, leaving Hope by herself on the sand. With the sun nearing the horizon, the sky was painted in a kaleidoscope of red, orange, and pink. The slightest hint of a breeze caressed Hope's face as she stepped forward, the silky powder warm under her bare feet. The only sound was soft waves caressing the shore. She and Alex had decided against music, since nothing could improve upon the natural setting where they chose to say their vows.

Hope approached the small assemblage.

A few orderly rows of white chairs were lined up with an aisle in the middle. Bouquets of stargazer lilies accented with white roses graced each row, complementing the arrangement she clasped in both hands. Robert crouched nearby, moving his camera up and down as the shutter clicked.

Hope soaked it in, trying to memorize every detail, then continued into the aisle. The sand before her was adorned with scattered red rose petals. Finally, she took a deep breath, and lifted her gaze to the front of the lane.

And stopped dead.

At first, she couldn't comprehend the vision her eyes beheld. It was Alex, yet no Alex she had ever seen.

He stood ramrod-straight at the head of the aisle, resplendent in his Navy dress white uniform, and brighter than the sun behind him.

Hope gripped her bouquet tighter, emotion trying to overcome her. Sheer astonishment weakened her knees as she took him in, from the black-and-white peaked cap on his head to his fitted coat. His left breast was positively covered in medals, with additional ribbon bars on his right. Even from where she stood, there was no mistaking the inner top medal he wore in the most prominent position.

His Navy Cross, and his Purple Heart hung next to it.

White dress pants and shoes completed the sight. Where others might have looked stiff and uncomfortable, instead Alex was completely at home, as if the uniform were an extension of him. Hope blinked away tears and her breast swelled as she moved her gaze up to meet his eyes. The look in them staggered her.

He looked upon her with pride, indelible love, and something approaching complete awe.

She was vaguely aware of Mike standing behind him, dressed in a Navy dress blue uniform, but she couldn't take her eyes off Alex. Snapping her open mouth shut again, Hope jerked forward and began walking once more.

After she took another few steps, both men saluted her, then lowered their hands extremely slowly and in complete unison. The entire audience breathed a captivated sigh. As she stared at the long column of brass buttons on his coat, Hope's mind flashed to the pictures of Alex in his dress blues. They were the only other time she'd seen him in uniform, though a mere photograph paled to the vision before her.

Did he sneak out for a military haircut?

She darted her eyes back to his head. No, his hair was the

same as she'd last seen it. The man before her was different from the one in the pictures.

This was *her* Alex.

Finally, Hope wrenched her eyes away and continued walking. Patti wept, and next to her, Cindy dabbed her eyes with a tissue. Tommy stood to Alex's right, dressed in a light-blue Cuban shirt and black slacks, and she exchanged a quick nod with him.

Then she was standing before Alex, understanding better than anyone else here, even Mike, what wearing his uniform at this moment meant. Tears threatened to overwhelm her, but she bit them back, swallowing hard. She passed her bouquet back to Sara and stepped forward. Bride and groom clasped hands, gripping tightly. Her hands were enveloped in his larger ones, cradled and protected.

The expression in his eyes beamed into her soul. She did her best to return it, trying to match the wonder and depthless love.

Tommy gave a short welcoming speech, informal and funny. Hope hardly heard it. She kept returning her gaze to the incredible image before her. From the black-and-white cap on Alex's head, to the medals on his chest, and back to those crystal blue eyes, this was home.

"Now it's time to exchange vows," Tommy said before pulling both rings out of his pocket and holding them out.

Alex picked up her ring and slid it onto her finger as her heart pounded in her ears. He took her hands again, staring into the depths of her, and recited his vows.

"Today, I promise to love only you. Always.

"I promise to laugh with you in the good times, and comfort you through the bad. I promise to help you when you need it, and step aside when you don't." He twitched a corner of his mouth at that, but his smile fell quickly as he continued.

"I promise to care for you, and share with you all that life might throw before us, both the adversities and the joys, from this day forward, and all the days of my life."

Hope slid Alex's ring onto his finger and repeated the same words back to him. The emotional tide rose within her, but she called out the words in a strong, clear voice. A lightness built from deep within, and a radiant smile lit her face as she finished her vows.

Tommy stood next to them, tall and grave. "By the power vested in me by the Territory of the US Virgin Islands, I now pronounce you husband and wife. You can kiss your bride."

Alex encircled his arms around her waist as Hope moved her right hand to his chest. The medals were cool beneath her palm. As he pressed his lips against hers, they were warm, relaxed, and promised more to come. He started to pull away, but Hope flung her arms around his neck. She lengthened the kiss as the crowd's applause strengthened. She could have been made of helium, ready to float away at any moment.

Without warning, Alex broke their kiss and slid his arms down her back. He lifted her up and even with his eyes as an enormous smile lit his face. Heart soaring, Hope bent her knees behind her and lifted the cap off his head. With a laugh, she set it on hers. Alex's laughter matched her own—they had eyes only for each other.

The crowd cheered wildly, and Robert dashed around, taking pictures from every angle as the sun set behind Mr. and Mrs. Monroe.

As Alex set her down, Hope put the cap back on his head. "It looks better on you."

"No, it definitely does not."

She stroked his face. "Don't you know it's bad form to upstage the bride?"

His eyes became glassy. "Believe me, that's not possible."

They turned, standing side by side, and Hope swept her gaze over the applauding crowd. Dave wrapped an arm around Kate, who was openly weeping now. Emma sat next to her, dabbing her eyes. The two kids wore politely interested expressions, like they'd been told to look happy or else. Tommy's wife Priscilla and their two kids were there, and both Clark and his pregnant wife Kamila were present as well.

Next to them sat Patti, who was busy blowing her nose into a succession of tissues. Her husband Gary comforted her, his gray-haired head nodding over her. Cindy sat on her other side, smiling as tears rolled down her face. Gerold and Charlotte sat in the back row, prepared to make a quick exit to start the dinner service. And next to them was Steve, dressed in a white linen shirt and applauding, wearing a smile that might crack his face.

Finally, Hope looked over her shoulder, and Sara stood just behind, dabbing her eyes with a tissue. "Here," Sara said. "You need your bouquet back."

Hope took it and she and Alex posed for a picture, his arm around her shoulders. Her entire body turned to melted butter, and she beamed at the camera. Robert moved sideways in front of them, shutter clicking the whole time as Alex stroked her tattoo with his thumb.

Her dream had come true.

Patti finally got herself together and stood. "We'd like to invite everyone to a champagne reception on the patio, to be followed by a dinner celebration. Please join us in welcoming Hope and Alex Monroe."

CHAPTER 39

Alex's head spun as he pulled Hope tighter. He looked at all their friends, applauding and crying. Fierce pride rose within him at wearing this uniform right now. He was acutely conscious of the ring on his left hand and everything it symbolized. He gazed at his wife beside him as Robert took several pictures.

Then Alex turned back to Mike, giving him a handshake that turned into a hug. "Mission accomplished."

"Judging by everyone's expressions, you pulled off your little surprise."

"Nice to know we can still conduct covert operations, huh?"

The main reason Mike had rented a car was so he could sneak the garment bag containing his uniform into the bungalow without Hope seeing it. She came over to speak with Mike, so Alex turned to Sara, who stood back. She was still wiping her eyes with a rumpled tissue.

"I can find you another one of those if you want."

"Don't be silly. The sun was in my eyes and made them water. Now that it's gone down, I'm fine."

"I understand. The sun's blinding as it sets."

Sara gave him a mock glare. "I hope you're happy. You've ruined my plans. I was all set to rake you over the coals for wearing some stupid outfit to your wedding. Instead, you steal the show."

Alex's eyes were drawn to Hope, now embracing Patti, and his breath caught. "No, I definitely did *not* steal the show. And I'm very happy." He turned back to Sara and bowed. "You look lovely."

"Thank you. I managed to finish our hair before the power went out."

Alex burst into laughter. "I never even thought about that! Though I imagine if you can survive five gallons of water pouring over your head, a power outage wouldn't have been any difficulty."

Sara narrowed her eyes as her mouth thinned. Alex lifted both hands, grinning broadly. "Sorry, I couldn't resist." Then he sobered. "Hope looks beyond beautiful. As long as I live, I'll never forget my first sight of her tonight. Thank you for that."

"You're welcome. I'm pretty sure she feels the same about you."

Sara made her way to the patio, and Alex turned to find Katie in front of him.

"Oh, big brother. You always could command a room just by walking into it."

"I think you need glasses, Halfpint. We're not in a room. We're standing on a beach."

"Would you shut up and accept a compliment for once in your life?"

"Temper, temper." He drew her into his arms, and she held him tightly.

"You have no idea what it means to see you in that uniform. I never thought I'd see it again."

"For a long time, neither did I. Let's head to the patio and get a glass of champagne. I forgot how hot this damn thing is, especially when the collar's choking you."

As they started walking, movement caught Alex's eye and he paused. Hope stood in front of the ocean as Robert photographed her. The sky behind her was painted in orange and purple, fading to deep indigo. A lump formed in his throat. He couldn't find words to describe how magnificent she was. Her dress was stunning—all of her was. As if she sensed him, Hope made eye contact and broke into a spectacular smile, which he returned.

Robert glanced over and brightened. "Get over here, Alex. I need some pictures of you before I lose the light!" After taking several of Alex alone, Hope joined him, and Robert got more shots of them together. Eventually, he was done, and they strolled to the patio.

At last, Alex got his drink from Charlotte, who gave him a shy smile. He finished the whole flute in one shot before grabbing another from her tray. Hope had already moved off to talk to Tommy, so he headed toward Katie to resume their interrupted conversation.

"There you are," Katie said. "First you're thirsty, then you're all paparazzi. Now you're thirsty again. Make up your mind."

"You sure are cranky on such a happy occasion." Alex shook Dave's hand as the two kids stood next to their parents. Monica stared at him, as if she'd never seen him before. *I suppose in some ways, she hasn't.*

Jason came forward, his eyes glued to Alex's chest. "How many medals do you have?"

"Enough. You want one?"

Jason snapped his head up, his eyes becoming even rounder. Alex removed an Afghanistan campaign medal and pinned it on Jason's shirt. He had several. "Thanks!" Jason shot him an awestruck glance and Katie started crying again.

"And you say I need to make up my mind. Come here." She

crumpled against his chest, bawling, and Alex patted her back as he gave Dave an awkward smile.

∾

Alex stepped into the men's room to wash his hands, breathing a sigh when no one else was there. After turning off the faucet, he caught sight of himself in the mirror and straightened, coming to attention.

As he stared at his reflection, the full weight of it hit him—wearing the uniform and now happily married, fully launched into his new life. Alex rushed to lock the door and returned to the mirror. His eyes filled with tears, and he let them come.

They were happy tears.

The last time he'd worn dress whites had been before Syria, and wiping his face dry, he studied himself. The uniform was a little looser now—he wasn't packing as much muscle as he had in the old days. It still fit well, but he was different. A smile crept across his face.

A better man stared back now.

After he got it back together, Alex stepped back to the patio. Patti stood alone, and he broke into a grin as he was brought back to earlier in the evening, when she had come to escort Mike to the ceremony. Emma had already left to take her seat. Alex was in the bathroom, fully dressed, when Mike opened the front door.

"Oh my," Patti said, her voice clear even from where he stood. "Don't you look sharp. You're not goin' to show up our Alex, are you?"

He came out of the bathroom and said, "I don't know. You tell me, Patti."

When she saw him, her eyes nearly bulged out of her head, and she raced both hands to her mouth.

Then she burst into noisy tears.

Alex hurried to give her a hug, but Patti pressed back against the front door, whipping her head back and forth. "No! Don't come near me—I don't want my makeup stainin' your white uniform. Oh, Alex!"

She started crying again, waving a hand in front of her face. Alex threw a beseeching glance at Mike, who just shrugged and looked like he was trying not to laugh.

Alex grabbed a tissue and gave it to her, and she got to work with it. He held her at arm's length, awkwardly patting her shoulders. "Take Mike out, then come back for me, just like we practiced, ok?"

He glanced again at Mike, who smirked back. Alex mouthed "Asshole!" and Mike grinned, holding his hands up.

"Come on, Patti," Mike said, pulling several tissues out of the box. "Here, pull yourself together."

Patti blew noisily and rushed to the bathroom to wash her hands. When she came back, she looked more like her usual self.

"That's better," Mike said. "You and I have an important job. We've got to get Snow White here through this ceremony. So how about we get this show on the road?" He gave Patti his elbow and led her through the door, nodding to Alex on his way out.

As the door closed, the nerves slithered up from Alex's gut. "I really hope I don't screw this up," he said to the empty room.

Soon, Patti opened the door and walked into the bungalow. She straightened and looked him up and down, a big sigh escaping. "I've loved my Gary for over thirty years. But right now, I think you might be the most handsome man I've ever seen, Alex Monroe."

She was getting misty eyed again and Alex stepped in. He placed his hands on her shoulders, concentrating on the mission at hand. "Thank you. But Patti, I need you to keep it together, ok?"

She blinked rapidly, her fists clenched. "I'm tryin'!"

"Hey, you have an important job coming up. I need to know you won't give anything away when you escort Hope. She has to be surprised when she sees me. Ok?"

At that, Patti snapped her head up, and a remarkable change overcame her. Her eyes clearing, she straightened her back and held her head proudly. "Don't you worry. Hope won't know a thing until she steps down that aisle."

Now he walked toward Patti, standing on the patio in her fancy light-yellow dress, and finally embraced her. She still tried to pull away, afraid to mar his uniform. "Stop it, Patti. You and I have been through too much to worry about a stain or two. And stains do wash out, you know."

She relented and wrapped her arms around him, though she still kept her head away from his coat. "I'm so happy for you two. I can't even begin to tell you."

"I know you are. *We* know. Thanks for all your help—we couldn't have done this without you. Where's Gary?"

Patti rolled her eyes. "He went to talk to Gerold. Gary thinks he's a gourmet cook. I'll go rescue Gerold in a little bit."

Alex cracked a small smile, almost shy. "You did great. Hope looked pretty stunned when she saw me."

"I'll carry that memory forever." Then she gave him a teasing smile. "But that goes both ways, you know. You were a little stunned yourself."

Alex laughed. "That doesn't begin to describe it. In my wildest dreams, she didn't look as spectacular as she did tonight." He embraced her again. "Thank you. I love you."

"Oh, you dear man. I love you too." Then she took a step back. "I need to go pull Gary away, or we won't have dinner tonight."

Patti disappeared through the swinging double doors as Alex checked if Hope was available, but she was speaking with Cindy.

With a sigh, he grabbed another glass of champagne, searching for someone to talk to. Priscilla was heading toward the pier, her arms around the kids, while Tommy stayed on the patio. A smile rose on his face as he watched his family.

"Where are they going?" Alex asked.

"David's starvin' and actin' up a bit. So Priscilla took them to the pier to look around."

"Sorry. Weddings aren't real fun for kids."

"Hey, they weren't here for you. They were watchin' me."

"And you even got to stay dry this time. Drier than me, that's for sure." Alex pulled at his collar.

"Yeah, aren't you Mr. Fancy Pants?" Tommy laughed, his white teeth flashing, and Alex joined in.

"Mike called me Snow White earlier."

"That works too!" Then Tommy became serious. "Congratulations. You both looked pretty incredible tonight."

Alex clapped him on the shoulder. "Thank you. You were fantastic—the ceremony was perfect. You're the only man I wanted for that job."

Tommy moved off to join his family and Alex turned, making eye contact with Steve, who approached with his hand out. They shook as Steve's gaze traveled up and down.

"Congratulations. I didn't realize you were going to wear the uniform. It suits you."

"Well, a wise man once told me not to let Syria define my life. I decided to listen to him." At the same time, they broke into wide smiles and ended in a full embrace, no awkwardness in sight. "Thanks for coming, Steve. It's good to have you here."

"Sure, you say that now. Good thing we're not on the pier."

"I'm in a mellow mood tonight. Pretty sure I won't be tempted to throw you in the ocean."

They were both laughing again when the sound of clapping came from behind. Patti stood next to two big tables set on the patio.

"We're ready to start dinner now," she said, and Alex's gaze was drawn to Hope. She was still standing with Cindy. They were watching Patti, then Hope turned to look straight at him.

Alex nodded to Steve and crossed the patio to escort his bride to their table, his chest proud and head held high.

CHAPTER 40

As Hope chatted with Cindy, she'd caught sight of Alex several times as he circulated around the patio. She tried to concentrate on her friend instead of her husband.

Which was impossible.

After Patti announced dinner, once again Hope searched for him. She turned and he was walking confidently toward her, breathtakingly handsome. She swallowed the lump in her throat as Cindy excused herself.

He offered her his elbow. "May I have the honor of escorting you to dinner?"

"Yes." She wasn't capable of saying more than that as she stared into his eyes. Then she was floating at his side. The brick pavers were cool under her bare feet as the dark ocean whispered softly against the beach. The night sky was completely clear, with the Milky Way streaking overhead.

White cloths covered the two tables, and floating votive candles flickered inside hurricane lamps. Strings of her beloved Edison bulbs crisscrossed overhead, bathing the patio in soft romantic light. Arrangements of stargazer lilies decorated each table, and Hope had added her own bouquet to theirs. She and

Alex sat in the middle, Sara on her left and Mike, then Emma, on Alex's right. Every time Hope had asked about the reception decorations, Patti had just waved her off, saying, "You just leave all that to Clark and me." And so she had, knowing she was in good hands.

Hope could have been inside a dream—wanting never to wake.

Ice buckets filled with champagne bottles rested on both tables. The bubbles were soon flowing, and the volume of conversation rose.

"How's it feel to be an old married woman?" Sara asked, finishing her lobster bisque.

"Wonderful!"

Sara laughed and shook her head.

Alex squeezed Hope's knee, his fingers lingering as he whispered in her ear, "I cannot even begin to tell you how stunning you are. I'll never forget how you looked, silhouetted against the sand. Ever."

"That goes double for me. You're just full of surprises."

A lazy smile spread across his face, and he winked before taking a sip of champagne. He was now bareheaded.

"Where is your cap?"

Alex tipped his head. "On that table behind us. The uniform is hot enough. The cap only makes it worse."

She and Alex raised their glasses as several toasts were given. She kept sneaking peeks at him, still not believing he was wearing his uniform, or how good he looked in it. Though that part wasn't really a surprise.

She had so many questions, but they were private, and this wasn't the place. Instead, she settled for stroking her hand down his thigh. He darted his eyes to her and covered her hand with his.

Hope caught movement to her left. Her heart lurched as Sara scraped her chair back and stood. "Ladies and gentlemen, if I could have your attention for a moment? Hope told me not to say anything, but when have I ever done what she told me?" She smiled at Hope. "Don't worry, I won't give a long, boring speech. I just have a few things I'd like to say." Sara gestured at the decorated patio with a broad sweep of her arm, the party lights reflecting in her brown eyes. "Look at what Hope has accomplished in the past year and a half. I thought this place was beautiful when I was here last year—now it's incredible. And incredibly successful."

Sara made eye contact with everyone. "You've all been a part of that, and I can tell how close you are to each other and to Hope. Until she moved here, I was the only family Hope had. She was the only family I had. It's always been us Collins girls versus the world. That's changed. You've all become her family now, and by extension, mine too. And today, I gained an actual family member."

She gave Alex a crooked smile. "When I visited last time, I told you what an amazing woman my sister is. I'm glad you finally figured that out." She stopped until the laughter faded. "And if you ever forget, I'll be the first to remind you."

Alex laughed and held his hands up in a surrender gesture.

"Hope is incredible. You see how beautiful she is?" She paused for the applause and a few whistles, beaming. "I'd like to think I had a *little* to do with that, having done her hair and makeup." Sara paused. "But I'm not fishing for compliments. My love for cosmetology started when Hope and I were much younger. We'd sit for hours, getting me ready for my school dances and proms. She never missed one."

Sara looked down, gathering herself as her eyes teared up. "Look, I know that doesn't sound like much. But I'd like you to understand this. That she never missed helping me prepare for my big nights, even though she never had one herself.

"Alex's story is pretty heroic. Hope's is different . . . but no less important. Why wouldn't a smart, beautiful teenage girl have her fun nights out? It wasn't because the guys weren't interested. And believe it or not, she has some pretty good dance moves if the need arises."

She and Hope exchanged a small smile. Hope was surprised. Sara was dramatic, but not overly open in her affections.

But she was tonight.

Sara sipped her champagne before continuing, her face hardening. "No, the reason Hope never went to a single dance or prom is because she worked up to three jobs, in addition to getting top grades. She didn't have time to be a fun teenager because she supported our family. All through high school. And after.

"Again—why, you ask? I'll tell you. Because our dad ran out on us, and our mom couldn't make ends meet. And Hope had a snotty little sister she moved heaven and hell for, to make sure I was ok. Hope gave up her best teenage years so I could have mine. And I've never even said thank you." Sara had to stop for a moment, and her breath hitched as she turned toward Hope.

"So I am now. And you've finally got your night, big sister. It's been much too long coming, but I'm so proud of you. I love you."

Tears streaked down Hope's face as she rose to embrace Sara, both of them trying to hold it together. "I love you too," Hope whispered to her.

"Don't worry!" Sara called to the crowd. "I brought the waterproof mascara. All is well."

As expected, Gerold's dinner was exceptional. Hope had the blackened mahi-mahi, and Alex the filet mignon. She enjoyed every bite of the fiery flavors. Both the red and white wines were flowing, and the hum of voices drifted over the patio. Gerold and Charlotte had sat down too, and he could be overheard telling Steve about the triathlon he'd completed with Hope and Alex.

Sara was right. These people were her family now. She had

accomplished a lot, but not without help from everyone here. And none of it would have been possible without Alex. He'd been her rock. The one person she could always depend on. He was talking to Emma, gesturing with his left hand, and a thrill shot through Hope at the ring on it.

Charlotte and Gerold cleared the dishes, and the conversation lulled. Mike stood up, tapping a spoon against his red wineglass. "Can I get your attention?"

"Sit down, Baker," Alex muttered as Hope perked her ears up.

The room quieted. "Alex ordered me not to give a speech," Mike said. "But this isn't a speech, just a little chat. Cool?" Mike waited for several answering nods, but avoided the groom's eye. "Alex and I have known each other for a long time, though we just recently got back in touch. He was my commanding officer for over ten years. We were SEALs together. Until we weren't. I saw that article about Alex, and I'm sure you all have too."

Hope stole a quick glance at Alex, who wore an even expression, watching Mike. He wasn't tense and she relaxed.

Mike continued. "I was there that last night. In Syria. The article mentioned Alex pulled a bunch of civilians and SEALs to safety before he was almost killed."

Mike paused, staring at the table before lifting his gaze to make eye contact with the group. "I was one of those guys. I wouldn't be here right now if it weren't for him. I got through that disaster with hardly a scratch—because of him. You'd think most guys would want to brag about that, wouldn't you? But Alex was just the opposite. He convinced himself that because he was in command, the whole thing was his fault."

Finally, Mike met Alex's gaze. "Can you hear how ridiculous that sounds, man?"

Mike turned back to the crowd. "You see that medal on his chest? The cross with the blue and white ribbon? The article mentioned that too. That's the Navy Cross, and it's the highest honor the Navy awards. God knows Alex deserves it. Seeing him in uniform tonight, wearing that medal, is a pretty big deal. I think everyone here understands that."

Mike met Hope's gaze, and she nodded before he turned back to the audience.

"You all know Alex. He can be a stubborn, grumpy son of a bitch." Laughter rippled through the crowd. "But if you're ever in a dicey situation, this is the man you want guarding your back."

Mike lifted his wineglass. "I want to say thank you. Alex was hurting when he first got here, inside and outside. You had a lot to do with helping him get better."

He turned to Hope with a slight smile. "And you might've had a slight effect too."

He clapped his hand on Alex's shoulder. "Thanks to *all* of you, I got my best friend back. Cheers, sir." Mike and Alex toasted glasses and drank.

Then Mike came to attention and saluted him. Alex immediately stood and saluted back, then they both fell into a back-slapping hug as the crowd erupted into cheers.

CHAPTER 41

The moon cast a silver shimmer along the placid sea as Hope strolled along the beach, hand in hand with her husband. Alex's cap was firmly back in place. She kept sneaking peeks at him, just to convince herself that what she saw was *real*.

They approached the Hibiscus bungalow, the only northern one with its porch light on. A soft glow flickered from within. The party was still going, but the newlyweds had ducked out early to raucous cheers. Since they had decided against music at the reception, it was a quiet, peaceful evening as they climbed the steps.

Alex opened the door, then turned back expectantly. Hope broke into a smile. "I wondered if you were going to carry me over the threshold."

He bent down to kiss her, brushing his tongue over hers. Then he pulled back and arched a brow. "Play your cards right, and I might carry you over more than one tonight."

"That's the corniest thing you've ever said to me."

"We're married now. I don't need to impress you anymore." Then he sobered, taking her left hand in his and bowing over it. "Mrs. Monroe, will you allow me to carry you over the threshold?"

"Yes," she breathed.

Alex picked her up in his arms, their eyes never leaving each other's as he easily carried her through the door. He kicked it shut behind him before setting her on her feet. As he bent to kiss her again, Hope pressed against his chest. His medals clinked as she rubbed against them. She opened her eyes to his rugged, handsome face before being distracted by the soft glow surrounding them.

Stepping back, Hope glanced around the bungalow and caught Alex's grin as he set his cap aside. White candles were scattered around the room, dozens of them. Red rose pedals were sprinkled over the sheets of the turned-down bed, and the gauzy mosquito net was draped around it. On the coffee table, a champagne bottle filled an ice bucket and two flutes stood at the ready. A box of chocolates sat next to it.

Hope took it all in, awed and delighted. "Patti told me she was getting a room ready for us but didn't say anything about this!"

"It was a special request of mine. I didn't want to spend tonight in the house and asked her to take care of decorating a bungalow. Just before we left the reception, she ducked out to light all the candles."

Hope had been clasping her hands to her breast, and now she let them fall to her sides. "Honey, it's beautiful, but I feel guilty. You always surprise me with the most wonderful things. I don't do nearly enough for you."

Alex burst into laughter, bending over at the waist.

"What's so funny?"

"I can't believe you said that! Have you looked in a mirror today, baby?"

She couldn't help the smile that rose as she fanned out her silk skirt. "Well, I guess this is kind of a surprise, isn't it?"

His smile faded as another expression filled his eyes. Desire was there, but it was mostly bare, naked love. "You are the most beautiful thing I've ever seen."

Hope drank him in from head to toe as she sidled closer. "I still can't believe you're wearing that uniform. I know men are supposed to be called handsome, not beautiful. But you are. When did you decide on it?"

Alex broke into another enormous grin. "About thirty seconds after you nodded yes."

"*What?*"

His smile faded. "I wanted to honor you tonight. This is the best way I knew how." He looked at his chest, running a finger over the left side. His medals jingled in the still room. "I decided on the uniform right away. Wearing the medals was a recent addition. One Mike helped with. And you."

"I'm so proud of you. I can't even express it."

Standing this close, a sensuous ripple traveled all through Hope's body—she was finally alone with him. She pressed her lips to his, and he opened his mouth, sending desire roaring through her. Hope broke away, her heart already pounding. She ran her tongue over her lip, and his eyes were locked on her mouth.

Not yet.

Taking his hand, she led him to the couch, and they sat. She smiled as something occurred to her. "So, all that business with the shorts versus pants, and all those shirts. It was just a ruse?"

"Of course. I've seen you poking through my garment bag and exclaiming over my service uniform. I was scared to death you'd take a liking to the ones behind it and spoil my surprise."

"It was definitely a surprise. Why were you and Mike in different uniforms? You're in white and he was in blue."

Alex's brows flew up. "Because you told me we couldn't match. Just following orders."

She laughed. "You chose wisely. I'm partial to the white one, for sure. And if you're in the mood to follow orders, then follow this one. Open us a bottle of champagne, sailor."

"Yes, ma'am."

They held their full glasses up. "What shall we drink to?" Alex asked. "We really need a new toast besides *new beginnings*, even if it is apt."

"It's apt because I feel like my life didn't start until I met you. But if you don't want that, how about we drink to the rest of our lives?"

He brushed a finger down her cheek. "Excellent toast, Mrs. Monroe."

She settled closer to him, drawing her knees next to her while smoothing out the white silk. "Why do I get the feeling you're going to drive me to distraction with the Mrs. Monroe stuff?"

"Uh-oh. You're sick of it already? We've only been married a few hours. This isn't good, Hope."

"Shut up and kiss me."

He took his time, tracing his way from her mouth to her ear, and sending a jolt through her as he darted his tongue in.

Alex laughed softly at her moan. "That gets you every time."

"Already have me figured out, do you? Maybe there's nothing left to discover."

"I plan to spend the rest of my life discovering."

Hope gave him a long stare in response and took a sip of champagne. Then she laughed at what was on the coffee table, picking up the issue of *Entrepreneur Today*. "Oh, Patti."

With a grin, Alex took it from her and thumbed through it. "I'm not even the slightest bit surprised you're on the front. You're cover-girl material all the way. It's a great article, and I'm really proud of you."

"I hope she didn't put these in all the bungalows. I let her place a stack in the lobby, but I don't want to look conceited."

"You don't need to worry about that. And now you've got the bank account to go along with the entrepreneur title."

Hope sighed. "It was a little depressing how much was gone after Prodigy took their cut and the CPA took out the amount for taxes."

"It's still over two million dollars."

"I'm not complaining, believe me. Tomorrow or the next day, we can start planning what to do with it." She drew her finger over his medals, smiling as they rang softly under her touch. "But not tonight."

He set the magazine back on the table. "Oh, if you get hungry, Patti told me they put some extra wedding cake in the fridge."

"No, I'm good on cake for a while," she said. "And thank you for behaving on that, by the way. I wasn't at all sure you weren't going to smash it all over my face."

Alex twitched a corner of his mouth. "I won't say I wasn't tempted, but I wouldn't do that to you. Besides, I might get another opportunity later tonight."

"Indeed, you might." Hope was drawn to his uniform once again and stroked her finger over the SEAL insignia. "How did it feel to pin this on again?"

"Like it belonged there."

Her eyes zeroed in on his. "Because it does." She brushed another pin below the mass of medals on his chest. "And you're wearing the parachutist badge too."

"It's usually what we wear as the secondary beneath the SEAL insignia."

"This is really quite fascinating, you know. I'm very dull in comparison."

He tilted her chin up. "You're anything but. You just have a different story, is all. I was really touched by Sara's speech tonight. Taking care of people is what you do best."

"You too. Mike was one of the people you saved?"

"Yes. Though I still don't remember any of it."

"And you were all right with him talking about it in front of everyone?" She dropped her eyes to his Navy Cross. When she looked back up, he wore a slight smile.

"Yeah. It's his story too, and I seem to be hearing from people lately that I'm stubborn. Maybe it was time to start listening. And after hearing firsthand that Mike and the rest of the Team didn't hold me responsible, I understood it was time to stop blaming myself and finally move on." He touched the Navy Cross. "That's what tonight meant, wearing this. And the Purple Heart too."

"I can't describe what I felt, seeing you in uniform. I understood right away what you were saying with it." She stroked the two medals. "You're finally healing, and so am I. Because we found each other."

Alex nodded. "That's exactly what it meant."

"My head's still spinning. About all of it. I am *so* happy."

Hope let her eyes travel around the remodeled bungalow, then broke into stunned laughter. "It's fitting we're in Hibiscus. Would you believe I spent my first night at Half Moon Bay in this very bungalow? I cried myself to sleep, afraid I'd made the worst mistake of my life."

She was drawn once again to those crystal blue eyes. "And now I'm here again, married to you. This resort, and most especially *you*, are the best things that have ever happened to me."

"Not just you. The day you arrived here, everything changed for me, in the best possible way. I'm an incredibly lucky man."

"We're both lucky. But we also made this work—we both took the leap."

After they finished their champagne, Alex set their flutes on the coffee table and leaned back. He tilted Hope's face up, silent, and just studied her. She focused her gaze on his mouth. His full lips were parted and flushed. As their eyes locked, her breath deepened, and they moved silently toward each other. Her lips melted into his as she held his face in both hands, stroking his chin. It was smoother than usual this time of night. He must have shaved shortly before the ceremony.

She rested both hands on his broad shoulders. The shoulder boards of his uniform were firm beneath her fingers. As she moved her hands to his chest, she crushed her mouth to his and slipped her tongue into his mouth. In response, he rumbled deep in his chest, deepening the kiss.

Hope unfastened the brass buttons, opening his coat to reveal another button-down shirt beneath. She pressed her palm against his chest, which was slightly damp with sweat. Now it was her turn to moan as she pictured herself tasting his skin underneath.

She broke the kiss and watched Alex's chest, running her hands over his medals and bars one last time. She committed the sight to memory before sliding the open uniform over his shoulders. He shrugged it off and tossed it on the nearby chair and turned back to Hope, stroking his index finger across the swell of her breasts. Then he slid his hand behind her neck and pulled her toward him.

She fumbled to open his shirt, rushing now, and spread her fingers, tracing them down the warm, damp skin of his chest. His shirt quickly joined the uniform top, and Hope pressed him back against the couch.

His tan skin was hot and soft to the touch, but he was all hard muscle underneath. Her gaze continued downward, past his taut, defined abdominal muscles. Without the uniform top, the evidence of his desire was prominent and straining against the fabric of his pants. There was a pull deep inside her as she looked at it. She ran her tongue over her top lip as she returned her eyes to his. "You are the most glorious man I've ever seen."

He lifted a corner of his mouth and brushed a finger over her jawline. "If you say so."

"Oh, yes, I do. Sometimes I can't believe you're real." She reached for his hand, twirling the ring on his finger. "It's even harder to believe you're mine."

"I'll always be yours."

Hope rushed toward him, smashing her mouth into his as she ran her hands over his back. She was acutely aware of each muscle flexing as he slid his arms around her. Catching herself, she softened the kiss, wanting to enjoy every second.

They had all night.

Eventually, Alex pulled away and took both her hands in his, rising and pulling her to her feet. He kissed her feverishly, her lips aflame now as his tongue swirled in her mouth. He pressed hard against her, forcing her back before his hold tightened and he steadied her against him.

He broke away and stepped back, breathing hard. He slowly moved his gaze from her head to her breasts, lingering there before continuing downward. Finally, he met her eyes. "You look so incredible I almost hate to take that dress off you. Almost . . ."

An easy smile spread across his face. He moved back to her and traced his hand across her shoulders. Yet his soft, delicate touch lit her on fire.

Alex ran a finger across her tattoo. "Thank you for showing this tonight."

"You were right. It's symbolic for both of us."

He bent to kiss her, tender once again, his lips barely touching hers. He drew down the zipper in the back of her dress, then pulled away, catching a handful of silk to prevent it from falling. He moved his hands to her breasts, cupping them before slowly drawing the dress downward, and watching intently, as if he'd imagined it a thousand times. He widened his eyes as her strapless white lace bra was revealed. From there, the dress slid more easily, and he let go once he'd reached her hips. His breath hitched at the sight of her sheer white panties.

Their eyes met again.

His glittered in the candlelight. "Oh my God, Hope. Is this real?"

"Oh, yes. You and I are as real as it gets. Never doubt that."

They embraced again, and Alex unclasped her bra and tossed it aside without breaking their kiss. Hope pressed against his naked torso, her breasts incredibly sensitive as she rubbed against it, and brushed her lips down his neck. She moved to the center of his chest and opened her mouth. Languidly drawing her tongue down, she was completely ignited as she finally tasted the saltiness of his skin.

Lowering to her knees, Hope unbuckled his belt, then his pants, sliding them over his hips along with the boxers underneath. After Alex kicked off his pants, she kissed his scattered scars, loving each one. Then he groaned as she took him in her mouth. She savored the pleasure she was giving him, and his breathing grew deeper and deeper. Then he stepped back, drawing her to her feet again.

He softly traced his hands over her hair, touching the pearls. "I don't even know where to start with this."

"Here." Sara had artfully twisted the mass into a French roll with two large pins. Hope removed them easily, shaking her hair free around her shoulders.

She smiled as Alex gaped at her in open-mouthed wonder. Then his expression changed, and he put his mouth to good use, crushing her lips to his, wet and frantic as his need pressed between them. He bent and slid an arm under her knees as he lifted her into his arms, carrying her to the bed. He set her down gently next to it.

Hope arranged the gauzy net around the bed, then brushed a hand over the rose petals, and their delicate scent filled the air. "This is pretty romantic."

Alex just smiled and kissed her again as they stood together next to the bed. He kissed a slow, wet line down her neck and settled at her breasts. Waves of desire crashed through Hope. Alex moved to her other breast, repeating the motions with his tongue as she tipped her head back.

He moved down her stomach, settling on his knees as he brushed his lips over her three scars. He kept his eyes closed, his hot breath warming her skin, and she felt incredibly loved. "Oh, Hope. You are so perfect for me."

Finally, he hooked his thumbs over the sides of her panties, drawing them slowly over her hips. He slid them down with one hand, following with his mouth all the way to her feet. She stepped out and he tossed them aside, rising to his feet once more as they slid into the cool sheets together.

His eyes were a darker blue in the muted candlelight. The warm glow lit up the gauze around them and she took a deep breath of the rose-scented air. Hope pressed her body against her husband's, gasping at the heat radiating off him as their eyes locked.

At the same time, the tenderness fled from both of them, and they smashed their mouths together. Hope raked her fingernails down his back. Alex responded by grabbing a handful of her hair and yanking her head back as he kissed her even harder.

Hope couldn't wait any longer. "Come to me, love. I've been waiting for you my whole life."

She wrapped him tightly in her arms and urged him on top of her, opening as he powerfully entered her. As she arched her back and cried out, he slid his arms to her ass, cupping her tightly as he drove into her. Again and again.

They were both escalating quickly, and Hope rolled them over, sitting above him.

She held him with her eyes. His mouth was open, and he breathed in gasps as she started moving above him. He closed his eyes again, bringing his hand to her center. Hope tipped her head back, using both hands to dig into his chest as they both climaxed, crying out for each other.

She collapsed forward, lying with her cheek next to his, and Alex drew her tightly to him, wrapping her in his love. Her tears slipped down and mixed with his as they lay entwined.

For several minutes, they were silent as they stroked their hands slowly over each other. The candles cast a soft light around the quiet room.

Hope lifted on an elbow and watched him, drinking in every detail. They wiped the tears from each other's faces, their eyes locked together.

She stroked a finger down his face. "I love you. You are the only man in the world for me. Do you understand that?"

"Yes. I've known for a long time that you were made for me, and me for you. I love you. Always."

"Forever?"

"You've always been my forever, Hope."

EPILOGUE

January...

DEBRA HARTFORD WAS TIRED. Really tired.

At least the kids were quiet in the back seat. Will gripped the wheel of their rental car, white knuckled, as he concentrated. Driving on the left side of the road was a new experience. The tension was making Debra hot, and she pulled her shoulder-length blonde hair into a ponytail. She stared out the window at the glinting turquoise ocean, trying to absorb the peaceful scene.

A family vacation had seemed like such a great idea two months ago. She and Will had been growing distant for several years now, and their demanding jobs and demanding children didn't help.

She glanced behind her. Connor was seventeen and had just been accepted at Columbia. Hannah was sixteen, going on twenty-five. Debra had been desperate to find some common bond to bring them together again and was thrilled when Hannah had actually liked the idea of learning to scuba dive. Debra had immediately signed her up for a course. Connor had learned to dive a couple years ago. So he, along with Debra and Will, had taken a refresher, and they started to think about a family dive vacation.

Pure luck had intervened when Debra sat in the lobby of her dentist's office, thumbing through a magazine to pass the time. The issue was about female entrepreneurs, and the lead article featured a dive resort owned by a woman.

The pictures were jaw-dropping—a white sand beach, palm trees, and warm breezes.

Debra jotted down the name and Debra jotted down the name and hurried home to check out the resort's website, growing more excited by the minute. Will had amazed her by agreeing it was a great idea, and they started planning.

The difficulty had been finding a time when Half Moon Bay Resort wasn't fully booked. But she finally found some free dates after the holiday season. Debra splurged, booking two bungalows so she and Will could have a little privacy and maybe rekindle the flame a little.

The kids had started squabbling as soon as they left the house, arguing for the first hour of the plane ride from Cincinnati. Debra normally discouraged screen time, but she relented and practically begged the two kids to watch movies instead of ripping each other's heads off.

Even descending from the plane, Connor had sighed impatiently as they waited in the line of people. He didn't even notice the warm tropical air. Everyone was tired and cranky as they waited for luggage—all there, thank God—then it took forever to get the rental car.

Eventually, they passed through a beautiful little town called Frederiksted, but even the colorful buildings with the long pier jutting into the ocean couldn't help Debra relax.

Have I made a huge mistake? She tried to concentrate on the vivid colors around her but stayed silent, not wanting to add to the tension.

The jungle reasserted itself, and Will turned left off the highway. They rumbled down a long tree tunnel, the sunlight filtering through the tree canopy. Some of the stress eased out of Debra as she craned her head, looking more closely. The trees thinned out to reveal a circular driveway with a lovely cottage-style building behind it. Will parked in the small lot and they got out.

The azure ocean peeked from behind the building and a gentle breeze whispered through the trees around them. A grassy lawn sported several flame trees, alight with bright orange blossoms. A nearby frangipani bathed them in its incredibly fragrant blossoms. And the area was nearly silent except for the breeze and the ocean waves. A row of waving palm trees fringed an impossibly white sand beach.

As she took it all in, a calm peace overtook Debra. She turned her attention to the kids and exchanged smiles. Both were more alert now, eagerly inspecting their surroundings.

"This looks *nice*," Connor said in his disturbingly manlike voice.

"Mom, you might have done ok. Might, I said." Hannah gave her a small smile to soften the words.

Will darted his eyes around, evaluating the condition of the resort, then turned to her with a wink. They climbed the stairs into a building under a sign reading Lobby, with Debra in front. She entered a brightly lit room. Ceiling fans spun a cooling breeze, and soft island music filled the area. It smelled fresh and clean, and a smile came to her face as she soaked in the peaceful room.

Her tension dissipated further.

A wall of pictures immediately drew her eye. There were several rows of staff photos, but Debra's breath caught at the large, modern glass portrait prominently displayed just to the left of them. She was vaguely aware of a woman standing behind the front desk, but her feet moved of their own volition toward the portrait. The rest of her family followed. They must have felt the same inexorable pull toward it.

The picture was breathtaking.

It was a poster-sized, vertical photo taken on the beach, featuring an elated couple. The woman wore a strapless wedding dress, and the man a Navy uniform. They were impossibly gorgeous and impossibly happy.

Debra raised a brow. *Definitely models.*

But models or not, the photo was stunning.

The photographer had captured a perfect moment in time. The man had lifted the woman into the air as she was lowering his Navy cap onto her head, her knees bent behind her. Doubt rolled through Debra's mind at the look of transcendent joy on both their faces.

You couldn't fake that.

Was I that happy on our wedding day? Will sure hasn't ever looked at me like that.

No, it couldn't be real. Still, they couldn't ask for a better advertisement if the photo shoot had occurred here at the resort.

Connor breathed behind her, "Look at all those medals!"

Debra turned her gaze downward, and her stomach lurched at the sight of a framed copy of the same magazine she'd seen in the dentist's office. The woman was quite similar to the one in the wedding photo, but much more serious on the cover. Next to the magazine was a third frame, which held a newspaper article about a trial witness who had once been a Navy SEAL.

But Debra couldn't keep her eyes from the glass print. And the look on those two faces.

It has to be fake, doesn't it?

"Are you folks checking in?" A woman's low, husky voice spoke behind them, and Will snapped his head around. Debra rolled her eyes. He was such a sucker for a sexy voice.

He approached the front desk. "Yes, reservation for the Hartfords."

With regret, Debra tore herself away from the photo and the timeless dream it exuded, moving toward the check-in area. Her mouth dropped open at seeing the woman behind the desk. Then she came to a dead stop, jerking her thumb at the photo. "That's you!"

The woman, whose lovely chestnut hair fell to her shoulders, looked up with a smile. "Guilty as charged. The general manager wanted to hang it in here. She said it brought life to the room."

Debra's heart pounded. The photo *wasn't* fake.

The sultry-voiced woman shrugged and typed on her computer. She was dressed somewhat strangely, wearing a staff polo shirt, but with a long-sleeved desert camo shirt loosely draped over it. The name Monroe was embroidered on the right breast.

Connor was behind her, still at the wall. "Whoa! That guy was a Navy SEAL?"

"He was." The woman said. "I see you have two bungalows booked. One with two queens and the other with a king. Sounds like a wonderful idea."

Connor quickly approached the counter. "So, can we meet him? The SEAL guy?"

She typed on her computer again, then smiled at Connor. "Looks like all four of you have booked a dive package. So, yes—you will definitely meet him. That's my husband. He runs the dive operation here and leads a lot of the dives himself."

She turned her smile to all of them.

"His name is Alex, and I'm Hope Monroe. We own this place. It's our home. And for a little while, maybe it will be yours too."

The End
for now...

But keep reading to find out what happens next...

AUTHOR'S NOTE

Well, there you have it. I'm not going to lie—writing the end of this book hit me right in the gut. It was quite a journey taking these two characters from closed-down, untrusting souls to soulmates, and now it's finished. I only hope I've done them justice.

I knew midway through the first book that Hope and Alex's story was going to end in a sunset beach wedding, with Alex wearing his uniform. The question became: how do I take this man who was so traumatized he couldn't even talk about his military days, and get him to the point where he *wants* to wear his uniform? And that, Dear Reader, is why this story took four books to tell. Both Alex and Hope ended up massively changed compared to where they started. But isn't that why love stories are so eternal? Nothing else is so transformative.

The dive site Washing Machine is a combination of sites, including Fish Rain off Molokai, in Hawaii. It's a wonderful dive, and very like being in a three-dimensional aquarium. There are various sites around the world named something like Washing Machine, Maelstrom, Spin Cycle, etc. I'm firmly on Team Hope with this one. I can't say getting spun around like that appeals much to me—with or without the company of Navy SEALs!

I also thought it was very fitting for them to return to Horseshoe Key, where it really all began for them. And the dolphin encounter really cemented Alex's growth. I've never had an experience like that with a dolphin, but I've been on several dives where an animal will ignore all divers except one. I've had turtles approach very closely, and it's a very special experience.

Writing about these two characters has been such a strange experience. They've been chattering in my head for so long, and now they've gone silent. I'd like to think it's because they're busy with each other. But I have a feeling they won't stay silent forever, and another Hope and Alex book may come along in the future. When they start talking to me again, you'll be the first to know.

But for now, it's time for the Half Moon Bay series to move in a new direction. Are you looking forward to the couple in the next book? You know who it is, right? Wait—you don't? Go back and read Chapter 36 again. Seriously . . . I'll wait.

Yes, it's time for Hurricane Sara to take center stage! It doesn't sound like she's too fond of Jack, though, does it? Then again, who would be? Not exactly an auspicious beginning. I think they've got their work cut out for them. But they won't be alone. Hope and Alex are the beating heart of Half Moon Bay, and will be there too. And they've got some big plans in store for our little resort!

∼

Half Moon Whim: Half Moon Bay Book 5
Coming, Fall of 2022!

★★★★★: *"I really don't know where to start with the praise. Each book in the series has been enthralling and captivated the interest from beginning to end."* -Amazon reviewer

SARA AND JACK... Will her searing flame scorch him to the bone?

Sara Collins never wanted to put down roots. When her sister offers her a job at the sunny Caribbean scuba diving resort she owns, Sara jumps at the chance to manage her own spa. Even if it means interacting with the divemaster who humiliated her.

Jack Powell is finding out his dream life is more challenging than expected. Especially after his boss's sister moves to town—they don't exactly get along. He tries to avoid the situation, which is difficult when he can't stop thinking about her.

Throw in a handsome, successful developer who offers Sara everything she ever dreamed of, and she finds St. Croix might be exactly what she's always wanted. But which man holds the key to her heart and her greatest dream?

Half Moon Whim is a sensual love-triangle, enemies-to-lovers beach romance, and Book 5 of the Half Moon Bay series. It can be read as a standalone, and is the springboard into the next phase of this captivating series.

Half Moon Whim: Half Moon Bay Book 5

Know when it's released by
following me on Amazon
(Click on my author name on Amazon, then click the yellow +Follow button on the left side of the Amazon page below my picture)

Or better yet ...

Have you signed up for my Beach Read Update yet? You'll stay up to date on all my new releases and get free stuff too!

Want more of Hope and Alex? How would you like a free short story featuring them? Sign up now at www.erinbrockus.com/vip.html, and I'll send you an electronic version of my short story, *Tropical Hope*.

This is a quick, fun read that is set between books 1 and 2 of the Half Moon Bay series. Hope and Alex are trying to reunite after she has been off the island for several days, but obstacles keep getting in the way!

My Beach Read Update subscribers hear about all my free content, plus exclusive offers and sales. I'd love to have you along! Sign up to download this exclusive bonus today.

Last, but certainly not least, thank you, Dear Reader, for your continued support and encouragement. Without you, none of this would be possible!

Erin Brockus
May, 2022

Keep reading for the first chapter of *Half Moon Whim*, Book 5 of the Half Moon Bay series . . .

HALF MOON WHIM EXCERPT

October...

THE WARM CARIBBEAN SEA washed over Sara Collins's feet as she walked barefoot down the beach, carrying her flip-flops in one hand. Shading her eyes from the late-morning St. Croix sunshine, she squinted at her destination.

A cottage-style house with a lovely, full-length covered porch faced the ocean a fair distance away from the bungalow where she had spent the previous several nights. Half Moon Bay Resort had been closed for the previous several days, only this morning returning to normal. Since guests would begin arriving in a few hours, she was leaving so her former bungalow could be prepared for them.

As she approached, her sister Hope's house looked the same—everything around her did—but the world was fundamentally different now. A massive shift had occurred, and a new era had started. Sara lifted the skirt of her breezy yellow sundress and climbed the short flight of stairs onto the porch. A quiet *woof* greeted her as a short-coated yellow dog sat up on his padded bed, watching her closely.

"Hello there, Cruz. I'm going to crash here until my flight. You're not going to get all protective and bite me, are you?" Sara used a soft, friendly voice and Cruz responded with a thumping tail, approaching so she could pat his head.

With a relieved sigh, she scratched behind his ears. He'd been mistreated by his former owner, who was euphemistically known as Creepy Guy, and he was wary of people unless he knew them well. Though Sara had never met the man, the aftermath he'd left on Cruz was evident. Apparently, she had been around enough the past few days to pass muster, which made her smile. "Thank you for not running away or attacking me. Creepy Guy sure did a number on you, didn't he? Poor baby." She glanced around, locating her packed suitcase near the sliding glass door. *Well, I won't be needing that for the next few hours. It can just stay there.*

Sara slid open the unlocked door, and Cruz shimmied through the narrow opening as soon as he could, eager for the cool interior. She entered more hesitantly. Shutting the slider behind her, her gaze took in an expansive great room with a kitchen at the far end. The house was silent, and despite the cozy, welcoming decorative touches, Sara was uncomfortable. This wasn't just her big sister's house anymore.

This was Hope and Alex Monroe's house.

Hope had owned Half Moon Bay for a year and a half, and Alex had been the dive operations manager and head guide for over six. But the resort wasn't Hope's anymore—it was officially *theirs*. Their wedding had taken place two evenings ago, an intimate sunset ceremony on the resort beach.

The bride and groom had retired to a guest bungalow and hadn't made another appearance until the previous afternoon, when they had joined the rest of the small wedding party at the infinity pool. Hope and Alex radiated happiness as they embraced their family and close friends. Now Sara was the last of the wedding party to leave. Best man Mike Baker and his wife Emma had left the previous evening, and Alex's sister Kate Fletcher and her family departed earlier that morning.

Still standing near the slider, Sara took in a deep lungful of the cool air, trying to convince herself she wasn't an outsider. Her musings were interrupted by a loud thump from the kitchen corner. Cruz stared at Sara, his water bowl tipping back and forth on the floor before finally settling.

She grinned, glad to have something productive to do. "Thirsty, huh? I can take care of that. It's just you and me for a while yet, Cruz. You're probably glad to have things back to normal around here." She padded over and filled his bowl with water, trying to avoid his wagging tail as she set it down. "Hope and Alex are both working. She's getting the resort ready to accept guests, and Alex is taking out a group of divers staying in a condo. He wanted to give Tommy and Robert some time off, so he's driving." She scowled. "Apparently, that asshole divemaster Jack is working too."

Cruz ignored her, not as interested in Hope and Alex's whereabouts as quenching his thirst. And even less interested in the work schedules of Captain Tommy Williams and Divemaster Robert Davis. And as far as she was concerned, Jack Powell wasn't even worth thinking about.

Sara straightened and caught sight of Hope's bridal bouquet, sitting in a vase on the kitchen table. She shook her head, still not able to fully process the image of the two of them exchanging vows. Or, more specifically, her own reaction to it. As maid of honor, she'd had a full view of Alex during the ceremony.

Sara had never been traditional or domestic, so it was all the more surprising that seeing Alex stare at Hope like she was the only thing in the universe had induced such longing in her. Wanting a man to look at *her* like that. Hope was fond of saying she never thought marriage was in the cards for her. Until she fell in love with Alex.

Sara breathed a deep sigh, then shook herself. *Stop being a sap.*

Cruz finished drinking and curled up in his bed in the corner, closing his eyes with a happy sigh. "Well, I'm not going to get any stimulating conversation from you. Maybe I'll head down to the pier and see if Selena is back at work yet." He cracked an eye open, then closed it again and she smirked. "The only thing worse than talking to the dog is talking to yourself. Get a move on, girl."

Soon Sara was climbing onto the pier, the wooden slats creaking pleasantly under her feet. Though Half Moon Bay was primarily a scuba diving resort, Hope had opened a spa recently. She'd spoken with the new massage therapist, Selena Allen, several times prior to the wedding, and immediately bonded with her enthusiastic personality, especially since the spa was Sara's kind of place.

Halfway down the pier, she passed through a tunnel of buildings and made her way past the dive shop to a long staircase at the north end. A covered deck with an incredible ocean view dominated the area at the top of the stairs and served as the outdoor massage area. Next to the glass entrance door, a wooden wall formed a privacy screen, and a second, more nondescript door led to a restroom. Sara entered the clean, brightly lit spa, where Selena stood behind the glass check-in counter, refilling a small bottle with massage oil. The warm scent of sandalwood filled the air.

The massage therapist glanced up at the door's opening, her dark face bursting into a wide smile at Sara's entry. She was a trim, small woman in her mid-twenties, wearing a light-blue staff polo shirt. *What I wouldn't give to have her small, petite frame... Lucky girl.*

Sara made an effort to dress well and appear professionally styled and made-up, partly to compensate for her voluptuous and curvy figure. No manner of diet or exercise had ever changed that and now, at age thirty-three, she was resigned to her fate. But that didn't mean she wasn't self-conscious about it

"Sara! You stayin' a few more days?"

"No, I'm flying out this evening. Hope's working, so I thought I'd come up here." Her gaze took in the mani-pedi station along one wall, with a full stylist area in the corner. Like a magnet, she was drawn toward the hair salon. Several windows let in plenty of light. "You have a massage scheduled?"

Selena finished filling the bottle, shaking her head. "Not till tomorrow. I'm just gettin' ready."

Sara ran a hand over the back of the stylist chair where she had cut Hope's hair and given her a deep-conditioning treatment the day prior to the wedding. They had chatted throughout, almost like old times. Immediately afterward, they had met the rest of the wedding party on the resort dive boat, *Surface Interval*.

Heat crept up Sara's neck as she tried to push away the memory of what had happened next. The resort's newest employee, the divemaster Jack, had tripped and dumped an enormous bucket of water over her head, drenching her from head to foot. In front of everyone. She'd been mortified and embarrassed but determined not to show it.

As Sara passed by a window next to the stylist station, movement at the end of the pier caught her eye. A gleaming white boat was tied up and the group of divers was already headed away. "There's good sound insulation in here. I didn't even hear the boat come in."

"They did a great job on the construction. It always stays nice and cool in here, too."

Sara turned toward the front door. "I'd better get going. Hope said she'd be finished about lunch time." The two women said their goodbyes, then Sara opened the door, turning left to descend the stairs.

And collided right into a warm body, smashing her nose into a shoulder. "Oof!" Wincing, she rubbed it as she staggered back. She was preparing to apologize as she looked up into a pair of huge, gorgeous brown eyes that widened in recognition.

Unfortunately, the eyes belonged to Jack. The horrible divemaster.

Her chagrin instantly erupted into fury, and she dropped her hand from her face. "Goddammit, watch where you're going. Pouring water over me wasn't enough? You have to break my nose too?"

Jack's face flushed crimson as he took a big step back, holding up both hands. "I'm sorry! I need to use the restroom and wasn't watching where I was going."

He was of average height, but at five feet three, she still had to look up at him. He spoke with a very slight twang. Texas? "Yeah. No kidding. You really need to stay the hell away from me, understand?"

His obvious embarrassment was replaced by a flash of anger that he quickly covered, raking a hand through his short, dark-brown hair. He had a strong jaw and sharp cheekbones, and really was rather good looking.

Too bad it's all wasted on him.

"Look, I'm not doing it on purpose. Lighten up, princess."

Clenching her jaw tightly, Sara drew herself as tall as she could. "No. I won't. But fortunately for both of us, I'm leaving later today." She breezed around him toward the staircase. "Have a nice life, Jack."

Sara stomped up the pier, but by the time she turned to walk north along the beach, her irritation had dissipated. It was quickly replaced by tranquil peace as a soft breeze blew through her long brown hair, and the line of palm trees waved gently back and forth. They stretched along the back of the long crescent of white sand that gave the bay its name. Half Moon Bay sat on the western side of the island, but she'd be gone before the sun descended to the ocean.

Sara had intended to head toward the lobby office, but changed her mind, strolling north along the beach instead. *Enjoy it while it lasts. I'll be sleeping in Charleston tonight.* She kicked off her flip-flops and let the waves wash over her feet, a small smile on her face as she soaked in the peaceful setting.

"Hey! Wait for me. Where are you going?" Hope called out behind her, and Sara stopped as her big sister hurried toward her, dressed in a dive-themed Half Moon Bay T-shirt and long black shorts. Her hair was much lighter than Sara's, especially since moving to St. Croix. She had it loosely wound in a clip and wore no make-up, yet she was still gorgeous. Totally not fair.

"I thought you'd be waiting in the cool house," Hope said.

"Are you kidding? These are my last few hours in paradise. No way am I wasting them." Sara turned and they continued north. "I've never walked to this end of the beach, and thought I'd check it out. So, how's married life?"

Sara rolled her eyes as Hope broke into a face-cracking grin. "Incredible! We've been living together for over a year, so it shouldn't really make a difference. But it does."

"Who would have thought you'd become the face of wedded bliss?"

Hope arched a brow at her. "Careful. That sounds suspiciously close to sour grapes."

Sara had to laugh. "I'm very happy for you. Both of you." They were nearing the north end of the beach. The sand competed with iron-shore rocky ground as the crescent swept out to their left. As it narrowed to a point, the rocky ground won. Sara put her flip-flops back on and the two women picked their way carefully onto the thin spit of land.

Sara shaded her eyes with one hand as she took in the expansive view. "This is beautiful. Nothing but ocean ahead and the resort behind us." In the other direction was nothing but wild jungle. She itched to paint it. *Oh, these colors!*

To their left, a large expanse of dark coral reef descended from the rocky edge and disappeared into the depths in a stunning variety of blue shades. Hope pointed at it. "That's the house reef.

We're lucky to have it so close. Most resorts don't have something this nice. It gives the guests something to dive or snorkel, even if it's too rough for the boat to go out."

Her sister had gotten off to a rocky start at the resort, but she had turned it into a resounding success—with Alex's help, who was a great deal more than dive manager and instructor. The women picked their way back to the soft sand and continued toward the resort. "No plans to develop this end?" Sara asked.

Hope laughed. "Actually, Alex and I don't own this end." Sara caught her unconscious *Alex and I,* but remained silent. Hope pointed to an orange wooden stake pounded into the edge of the sand just south of the spit. "That's the property marker there. I met the owner once, who comes out here occasionally. As politely as possible, I asked for right of first refusal if he ever wants to sell it. He wasn't interested in selling, but at least he likes it undeveloped. It would be terrible if he built a big restaurant or something here."

Sara laughed. "Big sister. Resort mogul."

They continued past four northern bungalows and a central complex of buildings. As they passed by the pier on their right, Alex was strolling toward them, and they paused to wait. He was tall and gorgeous, with bright blue eyes and short, light hair—he and her sister were a stunning couple. Alex broke eye contact with Hope long enough to say hello to Sara before sweeping up to his wife and enveloping her in a long kiss.

Sara propped her hand on her hip. "Hey! I'm standing right here, you know. Don't you two have any decency?"

They both ignored her, but finally pried themselves apart. "Good trip?" Hope asked, a dizzy smile on her face.

He nodded, stroking a finger across her chin. "Perfect day to drive and very experienced divers. It was a walk in the park for Jack."

At the divemaster's name, Sara scowled and resumed the trek toward their house. The couple fell in beside her. They entered the house, and Cruz was much happier to see them than he had Sara. After a quick shower, Alex joined them in the kitchen as Hope prepared lunch.

"So Kate and her family got away this morning?" Sara asked, standing behind one of the kitchen chairs.

Hope stopped stirring the salad and a long look passed between her and Alex. Sara could practically see information being passed between them. *Jeez, they've only been married two days and they're doing that already?*

Alex turned to her. "Yeah. They didn't have any problems. Katie and Dave were sad to go, but we talked to them about something that cheered them up a bit."

Hope wrapped one arm around Alex's waist as she gestured at the chair Sara was standing behind. "Please sit down. We have something to share with you."

Half Moon Whim...coming Fall, 2022!

ALSO BY ERIN BROCKUS

Tropical Chance: A Half Moon Bay Novella
Tropical Hope: A Half Moon Bay Short Story

Half Moon Bay Series:

Finding Hope: Half Moon Bay Book 1
Defending Hope: Half Moon Bay Book 2
Rising Hope: Half Moon Bay Book 3
Forever Hope: Half Moon Bay Book 4
Half Moon Whim: Half Moon Bay Book 5 (Fall 2022)

ABOUT THE AUTHOR

Dive into a romantic escape!

Erin Brockus writes sensual contemporary romances set in exotic, tropical locales. She features mature, realistic characters you actually enjoy getting to know. Count on plenty of adventure with a focus on the ocean, especially scuba diving.

She was born in 1969 in Washington state. A great love of creative writing as a child got pushed aside by the expectations of Real Life and she went to college to become a pharmacist. After practicing pharmacy for over 25 years, it was time for a change. So she reduced her hours as a practicing pharmacist to devote more time to writing.

She was introduced to scuba diving in 1998 by her husband. They have since traveled worldwide enjoying diving, and the breezy locales they visited formed the ideas for her characters and stories. Erin has even been known to don a drysuit and explore the cold, murky waters of the Pacific Northwest. She is also an avid runner and cyclist.

Erin lives with her husband (a scuba instructor) in eastern Washington state. She is currently at work on the next Half Moon Bay installment.